LOVE AT THE MAYO

MAYO LOVE

SARAH SOON

W
Winter Orchid

COPYRIGHT

Love at The Mayo
Copyright © 2024 by Sarah Soon
All rights reserved.

No part of this book may be reproduced, distributed, or transmitted in any form or by any means, including photocopying, recording, or other electronic or mechanical methods, without the prior written permission from the publisher, except permitted by U.S. copyright law.

This is a work of fiction. Names, characters, places, and incidents are the product of the author's imagination or are used fictitiously. No resemblance of persons (living or deceased) or products are coincidental.

Scripture quotations from The Authorized (King James) Version. Rights in the Authorized Version in the United Kingdom are vested in the Crown. Reproduced by permission of the Crown's patentee, Cambridge University Press.

Scriptures taken from the Holy Bible, New International Version®, NIV®. Copyright © 1973, 1978, 1984, 2011 by Biblica, Inc.™ Used by permission of Zondervan. All rights reserved worldwide. The "NIV" and "New International Version" are trademarks registered in the United States Patent and Trademark Office by Biblica, Inc.™

Library of Congress Cataloging-in-Publication Data
.Names: Soon, Sarah, author
Title: Love at The Mayo
Description: Tulsa: Write by Grace, LLC, 2024
979-8-9879644-3-9 eBook
979-8-9879644-4-6 Paperback
979-8-9879644-5-3 Hardback
Book Cover Photography: Mike Tedford Photography
Book Cover Design by 100 Covers
Book Editing: Two Birds Editing, Jill Butler Wilson, and Kristi Bridges

CONTENTS

*I dedicate this book to my husband, Robert,
and my friend Andrea Moniz.
Both encouraged me to breathe life into a story idea—now, it's a book
series!*

PROLOGUE
DECEMBER 30, 2009

"Times were simpler for you," I said to my nana as I glanced at the Imperial staircase. "You found Papa and married."

Nana closed her eyes, perhaps praying or reminiscing about when she and Papa met here at The Mayo hotel in 1948. Today, my family gathered at the newly renovated hotel for my cousin's wedding.

I waited for Nana to open her eyes. "Why can't Lance realize that waiting five years to start a family is reasonable?" I asked.

"If you knew you couldn't live without him, you'd fight to make it work."

"Humph! He's too stubborn."

Nana raised her brows. "Hasn't he waited a few years before proposing?"

"That was a mutual decision." I raised my voice. "Sorry, I didn't mean to snap. Everyone expects me to marry him." I frowned. "How did you endure your family when you called off your engagement?"

Nana looked down at the cream-and-black checkered marble floor. "It was very difficult."

Born and raised in Philadelphia, Nana grew up in a privileged home. Private schools, a debutante ball, chauffeur. She'd laugh, saying she woke up wearing white gloves, fresh makeup, and even fresher breath.

Nana's mother chaperoned her and her fiancé for a New Year's Eve weekend trip to Tulsa, where he was visiting his former boarding school buddy returning home after serving in World War II.

As Nana descended the staircase to meet with her fiancé, my eventual papa, sitting in the Grand Hall on the ground floor, sprang up from a tall armchair. He approached her despite a two-carat solitaire rock on her finger. A month later, she moved to Tulsa and started a new life with him.

"When I met Papa, I realized I'd been asleep." Nana took my hands. Hers were velvety soft and warm.

"I see. Did his confident charm and down-home personality awaken you to the stodginess of society?" Since Nana's life had long been embedded in Tulsa, I sometimes forgot she wasn't a native.

Nana shook her head. "That wouldn't have been enough reason to leave the life I knew."

"Then I don't understand."

"When I first noticed him waiting for me at the bottom of that staircase, I saw this iridescent glow emanating around him. Compelled by the light, I forgot about anything or anyone except him. Once we were face-to-face, I felt an unmoving peace and joy. I wanted whatever he had."

I released my hand from hers, more confused than hurt she'd kept this facet of their love story from me. I thought I had heard every iteration. "Why haven't you told me this before?"

"It wasn't time, dear. Papa and I pray you'll not only find a partner in life but embrace God's love. If I hadn't discovered divine love, I would've married my fiancé."

"I didn't know." I rested my forehead in one hand, shielding my expressive eyes and face. Although I believed in God, I'd become skeptical about many tenets of traditional Christianity, especially surrounding money, purity, and community. I feared questioning some beliefs might get me accused of heresy, deconstructing my faith, or being lukewarm. Nana wouldn't hurl stones, but I was concerned about others at church.

"If you aren't sensing you could enjoy a lifetime partnership with Lance, I'm glad you moved forward." Nana's return to the original topic was gracious.

Grateful she understood, I hugged her. Keeping me in her embrace, Nana said, "There's a prayer I use for times like these, from one of my favorite Psalms—Psalm 139:12: 'Yea, the darkness hideth not from thee; but the night shineth as the day: the darkness and the light are both alike to thee.' "

I usually found the King James Version cumbersome to read, but in Nana's soft, rhythmic tone, the verse sounded poetic and moving. Tonight, I'd look for the leather-bound KJV Bible Nana and Papa had gifted me.

We returned to the ballroom shortly. I sensed a lightness in my step, confident I'd not only made the right decision but would find sustaining love. Perhaps at The Mayo.

CHAPTER I

MAY 5, 2018

I turned off the light in the living room of the condo. A handwritten note on his desk was the only trace of my presence.

Jordan, I can't pretend anymore that we love each other. So, I moved out. Our business relationship will benefit.

He was on a two-week business trip to London, making it convenient for me to move out.

The steel front door closed quietly behind me as I trekked into the complex's empty hall, blah with grey stone walls and slate-speckled marble floors. Why did I ever covet living here?

As I hustled to the elevator, I carried the last cardboard box of my belongings, my diploma jostling on top of other keepsakes. I pressed the down button for the last time.

The elevator doors opened. Warner, our neighbor, emerged. Seriously? I'd come from ten until noon, when the retired attorney golfed; otherwise, I would've moved everything in a day, instead of in four.

A condo community was ideal for Jordan's investment client, a recent widower. Warner acted as though Jordan's referral for residence granted him a kingdom. When Warner got on the HOA board, I wondered if he did that to keep Jordan abreast on the community gossip and HOA news. He referred many investment clients to Jordan, so Jordan didn't mind when Warner would unexpectedly visit. My time alone with workaholic Jordan became a rare commodity, so Warner was a nuisance.

"Glad I caught you, Celine," he said, blocking the elevator door. "Is Jordan enjoying England?"

"He's working hard." I smiled wide.

The snoop peeked at my box. "Decluttering?"

I hugged it close; he needed to mind his own business. "Yes."

He pointed to my diploma. "You also graduated from TU? I'm surprised Jordan never told me. I got my JD there."

"Yep." The elevator doors closed with Warner still standing in front of them. What was the universe trying to teach me?

"You wouldn't move without letting him know?" He knitted his brows.

I smiled but tightened my body. "I found an office."

"Oh... good for you." He shrugged.

My phone rang from my purse. It was Dad, but I needed to free my arms to answer. "I've got to take this," I said with more impatience than I intended.

"Jordan will be thanking me, then, that he didn't get tethered to a joint tenancy."

After getting a unit close to cost for referring ten buyers, Jordan offered me joint tenancy. I wanted to invest and was livid when out of nowhere, he changed his mind. I should've known that the former divorce attorney would advise Jordan against it.

"I wondered why Jordan did a 180 on the joint tenancy." I advanced toward Warner.

He crossed his arms. "Where's your office located?"

"Nearby." I took another step, standing only inches away. Warner moved back until nearly flush against the elevator.

"Did Jordan find it for you?" He raised an eyebrow, issuing a challenge. I had seen him do that exact gesture when he was extracting info from the HOA President.

"What was your reasoning?"

"I thought that agreement unwise considering he'd have to buy your share at market value." He narrowed his eyes. "Does he know you found an office?"

"When did you advise him?" I asked.

The interloper winced for a split second but recovered with a smile. "It's not important."

"January?"

He bobbed his head. "Something like that."

I stepped back, giving him space. "Thanks. Well, I better get going."

He stepped aside, and I pushed the elevator down button again. The door opened immediately, so I rushed inside and hit the close button and then G for ground floor.

After the doors shut, I leaned against the elevator wall, relieved I didn't invest, hurt Jordan lied. Did integrity ever exist in our relationship?

CHAPTER 2
MAY 2

In the parking garage, I rushed to Addy, my sedan, stuffed the box into the crowded trunk, then stared at the building. Should I return to the condo and remove the note? Call Jordan before Warner did?

I only left the note because Dad and my bestie insisted. Dad and Jennifer were afraid Jordan would talk me into staying, especially because (Dad argued this part) Jordan had this inexplicable control over me. Since he cheated, I was sure I wouldn't stay, though my self-image was at an all-time low. Overly tired from packing, moving, and working, I left the note.

Dad called again.

"Hi." I swiped sweat off my forehead. Eighty-one degrees and only the beginning of May. We were in for a long, sweltering summer.

"Are you completely moved out?" His voice was riddled with angst.

"Yes, but..." I paused, so I wouldn't panic; otherwise, Dad would jet out here. "Warner just interrogated me, asking if I was moving."

"You didn't tell him anything, did you?"

"No... I said I found an office. He might not pull the emergency cord with Jordan today, but he might this week. Why didn't I leave ten minutes earlier?"

"I doubt Warner contacts him before he returns."

"I don't want to chance it. I'm going to destroy the note and tell Jordan in person."

"No!"

I jumped, not expecting him to yell.

"Stick to the game plan," Dad said, voice lowered.

"Hear me out." I slid into the driver's seat and turned on my car. "Warner catching me alters—"

"The worst-case scenario, Jordan suspects. The best case, he thinks you've found an office. Leave the note."

"I must prioritize my business. There's a chance he'll be relieved we're no longer going through the motions. If I salvage our working partnership, I'll retain clients." I didn't care if I defended arguments from an earlier discussion; I needed to remind Dad to think rationally. He had tunnel vision when it came to Jordan.

Dad immediately responded, as if his quick reply would defeat my argument. "He'll feel disrespected because you broke it off and moved out. He doesn't want you to show him up."

Even though Jordan was an investment advisor, he referred clients to me. I quit my job at a marketing agency to go fulltime as a marketing consultant. Since we dated, he didn't ask for a referral fee saying my services helped his clients. So, the odds of them staying if he advised them to switch to a different consultant weren't in my favor.

"If you're worried they'll leave," Dad continued. "Your maman and I want to invest in your business as you rebuild. You'd completely cut ties to him."

"No, I have to do this myself." I groaned, tired of reinforcing my independence.

"Come here for a month or two to clear the air. And we'll figure out how to grow your business."

I closed my eyes, tempted to escape to paradise. The Villages, a retirement city in central Florida, catered to residents' needs with three squares of restaurants and shops, live entertainment every night, and a pool and recreation center in each neighborhood. I could work while lying by the pool and sipping on a frozen mai tai. Shop with Maman on Saturdays. Golf with Dad on Sundays.

Jordan's voice interjected in my mind. *You'll never reach your potential with your old man calling the shots.*

I opened my eyes. "I need to face him."

"Absolutely not!"

"Stop yelling. Just stop!" I gripped my head as an invisible claw squeezed my temples. Jordan often castigated me with an ear-splitting volume when we'd argue, or I'd make a mistake.

"I'm sorry," he said. A long pause. "How about I fly there and help?"

"Do we have to talk about this now?" I gripped the steering wheel I'd sacrificed for, saving money when I landed my first job. I wouldn't let Dad buy me a new car, so I drove an old clunker until I had enough to buy this gently used sedan with cash. The pride of buying my own car outweighed the need to subsist on beans and rice while declining invitations to eat out with friends.

In hindsight, buying Addy was a rite of passage, not a means to enforce my independence. When I moved in with Jordan, he got irritated by how much I depended on Dad for "everything." Assuming Jordan exaggerated, especially since he hardly talked to his own father, I argued I only checked in with Dad a few times a week.

A seed of self-consciousness planted, I kept a mental tally of every time I talked to Dad and realized we chatted daily. To show I wasn't dependent on him, I weaned our talks to three to four times a week, telling him I needed to invest in my relationship with Jordan. Dad got angry but caved to my boundary somewhat. He texted more frequently, but I didn't mind, especially because I could hide texts from Jordan.

"Aren't you relieved you didn't invest in the—"

"Is that Celine?" Maman's melodic joy echoed faintly in the background.

"Hold on, Celine." Then Dad addressed Maman. "Yes, I'm talking to her."

"Ask her to call me after you finish talking," Maman shouted, wanting me to hear.

"Sorry," Dad said into the phone. "She's eager to hear from you." I didn't blame him for the irritation in his voice. Maman, the social butterfly loathing to miss anything, frequently interrupted conversations, especially between Dad and me.

"Can you fill her in? I'm not in the mood to ticket her questions. And I need to get to Jennifer's, take a shower, and plan my week." My chest burned, but I'd run out of antacids in my purse.

"Sure, but please text her. She's concerned."

"K."

"Remind me. When does Jordan return?"

"The seventeenth."

"That gives us time to come up with a strategy to retain your clients. We must be three steps ahead."

I envisioned Jordan dragging his jet-lagged body and suitcase into the condo. He'd go to the den to check urgent mail I would've placed on his desk. Once he read my note, he'd rip it up, crumple it into a ball, and toss it into the trash. He'd call, violently cussing me, mostly because I caught him off guard. I wouldn't crawl back to him, but I'd overpromise something... Pay rent for a few months. Give one of his start-up investments free marketing sessions. Whatever it took to defuse his anger.

"Celine? Did we get disconnected?"

I turned off my car. "I'll remove the note and call him. I'll plant enough seeds about our inability to get along that he'll think he broke up. But… I'll wait to retrieve the note until tomorrow, to avoid Warner."

"Celine Elizabeth!" Dad's voice boomed. "Drive to Jennifer's and forget about telling him in person." He paused and took a deep breath. "Sorry, I'll try not to raise my voice. Please, just stick to the plan."

"He'll be upset because he'll have to fork over a thousand a month extra toward the mortgage. But since he's into this reception-ist, he should ask her to move in and take over my payments."

"His mortgage isn't your concern. Focus on retaining clients."

"I am. If he thinks he broke up, he'll work with me."

"You're not on his side, so he'll advise your clients to work with a firm where he'll receive a referral fee. You have to think like a serpent."

"He lied, by the way. About why he changed his mind on the joint tenancy."

"That reinforces my point. How did you find out?"

"Warner blurted it. He advised Jordan to not get entangled in a joint tenancy. So, Jordan convinced me I needed to invest in an office."

Sweat ran down my forehead. I turned the car back on.

"Stop playing games. Warner provided great advice. Now, you have a financial cushion if you lose clients."

"Kind of…" I tapped my steering wheel then pulled onto the street and glared at the twenty-story condo building, mostly glass and steel with tan bricks in the middle. It no longer seemed modern or upscale, just frigid and dull.

"Explain."

The traffic moved slow, so I took my time leaving. "I was upset Jordan backtracked, so he offered alternative investments. I bought three paintings and new furniture for the condo. Spent twenty grand altogether, but that's half of what I would've paid toward a down payment. The paintings should have appreciated, since the artist is in demand."

"You're letting him keep the furniture, right?"

"Of course. I'm hoping Jordan will interpret my leaving them behind as a gesture of goodwill."

"Don't count on it," Dad deadpanned.

"I do have the paintings at Jennifer's."

"Good. Also, is Jordan still managing your inheritance?" Dad's voice was strained. Initially, I invested the inheritance with the brokerage firm Dad used—until Jordan offered to manage my investment. He assured me he'd double my earnings, so I jumped at the opportunity.

"Yes." Needing to fast-track Dad off this topic, I took a chirpier tone and spoke quickly. "I have it in a high-growth investment yielding about 20%, so I have a cushion. How's your fund doing?"

"Switch now!" Was Dad angrier at me or Jordan?

"It's insurance, so he'll still partner with me. Win-win." I knew what I was saying wouldn't cut it with Dad.

"Transfer to Raymond James immediately."

"Why not hunt down Jordan in a meeting in London and tell him and everyone there that I left him? Because *that* wouldn't cause him to retaliate." I didn't mean to raise my voice, but Dad's obsession to completely disengage with Jordan could derail our exit strategy.

"I'd rather you lose clients than your inheritance."

I sat straighter in the seat. "I'm confident I can retain both."

"You're testing my patience. That boy isn't someone to toy around with."

"I understand that better than anyone."

"Then act like it."

"I'm not arguing about this. I'm headed to Jennifer's."

"Alright… Just keep me updated on Jordan."

"I will. Bye."

It took me fifteen minutes longer than usual to get to Jennifer's, since I drove about thirty miles an hour. I stopped at the yellow lights (earning some honks and birds in the process) and rerouted a few times after I turned onto wrong streets. Although the sun shone bright, few clouds in the sky, my mind drifted into a thick fog.

I drove past the street to Jennifer's. Blood rushed to my head. Only a few blocks down, in a seedy part of town, was the restaurant where I caught Jordan and the receptionist holding hands. At first, shock hit me—I couldn't believe they were together or that he patronized that hole-in-the-wall. Then, I couldn't get out of my mind how easily he replaced me. So, today, I refused to see that eatery again. I turned into a parking lot to get back on the road, heading north.

Once I pulled onto the side street where Jennifer lived, I exhaled. I drove to the gated condo complex and entered the code. A tall dogwood with white hoary blossoms stood just inside the entrance. This neighborhood contained five powder-blue buildings with white shutters, each with four, two-story units. Citrus dahlias, yellow snapdragons, and pink cosmos bordered the sidewalks.

After I pulled into the parking lot in front of Jennifer's unit, I rested my head on the steering wheel. Although I'd physically left Jordan, what if it took months before I was completely free?

CHAPTER 3

As I walked inside the condo, carrying a heavy box, light instrumental jazz and delicate diffused eucalyptus welcomed me. My racing thoughts slowed. I felt at ease in Jennifer's Mediterranean-style home with cream walls, sea-green throw pillows, blue denim furniture, and fuchsia orchids in terra-cotta vases. Much more at ease than in Jordan's industrial modern condo, with its grey, black, and white color scheme and metallic and glass furnishings.

Although Jennifer's home was placid, nothing about her was slow. A spring storm, she moved quickly, but always with a refreshing aroma. She worked long hours as a Realtor and single parent to her daughter.

Standing over the stovetop, earbuds in, she mouthed *Client selling her home.* I nodded, then continued toward the stairs, greeting Sienna at the kitchen island. A stunningly beautiful ten-year-old, she shared her mom's deep chestnut hair and her father's aquamarine eyes but had her own bronze complexion.

She glanced up from staring at her cell phone. "Hi, Celine. Want help?"

"Sure. My trunk's full of boxes."

Once we finished emptying my car, Sienna complained about having to write a book report. Although mentally and physically exhausted, I wanted to return her favor. "English was one of my favorite subjects. Do you want help?"

"Yes!"

We spent thirty minutes discussing the book's theme. She enjoyed painting, so I used painting metaphors to explain writing principles. Fortunately, she caught on and breezed through the report.

"You make writing fun," she said, giving me a high five.

I enjoyed helping someone else for a change, especially someone as endearing as Sienna.

"Alright, literary scholars, let's eat." Jennifer sat at the dining table. "On tonight's menu, braised short ribs, creamed corn, and collards." She pointed to me. "We need to put meat on your skinny bones."

The aroma of savory ribs reminded me of our university days. Despite Jennifer's busy schedule, she'd make time to cook comfort foods, like three-cheese mac and cheese, savory oxtail and butter beans, or pecan-crusted fried chicken.

I headed to the table and sat across from her. "Don't have to ask me twice. Hopefully, I'll gain back the ten pounds I've lost these past two weeks." All my clothes hung on my body as if on a clothesline.

Jennifer said a brief prayer then asked, "Which grade were you in when you and Aimee transferred? Sienna asked me, but I couldn't remember."

"Fifth," I said. Going into high school, my sister begged our parents to let her switch to Metro Christian, where her boyfriend and best friend attended. My parents visited the school and preferred the friendlier staff, so I had to switch too. I vowed to never talk to Aimee again, but that only lasted a day. Maman warned that if I didn't talk to my sister, I'd have to cover her chores as well as mine.

"That's my grade," said Sienna, seated next to Jennifer. "Was it hard to make new friends?"

"It would've been harder, but your mom was my lifeline. On the first week of school, she invited me to her lunch table, where the popular kids sat. Then, I didn't struggle to have friends."

I grabbed a few short ribs. The smoky garlic from the BBQ sauce wafted. I'd enjoy living here.

"The invitation wasn't all altruistic. You were competition, so I had to scope you out. Make sure you didn't make a move on my boy." Jennifer winked.

"Baby-faced Benji?" I squeezed my cheeks.

She laughed. "He had it so bad for me."

"I returned the favor by rescuing your butt from Joselyn."

Sienna stared at her mom, probably incredulous Jennifer was involved in a love spat.

"Joselyn was the school's Scarlett O'Hara," I said. "When Benji and your mom held hands at recess, Joselyn yelled at your mom to get away from her boyfriend."

"Celine stood in front of me, telling Joselyn to find a different boy." Jennifer scooped collards onto her plate then gestured air quotes. "So, 'Scarlett' shoved her on the chest and—whop—Celine fell hard to the ground."

"Did you get in a fight, Mom?" Sienna asked, tilting her head.

"No. I told her she didn't want a part of me, and she walked away. That's how it's done. You set boundaries and let bullies know you don't play games."

"I need to learn that myself," I said. But not wanting to usher heaviness into the conversation, I glanced at Jennifer. "Do you know what I appreciate about you?"

She smiled. "My cooking?"

I laughed. "That helps. No, your strength and authenticity. You'd tell me what you thought about me to my face, not behind my back.

You were my Elizabeth Bennett, entertaining me with social commentary on the gossiping girls."

She pointed her fork toward me. "My momma taught me to shoot from the hip."

After dinner, I insisted on washing the dishes, but Jennifer informed me that was Sienna's job. So, armed with chamomile tea, we sat on the cream sofa in the upstairs hangout Sienna called "the Haven." Jennifer assured me Sienna was cool with temporarily surrendering the space for my stay.

The Haven was shabby chic, with cream furniture, a beige jute area rug, and fuchsia throw pillows. Its chartreuse walls were too vibrant for me but reflected Sienna's style, which bled into the nearby guest bedroom, conveniently situated next to an enclosed kitchenette with walnut cabinets, a single sink, a compact fridge, and a microwave. During my stay, I could heat a prepared meal and continue working upstairs many nights without interruption.

"How are you doing?" Jennifer's radiant ebony skin contrasted perfectly with her white pantsuit. Her caramel eyes and angled cheekbones exuded natural beauty.

"Still adjusting," I said.

"I understand. It'll take time."

"How did you do it?"

Five years ago, she filed for divorce from Sienna's father. I never liked him. Graced with sandy blond hair and deep hazel eyes, he attracted many of the female students at TU with his West Texas accent. After graduating and leaving his thrilling days as a collegiate tennis star, he married Jennifer. But within a few years, he deflated under the stress of supporting a family. He found sanctuary gambling at the casino and betting on sports online, anywhere he could attempt to restore his former glory.

"Divorcing A.J. was harder than I expected," Jennifer said. "I second-guessed myself for months, especially when Sienna got angry about the split."

"Did she understand why you left?" I asked.

"She does now, but back then, A.J. hid his abuse from her."

"Abuse?" I never considered him violent, just smug.

"Verbal. He never hit me." She paused, touching her forehead. "Sorry, I can still hear his voice screaming expletives."

"I understand." I set my tea on the coaster on the side table.

A scene with Jordan flashed through my mind, him screaming a variety of colorful names as he hurled the glass vase I inherited from Nana Monroe onto the hardwood floor, me crying as I swept up the shards of glass. "Jordan did the same whenever we'd get in a heated argument. He'd always blame me for our fights."

"I'm sorry you endured that, too." She set her tea next to mine then reached for my hand and squeezed it. "If we had reunited earlier, I could've been there for you. Maybe you would've left him sooner if—"

"I wouldn't have listened. My family begged me to leave, but I thought I loved him. Even when I felt like trash. It all feels like 'wood, hay, and stubble,' as Nana would say."

"We were starry-eyed out of TU, looking to change the world. Now, we're two broken women on the mend. So, stay here as long as you need."

"Thank you," I murmured. I didn't want to cry. I'd shed too many tears these past two weeks. "I wish we hadn't gone our separate ways after TU. I was focused on my career, but—"

"Don't take all the blame. I was focused on keeping my family together."

Jennifer and I lost connection a few years after she had Sienna. Because my friend was in a different stage of life, I didn't reach out much. While she engaged in playdates with fellow moms, I worked overtime or socialized at happy hour. Thankfully, six months ago, we ran into each other at a TU football game and vowed to keep in touch.

"Look, if I'm ever in the way between you and your girl, let me know. I hope to find a place in a month. That way, Sienna can have the Haven back."

Jennifer tucked her long legs underneath her. "It's going to take time to get your life sorted out. If there's anything I can do, I'm here. I had an angel when I went through my divorce. The best advice she gave was to not make any major decisions for the first three months."

My back stiffened. *Major* described all the decisions I faced from establishing a permanent residence, rebuilding my business, and finding a new network of friends. "That seems like odd advice considering your life had been so upended." I frowned while Jennifer nodded.

"Outside of the cyclone of decisions around the divorce, I tried to keep life simple and not add more drama. I made some mistakes during that time." She sipped her tea as sadness filled her eyes. "For a year, Sienna and I remained in the house. As my emotions leveled, my mind cleared until I knew what I wanted. Your journey's different, and maybe you don't need as much time. But it'd help to slow down and keep life manageable."

"Three months is a long time to mooch off you. I'm paying rent even if I only stay a month." I wagged my finger. "It's nonnegotiable."

"Fine, how about five hundred dollars per month for groceries and utilities?"

"Agreed, but don't plan on me at dinner every night. I work strange hours and might meet a client at night or work late upstairs. When I get in a groove, I don't stop."

"Oh, I know."

Memories played of Jennifer and me accommodating each other's schedules in our college days. Determined to graduate top of my class, I studied late into the night, even though I was juggling an internship. Now, I'd probably need to hustle just as hard or even harder.

But what if, even working hard as I could, I lost most of my clients? Would I need to stay here longer than three months? I shuddered, concerned what Jordan's return from London and discovery of my note could do to my business.

"Give yourself time." Jennifer narrowed her eyes like a mother reiterating instructions.

"I'll try." I said, gazing up at an eight-by-ten wall portrait of Sienna and Jennifer. They stood near the reflection pool at the Philbrook, a local art museum. Both wore half smiles, Sienna stood stiffly, Jennifer's shoulders hunched. My eyes stung, so I stood. "I'm calling it a night."

Jennifer stood too and gave me a hug. "I'm glad you're here. Sleep well." As I got ready for bed, I pondered her words, wondering. What would my next three months entail?

CHAPTER 4

MAY 6

From an early age, my sister aimed to marry and raise a family. Five years old when I was born, Aimee treated me like I was her baby. Maman would brag how Aimee bottle-fed me, rocked me to sleep, and put me down for a nap.

Growing up, I went through different phases: nearly worshipping Aimee, shadowing her and her friends, then getting advice about boys. While I attended university, she got married, and I stopped looking up to her. I didn't want to marry out of the gate but preferred to earn a degree and launch a career.

Even before Jordan, I was only semi-involved in Aimee's life, especially after our parents moved to Florida. She'd invite me over, notify me of her boys' activities, and occasionally treat me to lunch. I'd advise her about marketing the custom headbands she sewed and sold online as a side gig.

That cordial relationship ended last summer. Aimee called on a Thursday night, alerting me about John's championship baseball game on Saturday.

"I wouldn't miss it," I said, excited for my nephew.

The next evening, Jordan informed me that we'd host Saturday cocktails for his new investment client before going out for dinner. Of course, Jordan wanted to show off the condo. Richard Pine owned an appliance store and wanted to hire a marketing consultant to promote his upcoming expansions throughout the state. Amped to acquire a lucrative client, I forgot about John's game.

Aimee called again Saturday morning, inviting me to dinner following the afternoon game. Realizing my dilemma, I brainstormed a plausible excuse. Meeting a client wouldn't fly with her.

Aimee broke the silence. "No worries if you have dinner plans. John will be thrilled you came to the game."

"That's not the problem. I was so excited about watching him play in the championship, I forgot about my prior commitment. Unfortunately, I can't reschedule. Will Heath video the game?" Her husband usually did.

She sighed. "This is the first time John's team made it to the championship."

An excuse popped in my head. She'd respect a family event. "Jordan's throwing his mom a surprise birthday party here. He'll need my help."

"When will it start?"

"Five."

"I see... Fine."

On Saturday afternoon, Jordan and I sat in our condo's living room with Richard and his wife, enjoying our cocktails and getting better acquainted. Richard was the most lively, entertaining us with vignettes. As he shared his marketing needs at the restaurant later, I lost awareness of people around us. Until I heard my name.

"Celine?"

I looked up. Uh-oh. Aimee glared as if ready to scold her child. Heath and the boys stood a few paces behind.

"Hi." I smiled and placed a hand on my knee to stop it from shaking. Hopefully, she wouldn't call me out in public.

Aimee pounced. "Aren't you hosting a birthday party?"

"She goes to bed early, so the rest of us are here for the after-party." Both knees shook as I stared at Richard. I'd iron out my lie with *him* after Aimee left.

"Was your mother surprised?" Aimee glared at Jordan.

"Very," he said, smiling. Fortunately, I had told him earlier about the conflict. "Celine's the epitome of grace under pressure. Mom—"

Aimee turned toward me. "You missed an incredible game. John's team pulled out a victory in the final inning." She left, and the family headed to their table.

Fortunately, Richard didn't care about the lie, saying success requires sacrifice. Jordan waited until we got home to rebuke me. "You need to practice boundaries with your family. Let them know work comes first, not a Little League game that won't mean anything to your nephew ten years from now."

I felt justified until Aimee called the next day, asking if I planned the client dinner before she invited me to John's game.

"I'm sorry I didn't make it," I said, carrying guilt for backing out of a commitment. "But I don't owe you an explanation."

"I should've known you'd choose your career over us."

"Your family *is* your career."

"You're driven by an insatiable desire to be successful—whatever that means. You'll lie to everyone, including yourself."

My claws came out. "You're so high and mighty you think anyone with different values than you is wrong. Heaven forbid I have a career and ambition. That's not a sin."

"I'm not wasting my time talking to the wall," Aimee said calmly. "Next time just tell me the truth." The angrier she became, the more low-toned and controlled she got. I was the opposite.

"I would!" I paused since my voice boomed. "If you'd stop preaching every time my values don't align with yours."

"Then respect me enough to be honest."

"Don't give me flack when you don't approve or agree when I tell the truth."

"That's the problem. You want to live life any way you want, as if you're on an island and your actions don't affect us. We're family, not a client."

I hung up, wishing she'd understand just once.

After that, she quit notifying me of family events. We only saw each other during visits with our parents on major holidays, the last time at Christmas.

When Aimee texted on Sunday night, I sat in the Haven and stared at the message.

> Maman informed me that you left Jordan.
> Do you want to meet for lunch tomorrow?
> Panera on Cherry Street?

Really? Was I up to meeting with her? My emotions were riding a teeter-totter, so I might not handle her well if she lectured or invited me to church.

But I missed my nephews. Since I wasn't with Jordan, I could be more involved in their lives. That was a good enough reason to text back.

> Definitely!!! How about at 11:30? 😊

Aimee responded right away.

> Great, see ya then, sis.

CHAPTER 5
MAY 7

I arrived at Panera by eleven twenty, wanting to nab a booth before the lunch crowd hit. I'd research a lead, contact an interior designer I met briefly last week at a networking lunch.

Fifteen minutes and an unanswered call later, I slid out of the booth, wanting something to drink. Aimee entered the restaurant looking effortless in a coral maxi with spaghetti straps and a coral headband. I waved as she scouted the room. Seeing me, she smiled and approached. I quickly placed my laptop in the satchel lying on the booth seat. My assurance I'd give her my undivided attention.

"Hi, sis," she said, briefly hugging me. Vetiver mingled with vanilla and lavender wafted.

"You look luminous," I said.

A contemporary Helen of Troy, Aimee radiated from her coarse, blonde hair and olive complexion. With my baby fine hair and blanched almond skin tone, I envied her goddess beauty.

"Thanks." She inspected my sleeveless grey pantsuit. "Are you meeting a client later?"

"Nope," I said. I dressed sharp in public in case I'd make a business connection. "Ready to eat?"

Her extended hand invited me to go ahead of her. I ambled to the ordering counter then gracefully turned to Aimee. "You first. It's my treat." I stepped aside.

She hesitated then stepped forward. After ordering her usual, she grabbed her wallet from her coral knitted handbag and pulled out cash.

"I'm paying," I reminded her. Why wouldn't she accept my courtesy?

"Habit." She tossed the cash and wallet back into her bag.

I chose to give her the benefit of the doubt. Otherwise, my patience might not last through lunch.

After I ordered, we went to the beverage station.

Aimee turned to me. "Where are you living?"

"At Jennifer's." I stared at the myriad of beverage options. Did I want something highly caffeinated or something more subdued?

"I like her. Is this temporary until you rent a loft apartment downtown?" Aimee filled her cup with acai tea.

"I don't know, just taking it a day at a time." *Clunk, clunk, clunk.* I dispensed chunks of ice into my plastic cup then filled it with lemonade.

"Hard for you, isn't it?" Couldn't she drop the maternal tone?

"I prefer planning months ahead." I flashed a fake smile. It's true I was always scheduled and ready for the next event, while Aimee traipsed through as though life moved on her time.

"I was shocked when Maman informed me you left him," she said.

"Our relationship deteriorated months ago." I took a sip of my drink as we headed to the booth.

"Really?" She stopped walking. "I didn't know where you two were. What made you leave?"

"I'll tell you when we sit down." I didn't want eyes on us as we stood in the middle of the restaurant. I refused to air my dirty laundry in public.

She headed to the booth. I sat across from her, placing the number for our order at the front of the table.

Leaning toward her, I whispered. "He cheated."

Her baby-blue eyes expanded. "I'm sorry. When did you find out?"

"A few weeks ago, but I'm moving on." I cringed as a scene of Jordan and the receptionist replayed in my mind, me in my car, mouth gaped, watching them as they sat near the restaurant window.

What bothered me most wasn't the receptionist's low-plunge, vixen-red tank but that he never held *my* hand in public. I wasn't into making an exhibition of our relationship, but I wanted to hold hands. He refused, explaining he loathed public displays of affection. Eventually, I realized that wasn't the reason, since he quit showing much affection privately over the past year.

Why was this woman different? Did she make him laugh? Charm him enough to forget about me? Lure him with her sex appeal? The answer came like a newsflash: *She doesn't need much from him. Yet.* I'd been angry he worked late and wasn't around to help with my business.

"Glad you've finally left him." Aimee nodded as though she, not my parents, had advised me in this direction.

To detour from her opinions of Jordan, I sought a neutral topic. "When do you need to get home?"

"An hour or two." She looked at her blue nacre watch, a gift from Heath when he became fed up with her running late. "The boys don't get home until after three."

"Great!" I hoped we'd talk about them.

"Did you know the other woman?" she asked.

Of course she wanted the gory details.

"She's the receptionist at Jordan's office. No older than twenty, so probably attracted to his charm and money." I stiffened, embarrassed by how impressionable *I* was when I met him.

"If it were me, I would've stormed into the restaurant and

confronted her. Reminded her that he was taken." Aimee scowled. "Anyway, I wouldn't have let them off the hook that easily."

I wasn't surprised Aimee would interject herself into the situation, although I doubted she'd react like that *if* her husband cheated. "It's easy to assume what you'd do until you're in the situation. I was too shocked and hurt to confront him." Rather than raise my voice, I took a long sip of lemonade. "I still haven't. He's in London and doesn't know I moved out."

Aimee furled her brows. "It's a mystery how you're a lioness in business but a lamb with him. Let him know he disrespected you. Direct is the only language men like him know."

Of course she knew what I should do. I looked at her steadily, hoping she'd reconsider her words. But she stared back like she hadn't said anything offensive. "You don't have a clue what our relationship was like," I told her. "I know how to confront Jordan."

She waved her hands. "Now isn't the time to advise you. I suppose between Dad, Maman, and Jennifer, you've received plenty of counsel."

"Yes." I looked away, wishing I hadn't disclosed Jordan's cheating.

"I'm here if you need support. And if you want to meet new people... make new friends..." Her shoulders raised, framing her swan neck. Nothing thrilled her more than matchmaking. She was probably making a mental list of eligible bachelors.

"I don't do *new* well," I said to deter her.

"I know, hon." Aimee extended her hand.

I grimaced. Even though she called everyone "hon" as if she were a pageant mom at a beauty contest, I took it personally.

"What's wrong?" she asked, returning her hand to her side.

"Just getting used to us being together." I flashed a weak smile.

"Let's make up for lost time. We can put all the mess behind us."

What mess did she mean? The way I handled our relationship? Our lack of camaraderie?

I didn't respond but fought thoughts in silence while she chattered about Heath and how business at his insurance agency was steady. Yada, yada. I was relieved when our food arrived.

"How are the boys?" I asked.

She smiled. "They're fine. Busy."

My phone rang from beside my plate. The interior designer's name flashed bright like a Broadway marquee. I almost touched the phone, but I set my hands on my lap.

"You want to answer that, don't you?" Aimee asked.

"No." I put the phone on silent then set it in my unzipped purse. "Where were we?"

"Is it a client?" she asked.

"How are the boys?" I countered. Oops... I just asked about them. "Will they be attending any summer camps?"

"Probably, but I'm focused on getting through this week, since they're still in school."

"Don't you need to sign up for camps now before they fill up?" I stole a glance at my phone. No voice message yet. I hoped the designer wanted to meet. I needed another client before Jordan returned.

"I'm not used to you being so enthusiastic about the boys." Aimee sliced a chunk of chicken in her salad in half. "I understand you were divided between Jordan and us, but even before, work distracted you at family gatherings and the boys' events."

"Wait." I slammed my cup on the table. It tipped to the side, but I caught it and set it upright. "Are you saying I was distracted *before* Jordan?"

"You were always on the phone and left early from gatherings and the boys' events."

"I left work at the office and rarely answered my phone. There were plenty of times when I listened to you about the PTA, your Bible study, and your headbands." I peeked at my purse, hoping this lead wasn't backing out.

"Like now. You're distracted." Aimee took a bite of her salad.

"I'm wondering why we're fighting." I glared at her.

She rolled her eyes. "Call them back."

"Later." I forced a smile, not wanting to lose this tug-of-war.

"Just address it. Your wheels are spinning, wondering what they want."

Aimee reached into her purse and applied coral lip gloss on her cherub lips. Why did she inherit the pouty, thick lips while I had papier-mâché thin ones? Obeying her signal to check the call, I grabbed my phone.

"Fine." I listened to a fresh voice message.

"Celine, it's Lauren Maxwell returning your call. Since we met at the networking lunch, I've wanted to get together to discuss your marketing services, so please call or text to set up a time. Have a beautiful day."

"I'll just voice-text her," I said. Aimee shrugged.

"Got your message," I said into my phone. "How about Wednesday at eleven thirty at Shades of Brown?" I turned my phone off and tossed it in my purse. "Now, where were we?" I asked.

She smirked. "You and Père are so alike."

Like Maman, Aimee used the French term for dad. Aimee seemed to identify with her Franco side, speaking French with Maman. I used to speak French fluently before grade school, but I wanted to fit in with my peers and spoke English. That's when I started using the American term for Dad.

"What now?" I groaned. I couldn't win.

"Business before pleasure."

"That's unfair. Maman said Dad changed after we came along."

"He came home at a decent time, but he still worked after we went to bed. Maybe you think that's normal, but Heath rarely works on weekends."

"Do you want to go there?" I asked, ready to engage in a memory battle. Always assuming Dad favored me, Aimee didn't acknowledge how much he doted on her. Anytime I insisted she cut Dad slack or try to understand him, she'd deflect, saying I was blind to his faults.

"I'm encouraging you to set work boundaries. Make time for family and enjoy life. When you're ready to get back out there, I know some eligible men." Again, her shoulders framed her neck. "Life is meant for enjoying relationships. Healthy ones, that is."

Irritated by her bachelorette campaign, I glanced at the door. "Seriously?" I dropped my fork and paused, frustrated I was losing my composure. Could she even help herself? Aimee anticipated her wedding since she was an adolescent. She staged weddings with friends serving as bridesmaids and me as the flower girl. Her life began at the wedding.

"You don't realize how self-absorbed you've been," she continued. "But why should you? You only have yourself to worry about. Your life is about having a prestigious career, pretentious clothes, and a prominent boyfriend. But I'd think you'd realize by now that you need something more."

I straightened the napkin on my lap. "Some of us aren't fortunate enough to find our man before we receive a diploma."

She pointed her plastic fork at me. "You refuse to see what's important, don't you?"

"I could say the same of you." I leaned back.

"I worry you'll wake up alone one day with only your career and money in the bank keeping you warm. That's not an abundant life, no matter how much Dad pushes that on you. I don't want you to regret not having meaningful relationships, especially with family."

I tossed my napkin on the table. "You've never understood me. My desires are different, but they're not shallow."

She looked down. "I do this to myself every time." Scrutinizing me as if counseling her boys, she added. "But I suppose I can't expect you to change overnight."

Fearing I might say something I'd regret, I took a bite of pasta. She stabbed a chunk of lettuce with a fork, surprisingly silent.

Wanting to sound composed, I waited until my pulse slowed before I spoke. "I'm sick of you lecturing, especially after I've suffered something upsetting. Maybe you've forgotten what a breakup feels like. Even the one doing the breaking experiences pain."

She studied me, probably assessing if I'd given her a line or was sincere. "Fine." She pursed her lips.

I waited, hoping she'd apologize. After about twenty seconds of silence, me fidgeting in my seat, she cleared her throat. "I'm sorry for your heartbreak." She nodded in empathy. "How about you attend church with us this Sunday?"

Another invitation to her church I used to attend. I liked the pastor and the large congregation where I could slip in and out without notice. But three years ago, the pastor dove into a month-long series about marriage and money. Since he never preached a message specifically for singles *once*, I felt he viewed singles as lower on the social and spiritual hierarchy.

After I left that church, I joined a traditional one with stained-glass windows and clergy in robes. Prominent people in my industry, clients and coworkers, filled the pews alongside other stalwart influencers in the community. When I dated Jordan, he attended with me, realizing the connections he could make. But I stopped going months ago, when we started to struggle more in our relationship.

I tapped my heels on the carpeted floor and summoned my sweetest voice. "I'm going to church with Jennifer."

"Really?" Aimee sounded skeptical.

I shrugged. "It's more my pace."

Her blue eyes blazed. "You're lying."

"How dare you accuse me." I dropped my trembling hands underneath the booth.

"I can always tell. Your lips tilt to the left and your eyes narrow. You still spread white lies as if doling candy on Halloween."

I repositioned my lips into a line. "What difference does it make if I attend church or not?"

She shook her head. "You don't want this lecture."

She was right—I didn't. I wanted to redirect the conversation to what mattered. "I want to reconnect and build healthier relationships with you and the family." I touched my cup as I paused. "Can we meet in the middle? I'll work on being more involved if you patiently let me find my way."

She sighed as if my request was a burden. "I'll let you know when the boys have games."

"Thank you." I thought about what happened with John's game. "I can't promise I'll make every family event, but I'll do my best."

"That's fine... Just don't promise you'll come and then change your mind at the last minute because something better came up."

I tapped my nails on the table, holding back frustration. If I didn't answer wisely, we'd continue talking in circles. "I won't."

"Fair enough." She raised a brow. I'd need to prove it to her.

We managed to finish our food and chatted about our parents. When we exhausted that topic, we said goodbye and she left. I stayed, working until five.

On my way back to Jennifer's, I chastised myself. I shouldn't have met with Aimee until I came down from the emotional whiplash of leaving Jordan.

CHAPTER 6
MAY 8

Since the bay window in Jennifer's guest room faced east, I moved the desk flush against the window. Maman often challenged me to always catch the sunrise. Once I began free-lancing and could set my own hours, I faithfully welcomed the sun each morning.

Today, shards of tangerine light emerged through salmon clouds below a charcoal blue expanse. Once the sun settled on her throne, I closed my eyes, took a few yoga breaths, and chose a mantra for the day. "I owe this day my best." I didn't always recite a mantra, but lately I was attentive to what I could control.

As though she was observing me, Maman texted.

Are you acclimating at Jennifer's?

I didn't respond, needing to tackle work. She could stretch small talk for an hour, and I didn't have time to listen about her garden now. I'd reach out on my lunch break, though the delay would frustrate Maman.

Born and raised in a Pyrenees village in France, she emigrated to the States after marrying Dad. They met when Dad spent a summer in Paris as a college student on a European study program. They married a year later. Despite her willingness to live in the States, she adhered to her French culture and instilled those values in Aimee and me. Assimilating Maman's *savoir faire* and appreciation of art served me well professionally.

I couldn't fully embrace the French's *joie de vivre*, though. They believed you should work hard but play harder. Indulge in a two-hour lunch break, stroll for hours at a botanical garden, dine with friends for four to five hours at a restaurant or dinner party.

Dad's family, the Monroes, embraced the American philosophy of enjoy life but work harder. The lines between joy and work often blurred. Why not invite coworkers to social gatherings and discuss work? Meet clients for a power lunch or on the golf course? Enjoy haute cuisine while diving into business?

My phone rang. Maman, of course. I was in a good rhythm with work and let the call go to voicemail. Fifteen minutes later, she texted.

> Call me. Urgent.

For Maman, everything was urgent. Could I order Pyrenees wine for her because she didn't like shopping online? Would I text pics of the sunrise or the azaleas at Woodward Park? Did I attend John's or Daniel's game? No need to stop my work. If she experienced a genuine emergency, she'd ask Dad to call.

I continued researching the interior designer's website and social. The copy was verbose. I'd have to teach her that you can say much with little. I should've scheduled a two-hour block for our meeting.

Maman rang again, wanting to FaceTime. Unable to ignore her anymore, I rested the phone against my laptop screen, then answered.

"Why didn't you answer earlier?" She leaned close to the phone, nose squished, eyes slanted. Her angry face. The sunlight shined on her dewy, olive skin. She wore her wide-brimmed gardening hat, and dirt sat on the tip of her nose.

"I was talking to a client." Oops... my mouth tilted to the left and my eyes scrunched. Aimee's diagnosis yesterday made me self-conscious.

"I'm your maman." She grabbed a tissue from her gardening apron and removed the dirt from her nose.

"I called you back." I wished she'd set the phone down. As she moved it around, I got dizzy.

She shook her head. "Did you listen to my message?"

"Why don't you fill me in?" I glanced at the computer screen. The interior designer's portrait on her "About" page was only a thumbnail. I made a mental note to inform her to enlarge the image to medium or large.

"Are you staring at your computer?" Maman asked.

I grabbed my phone and closed my laptop as if caught passing a note in class. "That happens when you call while I'm working." I sighed. "I'm here." What was "urgent" today?

"You're not with Jordan, so why is work more important than family? Aimee says you were distracted with work when you met yesterday. Why didn't you take the day off and spend it with her?"

Maman excelled at the French's art of critique, questioning your performance because you could "always strive to do better." Growing up, she'd dissect everything, especially academics, asking why I didn't get an A on my test or invest more time on my art project? I'd accuse her of being overly critical and not appreciating what I did *right*. "To improve is to grow," she'd argue.

"Please sit back," I said. "I prefer seeing you, not your hat."

She complied and pushed her sunhat behind her head, exposing her blonde bangs. "You have no *joie de vivre*. Work will always be there. You're not present with us."

"Aimee insisted I respond to a work text," I said.

"Even worse, you lied about church. We didn't raise you to lie!" Maman pursed her cherub lips.

I grimaced because Maman was right. My parents instilled integrity and honesty all my life, yet I didn't appreciate Aimee tattling. I narrowed my gaze. "It's none of her business if I attend."

"Je suis ta maman!" She pointed her long, slender finger toward me.

I understood French better than I could speak it, and Maman spoke English with me unless she got angry. Then she'd speak Metropolitan French. But if she slipped into the Gascon dialect—the language she was raised around, identifying, like many French people, with her regional identity more than her national one—it meant she was blowing a fuse and couldn't keep her emotions in check.

"That's it exactly. *You* are my maman. I don't appreciate when Aimee interrogates me as if I'm on trial."

"She invited you to church because you need a healthy community."

I removed my black shrug, feeling warm and confined. "You both need to realize I can't become a saint overnight. I'd think you'd cut me slack since I'm living with Jennifer..." I paused, so my words could take effect. "A genuine Christian."

"Your attitude is the problem." Maman sighed then forced a smile. "Will you attend church with her?"

I refused to step foot in any church, but I needed to pacify Maman. "If I will, do you promise not to drill me with twenty questions about the pastor and what they believe? I don't have time for small talk."

She put her free hand on her forehead. "Celine Elizabeth Monroe, do you think God is *petit*? *Non!* He's grand. Oh, how you worry me." She set the phone on her chair, stood, and spoke in the Gascon dialect as she talked to God about extending mercy to her confused and worldly daughter. At least, I think that's what she said. Although Gra-mere taught me that dialect, I still struggled to understand it.

Worn out from her cross-examination, especially since she was now absorbed in interaction with God that could last an hour, I cleared my throat. "Your preference for Aimee is my problem. Doesn't matter what I say, she's always right. I can't take it much more." I held my breath, not wanting to mad cry.

Continuing in her native dialect, Maman asked God to help her explain to her daughter. She sat on her chair, face cherry red but eyes clear blue. She wiped the sweat from her forehead and stared hard at me.

"One day, you'll have children and understand I never take sides. I defend you to her, but self-pity blinds you." She placed her index finger on her cheek as if contemplating sharing a secret. I waited, hoping she would. "Extend an olive branch," she advised, "so Aimee knows you care. She struggles with Heath about the boys. He wants John to work at the insurance office over the summer, but she wants him to wait until he's sixteen. We're concerned Heath is trying to place too much responsibility on John's shoulders. So, be patient with her."

"Obviously, she didn't share that with me because she knew I'd support Heath."

I loved interning for Dad's firm when I was fifteen. Even as a little girl, I insisted on accompanying him to his office if he'd go in on weekends. I'd sit on his lap as he explained balance sheets and income statements. Or I'd play office with my dolls while he worked. Maman wanted me to get fresh air, but I'd throw a tantrum if she wouldn't let me go to Dad's work. So, Maman compromised. If I'd play outside for a few hours, she'd drop me off at the office.

"No, she didn't tell you because she was focused on you." Maman's blue eyes became lighter. "You need each other."

No, she was focused on mothering me, I wanted to argue. But I wanted to get off the call more. "I'll work on bridging the gap."

Maman wiped a tear from her eye. I wasn't sure if she was sad about her daughters struggling in life or happy we were attempting to rekindle our friendship. She smiled. "Since you're not with *him,* join us in France. Gra-mere's heart will swell seeing you."

Every summer, my family spent a month in France, visiting our maternal grandparents. Since Papi died ten years ago, there was just Gra-mere, dedicating her time to serving her community. This July, Aimee and her family were visiting Gra-mere along with my parents.

I used to go every year until I worked at Specter, then I'd go every other summer. I stopped altogether once I started dating Jordan. "Save vacations for retirement," he'd say. I embraced his philosophy, appreciating his dedication to his career. Now, I realized he might die from a heart attack before booking a getaway.

"June is too soon. Next year, I promise." I nodded, hoping she'd be satisfied.

Maman shook her head. "Go with us now. Père can help your business."

"I've got an important call that I need to take."

If I didn't end our back-and-forth, she could endure for another hour. After all, the French I knew lived for debates. Their business meetings consisted of spewing opinions, challenging views, and swapping insults, but they'd end with *bisous.* No matter how many times I implored Maman not to engage in contentious rapport with Americans, she didn't back down.

"How come you prioritize clients over me?" She pouted.

"You're important, but I've got bills to pay. I'm walking a tightrope. Once Jordan returns to the States, I might not have any of our mutual clients."

"I've been praying for your business." She talked slowly, probably discerning I didn't have another call. "Take breaks. Stroll Woodward Park or the Botanic Gardens. Invite Aimee. Nature will rejuvenate your creativity, helping you with clients. And you'll need it when that boy returns." She blew me a kiss. *"Au revoir, mon petit chou."*

I winced, feeling like anything but my maman's sweet "little cabbage." If I lost clients when my ex returned, I'd need to work seventeen-hour days. Could I survive Maman and Aimee's pressure to practice *joie de vivre*?

CHAPTER 7

By late afternoon, my eyes were strained from staring at the computer screen for hours, my mind exhausted. When the words on my screen ran into each other, I turned off my computer.

As I stared out the window, Maman's voice echoed. *Nature will rejuvenate your creativity.* I might as well explore Woodward Park, my favorite local refuge. I clicked *Do Not Disturb* on my phone, then changed into a grey lounger set, its loose-fitting sweatpants with a crop top at midriff still fashionable. I donned a baseball cap and dark aviator sunglasses to go incognito. I wasn't in the mood to socialize if I ran into someone I knew.

Woodward Park, a forty-five-acre nature center near downtown Tulsa, featured a menagerie of landscapes. The wild northern section encased grassy fields, delightful wetlands, and variegated woods, while the cultivated southern landscape showcased a garden center and a rose garden.

Maman, a Master Gardener, used to volunteer here, caring for the extensive flora and teaching novice gardeners. When I'd accompany her, I'd always explore the tree arboretum on the northeast or the woods, where I'd cloister under a willow, count the yellow flowers on the golden rain tree, and collect fallen magnolia blooms.

Today I'd explore the wild section. As I neared a towering pin oak, I paused to soak in the quiet. The breeze blew on my face, cleansing me of urban toxins. Wanting to indulge in walking barefoot on the grass, the grounding Maman insisted we practice daily, I removed my slip-on tennis shoes and carried them. The lush grass and lemon dandelions massaged the soles of my feet.

A young couple on my left lay on a blanket. The woman, bestowed with beautiful almond eyes, glanced up. Her man, too occupied to notice me, played with her jet-black hair. I looked away, not interested in observing their love.

I trekked ahead. A father and daughter played hide-and-seek. The daughter giggled as she hid behind a juniper while the father called her name, pretending he couldn't find her.

Two elderly women on a wooden bench conversed freely. One waved at me, and I greeted them with "Hi" but continued onward.

When I reached the sandstone steps of the dense woods, I slipped into my shoes and pulled my phone from my pocket. I captured pictures of the wildlife, especially zooming in on a pin oak's yellowing catkin with male flowers hanging from a leaf bud. So promising and bountiful, ready to harvest.

What a great time to explore. I crossed the wooden arch bridge leading to the wetlands, my favorite portion of the park. Azalea bushes in blush pink, rose wine, and cotton white ushered me to a quaint grotto and a lily pond. Life slowed here, as if all my troubles could fly away like dogwood blossoms.

Once I stepped off the bridge, a vibrant yellow light flashed. What was that? The partial clouds slightly impeded the radiance of the sun. It must've been a camera flash.

In the field to my right, a twenty-something woman posed in a flattering bridal gown, an ivory sheath. The golden hour gave her ebony complexion an angelic glow.

The pleasant tenor of a tall, male photographer echoed. He hovered farther on the right, on the narrow, unpaved path. He sported a short-sleeved tee in royal blue and khaki shorts more suited for hiking than for capturing a styled bridal session.

He focused on her. I focused on him. Where had I seen him before? A wedding? No. All the wedding photographers I remembered were clean-shaven. A client's photo shoot? Nope. Since I worked so closely with those photographers, I would've recognized him immediately.

I took a few steps closer, magnetized by his hike-the-Rockies vibe, completed by a five-o'clock shadow and the wavy, chestnut-brown hair skimming his broad shoulders. He moved slow and steady as he captured the bride. His comfortable-in-his-skin type, unconcerned about social status or financial standing, was an enigma. How could someone blow status off and sustain a business like his?

Why was I drawn to someone this unassuming anyway? Was it because he was such a contrast to Jordan? My ex captured a room's attention by his charm and drive, but this man exuded a quiet pull from his inner world.

The bride stood stiff, barely smiling as she asked about posing. When he gave directions, he assured that the camera captured her beauty and poise. She bit her lip as though she was unsure.

"Stare at the camera as if Darren's admiring you," he said.

She smiled and raised her arms high, chin up, back straight, with supermodel ease. After he snapped a series of shots, he peered at the camera hung around his neck.

"Do you want to see this one with your arms raised? The sun's shining directly behind your head like you're reaching toward heaven." His dulcet tenor tone was like listening to someone share stories by a campfire.

The bride stepped toward him but stumbled. She caught her fall then carefully straightened her body. As she took a step, her head jerked back. She tugged lightly on her train, but it was caught on something. The photographer asked her to stand still, jogged to her, and crouched to investigate what impeded her. With the delicacy of a surgeon, he freed a branched twig from her train and tossed it far behind her.

She pointed to her train and whimpered. Did she rip it? He inspected it, stood up, shook his head, and whispered something. She laughed. Did he tell her a joke?

As I stepped closer to hear, she turned toward me. Her shoulders slumped. Oops... I strolled toward the open field behind the photographer.

"Excuse me," he said to me kindly.

He leaned his head toward me, becoming still. His hand off his camera but it laid near his chest. He smiled as though he recognized me. In an instant, I forgot where I was as though the photographer and I were in this space by ourselves. He took a step toward me, so I took a step toward him.

"Garrett," the bride said. "Is everything alright?"

"What?" He turned to her abruptly.

"Why don't we call it a night?" the bride said in a strained tone.

"Sorry, I'm just passing through," I said holding up my hand. Neither the photographer nor the bride looked my way.

He approached the bride then placed his hand on her arm. "No," he said. "This is Darren's gift. I'm sorry I got distracted, but we'll get through this."

She nodded.

He turned back toward me and smiled, exposing his straight, white teeth. "Do you mind giving us the field for about fifteen minutes? I'm wrapping up a bridal shoot. I only have a brief window to capture the bride during this golden hour." His tone tender as though reassuring an impatient child.

"Of course." I smiled. "I'll get out of the way."

"Thank you." He stared at me but with less intensity than when we initially caught each other's eye.

To give the bride her time, I strolled to the west end of the pond, away from the shoot and closer to the street. Sitting on a wrought-iron bench, I faced the pink azaleas, white dogwoods, and green shrubs on the hillside. Two Canada geese shrilled as they flew overhead and landed gracefully in the water. Once content, they stopped honking.

After I removed my ballcap, I ran my hands through my medium-length hair. I'd been growing it for six months from a blunt bob. Jordan convinced me that clients took a short-haired brunette more seriously than a billowy, long-maned blonde. When he went MIA from my business, I ignored his theory, and he'd said nothing about my growing hair. I couldn't wait until my blonde roots grew, since I preferred the lower maintenance of retaining my natural hair color. Plus, I looked softer as a blonde.

Lying my head back and closing my eyes, I wished my life was simpler. Scenes of my time with Jordan flashed. Him caressing my face on our first night in the condo. Us screaming at each other over the electric bill. Me escaping to the balcony while he stewed in our bedroom. We spent several nights shielding ourselves from each other behind locked doors and silent spaces.

I opened my eyes and sought a fitting affirmation. *Focus on the beauty around you.* An orange-breasted robin hopped near me. Just as I leaned toward him, sirens from an ambulance invaded my refuge.

Where could I find peace? I plugged my ears but couldn't escape the deafening warning sounds from more emergency vehicles. I sprinted toward the lily pond, but the photographer and bride were still there.

I ran into the open field, near the bronze statue advising "Appeal to the Great Spirit." Its Sioux chief rode bareback on his horse. Arms spread wide, head and eyes lifted toward the sky. If only I could be that free.

After I caught my breath, I peeked beyond the statue. The photographer and the bride were at the same spot, so I jogged toward the woods. But the photographer instructed the bride to head to the open field.

"I'm leaving. Don't mind me." I extended my hand. He nodded then returned to focusing on the bride.

I fast-walked to the arch bridge then stopped to catch my breath. After a minute or so, the couple I'd seen lying on the blanket earlier approached on the bridge.

"You might not want to go that way." I pointed toward the wetlands. "A bridal photo shoot is ahead."

The boyfriend raised his brows, flashing a cheeky smile at his girlfriend. I didn't see an engagement ring on her finger. *Is he dropping a hint?* That he cherished her was written all over his face.

The girlfriend nudged him away. "Let's not hinder them," she said, flatly.

I wondered if she wasn't ready. If only her young heart knew how rare the security of a man cherishing her was. I had two serious relationships before Jordan, but they each wanted to get married and start a family immediately. That's when I broke off the relationships, panicking they'd hold me back. Jordan never pressured me about marriage but never cherished me either.

"We can just watch," the boyfriend said. The girl shrugged.

"Enjoy your stroll," I said, waving.

They both smiled, then held hands, watching the photo shoot from a safe distance.

I needed this refreshment from nature. Yet, as I watched the boy's gentle affection for the girl, I couldn't help but to compare it to the harsh reprimands Jordan directed to me. I wondered if I'd be enough for any man to cherish.

CHAPTER 8

MAY 9

Jordan hadn't reached out since I crossed paths with Warner. Obviously, Warner hadn't contacted him, but I feared Jordan's silence meant he didn't land the wealthy client in London he was courting after befriending the client's son, a local entrepreneur. Jordan and his boss, the owner of the investment firm, were meeting with the son, his four brothers, and their dad in London, where the dad moved recently.

Knowing Jordan would retaliate if he didn't land the account and then found my note, I called all my clients to confirm their account renewals. My desperation grew when Richard Pine, my most profitable client, didn't answer.

Don't get paranoia. Remain confident. Your clients know you work hard for them, so you'll retain them regardless of Jordan.

Needing to recharge, I retrieved more coffee from the Haven's kitchenette. As I filled my mug, my phone rang. I bolted to the bedroom. *Please, let it be Richard.* I answered without checking caller ID. "Hello, this is Celine."

"Hey, Bobbie," Jordan said in a cheerful tone he hadn't employed in months.

My body tightened. *Bob* was his moniker for me. Some men use *baby* as a term of endearment. Jordan, of Irish descent, used the Irish word for money. I initially thought he was clever. Since his thirty-fifth birthday, though, I realized he viewed me as a transaction, like everything else.

We'd gone to dinner at his parents' new home, but not really to celebrate. Brooks, Jordan's older brother, worth millions before he turned thirty-five, paid to have the home built two blocks from his. Jordan didn't yet have even one million dollars in an investment account and wanted to scope out the construction.

Brooks and his family were at the dinner, since the brothers were cordial. After all, Jordan was Brooks's financial advisor. We were eating at a long cherrywood dining table when their dad told Jordan, "Boy, you could be starting your own investment firm if you had heeded my advice. But I suppose it wasn't your fault your mom coddled you."

Ten years ago, his father pushed Jordan to work for Brooks's company, but Jordan declined the offer, wanting to steer his own course. I squeezed Jordan's hand, hoping he'd avoid a scene.

Brooks leaned toward his dad. "Jordan is where he needs to be. He's grown my portfolio by twenty percent."

Jordan stood abruptly, knocking over his dining chair. No one else moved as we stared at him. He pointed to his brother, sitting across the table. "I don't need your defense, Brooks." He turned to his left, facing his dad. "I'll be able to have ten of these homes built. You'll see."

"Of course." His mom stared at her plate.

His dad placed his arm on his chair's back and glared across the table at his wife. "You prove my point."

"Leave her alone!" Jordan's fist was only a few inches from his dad's face.

"Don't you threaten me, boy." His dad swiped Jordan's fist away.

I wanted to defend Jordan, but that would feed into his dad's accusation.

Jordan nodded at me. "We're leaving."

I stood, gently laying my napkin on my plate of half-eaten food. I glanced at his mom and mouthed *I'm sorry.*

She nodded. Poor thing. After years of suffering her husband's hammering, she was in a million pieces. I wondered if she could put herself back together.

Jordan approached her and gave her forehead a peck. "Thanks, Mummy." We left with Jordan's unsliced birthday cake, a Black Forest his mom made.

That incident stamped its mark on Jordan. He became obsessed about reaching his financial goal. That night, he wrote on an index card and taped it to the bathroom counter.

1 million in my investment account.

He was hardly home after that, working on weekends and twelve to fourteen hours each weekday. When he was home, he was impatient, groggy, and inattentive. We bickered more than we laughed. I became a shell, reminding myself I wanted a man who'd reach the top in his firm, so I needed to sacrifice for him.

Even now, I'd sacrifice when he returned. If he continued to support my business, he'd expect the referral fees he had waived. Otherwise, I'd have to work longer hours to acquire new clients, as insurance for whatever he might do.

"Hey," I said casually.

"You don't sound happy to hear from me." His tone reflected a rebuke, not hurt.

"I'm calling clients about renewing."

"You should have better results than I've had. We didn't land the patriarch's account."

My mind raced as dread filled my lungs. I could hardly breathe.

Should I tell Jordan I left and talk it over? No surprises? I'd go to the condo and remove the note. "Did you acquire the brothers?" I asked, crossing my fingers.

"Of course. All but one were sharp enough to understand we're as profitable as any firm."

"Good for you." I exhaled louder than I expected.

"How's Richard Pine's account?" he said with an urgency demanding respect.

"Why do you ask?" I blurted. He hadn't cared about my business since his birthday fiasco.

"What's up with you?" he asked after five seconds.

Do this for your business, Celine. I forced words out. "I'm meeting with him on the 30th to solidify the expansion strategy."

"Good. Speaking of expansions, have you talked to Uncle Sonny? He wants to open a second location."

Jordan's uncle owned Okie Pawn and only tolerated me, even though my marketing strategy translated into increased sales. "He wanted to discuss it with you first, like always."

"Of course. Keep me in the loop."

I tightened my grip on the phone. This was my chance to break the news softly. He might not appreciate it now, but he'd see it was for the best. Once our relationship was strictly business, we wouldn't have to pretend we were a couple.

"There's something I need to tell you." I closed my eyes to focus.

"Can you tell me later? I've got another call." *Click.*

Typical Jordan. Not that interested in helping, only in feeling needed. I hated how much I missed the old times when we'd talk business. Not when he'd tell me what to do, but when he encouraged me to push my limits and asserted how creative, intelligent, and savvy I was.

Let him read that note. I could sacrifice that referral fee of ten percent if he'd still support my business. Probably the type of relationship we should've had from the beginning.

CHAPTER 9

As I drove north toward the coffee shop, I caught a glimpse of a billboard featuring an attractive woman wearing a ruby necklace. A man's hand touched the ruby. Show Love was written above her head.

I got flashbacks to my time at Specter Marketing Agency, my former employer before I freelanced. The jeweler was one of my accounts. My boss at the time, Bill Plaxton, almost kicked me off that account because I became possessive and overly passionate. I enjoyed that client, so I pushed everyone on the account, expecting perfection on all our work. Although I didn't apologize to my team, I assured Bill I'd tame my zeal.

My goal was to run the agency at fifty, and I was on that trajectory. I got promoted to strategy director earlier than the person formerly in that position. But I got derailed. Seeing that ad reminded me of what might've been.

I called Dad. Shortly after our customary greetings, I unleashed my paranoia. "Tell me I made the right decision leaving Specter."

"Did Jordan return early?" he asked.

"No." Needing Dad's advice, I dropped the bomb. "I talked to him briefly today."

"You did what? Why? Did Warner call him?"

"No, Jordan contacted me. He checked in a couple of times before I left too, mostly to brag about his time there." Jordan's failure in London was inconsequential, so I didn't tell Dad. "Anyway, today he was engaged in my business like when I went full-time."

"You didn't tell him you moved out, did you?"

"No."

"Good, good." Did he wonder if I'd return to Jordan? Before I could reassure him, he continued. "Back to your question. It doesn't matter whether you should've left the agency. We need to focus on building your business and retaining your clients. I tell you what—"

"I've got this," I said curtly. Once I decided to leave Jordan, Dad and I hashed through my business strategy multiple times, they were set in concrete in my mind. "I'm headed to meet a prospect now. I've already renewed my B2B membership and scheduled networking events."

"Let me know how it goes after your meeting. Remind me. How many clients do you need to replace if you lose Jordan's referrals?"

"Seven, although Midwest Appliances shouldn't be a problem. He's paid up until July. So, if I acquire five to six platinum or gold clients, I'll stay afloat even if Jordan's referrals jump ship."

When I launched my business, Jordan pushed me to create three tiered packages. The lowest was bronze: hail to the minnows launching their small businesses. Hurrah to the guppies at silver; they were often rebranding, growing their audience reach, or introducing a new product or service. Lay the red carpet for the flounders at gold, needing a marketing strategy and corresponding services such as branding, digital ads, and social media campaigns. Champagne toasts to the sharks at platinum, either small businesses expanding to mid-level or mid-level businesses pushing an expansion. They often implemented my strategy with a marketing agency or their in-house marketing team.

"I'm working on sending you leads with some interested people here in Florida," Dad said.

I already had two clients Dad referred, but they were content with their bronze package. Retirees usually preferred spending their time golfing and chumming with their buddies, not growing a business.

"Thank you," I said. "Well, I better go. I've arrived at the coffee shop."

As I turned into the parking lot, I wondered what might've happened if I hadn't met Jordan two-and-a-half years ago, when I was still working at Specter but servicing Dad's referrals on the side. Wanting to grow my business, I attended a fundraiser at The Mayo Hotel for a charity the agency didn't support. I stood alone by the bar, scouting people to network with. Jordan approached in a navy suit with a gold tie tack. He carried a wine glass in his hand and swagger in his step. His hair slicked back, each strand stayed in queue.

I was attracted to his energy, a typhoon swirling with confidence and intention. He asked what an attractive woman like me was doing alone. Said if I was his date, he wouldn't let me out of his sight. I was flattered. Now, I wished I'd had more sense to run.

After that night, we were inseparable. I was intoxicated with him, not just his Irish green eyes focused on me, but his business acumen. Within a year, I had enough clients to leave Specter and freelance full-time as a marketing consultant.

I shook my head. I couldn't afford to replay what might be my biggest regret when I needed to focus on finding a vacant spot in the crowded parking lot. Fortunately, a car pulled out, freeing a space.

Before I could get out of my car, Lauren Maxwell, my lead, texted.

> Sorry. I'm running late. I should be there
> within ten to fifteen minutes.

"Seriously?" I wanted to cancel the meeting. I didn't want a client who disrespected my time, but I couldn't afford to be fastidious. So, I headed into the coffee shop.

As I stood in a long line inside, I focused on the boho interior. The furniture resembled a college apartment. An eclectic set of Victorian sofas and mismatched midcentury chairs at round walnut tables added to my nostalgia for the time I was a visionary believing I could change the ad world. My eye caught on an abstract painting of a woman emerging from an egg, her arms raised toward cotton clouds. I hadn't seen that one before, but the shop rotated artwork, promoting local artists.

The inspiring atmosphere must've been why I suggested this place. It used to give me hope, but now I regretted the decision. The constant whir of the espresso machines and the sight of college students huddled at their laptops reinforced I might be rebuilding my business. If my clients left, I might be looking for a part-time job.

"Focus on your presentation," I told myself, not wanting to learn how to make a latte. I reviewed the main selling points I'd devised to hook the interior designer. The last one made me smile. Busy brainstorming how a campaign created around the designer's living room could attract the hottest leads, I wasn't ready to order when I reached the barista counter.

"Sorry, you can take the next person in line." I stepped aside and reviewed the menu on the wall.

"Celine?" I turned to the voice from behind and did a double take, hardly believing. There stood Bill Plaxton, my former boss at Specter. I almost didn't recognize him in relaxed blue jeans and a grey polo, a far cry from his tailored, three-piece suits. I glanced down, wondering if he still wore Looney Tunes socks to remind him to enjoy work and not take himself too seriously. I once teased they announced that he was Bugs, devoted to outwitting the competition.

The last time I saw him was on my last day at Specter. When I told him I was going full-time as a consultant, he stiffly said he wanted the best for me, which I interpreted as *You're not ready, kid.*

"Hello, Bill," I said as he shook my hand.

"I see you returned to your blonde roots. You look—"

"Are you in line?" a young brunette woman asked Bill.

"Go ahead," he said to her. He stepped to the side, next to me.

What was Bill about to say? That I looked more bohemian—like a chilled freelancer? I didn't need him to confirm Jordan's belief that executives took brunettes more seriously. Mostly because it'd reflect who I was with Jordan; I didn't need to see that woman in the mirror.

"I recently ran into a friend who's one of your clients," Bill said. "He had only praise for your work. Monty Prize."

"Oh yeah." Monty, my landscaper client, upgraded to my gold package last month. While he expected excellence, he was friendly and open to my ideas. "Since we began targeting more affluent neighborhoods, I've successfully helped him double his client base."

"He mentioned his investment advisor referred you. Sounds like you've formed a strong partnership."

I plastered a wide smile, refusing to show discomfort. "He introduced them, but I'm servicing their accounts."

Should I implore Bill to encourage Monty to retain my services after Jordan returned? Or would I come across desperate?

"Looks like we both made the best choice for our careers," Bill said. "My cardiologist warned me to watch my stress. That's why I landed a slower-paced job."

Did I hear him right? Stress, slower-paced job...

"I retired from the agency to invest in the next generation of marketing minds at TU. I start this fall." I couldn't imagine Bill quitting Specter. His eyes narrowed. "I suffered a minor heart attack about six months ago, and my wife begged me to switch jobs."

"I didn't know." I took a step toward him.

"I'm ready for the change of pace." He tipped his head slightly. "What brought you in here?"

"Meeting a prospective client, although I'm shopping for an office space." I'd stopped looking once I realized Jordan wasn't on board with me, but I wanted to look professional with Bill.

"Good for you." He nodded. "I'm on my way to Specter now to meet with Stella. I like to stay current in the marketing world."

"How are they doing?" Longing to justify leaving, I used to follow up regularly with a contact who worked there. But once I acquired Midwest Appliances, I quit reaching out to him.

"Terrific. It's humbling because Stella is filling my position better than I did. She's pushed the agency to focus on measurable outcomes tied to performance, hired IT minds, and streamlined the account management team. Their reputation is spreading in the industry."

My stomach sunk. "Who's the VP of strategy now?"

"Morgan."

She had filled my position as strategy director when I left. I stepped toward the barista counter, my head swirling so much I almost lost my balance. What had I done?

"Are you okay?" Bill asked.

"Just need to eat something. I often work through breakfast and lunch."

"Go ahead and order." He motioned me toward the barista.

I wasn't hungry, but I got a blueberry scone and a drip coffee. After I ordered, Bill touched my elbow. "Wondering what if?"

I smiled, shaking my head. "No..." When Bill was my boss, I would've opened up, saying, *It sounds like I would've been climbing steadily up the ladder.* But Jordan drilled I should always keep a poker face. Confidence is an invaluable commodity. I straightened my posture. "Consulting fits me like a glove. And I prefer setting my own hours and helping clients excel. Like Monty."

Bill stared at me with scrutiny. I didn't flinch but kept my steady smile. He nodded. "Good for you."

"I enjoy collaborating with others. I work with a graphic designer and a production team for mid-level clients. You know, applying all my experience."

He gave a half smile, the same one he flashed when I asked why I didn't get the promotion from strategy to marketing director. "You've got a lot of experience to help small business owners."

My shoulders sagged as he said *small business owners*. Was he minimizing my talents? Assuming I could only support mom-and-pop businesses? I hoped Lauren wouldn't show up until *after* Bill left.

"Thank you. It's rewarding watching my clients' businesses grow."

He checked his watch. "I better order and get to the agency. Great seeing you, Celine. If you need referrals, I've got a Rolodex of contacts." He chuckled. "Listen to me aging myself."

"Thanks. Are you still on the same cell number?"

"Yep."

I nodded then grabbed my coffee and scone from the counter. Needing to nab a table and wait on Lauren, I checked the sitting area in the back, away from the noise of the barista counter. A three-seat table against the wall served nicely. I texted Lauren that I was in the back room, opened my laptop, and reviewed my notes. But I could only focus on my time at Specter.

On December 12, 2014, I stood in Bill's office presenting my argument about why I should've been promoted. "Yesterday, you assured me I was the top candidate. I know our clients' needs and have invested years into my team." He only nodded, so I continued as if he could alter the decision. "No one has heard of this Southern Cal import. Our Midwest clients have different needs than a corporate outfit in L.A."

I omitted that she was forty-something with an MBA, while I was only twenty-eight. Adding my four years of interning, I had eleven years of experience at the agency.

For a few seconds, he hadn't said anything, making me wonder if he was keeping something from me. Strange, because we were usually direct with each other. He shook his head. "I'm as shocked as you are."

"Did they give you an explanation why I wasn't hired?"

He'd popped a mint in his mouth, probably to buy time. "After discussing it with the team, they thought you needed a few more years to grow into the position. You climbed the ranks faster than anyone in their history. That's why they interviewed you though Stella has more experience. Trust me, you had my vote."

My youthful exasperation got the better of me. If I had listened to Dad, who advised me to stay and learn from Stella, Bill, and other executives, I could've been Strategy Director VP, sitting in a plush, corner office with wall-to-wall windows facing the Tulsa skyline. Not in a coffee shop resembling an antique store, with kerosene lamps, gilded candlesticks, and mismatched furniture.

I took a long sip of coffee and attempted to direct my thoughts. *Focus on the interior designer. You need this potential client.* But desperate affirmations couldn't drown my regret of what I lost by leaving Specter.

CHAPTER 10

Running into Bill distracted me from fixing my coffee to my liking, so I returned near the barista counter to add more cream and sugar. Swirling the stir stick, I faced the entrance, waiting for Lauren to arrive. And arrive she did. The sunlight through the window highlighted her bumblebee-yellow jumpsuit. A straw handbag embroidered with rows of Amalfi lemons hung over her shoulder, and thick gold bangles adorned her petite wrist.

As I approached, she greeted me first. "Celine, so sorry I'm late." She gave me *bisous* on each cheek. "I lost track of time chatting with my brother."

"Is he a designer too?"

She laughed. "Not at all! He took pictures of my design."

"Are they professional enough for social media?" Hopefully, he wasn't a hobby photographer.

"Of course. Garrett shoots high-end weddings."

"Perfect." Seeing the growing line, I stepped to the side. "I better let you order. I'll be in the back."

Lauren took a step forward in line but continued talking. "I'm excited about our meeting. I know you can get me in marketing shape. Your Insta is riddled with marketing tips."

I smiled, impressed she did her research. "Thank you."

"Mine needs rehab." She flittered, barely taking a breath. "I'm too random, posting pictures of my life and projects when I feel like it. It won't generate as much attraction, will it?" I got slightly distracted watching her hands soar here and there.

"Taja, my social media wizard, will transform your social media platforms."

"I can't wait to learn more, but I'm talking your ear off. I'll join you in the back."

As I returned to my table, my confidence rose. She was more extroverted than our initial meeting. I'd tap into her energy during my pitch. Since she wore her emotions on her face, I'd be able to gauge which ideas landed well.

When she returned, she sat next to me. *Doesn't she respect personal distance?* I wanted to scoot my chair away but worried she might interpret that gesture as unfriendly. I stared at my notes on my laptop, so I could focus on my pitch instead of my agitation. Close-distance people tended to be impervious to social cues.

"Excited to grow your business?" I asked.

"Yes. But—"

"Spicy latte grande," the barista yelled.

Lauren stood. "That's me. I'll be right back."

When she returned a few minutes later, she patted my hand. "So, what's your story?"

I counted to five, so I wouldn't pull my hand away. "I'll work directly with you to create and implement a marketing strategy. We'll set goals, launch campaigns, and review your progress monthly. Between reviews, I'll update KPIs—key performance indicators—on your marketing dashboard we'll set up."

She removed her hand then cupped her ear. "Sorry, it's getting loud." The people behind us were talking and laughing boisterously as if at a frat party. You'd think they'd be conscious of others in the small space. She scooted closer. "I appreciate your enthusiasm for your business, but I want to know more about *you*."

"Sure." I copped a faux smile. Would my résumé determine if she'd hire me? "I'm a Tulsa native and—"

"So am I! Oops... I'll let you talk." She covered her mouth.

"I graduated from TU with a double major in marketing and journalism. Started my career at a marketing agency before launching my consulting firm. So, I have fourteen years of marketing experience if you include an internship." I took a sip of my coffee, realizing I had forgotten about it.

"That doesn't tell me much about you. I need to know if we'd be a good fit." Her smile faded into a focused stare.

I looked away, but Dad's voice echoed. *Always give clients your focus.* I turned back and smiled. "I have a sibling who lives in town."

"We're blessed, then. I can't imagine if my brother lived in another state or, worse, another country."

"Sure," I said again. Did I appreciate Aimee living in town? It'd seem easier if she lived in Florida near my parents. That way, I'd knock out two birds with one visit and be spared a lecture about how I wasn't involved with family.

"Okay. Since I was late, I'll learn more about your life later. I'm excited to hear how you'll promote my business."

Despite the noise, we met for over an hour, conversing louder than I cared to. Having people possibly overhearing us violated my privacy. As we talked, I kept reminding myself to convert this lead. Once I nailed my closing, I stood and extended my hand. But she stood and hugged me like I was a long-lost relative.

"God's in this," she whispered.

I stiffened. Was she spouting religion to push me to go low on my services? *Here's a scripture for you,* I wanted to tell her. *A laborer deserves his wages.*

She patted my arm. "I think we're going to be good friends."

Good friends? This woman was hopped-up on caffeine or *extra*verted. I bit my lower lip, so I wouldn't say something snarky to Ms. Congeniality. Fortunately, a young woman walked past us, and the aroma from her coffee snapped me to attention.

"I'll email you a proposal. Let me know if you have any questions. Otherwise, sign and pay. A scheduler will pop up to set our next appointment."

"I'll be looking for that email." Lauren grabbed her handbag then waved goodbye.

I settled back at the table to make meeting notes. About twenty minutes later, she texted.

> Enjoyed our meeting. I'll take the
> platinum. See you soon.

"Yes!" I made a celebratory fist, and someone in the crowd behind backed me up with a cheer. Lauren was okay, not entitled or inauthentic. Since she signed up for my largest marketing package, I could tolerate her religious zeal and expectation for friendship.

CHAPTER 11

As I left the coffee shop, I trudged behind that boisterous block of young adults. I tried to veer past them, but they stopped abruptly near the crowded barista counter to chat with someone. To avoid running into a young woman in a red tank and denim cut-off shorts, I swerved around her but almost tripped over my feet. The group didn't seem to notice.

My irritation lingered as I headed to my car. Although I should bask in the victory of landing a client, I was bothered by the chaos of the coffee shop. What if I'd run into Jordan or someone else from our social circle next time?

Headed to Jennifer's, I looked around while at a stoplight. A **For Lease** sign stood in front of an office building. The sign was standard fare, but to me, it flashed neon yellow. I liked the building's bungalow style, its cream brick exterior with large twin windows resembling a home. Once the light changed to green, I turned onto the side street leading to the office lot. I parked next to a black Mercedes with the driver looking at his phone, just as another vehicle pulled away.

Shortly after calling the number on the sign, I realized that the Realtor, Russell Kirby, was the driver in the Mercedes. I asked if he could give me a tour since I was parked next to him. He turned to look at me and hesitated. Did he need to go? Fortunately, he agreed to the tour and gave me twenty minutes.

At least Russell remembered to hand me an application. Although he was professional, his impatience grated on me. I didn't appreciate feeling like a herded sheep prodded through a pen's gate. Granted, I was a last-minute tour, but I was a strong candidate. Maybe he didn't take me seriously because I was a thirty-something woman. Whenever Jordan and I toured offices, the Realtors treated us like VIPs.

Despite Russell's attitude, I wanted the office. I stood outside, soaking up the sights and sounds. Even at that busy time of night, the congestion seemed removed. The office space was at the end of a side street. Across the street was a sub shop and a grocery store, convenient for grabbing lunch or dinner. The best part? Jennifer's home was only a few miles away.

I called Dad. "I found my office!" My excitement grew.

"I didn't realize you were looking again."

Shoot! His cautious tone caught me off guard. "I need a private place to meet clients. At the crowded coffee shop, I struggled focusing on my pitch to the lead, so I refuse to experience that again." I groaned, heightening the drama. "I landed the client, but with all the noise, we could hardly hear each other. If I want to acquire mid-level clients, that atmosphere won't work."

"Can't you wait until June, when you know what Jordan will do?"

"Why this lack of confidence?"

"You don't need added pressure."

"What if I run into him while meeting a client?" I asked.

"I can't imagine Jordan at a coffee shop."

"I've searched for months and haven't seen anything this lucrative. Twelve hundred square feet for $2,150 per month. Jordan and I were looking at half that square footage for $2,500."

"Seems like a great deal," Dad said. "But can you fit it in your budget, especially if you lose clients?"

"I just landed a platinum account." I paused to get composed. "This office makes sense. It's the whole building, so I could sublease. It has a large conference room, a kitchenette, and a large private office in the back with a personal bathroom, including a shower. On the tour, I even got goosebumps."

I prided myself on being pragmatic, so I usually ignored physical signs, but after touring ten offices, I knew this was the one.

"How much do you need a month?" he asked. "To cover rent at Jennifer's, this office, and other expenses?"

"About six grand. I bring in about eighty-five hundred."

"How much of your expenses goes toward housing?"

"I'll look it up." I opened my financial management app. "Only around forty-four percent. If I acquire three bronze-tier clients, that'll pay the rent. And I'm confident I'll retain most of my clients."

"Is that doable for this month?"

"I'll have to hustle, but I always like a good challenge."

Through a long pause, I waited for his punchline. "What if Maman and I loaned twenty-five grand to cover most of your office rent for a year? You could pay us through interest-free installments once you rebuild your clientele."

I wanted to hang up. "Do you doubt I can cover the lease?"

"No, we want to support your business and lessen your stress."

The tired girl in me was yelling. *Take the money. They're your parents.* But Jordan's voice echoed. *You can't make it on your own.*

"You don't have any kids and have never asked for financial help."

"I'll make it, but thanks." My tone fell flat.

"If you change your mind, our offer stands."

Dad didn't need to talk to Maman. She'd agree—that's how the

French are. They helped adult children way longer than American parents did. Maman cooked every dinner for weeks after Aimee had John and Daniel.

"Thanks. I appreciate the support." I swallowed hard. I needed to adult, but would my pride get the best of me?

CHAPTER 12
MAY 17

As I prepared to work, Jordan texted.

Shoot! I had forgotten to plan for someone to be his taxi driver. What should I do?

Before I could text, Elise called. I let it go to voicemail. She was married to Matthew, Jordan's best friend who started a tech company. Jordan invested in it, believing it'd be his ticket to exceeding his brother's wealth.

I listened to her message. "Hey, we got four tickets for all of us to a charity ball on Saturday. Matt's beyond excited. There will be investors there, including Bryant March. Isn't this amazing? Call me so we can discuss riding together."

With all the chaos of moving out, I hadn't thought about our social circle. Most of them were Jordan's connections, so the women were spouses or partners of his buddies. Elise was my closest friend in the social circle. Yet her loyalty would be to Matthew, hence to Jordan, which it should be. So, I didn't want to call her back.

But her message gave me an answer to my dilemma. Matthew would be happy to pick up Jordan. I texted him.

> My potential client can only meet on Thursday night before he leaves the country. But Jordan flies in then. Could you be a lifesaver and pick him up at the airport? Just let him know, if you don't mind.

Matthew texted right back.

> Of course.

What a relief!

Five minutes later, Jordan texted.

> In the US, but my flight is delayed. Will stay in NYC 1–2 days. Will let you know.

I texted the info to Matthew, and he offered to still pick up Jordan. Awesome! Ten minutes later, Jordan texted again.

> Matt's picking me up. Will reach out when on my way.

> Great

His delay bought me a few days of peace. Yet I'd have to respond to Elise...

She beat me to the punch.

> We should have a spa day on Saturday. We'll need to look amazing. Let me know soon so I can book something.

Sorry, but my parents flew in for a few weeks. We have a family event on Saturday, but Jordan will be available. You know how he is about my family.

But this is uber important to the company and Jordan! Even if you can't make the spa day, surely your family will understand you needing to attend the charity ball.

I know but can't be missed.

She called, but I let it go to voicemail. She sent a text asking me to call soon. My life needed to get uncomplicated fast!

Sorry. About to meet a client.

Once everyone in our circle discovered I had left Jordan, I'd be an outcast and fodder for their gossip. Would Elise reach out, wondering what happened? And if she did, could I just explain without her expecting more?

CHAPTER 13

As I drove home from a meeting at the client's office, I passed the office building I had toured. Russell's car and a grey SUV were in the parking lot. Uh-oh! Another showing?

I wasn't sure if Jennifer's advice to not make a major decision for the next three months or the expense of an office had prevented me from already signing the lease. If I missed out on this property, I'd regret it. So, I called Russell, and to my surprise, he answered.

"Is the office still available?" Geez, could I be more quick on the draw?

"Which property?" he asked.

"Sorry, this is Celine Monroe. I'm inquiring about the property across from the Tulsa Ballet office on South Peoria." In my attempt to convey casual confidence, I sounded more like an automated voice message.

"It's available. I'm here if you want to stop by."

"Perfect!" I paused to temper my excitement. "I'm pulling in now."

Inside, he stood next to a beautiful blonde holding a baby. "Celine, meet my wife, Kathleen, and our boy, Dillon."

Kathleen showed me the sleeping baby. He had strawberry blond hair like his dad. There you go—Russell could've been anxious to get home to his family when he rushed my tour. I respected that.

"He's adorable," I said to Kathleen.

"Thank you. He's his daddy's mini-me." She kissed Dillon on his forehead.

Russell gave her and Dillon kisses before they left. Then he handed me the lease agreement. As I filled it out, seeing Sixty-Month Lease in bold font, my hand trembled. Where would I be in five years?

I put Jennifer's condo as my current address but didn't use her as a reference. She'd give me a glowing one, but I didn't want to justify why I was going against her three-month rule. I'd tell her after I got accepted. Instead, I listed the owner of the condo high-rises I moved out of and Bill Plaxton.

Russell confirmed he'd contact my references and gave me a copy of the agreement. We ended with a handshake and assurance that if everything checked out, he'd collect the first and last month's rent and hand me the keys. So efficient, I didn't have time to second-guess.

Not yet wanting to face Jennifer if she were home, I went to a local coffee shop to wrap up some work. Ecstatic about the office, I'd blurt the news. I called Dad, but it went straight to voicemail.

I arrived at Jennifer's around six. As I walked inside, she stood in the kitchen, cutting cucumbers. After a brief hello and inquiry about my day, she piped up. "Russell Kirby called about your lease application."

"Wait—what?" I set my purse on a barstool.

"He asked if you were my tenant."

"Is that legal? Isn't he violating some privacy law?"

She continued cutting. "He's checking a reference."

"You weren't on my list."

Jennifer looked at me. "Sorry if you think he violated your privacy, but Russell and I are friends. He actually referred this condo. If it helps, I gave you a raving reference."

"It's unprofessional to call you and pry into my business." Contemplating a back-out call to Russell, I turned to go upstairs.

"Look," Jennifer said. I faced her as she placed the cucumbers in a glass pitcher of water. "I'm not upset you're leasing the space, just surprised."

"It violates your three-month rule."

"I've been in your shoes." She paused. "Do you want some cucumber water?"

"I'm good... I've got to take care of something." I walked to the stairs, hand on the railing, prepared to call Russell.

"Alright. I'll be praying for you."

I stopped on a step. "What exactly does that mean?" I'd heard that before from Maman and Aimee and regarded it as code for *You need all the help you can get*. I appreciated Jennifer renting me a room, but that didn't give her access to my career.

She raised her brows. Uh-oh. That meant she was ready to engage, and she wasn't one to back down. "You need to slow down and process all the changes you've endured in the past few weeks."

"I've shopped for an office for months. It's not that major if you look at it in that light."

She smiled. "Got it."

"Thanks." I frowned, not convinced she approved.

"Are you eating here?" she asked.

I shook my head. "I'm exhausted, so I'm calling it a night."

"Sleep well." She poured cucumber water into a tall glass and took a sip. So typical. She could remain composed even if disappointed or flustered.

Once I was in bed, a cooler head prevailed. I needed the office, so it'd be best to confront Russell on the privacy issue *after* I secured the lease.

CHAPTER 14

MAY 18

Fortunately, the possibility of acquiring the office distracted me from obsessing about Jordan's arrival. I read the office's lease agreement three times. A fairly straightforward document, except it was a triple net lease. I'd be hit with any major repairs to the structure and appliances. Since the rent was lower to accommodate the extra expenses, I'd put money away monthly into an emergency fund.

To get excited about the office, I made a list of furnishings I'd buy and gave myself a budget of eight grand. A little risky to invest that much, but I needed to impress clients with something upscale, contemporary, and energetic, with pops of color.

When Jordan texted around six in the morning, my mind blanked.

> I'm flying into Tulsa at 3:35 p.m. I'll see you tonight.

Tonight for dinner? Or late at night, after he stopped by *her* place? I put his arrival details on my online calendar then got ready. As I applied makeup, I kept reciting something Dad would say.

"Conquer this hour, so you can conquer the day." I hadn't recited that mantra in a few years.

At eight, my phone rang. Though it wasn't Jordan's ringtone, I jumped then hesitated when I answered the call. "Hello, this is Celine Monroe. How can I help you?"

"Hi, Celine. It's Russell Kirby. Do you have a sec?" He seemed too chipper to deliver bad news, but maybe he was happy to get a task off his list, even if his news was received with gloom.

"Sure, what's going on?" I glanced at the lease agreement, hoping to sign it, not burn it.

"We approved you."

I pumped my fist. I was an eagle soaring above grey clouds. "Thank you. What do you need?"

"Can you meet at the office at one? My wife will serve as notary. I'll need first and last month's rent."

"Let me look." I checked my calendar. "I'm free."

"I think you'll be happy with the space."

"Thank you. See you this afternoon."

After kicking my legs under the desk, I opened my calendar and added an entry. 1 pm—sign lease.

I ambled downstairs to get coffee, Jennifer greeting me as I entered the kitchen.

"Beautiful morning," I said.

She secured the top of her coffee thermos. "You're eager to start the day."

"I..." I hesitated to tell her about acquiring the office, not wanting an unenthusiastic response to temper my excitement. "Jordan's arriving today, so I'm trying to get amped about work."

She frowned. "How about I make fried chicken tonight? That way, you have company in case he calls."

I smiled. "Are you sure? You're so busy."

"Miss out on making your favorite dish?"

"Alright."

Jennifer did friendship better than me. She was steady, faithful, and supportive, yet she did it subtly so you didn't realize she'd helped you. She always seemed to be around in your time of need, and you'd reflect back and notice how she wove her support into the difficult periods of your life.

When creditors blitzed her with calls, demanding she pay them—that's how she discovered A.J.'s mountain of gambling debt—she asked me to pray. I said a prayer and asked if she'd like to meet for coffee. But when she reached out, I kept asking for a rain check. Preoccupied with my career and ill-equipped to handle the emotional load, I avoided her. We eventually lost contact. So, I wasn't around when her marriage crumbled or when she fought for custody. I couldn't catch up as a friend, but I'd be there now if she needed me.

"By the way," I said, convicted about holding back. "I acquired the office and will be spending my days there."

"Oh, you did?"

"Yes!" I exaggerated my excitement.

"Good for you. This gives us something to celebrate. I'll pick up a cheesecake on my way home." Small creases appeared around her eyes. She meant it.

"Let me pick it up." I wanted to recoup my poor attitude from last night. "The office is symbolic. Jordan's flying in, and I'm moving on."

"For sure..." She glanced down.

I knew that tone. "What are you thinking?"

"I hope you make time to rest. Set regular hours and come home at a decent time. At least to eat a home-cooked meal." She tilted her head. "Self-care is nonnegotiable."

So is paying my bills, I wanted to say. "I'll try... I better start work."

"I'll be praying about Jordan."

"Thanks." I hugged her.

After she left, the condo felt empty. Silence ushered in troubling thoughts. I wished I had asked Russell to meet earlier, so I'd have a diversion.

When I went upstairs, I told myself not to think about Jordan, to get lost in work instead. A task reminder popped up on my computer screen.

Call potential clients:
>Ms. Kay's Bakery
>Koch Insurance Agency
>Kyle Linton, life coach
>Jeff Jones, Legal Services

I talked to three of four but could only set up an appointment with the attorney.

By noon, I couldn't contain my nerves about Jordan or my anticipation about the office, so I left the house. After grabbing a sub, I drove to the office's parking lot. Though I was early, Russell approached my car, asking if I'd like to come inside.

He gave me a final walkthrough, pointing out potential issues. Every time he mentioned a possible repair, the *beep* of a cash register resounded in my head. The bathroom shower worked, but the hot water heater sometimes made a gurgling noise. Beep! The A/C unit was older, so I'd be stuck with the cost of replacing or repairing it. Beep!! The roof was ten years old, so if it needed to be repaired, I'd be footing the bill. Beep!!!

Should I back out? "Is there a contingency if these expenses occur in the same month?" I asked.

"We'd work with you, especially if there's a steep bill." He paused. "My wife and I own this property."

"Can you add that provision in the agreement?" I asked.

"It's in there."

I forgot I had highlighted that clause in the agreement just this morning. I'd have to do better to mentally prepare for Jordan's arrival. "Oh good," I said.

"Do you have any more questions?" He placed his hands on his hips, showing his openness.

This was my chance to clear the air, especially to prove to myself that Jordan didn't snuff my voice.

"Why did you contact Jennifer for a referral?" I looked at Russell squarely but held my trembling hands behind my back.

He smiled. Again, I didn't trust him. Was I paranoid or discerning something? When Jordan copped a faux smile, I could sense his indignation underneath. "Jennifer's a friend and colleague. I reached out because I recognized her address. She gave you a bang-up referral."

I wouldn't back down. "Colleague or not, isn't asking her a breach of privacy? Were you concerned I wouldn't make rent?"

"Doing our due diligence... Actually, her referral was one of the reasons why my team and I chose you over another candidate." He crossed his right foot over his left, arms casually hanging at his side. No rigidity or tightly pursed lips like Jordan during a negotiation.

"Thank you." I laid my hands, finally relaxed, along my side.

"Ready to make this official?"

I glanced at my phone, wanting to call Dad, but he hadn't reached out. With uncertainties in my business, could I afford to sign this triple net lease? Could I pay for maintenance for the parking lot and structure, plus property insurance?

"Yes," I said, relying on that feeling of peace I experienced during the initial tour. I doubted I could find anything equitable that checked all my boxes.

By one, Russell and I, his wife holding Dillon, were huddled in the office's kitchenette. He pulled a manila folder from his briefcase and handed me a blue pen.

We signed and initialed all the sections marked Sign Here with yellow transparent stickers. He held Dillon while his wife notarized the agreement. As he cooed at his son, I relaxed. He was a decent guy.

I wrote the check for the first and last month's rent. The click of the pen snapped a ball and chain on my ankle for this five-year obligation. I took some yoga breaths to regain my confidence.

When he handed me a set of keys, my fingers tingled. Too late to back out now.

He led me to the front door and pointed to an alarm pad on the wall, giving me the disable and activate codes. I put them in my phone. Addressing protocol if the alarm should go off, he ended with a warning. "Although there are sensor lights in the parking lot and on the front door, don't leave alone late at night."

I waved off his comment. "I'm not worried about the neighborhood."

"Good, but I'd prefer if you don't work here late at night or stay overnight. And of course, you can't reside here—it's zoned commercial."

"Not a problem."

After he left, I reviewed the signed page. I touched my forehead, wondering if I ran a fever.

CHAPTER 15

Elise called and left a message. "Celine dear, I haven't heard from you. You're not working too hard, are you? Look, since Jordan agreed to the fundraiser, I booked the spa day. Call me ASAP, or I'll drive to the condo and whisk you away from the computer."

I doubted she'd go to Jordan's condo, but I didn't know how long I could hold her off. To distract myself, I went to my car and grabbed cleaning supplies. I inspected everything in the office, starting with the kitchen counters, the faucets, and the doors. The hardwood floors were scuffed in the sitting area. Crown molding in the back office had nicks. Corners of the rooms and baseboards had small strands of hair. The ceiling fan had sticky residue, probably from hair products. Rather unpleasant to deal with but much better than facing Elise.

I replaced the evergreen room fresheners with my diffusers. Lavender essential oil for my work space, citrus for the sitting area and entry. Now, this office channeled my work home.

Sherwood Forest trumpets blasted, announcing a text from Jordan. I nearly dropped the phone.

Just touched down. Will see you shortly. Exhausted.

I stared as if the text would self-destruct in my hand. When would he go to the condo? It was 3:45 p.m. Would he be too tired until tomorrow to go to the den and see the note on the desk? Would the receptionist bring him home from the office?

K

Not wanting to obsess about what he'd do, I left to rent a small truck, since I needed to bring my furniture and decor from a storage unit. When Jordan and I moved into the condo, I was excited to use the mahogany desk and chaise lounge I inherited from my grandparents, but he insisted we buy new furniture. After a few rounds of "discussions," he convinced me I could use the antique pieces when I leased an office. When I moved out, I was relieved he'd won that argument.

At the storage unit, I struggled with getting the solid mahogany desk on a dolly and into the truck's bed. Each time I tried to pull the dolly onto the metal ramp, I couldn't get enough momentum to pull it into the bed. Desperate to empty the storage and save a hundred dollars a month, I called Jennifer and asked if she knew a handyman.

Luck was on my side. The person she recommended was available. When he arrived, I was pleasantly surprised he was handsome—until I realized he was married. If he were single, I could flirt and see if I could attract a man. With Jordan neglecting me and cheating on me, I wondered if my confidence had sunk. I'd forgotten how to be feminine, flirtatious, and fun. The answer wasn't going to pay the bills.

After the helper and I moved everything into the office, I cleaned my eclectic collection of vintage and modern pieces. "Sorry, Nana, I haven't touched these brocade cushions in two years." Collapsing on the Viennese chaise lounge and caressing the gilt-bronze rosettes on the curved backrest, I laid my head on the luxurious soft back.

I finally had my own office. No matter what would happen with Jordan, I had something I could call mine. Something I accomplished without my dad's or Jordan's help.

CHAPTER 16

Jordan called. Was he home? He called three times, but I let every call go to voicemail. I wanted to turn my phone off, but I didn't want to miss a client reaching out. Hoping to drown out his voice messages running through my head, I listened to classical music as I returned to work.

When my cell phone rang about an hour later, I jumped a few inches. I slid off the desk chair, landing butt-first on the hardwood floor. Ouch! I stood and grabbed my phone from the desk. Dad wanted to FaceTime.

"Did you hear from Jordan?" He sat at the patio table on the lanai.

"Yes." I rubbed my butt, massaging away the pain.

"What did he say?" He leaned forward, and I could see more of his khaki newsboy cap.

"On his first message, he was composed, asking for an explanation and what I meant by 'leaving'. On the second, he asked why I didn't tell him in person. On the last one, he got irate, calling me a coward. Asking how I could do that after all the things he did for me."

The word *coward* played on a continuous loop in my head.

"Hopefully, this confirms why you needed to leave that..." Dad looked away.

"He's right. I knew I should've followed my instinct. I was cowardly not to confront him before London."

"I've thought about this situation more than anything else lately. The only way to have a spiritual disunion was to get away from his tentacles." Dad pointed his finger at me.

I didn't understand the spiritual component. But then, I didn't know what he considered "spiritual". Maman's understanding of the unseen dimension was something different—connecting with God in nature and living connected to others. Dad referred to it as justice. If you sowed truth, followed the golden rules, and walked in integrity, God, the Great Judge, would reward you. If I cut myself off from someone ungodly, I'd get rewarded. But I was as unspiritual as Jordan. So, was God Team Celine or Team Jordan? If we viewed it through Dad's justice lens, God wasn't beholden to either of us unbelievers—unless Dad thought I was covered under his policy.

"You don't agree?" he asked.

"Maybe." I glimpsed at the chaise lounge and pointed my camera toward it. "What do you think?"

My grandparents had the lounge refurbished in navy jacquard material with white outlining, so it appeared more contemporary. It fit in perfectly in this space.

Dad smiled. "I'm glad you claimed the piece."

"That inspires me. How about I call this room Monroe, in honor of them?"

"Thank you." He paused, took a deep breath, then continued. "How about showing me the rest of the office?"

As I gave him a tour, my excitement for the office grew, almost drowning the bits of Jordan's voice messages running through my head.

"Hold on," Dad said. He looked to his left. Maman must've

stepped onto the lanai. "I'm FaceTiming with Celine. She's in her new office."

Maman appeared on the screen and waved. Then she tapped him on the shoulder, "Seven, *mon chéri*."

Dad glanced at his watch. "Thanks." He smiled at me. "Need to call Heath. Office looks great. Will talk to you later."

"Love you." I blew him a kiss.

Maman sat in his vacated chair and stared at me through his tablet. "Can you give me a tour?"

"Is that about John working for Heath?" I asked.

"I don't know, although Père sometimes advises Heath on business." She shrugged. "I'm ready for a tour."

"Okay." I got slightly irritated, sensing she wasn't telling me the whole story. But I should be used to that. Maman told Aimee all things Celine but rarely spilled the news on Aimee. It'd be better for me to focus on the tour.

As I showed Maman around, she thought the office was too big. She wanted me to add a vase of fresh flowers in each room, but doubt she considered that I didn't have a bountiful cut flower garden in my backyard.

I walked to the front as her scrutiny sowed seeds of doubt about the office. Should I have leased a smaller space? I showed her the kitchenette, and she raved about the foods I could cook. Like Jennifer, Maman was concerned about my dietary habits, asking me to make time to eat three meals a day.

She urged me to show her the outside. "I'd like to know where in the city it is. The neighborhood. Is it safe?"

"It's safe." I walked outside and showed her the front door, avoiding any shots of nearby apartments. "The Tulsa Ballet's offices are across the street."

"Will you buy potted flowers for the front door? Get an artisan-created ceramic pot, not those boorish orange plastic ones at the hardware store. Your clients need a warm welcome."

"Maybe, but who'll water flowers? I don't have a green thumb."

"Buy a little watering can and set it near the flowers. If you buy geraniums, give them a small drink every morning in the summer. Once the temperature drops in the fall, water twice or three times a week. Keep them inside during the winter. I've taught you how to maintain potted flowers, *mon petit chou*."

"I'll think about it. Look, I'm about to head out." I didn't want to think about taking on another responsibility, even as low-maintenance as hardy flowers.

"Don't forget God's with you, and as much as I hate saying this, he's with Jordan too." Maman curled her nose as if forced to say those words. "We won't see him back down until we forgive and pray for him." She glanced up. "Why, God, must you reveal such difficult truths? Couldn't you send a donkey to tell him to stop harassing my Celine?"

"I tried to love him, but he doesn't want it," I said, interrupting Maman's little back-and-forth with God.

She shook her head, coming back to earth. "If he couldn't love you or receive your love, how does he love himself?" She shrugged. "*Je t'aime*." She blew me a kiss before hanging up.

Maman's question only reminded me of why I fell for Jordan in the first place. I cared more about what he represented than who he was.

I returned inside, went to the kitchenette, and grabbed a box of Bordeaux pecan fudge from the fridge. The creamy delight melted in my mouth, and the last remnants of pecan stuck to my tongue. The best feeling.

As I returned to Monroe, Sheridan Forest trumpeted from my phone. Jordan texted. I waited until my pulse slowed then checked the message:

> Call me or else I'll contact all your clients
> about what you did.

What was he wanting to convey with the red rose, the painting, and the pointing finger emojis?

CHAPTER 17
MAY 19

The next morning, Elise texted.

> I canceled your appointment at the spa.
> Jordan told me about your note. Call me,
> so I know you're alright. I'm worried sick.

She wouldn't relent, so I called.

"Sorry, Elise. It's been a hectic few weeks. I didn't reach out because I didn't want you to have to take sides, not that you would, but I understand your loyalty is to Jordan." I blurted the words fast as a preemptive strike.

"As your closest friend, why didn't you tell me you were moving out?"

She sounded hurt. In her world, I suppose, we were close. Yet, whenever I'd tell her about my struggles with Jordan, she'd minimize, saying all couples argue. Or she'd redirect, saying, "You'll work it out. You always do." She didn't want to consume anything negative unless I fed her gossip about our social circle.

"I couldn't take his neglect or our bickering anymore." Should I tell her about the receptionist?

"He thought you might be with someone else."

His jealousy ran thick. He often accused me of flirting with this guy or that. "You know me better than that. I wouldn't cheat like he did."

"I told Jordan you wouldn't cheat, but he's convinced that's why you moved out without discussing it with him first." She either ignored my statement or was too consumed with her narrative to hear clearly.

"It was the only way I could've left him; otherwise, we would've gotten into a big fight, and he'd try to talk me into staying. Our relationship was on life support anyway, so his cheating convinced me to pull the plug." I didn't want her to continue evading that fact.

"He's too crazy about you to cheat. The guy practically invests all his free time helping your business."

"Humph!" I gritted my teeth then took a deep inhale. "Like I've told you before, he stopped spending time on my business months ago. And now, you know why. So, I'd appreciate if you stop lecturing me that he's faithful just to relieve your conscience."

"I don't know what's going on with you, but you've changed. I hope you get professional help, because I'm worried for you."

"Don't be. Bye." I hung up, angry she wouldn't admit Jordan cheated. Did she call to spy? Trying to confirm his suspicions I was seeing someone? Money and success trumped loyalty and friendship in that circle, so I wouldn't put that past her. I regretted ever confiding in her as a close friend.

CHAPTER 18

The office doorbell rang. I glanced at my calendar. It must be Lauren, here for our first session. I'd need to put on my game face. As I walked to the door, I recited Dad's mantra. "Conquer this hour, so you can conquer the day."

Considering Lauren's exuberance when we met at Shades of Brown, I'd work on maintaining boundaries. Dad to some extent, Bill at Specter, and Jordan emphasized maintaining professional distance with clients. Be friendly. Talk about their personal lives if necessary. But remember you aren't friends. Otherwise, you might get emotionally involved and not make tough decisions that's best for the client and your business.

After my talk with Elise, I didn't need more so-called friends.

Lauren stood at the door, wearing a hot-pink jumpsuit. She gave me two *bisous* then entered the office. "I'm so excited about our first session! Although I admit, I need coffee. I got up before sunrise to watch the royal wedding. Did you?"

That's right, Harry and Meghan tied the knot. "No, but I liked the elegant simplicity of her gown."

Aimee texted Maman and me images and commentary from

the ceremony as though she was there in person. I was ambiguous about the British royalty, occasionally admiring their business attire on royal engagements, but too consumed with my life to really care.

"I love weddings, and a royal one, while over the top, reminds me of a fairy tale." Looking around, Lauren got excited. "Oh my gosh, this space has so much potential. Mind giving me a tour?"

"Sure. I want the vibe of an artist's studio. Abstract paintings and bold pops of color. Fused with professionalism. Highlighting my grandparents' Tudor-style furniture." I led her to the sitting room.

She stopped near the wall adjacent to the long narrow hallway and pointed to the blue, white, and gold abstract painting on the wall. "Is this Evan Painter?"

I nodded. "Impressive."

"He's über talented. I purchase his works for high-end clients, but I've never seen this one."

"I acquired two others from the same collection and hung one behind my desk and one in the conference room. He was experimenting with a new technique and doesn't usually sell practice pieces, but I tagged a free marketing consult with the purchase."

Lauren hugged me. "I'm going to enjoy working with you. You have exquisite taste."

"Thanks." I took a deep breath. I never experienced a client with her affinity for physical touch. As she put decor ideas in her tablet, I reminded myself silently that I'd have to reinforce boundaries without offending her.

After we discussed decor, we walked down the hallway and turned left at the end, entering through the open French doors of Monroe. I emphasized how I wanted to transform that space first, since it would be where I spent the most time.

"There's potential." Silently, she inspected the room slowly then turned toward the wall near my desk and approached the beige, three-drawer filing cabinet. "Would you be open to painting this navy with gold edges, using chalk paint? It'd highlight navy from your rug, the chaise lounge, and the painting."

"If you'll show me how. I've never painted anything before." My anxiety rose. I'd rather pull weeds in Maman's garden than endure the tediousness of prepping and painting, especially if it'd need to be perfect.

"How about I paint it during a brainstorming session? I'll get the paint and all the supplies."

I smiled. "Even better. Let me know how much I'll owe you for labor and materials."

"Consider it my office-warming gift."

A warning flag shot up. "This is for my business, so I'll throw in a few extra hours of marketing services."

She wagged her finger. "My goodness! Someone has a hard time receiving."

"I appreciate your generosity, but I've learned it's best to keep the lines of professionalism clear in business." I held my breath, hoping she'd understand and not take my conditional as a slight.

"In business, I adhere to the Golden Rule Jesus taught. Treat others like you want to be treated. My mentor provided office-warming gifts, so I want to bless you in return."

Was that attitude something I could trust later, when she knew more about me and discovered we held different values? At first in relationships, we seek commonalities and feel closer, until we realize our differences. That's when relationships could break down.

I took a step back, as if those hidden creatures of shame, regret, and angst living at the cold depths inside me could swim to the surface and become visible.

She tilted her head. "You don't agree?"

"I was raised with that Golden Rule too. But you have a different approach as a designer. You need to know your client's personal needs and preferences. In marketing, however, a client's private life and tastes could be different than their business needs."

"I see that, but I look at our dynamic as female entrepreneurs launching our businesses. Since we're in competition with bigger firms, we need to network. Through connecting and supporting each other, we're resourced like a large firm."

Hmm. She was more socially adept than her rah-rah, hip-hip-hooray routine let on. "I can get on board with that... Ready to show me your design work?" I could maintain professionalism as a fellow female entrepreneur. It wasn't as if she asked me to attend her birthday party or baby shower.

Lauren placed her phone on the edge of my desk and set her over-sized pink tote bag on the chair. Her phone cover was a photographic image of a sparrow with bright white feathers outlining the tiger stripes along its back. Dainty, yet alert. She tapped on her photos on the tablet, showing me the half bath she designed for the Designer Showcase. I liked her style. Warm, yet modern, with a tinge of Asian influences—the slate quartz sink with brass accents, miniature cream oriental figurines on one side, a burgundy orchid on the other. She had set a round beveled mirror above the sink, and oriental wallpaper with tinges of navy, cream, and beige enlarged the small space.

"These are terrific," I said, relieved her style wasn't too eccentric. "Minimal, yet inviting."

Lauren smiled. "Garrett's talented. He captured the best angles to make the space open up. Oh, I took a quick shot of him while he was at the Showcase."

She swiped to the next photo. Her brother smiled naturally with squinted eyes, a camera in his hand. I leaned closer. They shared the same cornflower eyes. He was the photographer at Woodward Park. I quickly looked away, as though he'd caught me staring.

I wanted to ask if he was single. But I thought it best to act nonchalant. "I saw him shooting a bridal session at Woodward Park, just the other day."

"What a coincidence. Do you know him?" Her eyes got large.

"No. That was the first time I laid eyes on him." I didn't want to admit that when I saw him at Woodward, he looked familiar. Since I couldn't put a finger on why, I didn't want to give her an impression that I was dropping a hint of interest. With his make-your-knees-shake good looks, I'm sure Lauren was used to women throwing themselves at him, so I didn't want to appear like I'd swoon as well.

"It won't be the last." She clapped. "I'll introduce you."

"Yes... for business." I got excited, more than I expected. Was I blushing? "What's his social media handle? So we can tag him."

Lauren grabbed her phone. "I'll have to look."

Shortly, she gave me his handle, so I followed him. Almost all his posts were of wedding couples, with only a few of himself usually backpacking in the mountains.

Lauren spoke up. "Ready to wow me with your ideas about promoting the Showcase?"

I set my phone on the desk, embarrassed. "Let's do it."

What were the odds this man who'd intrigued me was Lauren's brother? Just when life was complicated enough. Did I need another man in my life?

CHAPTER 19

MAY 22

On Friday, Lauren suggested we coordinate my office decor around Evan Painter's abstracts, by changing the sitting room's walls to a beige with specks of gold. After Russell approved yesterday, I contacted Javier, the commercial painter Lauren referred, and set up an appointment for an estimate.

Today, she and I drove separately to the home furnishing store, where I witnessed her genius at work even though she pushed my comfort zone. Although I appreciated the charm of my grandparents' vintage furniture, I wanted to create a more modern look with sleek, minimal lines. However, Lauren argued the office should reflect me —warm, professional, and sophisticated. I could see her view, so we settled on transitional decor—two-toned furniture sets, all slate blue with cherrywood edges.

We almost had to call a truce over an area rug, a spiral design resembling a sunburst in muted gold, beiges, creams, and slate blue. Initially, I thought the design was too busy, but she convinced me it'd marry with the other patterns and colors well.

Eight thousand dollars lighter (even with twenty-five percent off everything from a weeklong Memorial Day sale), I was satisfied. *You must look affluent if you want affluent clients*, Jordan would often say. They'd deliver the furniture within four to six weeks, giving Javier a reasonable timeframe to paint.

After I said bye to Lauren and got into Addy at ten thirty, Jordan called. Such bad timing since I was enjoying the morning. Despite sensing I should just delete his voicemail, I was obnoxiously curious to know what he said. "Meet me today at The Mayo, 11:30. Let's discuss business."

His choice of place had to be strategic. My paternal grandparents met, fell in love, and married in The Mayo Hotel. Opening in 1925, when Tulsa was known as the oil capital of the world, The Mayo was the city's premier hotel, with its art deco design, six hundred rooms, and running ice water. When the oil industry migrated to Houston in the eighties, Tulsa's economy sank. The hotel fought to stay open. Although it landed on the National Register of Historic Places in 1980, it closed the next year.

My grandparents, along with several other residents, lobbied the city to restore the landmark. By the 2000s, a private owner purchased the hotel and invested forty-two million dollars, in mostly private and some public funds, to renovate her to her former glory. The renovations kept as much of the original beauty as possible. When my grandparents, Dad, and I attended the hotel's grand reopening in 2009, it was like resurrecting our family's legacy.

Longing to experience a love story rivaling my grandparents', I planned a staycation there with Jordan on my birthday. I kissed him when he got off work early that Friday afternoon and sulked when he answered a business call during dinner. I held back tears when he arranged for Elise to pick me up for a spa day the next morning. Jordan asked her because he wanted to work.

I texted:

Daily Grill instead.

I have a meeting at Mayo. Show or there
will be no negotiation.

Unsure what to do, I drove north. Should I head to the office or the hotel? I couldn't allow him to ruin my memories, but I needed to secure my clients, especially after dropping all that money on furniture. At the next stoplight, I texted him a thumbs-up emoji and began reciting a possible script for our meeting.

"I'm sorry I left with only a note, but I'm doing us a favor. We don't love each other, but we make better business partners." I considered what he might say, my rebuttal, and a mantra to repeat if he objected. My confidence grew the more I recited.

When I pulled up to the hotel, I glanced at the classic Sullivan architecture with its terra-cotta stone facade and majestic Doric columns. A witness to Tulsa's gilded age of oil, the hotel prominently brushed shoulders with the city's other historic art deco structures, all giving a timeless charm to downtown. The hotel was built in the era when joint collections of master craftsmen composed architectural symphonies. A parapet violinist etched images of Native Americans to guard the hotel from above.

Rain pounded the car, so I pulled up to the hotel's valet entrance and rushed inside, my umbrella guarding me from the elements. In the marble lobby, I glanced at my watch. It was only a quarter after eleven, giving me time to get quiet and relaxed before meeting Jordan.

I headed directly to the narrow hallway. I always liked the hotel's coffee shop especially since it was like traveling back in time. The dark wood barista counter resembled an upscale saloon with a semicircular bar, bar stools set around, and a horse saddle lying on top of a stool. Wine and liquor bottles decorated the white shelves behind the barista.

They had restored the original flooring with animals hand-painted on the tiles. Mosaic bricks ran along two-thirds of the wall, and above them, vintage photos of the city hung on display.

I ordered English breakfast tea, Nana's favorite. Sitting by myself at a four-top, I faced the barista and the hallway. It was quiet. Only the whir of the espresso machine and a few people chatting occupied the room.

I'd chosen a metal chair, purposely avoiding the blue-green barrel-back chairs along the brick wall. Jordan and I sat in those during our staycation. Back then, he was preoccupied, checking the latest stock market figures, so I sat in silence, downing my frozen latte and feeling alone.

I recited my script under my breath, with affirmations. *Stay level-headed. Focus on business. Don't justify why you left.* Ten minutes later, I checked emails on my phone, irritated he was late. Twenty minutes later, I got up to leave, assuming he intended to waste my time and get me rattled.

As I headed toward the hallway, a slight shudder rained through my body. Near the lobby, Jordan and a distinguished older gentleman stood next to a framed photo of J. Paul Getty. The man shook Jordan's hand then left.

I couldn't remember my script. Jordan turned, buttoning his ebony jacket, then slowly approached, his hard-set face and eyes revealing that a sea of turmoil churned underneath his three-piece suit. I walked back to the table.

Thank God I was no longer attracted to his slicked-back, caramel hair, or hazel eyes. As he approached, he stopped to straighten his grey tie. The first line of my script returned.

"I'm ordering a latte," he said. His musky oak cologne drifted as he strode to the counter. Suddenly, I was back in the condo's bedroom, lying in bed, his cologne staying on the sheets longer than he did. Why did I agree to meet?

Only peeking up at the barista when ordering, he then stared at his phone, not moving forward when the next customer ordered and paid. When the barista called Jordan's name, I drank the last sip of my tea. As he set his latte on the table, I frowned at his name written neatly on the cup's side. I used to like that name.

He laid his leather briefcase on the spare chair to my right then sat across from me. "Ready to apologize?"

I nodded. "I'm sorry for only leaving a note. I should've told you—"

"Evan Painter sent you those red roses," he said through gritted teeth.

"Seriously?" I shook my head. After I bought Evan's paintings, he invited me to his showing at an art gallery. Jordan and I went, but after we got home, he accused me of flirting with Evan.

"I captured a picture of the roses before the cleaning lady discarded them in the trash." He gripped his paper coffee cup tighter. I was afraid he'd crush it.

So he thought *I'd* cheated. I smirked at the irony. "They were from my father." When the concierge delivered them, I put the card in my purse but forgot to take the roses when I moved.

He grimaced then stroked his hair, becoming stoic. "You think I'm naive? Your old man never sent you flowers when we were together."

My throat dry, I swallowed. "We weren't good as a couple. We're better in business. I appreciate all you've done for me, and I want to continue working with you." I extended my hand.

"You severed our partnership when you moved out without consulting me. How do you think I felt finding your note?" He leaned forward, arms on the table.

I looked away, wishing I hadn't met him today.

"Well?" he said.

I turned to face him. His eyes narrowed like he was looking through a rifle scope. Why was he such a bully?

"I'm sorry I hurt you, but we've hardly talked to each other these past few months. I didn't know what else to do but leave." I took a breath, irritated I sounded as though I read a script.

He took a short sip of coffee. "You're a quitter. You walked away from me and our social circle just like you left Specter. Elise was hurt when you wrote her off." His brows arched like an inverted V. "Only cowards run."

I turned toward the window along the alley of the hotel. Wrought-iron panes covered the window, protecting it from the outside. The Mayo's signature *M* logo was centered in the pane. "I'll pay rent for a few months until you find a roommate."

"Trusting Evan to send you clients?" he asked.

I leaned within inches of his face as I clasped the ends of the table. "Or you could ask the receptionist to move in."

He stared in silence, swallowing air.

"Are you still with her? I took pics of you holding her hands at a hole-in-the-wall restaurant on South Peoria." I pointed at his chest. "She was the last straw."

He arched back. "She's struggling with her old man. So, um...I advised her." He lightly slapped the table. "Stop gaslighting. Who's your boy toy?"

I stood and grabbed my purse and umbrella from the empty chair. "Don't play me."

He grabbed my hand. "I'm referring your clients to Grassly Marketing." He squeezed so hard my wrist hurt.

I pulled, trying to wrest my hand away. "We'll see, because they're loyal to me, too." I grabbed the back of his chair for leverage and jerked my hand free, stumbling forward a few feet before regaining my balance.

"I have an appointment with Richard Pine next week," he said.

As I jetted to the coffee shop's exit, I nursed my wrist. After I pushed on the door, I opened my umbrella. A sudden gust of wind blew and flipped it inside out, snapping one of the metal arms. Using both hands, I gripped the inverted umbrella so it wouldn't fly away.

Cold rain and quarter-sized hail ambushed me while I rushed toward the valet station.

Once the driver pulled Addy around to the entrance, I tipped him ten dollars then got in. In the rearview mirror, I inspected myself. My eyeliner ran, giving an appearance of a black eye. With a tissue, I tried to wipe it off but only smeared it further, as though I wore a patch. Melting hail stuck to my matted hair. I resembled a rescue kitten.

I drove to Woodward Park but stayed in the car, sobbing until the mental fog lifted. Why did I concede to Jordan's demands? I knew better than to meet him at my family's favorite hotel, ruining precious memories.

CHAPTER 20

By the time my mind cleared, the rain stopped. The sky remained ashen grey as I drove to Jennifer's to shower and change into a black jumpsuit before returning to the office.

Lying on the chaise lounge, I texted Dad that I was about to call but couldn't FaceTime. I didn't want to see his disappointment when I'd break the news about meeting with Jordan.

"Hi, baby." He sounded tired. "How are you?"

"It's Jordan." I held my breath to keep from crying.

"What now?" His voice conveyed tightrope tension.

"Um... it's bad... He..."

"Bad in what way?"

"I told you he'd get angry about the note."

"He's angry you broke up first. Just block his number."

"Trust me. It was the note. The way his eyes narrowed when he mentioned it..." Oops, I'd vowed to myself not to tell Dad I met with Jordan but act as though Jordan conveyed the threats on a voice message.

"Wait, wait, wait. You didn't meet him in person, did you?"

Uh-oh. "Don't get angry, but he texted about meeting to negotiate business." I touched my neck as my throat tightened.

"How did that work out for you?"

"He thinks I also cheated. I forgot to grab the bouquet of roses you sent when I moved out."

"I told you to think like a serpent. You can't engage without getting bit."

"I'll know for next time." Needing to gather my strength, I sat up.

"Why would there be a next time? If you'd have listened, we wouldn't be having this conversation."

I closed my eyes, trying to escape his rebuke. "You sound like Jordan. He'd always say he knew what's best and how I don't listen." My voice squeaked. "I made a mistake."

Awkward silence followed. I fidgeted but kept my eyes closed.

"I'm sorry I triggered you," Dad said. "I'm afraid you'll run back to him. I keep telling myself if *only* I had intervened when you were with him, maybe I could've prevented all this hardship."

"You warned me, but I didn't listen to you, Maman, or Aimee." I opened my eyes.

"Stop making the same mistake now."

"I'm trying. But it gets worse."

"What else?" His tone was curt.

I paused, holding back tears. "He warned that he's referring clients to Grassly Marketing and has an appointment with Richard Pine. Not only does Jordan know most of my clients better than I do, he's persuasive. And Grassly of all firms! The owner operates his business like a big-box store. Paying employees less than Specter yet requiring longer hours. Experiencing high turnover and always hiring kids straight out of college. Their clients got tired of acclimating to a new account manager every year and receiving standardized services."

"Exactly. Call every client. Explain you're no longer with Jordan, but this won't affect your professionalism. Market your strengths contrasted with Grassly. Emphasize you work with a veteran team and only take a limited number of clients, so you can provide personalized service with excellence."

"I can do this!" I tapped my steering wheel.

"If you're making them money, they'll stay. So, push your June special." Dad breathed hard between sentences. Did he just moan?

"Did you fall? Are you alright?" I gripped my chest as though I experienced heart failure. "Answer me." I held the phone close to my mouth, almost kissing it.

"Sorry... I'm okay... Just follow up with me." His voice was weaker.

"What happened?" I asked.

"Heartburn."

"See a doctor. That didn't sound like heartburn."

"I've been having odd pains here and there. Just old age. Spending too much time in the Florida sun drains the body. Eating too much rich food lights up the insides like a power plant." The hoarse edge to his voice, as if he'd inhaled smoke, revealed his deeper concern.

"Make an appointment after we get off the phone."

"At my age, I know my body. I'm good but take care of yourself. And I'll be praying about Jordan... Oh, I almost forgot. Have you withdrawn your investment funds?"

I held my head back. "Jordan threatened me about Grassly out of spite. If I withdraw my money, he'll follow through. I can't afford to lose clients."

"Stop letting him toss you to and fro like a mouse. I'll call my advisor, and he'll transfer your investment today." He was panting. I needed to de-escalate, stopping him from having an attack.

"No, I'll call your advisor," I said.

"Do it now!"

"Stop yelling! I care more about protecting my money than you do." I hated when he treated me like a child.

"Prove it."

"I'm calling now, K? Bye."

I called his advisor, and he assured he'd initiate the transfer immediately. I called Dad, hoping good news would slow his heart rate and alleviate my guilt for being difficult. His heavy breathing hadn't stopped. Once we hung up, I called Maman.

"What's wrong with Dad?" I asked.

The wind howled on the other end. "What?"

"He sounded short of breath. Has he seen his primary?"

"He's due for a physical, but he needs to get away from stress. I keep telling him to stop taking on all the family's cares. Did you talk about Jordan?"

I cringed, not wanting her to blame me. "I met with Jordan about my business."

"Did Père clutch his chest and breathe hard?" Maman asked a little too matter-of-fact for my taste.

"I didn't FaceTime, so I don't know about him clutching his chest. Why haven't you told me he's experiencing chest pains?"

"Just started a few weeks ago. Between you and Aimee, he's on edge."

I exhaled. "I'll do better."

"Spoon-feed Père your news. First, a bite of baguette. Later, a slice of Bayonne ham. Finish with a piece of sheep's milk cheese."

"That'll only make it worse. He'll call me, suspecting I'm holding back. Just have him see the doc or talk to Uncle Karl." Dad's brother was a cardiologist in Denver.

"I'll make an appointment, but I also need you to work with me. No bad news about Jordan... My friend is here for our walk. I love you, *mon petit chou*."

Omitting news to Dad would be hard. I disclosed nearly everything to him.

CHAPTER 21

round four, Jordan texted.

> So you transferred your money out of my firm. Does Evan want you to buy more paintings?

My stomach tightened. I loathed thinking he could persuade more clients to leave. I tried not to wonder who'd stay and who'd go, but paranoia buzzed around in my head.

I called Richard Pine. As it rang and rang, I wondered if Jordan was in his office.

"Hi, Celine." Richard answered on the fourth ring.

"Hello, Richard. I'm confirming our meeting on the thirtieth. I'll have your latest numbers from the ad, and we can discuss executing the next phase of our strategy. Do you want to meet at my new office? Might be quieter." *Don't throw everything at him.*

"Best to meet here because I might be in-between meetings. Hey, bet you're happy Jordan's back. When will we get a wedding invitation?"

"Well, about that—"

"I've got the Misses calling. Tell him I'm looking forward to meeting him tomorrow. You two have a great night."

"You too. Tell your wife hello."

After hanging up, I called five clients, but only Monty Prize answered. He assured that if I kept our marketing relationship professional and continued generating leads, he'd retain my services. I called Bill Plaxton to ask for referrals, but I had to leave a message.

The buzzing thoughts returned, but I tried to push through. After an hour, work wasn't driving fear away. I went to the kitchenette and sipped on a rosé. Usually drinking a glass or two to unwind after a full day, I was relying on this stress reliever earlier and earlier.

Around six, I shut everything down then went to the grocery store. At the deli section, I leaned forward to grab a roasted chicken in the warmer. As I straightened, I bumped heads with someone. I peeked at the person I collided with. It was Tony, my client and Jordan's personal trainer.

"Oh, Celine. Are you alright?" He took a few steps back.

"Fine." How convenient, since I had left him several messages. "I'm glad I ran into you... Well, not literally, but your analytics from our recent ad shows a hundred people clicked to learn more. What was your conversion rate?" I held my forehead, as it pulsated from the collision. He didn't look affected, but the guy had a thick forehead and about 250 pounds of muscle.

He massaged his neck. "About that... You've done an excellent job with my account, but I found a firm specializing in the health and wellness industry. I wish you all the best." He looked away.

My head reverberated as though I had gotten hit again, but this emotional pounding hurt worse. I should walk away, but I wanted an explanation. "Did Jordan refer you to them?"

He extended his hand. "My family's waiting in the car." I hesitated then barely shook his hand. He placed two roasted chickens in his cart and disappeared. I got a few sides and Hawaiian rolls. At least, he'd paid for the rest of this month.

After I left the store, I sat in the parking lot and called ten leads. I landed one meeting. The battle began.

CHAPTER 22
MAY 24

At nine, Lauren and Javier, the commercial painter Lauren referred, arrived. Oh no! I should've cancelled the appointment, but I forgot Javier was coming. Since Lauren was headed over to paint, she'd help me communicate what I wanted.

With Jordan threatening to refer my clients away, I should save money.

After Javier walked through the office and Lauren told him the style I was going for, he sat in the sitting area calculating the cost, while Lauren and I met in Monroe.

"Do you think he could paint the three rooms under a grand?" I winced because Lauren only used premium contractors. I liked that she'd only refer the best in their field, but excellence came at a cost. She shook her head. "No, I doubt it. You could have him paint the sitting area and leave the conference and Monroe alone until later."

"Maybe, but I'd want him to get the rooms done in one shot especially since we're waiting on the furniture to get delivered. Just be more convenient."

"Or keep the grey walls and have him come later."

"I'm afraid I'll have to." I extended my hand toward her. "I don't regret getting the furniture especially because it'll add warmth to the office. But I need to slow down spending."

I didn't want to tell her about my ex. Not that it'd frighten her off, but no one wants to hear someone else's drama.

"The furniture will show off your transitional style well, so the walls will just blend in."

"Thanks for the encouragement, but it won't make the space pop like I wanted." I hung my head wishing I had found all my clients even if that route would've taken longer.

"How about we paint on a weekend?" Lauren sat on the edge of her seat, voice raised as though she suggested a girl's weekend getaway.

"No. I don't paint. I could barter and give you free services if you'd paint."

"If you pay for the supplies, I'll paint for fun."

I shook my head. "Nope. You already used your office warming pass, so I'm throwing in…" I stood as a solution popped in my mind. "What if I barter with Javier?"

Lauren's smile radiated. "Brilliant. I've already suggested he use your services."

Shortly, when Javier came to Monroe, he gave me an estimate of three grand. When I suggested bartering, his eyes lit up and he shook my hand. I wasn't expecting him to bite immediately. I felt a surge of adrenaline rush through me. I just did that.

With Javier's hectic schedule, he couldn't work on my office until June 12th. As Lauren prepped to paint the furniture in Monroe, I coasted through the day, confident I could convince clients to retain my services.

CHAPTER 23
MAY 25

Lauren called at nine, reminding me she was headed over to paint the furniture. Yesterday, she sanded and primed it.

I didn't need that reminder though, since my office resembled a storage unit. Drop cloths and five empty drawers from my file cabinet lay in front of the bookshelves. I carefully veered around boxes of books and plastic totes of file folders.

When Lauren arrived, she sported cropped jeans and a white tee, with a pink, puffer duffel and a small purse slung over her shoulder. "Hey," she said at the door, barely giving me a hug. Uh-oh.

"Are you alright?" *Please don't bail out of working here today.* Needing to get my office back in order, I could only tolerate this chaos for a day or two.

"Do you think I'm overbearing?" she asked as we stood in the entry.

I tilted my head. "In our limited interaction, I'd say no. At least, not as a designer."

"No, as a sister."

"I can't help you there." After she stepped farther inside, I closed the door.

"Mind if I make myself a cup of coffee?" she asked.

"I was about to brew another pot. Just press Start."

She walked to the kitchenette. "Garrett's asking me to back off of matchmaking. He hasn't dated seriously since his broken engagement."

"Your brother, right?"

"Oh. Yes."

My heart raced, realizing he was an eligible bachelor. "How long since he was engaged?" I asked.

"Two years." She pressed the Start button. "That's why I'm nudging him into the dating scene." She made a pushing gesture with her hand. I forced myself to keep a straight face. Her nudge was probably more of a shove. "But instead of finding a wife, he threw himself into his business. Now, work is his excuse for not having time to date."

"Sounds like he's making the most of this time, developing his business." I knew there was something about him that I liked.

"He should be inspired toward love, since he spends hours capturing couples in their happiest moments."

"Two years isn't anything. He could meet someone in six months and marry within a few years." I didn't understand why married people pushed us singles to settle down early. Honestly, since marriage was for life, they should encourage us to take our time. What if I had married Jordan? I shuddered.

She crossed her arms. "He won't find love if he doesn't give a woman a chance."

Grabbing the vanilla creamer from the fridge allowed me to hide my smile. Kudos to her brother for investing in himself instead of jumping into another relationship. I set the creamer next to the wicker basket of sugar packets then stood next to her. "He'll figure it out."

"He excelled in business before the breakup. I'm concerned he's running from the pain. He's had this issue in the past."

I smiled. "Or just using his time wisely."

She touched my arm. "I've never asked if you're in a relationship."

"Not anymore." I instinctively pulled away.

"Do you want to get married?"

"One day, but I'd rather wait years for a supportive partner than settle for an unhappy marriage." I grabbed twin mugs from the cabinet above my head and handed her one.

"We won't be allies in this fight, will we?"

I shook my head. "Probably not."

She held the mug at an appreciative distance. "I like these mugs. Are they from Amalfi?"

"Yes." Impressed she recognized the region, I was even more relieved we were on a neutral topic. "I bought these from an artist there. The Amalfi Coast is one of my favorite places in Italy."

"Garrett's too. He wanted to visit on his honeymoon." The coffee maker stopped percolating.

Did Garrett also drink coffee? I appreciated it not just for the caffeine jolt but to inhale its distinct minty, woodsy aroma. I might enjoy snuggling next to him by a kindling campfire as we sipped on an organic, dark-roasted Colombian blend.

"Do you want me to fill your mug?" Lauren asked.

"What?"

"Coffee's done."

"Oh sure." I shook my head. Why was I daydreaming over a man I hardly knew?

Holding out my mug, I asked her to fill it about two-thirds. I poured in one part creamer to two parts cane sugar.

"I'm grateful he didn't marry Presleigh," Lauren said.

I fetched two spoons, handing her one.

"What's the story there?" I asked, taking a sip. Ah... perfect.

"She wanted Garrett to move to Vegas, her hometown. She came to Tulsa to attend Oral Roberts University then got a job here at

Believers church. But when visiting Vegas to shop for a wedding gown, she spent time at her dad's church and got this revelation that she was called to help him with the church's expansion." She crossed her arms. "Of course, she was confident Garrett would go along."

I scowled. "What kind of woman assumes her partner would move halfway across the country?"

She clapped. "Exactly. Garrett was willing to sacrifice what he wanted, just to be with her, despite how much he loathed Vegas." She extended her mug toward me. "I was careful to not judge her too quickly, but it was clear she was the spoilt youngest child. Believe me, I bit my tongue many times as she expected Garrett to be at her beck and call."

"What made him change his mind and call it off?"

"Technically, she called it off realizing he'd have to sacrifice too much. They did get back together for a brief time." She sighed. "Fortunately, he felt the walls closing in on him, so he came to his senses and escaped while he could."

"How long were they engaged?"

"A month."

"Not too long, then."

"Nope but now she's engaged to her ex-boyfriend. He works alongside her at her dad's church. Garrett wonders if she always cared for that ex more than she let on." Lauren rolled her eyes.

"Does happen." I needed to change the subject before I got triggered about my ex. "Let's work on creating your YouTube channel. That will be a great space for offering home decor tips and featuring your design projects."

"Sorry." She offered a sheepish grin. "Of course we need to work."

Shortly, I sat at my desk while Lauren changed into her painting clothes in the bathroom. When she emerged, she wore an oversized white painter's coverall with a hood over her hair and forehead.

I laughed, grabbing my phone. "Wait," I said. She turned to face me. "I want to take a shot of you for social. You look like you're about to walk the moon."

"Hold on." She picked up a paintbrush, held it in her right hand, and smiled like a child on their birthday.

I took several shots from different angles. Some serious, as she faked applying brush strokes on the bookshelf. Some whimsical, where she twirled the brush like a baton. Infusing creativity and humor into the post reminded me why I enjoyed my job.

Once she started painting, I stayed at my desk, since the navy chalk paint didn't give off an odor. We brainstormed ideas for her Step Into a Designer's Home series. She'd pair affordable decorating tips with vignettes about her and her business. To entice people to subscribe, she'd post three to four free videos a month. Fortunately, her husband, Shane, owned a production company and would shoot the videos. As someone who couldn't design a bathroom without help, I'd appreciate her walking me through the designer process.

Two hours later, she'd finished applying the first coat on the bookshelf and had moved on to painting the file cabinet, while I jotted six months of video content on a spreadsheet. Her phone rang from where it was charging on my desk.

"Would you answer my brother?" she said. "Tell him I'll call him back shortly."

I hesitated as I stared at the phone.

"No worries if you don't want to."

I quickly answered. "Hi, this is Celine Monroe. Is this Garrett?"

"Yes, is Lauren available?" I could hear his lower-register tenor better than at Woodward Park. I had a thing with registers, once declining a date with a concert cellist because his voice was too high-pitched. Garrett's had a slightly husky touch, making his tone appealing.

"She's in the middle of work, but she'll call you shortly." I bobbed my head.

"Thank you, Celine." He pronounced my name as smooth as silk.

"You're welcome."

He hung up.

With Lauren talking about him frequently, I felt we were practically acquaintances.

"Thanks," Lauren said. "Did he sound perky or depressed?"

"Casual." I wanted to believe perky, but I didn't sense that.

"Once I'm finished here, I'll call him. It's a good sign he reached out shortly after our argument. He doesn't hold on to grudges long."

Another great sign of character. If Lauren kept sharing about him, I'd anoint him to sainthood.

By the time she finished the first coat to the file cabinet, I wrapped up another client's campaign.

When she took a break and called Garrett from the sitting room, I stayed in Monroe. After about an hour, I checked on her. Lauren was slumped into the armchair, so I sat in the twin chair next to her.

"Garrett's down." Lauren frowned. "He scrolled through wedding pics of his ex on a mutual friend's social. I'd forgotten Presleigh got married last week." She waved her hand. "Anyway, he was shell-shocked seeing her in the bridal gown. I'm sure he wondered, *what if I were the one standing there with her?* Trust me, I know he's glad it wasn't him, but he still feels sorry for himself for being single at thirty-two."

Hmm. We were the same age, although I was content with being single. "Are most of his friends married with kids?"

"Yes, with kids." She took a deep breath. "Anyway, I better go. He's coming over for dinner tonight. I promised to cook shrimp scampi." She got up, collected her duffel and purse, and headed to her car. "I'll come tomorrow to apply the second coats."

"Great." I accompanied her to the parking lot. "With Garrett, maybe just listen to him and not give advice."

She crossed her fingers. "Thank you for listening."

Once I returned to the office, I texted Aimee since Lauren cooking for Garrett reminded me of pizza night. I wanted a close relationship with Aimee like Lauren had with Garrett.

CHAPTER 24
MAY 25-26

My phone rang. Sonny, Jordan's uncle, was calling. He was my least favorite client mostly because he liked to call the shots. Even when I advised him on a marketing strategy, he'd get Jordan's feedback as though Jordan was the marketing whiz. Once Jordan approved the strategy, Sonny would meet with me to discuss executing the plan. I'd struggled to maintain my composure during these sessions because he'd act as though he came up with the strategy and repeat the action steps as if ordering me to execute them. I might've fired him as a client if Jordan wasn't his nephew.

After I gave a greeting, Sonny talked fast.

"Celine, I'm expanding, so we better get the train moving. Figured you have a place, since you're not with my boy. But hey, no hard feelings. Show's gotta go on."

Talking to Sonny was always a buckle-your-seat-belt moment. Fast wheeling and dealing. The faster he'd talk, the slower I'd move, as I processed what he threw at me.

"Hello, are you there?" he asked.

"Sorry, I'm in the middle of work." I doubted he wanted to

retain me; more likely, he was spying for Jordan. "Sure, let's meet at your shop."

"Not a good idea. My office resembles a hoarder's workshop. Goods, paperwork, all a mess. We gotta meet at your office."

"Thing is, I'm not quite settled. I'm temporarily working at coffee shops and in my bedroom, wherever I find space. How about catching up at Shades of Brown?" I smiled. He considered artisan coffee pretentious, insisting coffee from a gas station tasted more honest.

"Nah. Obviously, you're suspicious about sharing your digs, so I'm cutting loose. Jordan wants me to switch firms. I always say it's better to play with the devil you know, but I don't play with those who don't trust me. Bye." *Click.*

"Good riddance!" I shouted at the phone. "I never enjoyed working with you anyway—a polyester version of Jordan!" I stared at the ceiling as though my ex was peering down from above, enjoying my downfall.

Immediately, I received a call from my attorney client informing me he was moving on. Uh-oh. This was news of an earthquake preceding a tsunami. He said the same as Tony—that he'd moved on to a larger firm but appreciated my services. I asked him about Jordan, but he wouldn't disclose the reason.

Afraid another client would dump me that night, I turned off my phone and worked late, brainstorming the best strategy for attracting leads.

After creating customized deals, I emailed each prospect their unique offer. I laid on the lounge just to clear my mind. When I woke up around ten, I had the worst crook in my neck. I drove home, anxious to get to work the next morning to rescue my business.

When I turned on my phone early Saturday morning, I discovered Aimee had left two voice messages last night. She called at seven fifteen, to ask where I was, and again at eight, inquiring if I had forgotten them.

I stared in the bathroom mirror. "What is my life?" Too ashamed to call, I got ready then drove to the office.

She called once I arrived, and I answered on the fourth ring. I might as well face her; otherwise, I'd be wondering what she'd say.

"Hi," I said. "I'm sorry for forgetting about dinner. I was despondent, so my mind blanked. I planned on coming, but I'm..." I held my breath, so I wouldn't cry.

"You worked late and forgot." She sounded flat.

"No excuses, but I'm losing clients Jordan referred, so I worked into the night."

"To acquire new clients?"

"To pay my bills."

"I'm sorry to hear that... Couldn't you have taken Friday night off? You're working all day today, right?"

If I could shut down her condescension, we'd get along just fine. "Sorry that I don't have a husband to rely on."

"Are you...? Forget it."

Was she about to lecture how I chose a career over a husband? "Just finish your sentence."

"Are you more concerned about not meeting monthly goals or about having to work for new clients?"

"Both! This isn't like, 'Oh well, I lost a client or two.' I'm holding onto the edge of the cliff with one hand. I didn't expect to have to spell that out, though!"

"Why can't you let people help you?" she asked in a gentler tone.

I held my breath, unsure what she meant.

"Are you there?" She seemed irritated.

"I'll make it out of this crisis, but I need people to listen and support me. Not shove God, church, or a husband down my throat."

Silence. Oh well, I needed to return to work anyway.

"If you didn't have such an attitude, you'd realize we're here for you. Heath and I will also refer clients. You never ask, so I don't think about it. We have friends who could use your services. At least if you'd..."

"If I'd what?" My voice raised. "Attend your church?" I closed my eyes to get myself under control.

"Not as if it's a networking opportunity but to get plugged into a healthy community. Your life would change."

"I'm good. I've got Jennifer and a Christian client networking me with other believers." I knew that wouldn't satisfy her obsession with getting me saved, so I had to be gentler. "I appreciate your offer. I was afraid to ask because I didn't want you thinking I was only interested in you if you helped my business."

"That's a safe assumption, but I'm willing to meet you halfway... The boys ask about you and were disappointed you didn't show, especially John."

"Tell them I'll be there next time." I added pizza night on my calendar for every Friday night.

"John has a baseball game a week from Thursday, on June seventh."

"I'll be there. What time?"

After putting the info she gave me in my phone, I asked her to give referrals my phone number and website. I offered free marketing services for her and Heath as a thank-you.

"No. We know you're talented, but you need to invest your time with paying clients."

"Thanks."

"Before I forget, there's a picnic at La Fortune this afternoon around six. They're having an ice cream truck, barbecue stations, and games."

"Through Heath's work?"

"No, our church."

"I'll pass."

"I'm going to say this because I love you. Realize there's a bigger picture at stake. Don't get caught up with work and lose sight that

God has bigger plans. He wants you to have a good business, but he's working behind the scenes to enhance your *life.*"

Our talks always came down to God. God this, God that. God, God, God. I didn't understand how Christians' love for people showed up as proselytizing. Why couldn't she try to understand *why* I was disconnected?

"Thanks for the sermon," I said.

She groaned. "I hope you don't learn about God's provision the hard way."

"Could you just listen for once? Instead of acting like God's recruiter?"

"It's you who's not listening. I'm saying this to help, not pat myself on the back."

"Whatever."

"There are no strings attached. Heath will be in touch."

"I will. And I'll be at John's game next Thursday."

Was I more frustrated that she lectured about my lifestyle or that I'd disappointed her by missing last night? Probably a little of both. Whatever would happen next Thursday, I'd attend John's game. I needed my family.

CHAPTER 25
MAY 30

I didn't enjoy balmy days where heat and sweat clung to your skin like mud and I never felt clean, even after a refreshing shower. Early Wednesday morning, the meteorologist issued a severe thunderstorm warning for the afternoon, with Tulsa County under a tornado watch until five. Welcome to Oklahoma's tornado season.

Since Richard didn't reach out to reschedule our meeting, I wasn't concerned about the weather. By noon, I drove to his office in only light drizzle descending from heavy grey clouds.

Wanting to focus on the meeting, I put my phone on silent. I entered the building from a side door that opened into a narrow hallway of offices and avoided the showroom floor. At the end of the hallway, I turned right, opened the glass door, and entered the secretary's office in front of Richard's, a large glass window and small glass door separating them. The secretary was in Richard's office, talking to him.

They looked at me, so I waved. Richard nodded, jotted something on a sticky note, and handed it to her. I could overhear him telling her something about his expansion, and I reviewed the main points I wanted to cover in our meeting.

Within a few minutes, she returned to her desk. I smiled, but she stared at the note in her hand.

"How are you?" I asked.

She laid the note face down on the desk then looked at me. "Could be better if it weren't for the severe weather. How can I help you?"

"Is Richard ready for our meeting?"

"Give him five minutes. He needs to make a quick call."

Normally, she'd offer me a chocolate bar and ask how business was going. Did the weather really have her in knots?

I sat and mentally reviewed the last point for the meeting. She typed something into her computer. After a few minutes, she put folders into a neat stack on her desk, placed her pen in the holder, and wiped the desk with a microfiber cloth. Maybe they were shutting down for the day.

Her phone rang. She nodded as she listened, then she hung up.

"He's ready for you," she said before cleaning again. Maybe Richard needed to cut our meeting short. Maybe he just had time to hear the latest metrics. We could reschedule the rest for another day.

Once in his office, I smiled, greeting him with "Good afternoon."

He stood, extending his hand across his desk. His handshake was loose. Uh-oh. Bad omen.

If he was dropping me, why tell me in person? He sat then leaned back in his leather chair. "I'm closing soon with the weather, so I'll make this brief."

He grabbed a pen and pressed on the end while I sat. Staring at his eyes helped me focus on him, instead of the repetitive *click, click, click*. "I've acquired another investor, one very lucrative, so I can expand faster. We thought it necessary to switch to a larger firm." He set the pen down then clasped his hands.

I couldn't feel my feet. A numbing sensation moved up my legs and toward my heart—did it stop beating?—then up my throat and toward my head. I couldn't move or speak.

"I'm sorry," he said, "but it's the best move for my business."

"You're making a mistake—"

"Bottom line, I have to work with the best in the city. Jordan... Well, anyway, this is the right fit." He stood, extending his hand as though a second handshake could make the news more palatable. When I remained sitting, he approached his office door.

I gripped the arms of the chair. "Jordan referred you to Grassly, right? Don't be fooled by their size. They have over twenty employees, but only three or four—mostly recent college grads—will commit an hour or two a week on your account. My team, with over fifty years of experience combined, have committed at least ten hours a week on your account—"

"No need to fuss. I've already signed with Grassly. Don't you worry your sweet little mind. I'll give you a fantastic referral. Thank you for your hard work and dedication."

Sweet little mind? No need to fuss? I stood. "How dare you treat me like a child throwing a tantrum."

He rolled his eyes then peeked his head out the door toward his secretary. "Get Celine's address, so I can mail a thank-you card with a testimonial for future clients."

"No need." I walked past, refusing to look at him.

"Don't be like that." He sighed. "Send my thanks to your team. And you have my best wishes on your business." He shut the door.

"Alright, dear. What's your address?" The secretary smiled. I half expected her to offer candy.

I shook my head. "I don't want anything from Richard."

She extended her hand, but I refused to shake it. "Celine, we've had a great working relationship. Please, let us do this. It's only business."

"Exactly, it's only business." I turned and left.

Outside, the sky was darker and rain pelted my head. By the time

I made it into the safety of my car, I was sopping wet. I grabbed my phone out of my purse to check the weather.

Uh-oh... I had a missed call from a client, Giuseppe, who ran the haberdashery where Jordan bought his suits. *Please, don't drop me!* He was one of my favorite clients. Always lively and entertaining, sharing about his humble beginning as an immigrant from Sicily. Working two jobs to save money to start his own shop. Dressing celebrities, a president, and a duke.

I called him back.

"Hi, Celine... Gosh, it's getting bad. If this turns into a warning, I'll run to my storm shelter."

"Did you receive my emails and messages, reminding you I had everything ready to promote your June special?"

"Oh dear. I got hacked recently. Hard to believe they'd trick an old man, but I had to get a new number. I forgot to give it to you. And I probably don't check my emails enough. I'm sorry." He sounded sincere.

"Sorry about what?" I asked.

"I didn't want to go with this other outfit. You've done an incredible job, and as the owner of a small business, I prefer supporting you. But—"

"You thought I dropped the ball, so Jordan convinced you to switch." I closed my eyes, wishing I could escape my nightmare.

"I'll refer my buddies to you. You're a swell consultant and affordable."

I tuned out his compliment. "Grassly, right?"

An ear-piercing shrill resonated. "The sirens are going off!" Giuseppe yelled. "Bye!"

The sky became eerily black, with ominous slate clouds. The wind howled and screeched like a captured wolf, adding chaotic torment to the atmosphere. I needed to find my way home.

CHAPTER 26

As I drove through heavy rain and wind, I struggled focusing on anything but the road. I held my breath, hoping I wouldn't hit a car, a tree, or the median. I was too young to die.

Once I arrived at the condo, I sprinted inside and sheltered with Jennifer in her bathroom. I preferred enduring the storm with her in the condo over hunkering by myself in the office, especially because I was volatile.

In the past, when I'd face trauma or a mountain, I'd drink. I wasn't addicted, but wine would help me forget for a day. The last time I got drunk was months ago, after Jordan and I got into an ugly fight. I got consumed with a client's campaign, losing track of time. Jordan came home early and assumed I'd have dinner ready. After he yelled "No man will marry you," I grabbed a bottle of wine, locked myself in the spare bedroom, and finished it in the night. Today, with my business in jeopardy, I couldn't afford to squander the day getting drunk.

Once the tornado warning lifted, Jennifer told me to chill while she made grilled cheese sandwiches before we returned to work. As I laid on the couch, Jordan called, but I let it go to voicemail then listened to the message with the phone to my ear.

"Can't believe you had the audacity to take the bracelet. Drop it off at the condo this Sunday afternoon, or else you'll hear from my attorney. Text when you're on your way."

"You gave it to me," I said out loud. "Need it to bribe your girl to move in and pay rent?"

"Gave you what?" Jennifer asked.

I sat up straight. For a split second, I'd forgotten she was there.

"Jordan gifted you something?" she asked.

I approached the kitchen, standing near the island. The buttered sandwiches she put on the steaming hot griddle sizzled.

"His heirloom bracelet in your safe." When I asked her to keep it, I didn't divulge its origin, only that it was worth about ten grand. I didn't want to justify why I kept his heirloom.

She frowned. "Why would you want to keep something that belongs to his family?"

"Every time I look at it, I get this surge of nostalgia, as if I'm attending a ball with Nana and Papa... I only inherited a few pieces from her jewelry collection, and this was something that she would've worn."

"Buy a vintage piece at an antique shop."

I flopped onto a barstool, shoulders slumped. "I'm also keeping it out of spite. Serves him right for messing with my business."

With the spatula in her hand, she pointed it toward me. "You do you... But take it from someone who's fought over possessions with an ex. Determine now how much you're willing to expend; it'll cost you time, energy, and probably money. Otherwise, you'll fight for more than it's really worth."

Why did she have to spout truth? Jordan's tenacity was endless, and he'd fight just to win. I stuck my tongue out. "I'll return it... No, I don't want to see him or his smug smile."

"How about delivering it to his office or his attorney?" She flipped over one sandwich and tapped its top with the spatula.

"I got it!" I slapped the counter. "I'll leave it with his mom, since it's her family's heirloom."

"That works."

I drank a glass of wine as we ate lunch. It helped soften the blow over losing another battle to Jordan.

CHAPTER 27

In high school, when I interned at the consulting firm Dad worked for, I dreamed of making a difference. Dad specialized in small businesses, and their owners clung to his advice like he was their life raft. They celebrated with him when they achieved ten, twenty years in business. I didn't know how I could earn that level of respect and undying loyalty from clients now.

Once I returned to the office, Dad called. "Hi, baby. Are you safe?" His breathing was heavy, like he had experienced the storm.

"The tornado was about thirty miles away but didn't touch down."

"Good. Did it prevent you from meeting with Richard?"

"What a waste of time and gas! I'm still reeling because he didn't just drop me over the phone but had me meet him at his office."

"Wait. He switched to Grassly?"

Oops. I'd just hit Dad hard with full-course news. "I'll be fine."

"I was concerned about you retaining him." He sounded as disappointed as I was.

"At least, he already paid for June—"

"Did he say he'd work with you until July first?"

"We didn't discuss it, but I'll give him a heads-up—more than he did for me—that I'll provide a refund in thirty days. Giving me time is only fair."

"That's precarious if he disputes the charge with his bank."

I turned on my laptop to check my bank balance. "Hopefully, I'll get a new client by then." I bobbed my head, convincing myself I was optimistic.

"I'd budget like it's not in your account."

"Why?" I moved to the couch.

"You need to prepare for the worst."

"I have some meetings with leads."

"I like to hear your confidence. We can build your business."

Dad didn't need more stress. "I'll call Heath and Bill Plaxton... and attend more networking events."

"How much money do you have in savings?"

"Five thousand. And the transfer went through with Raymond James."

I didn't tell Dad that I deposited five grand from the investment into savings. If I didn't acquire more clients, I'd have to withdraw more to cover my mounting credit card bill.

"Good," Dad said. "How about reconsidering and letting Maman and me cover your office rent? Don't need to pay us back— it'd take the pressure off you to keep your space."

Uh oh. He escalated their offer from a loan to a gift. Why didn't he have confidence I get out of this hole? I punched a couch cushion as Jordan's revised version of "Rich Girl" lyrics played in my head. *You can't make it without your old man's money.* Jordan sang that whenever he overheard my conversations with Dad about my business. "Appreciate that, but I can sustain myself without your money," I said.

"Keep in mind that we'd be investing in your business and expect a handsome return, mostly in the form of you growing your consulting firm."

Invest in your business. Exactly the words Jordan used when he offered to refer clients to me. "I'm outplaying him," I said. "I'll boost my social media videos that give tips and tools, push my clients to upgrade for July, and ask every contact I know for a referral."

"That's what I want to hear! And consider our investment as another part of your strategy. How about I fly out there next week and write you a check for the rent? And I'll help you strategize this July incentive and call your leads. Between the two of us, we'll get your business humming."

"On one condition," I said, trying to tame my adrenaline.

"What?"

"You can help with the calls. But let me support myself. I'll make rent on my own."

"We'll see."

After we got off the phone, I called Bill Plaxton. After a few niceties, I dove into business.

"I'm calling to ask for referrals. I broke up with my ex, Jordan, who referred Monty. And now Jordan's telling my clients to switch to Grassly. Since they offer inferior customer service, I'll wait it out and reach out to those clients in six months. They'll be banging on my door."

"Sorry to hear that." He cleared his throat. "Have you heard the latest on the agency?"

"On Grassly?" My hands trembled. I hadn't kept up with them because they weren't a threat before.

"A year ago, Keith Grassly's son took over the reins. He's implemented a new strategy to change the culture to a more tech-reliant firm. They've hired engineers, statisticians, IT gurus—not just fresh out of college, but from engineering firms and other nonmarketing companies. They've streamlined their operations, communicating with clients through an app and a centralized dashboard providing metrics and reports. It's paying off."

Jordan couldn't make the time to update me while we were

together? Keith's son was also Jordan's client, but I didn't know he had taken over Grassly. I blamed myself, too focused on servicing Jordan's referrals to pay attention to headlines on my competition as I advised my clients to do.

"I recommend hiring younger consultants with IT minds," Bill said. "The marketing world is all about the digital footprint."

"Hiring will take time, but I'll freelance now with digital marketers specializing in programming or IT. Fortunately, Monty's renewed for June, so I'm good with him."

"I'd ask him for referrals," Bill said. "Do you offer a referral program?"

"Yes. I give the referral a discount and give a free month of service to the one referring. Monty knows about my program."

"Great. Well, I'll make calls. Have you heard from Kris Murphy?"

I perked up. "Who's he?"

"He owns a fence company and is looking to penetrate beyond the Tulsa metro market to neighboring counties. He asked me for a consultant. Give him a call if he hasn't contacted you. Anything else you need?"

"No, that's a great start. Thank you for the referral. You made my day."

"Absolutely. I better go. I have downed trees to sort out."

"Sorry to hear that. Thanks for everything, Bill."

"Anytime."

I called Kris and left him a message.

Had Jordan kept the news about Grassly's renovation from me as his ace in the hole, in case we broke up? I had violated an important principle of war: win before you engage the enemy. I'd wanted to be three steps ahead of Jordan, but I was three steps behind.

CHAPTER 28
MAY 31-JUNE 1

I was usually swamped on the last day of the month, putting the final touches on next month's ad campaigns and emailing clients with reports on metrics and how we met marketing targets. Isla, my virtual assistant, was usually calling and texting me throughout the day, as she helped me get the reports ready.

When Jordan advised me to hire an assistant, I interviewed over twenty candidates and couldn't find anyone I felt compatible with. When Isla walked into the coffee shop with a command, I sensed I just found the person for the job. Fifteen minutes later, I hired her on the spot. Since then, I trained her not only to organize my business but to learn the job of a marketing consultant. During this time, she enrolled in and earned some valuable marketing certifications.

As I grabbed my phone to call Kris Murphy again, Isla texted.

> I'll email you Monty's newsletter this afternoon. I need to make sure everything's just right since this month's special is his largest ad campaign yet.

Before I could respond, Monty called.

"Celine, I got a minor tweak to make on June's ad campaign. I still want to apply the $100 discount to leads, but I want to extend the promo to current customers. This discount applies to any service over $1000."

"I like the aggressive approach. We'll edit June's newsletter and social media campaigns."

Although I normally loathed last-minute changes, Isla needed the work. Hopefully, Monty would value my flexibility.

"A lot is riding on June's campaign, so it needs to be perfect," he said. "Since we're targeting affluent communities, I just finished training five new employees."

"Don't worry, we're on this!"

Kris Murphy was calling.

"Alright, well, I value your support," Monty said. "If this campaign goes well, I'll upgrade to your highest package."

Yes! I made a victory fist. "Thank you. Can I call you back? I've got a meeting now."

"Of course. Bye."

I took Kris's call just in time. "Celine, this is Kris Murphy, returning your call. How's your morning going?"

"It's improving. How about yours?"

"Can't complain... Since Bill spoke highly of you, I'd like to hear what you can do for my business. Would you be available tomorrow at noon?"

Tomorrow? I touched my tight temples. I had never created a pitch in such a short time.

"Did we get cut off?" he asked.

"Sorry, I'm here. Someone's trying to call, but they can wait... Regarding meeting with you, tomorrow's a little tight. How about next week?"

"Let's see... Tuesday? I'll reach out to Grassly and see if they can switch appointments."

I squeezed the phone. I would not, could not lose to Grassly. "I'll be there tomorrow. What time?"

"Noon at my office. I'll text you the address."

"Sounds good. I look forward to meeting you."

"Same here. Have a great day."

I took a long inhale then created a to-do list, so I could get my racing thoughts on paper. With twenty steps written down, my organization couldn't ease my anxiety. Could I prepare a solid, you-won't-go-with-anyone-else pitch in twenty-four hours? I texted Bill then crossed off the first item on my list.

Fortunately, he promptly called back. "I'll provide a competitor analysis and get data from Kris. You'll get my report this evening."

"Thank you." I wanted to hug him.

I called Isla, asking her to help me compose a buyer persona for Kris's account. Having composed so many, she'd whip one out in half the time I could.

"But I need to polish the copy for Monty's newsletter," she said.

I touched my chest as unease pricked my heart. "Yes, you're right. Finish his account before creating the buyer persona."

"I only have until three today. I'm leaving at five for my bachelorette weekend in Dallas. At least, Logan's sister is footing the entire bill for the weekend."

As the unease crawled to my throat, I took a sip of water then a deep breath. "I don't have a choice. Just work on the persona. I'll add the finishing touches to Monty's copy and email everything to Brian before five."

Brian, the graphic designer, would upload the content to Monty's website.

"Okay. But don't forget." She sounded more stressed than I was.

I furled my brows. "Are you worried about Monty's account?"

"You've lost so many clients, and since Logan and I are paying for our wedding, I don't want to..."

"Look for another job?" I asked, slightly irritated.

"I don't want to work for anyone else, but I have wedding vendors to pay soon."

"It's fine. I've got this, K? You focus on work and let me handle client retention."

Once we got off the phone, I worked on Kris's pitch. By three, Isla emailed me the buyer persona, along with instructions.

> Email Monty at 3:30 and CALL him for
> confirmation.
> Email Brian by 4.

Her priorities were right, but my patience for them ran thin as the clock ticked. Though I needed every spare second to work on Kris's pitch, I spent the next few hours putting the final touches on Monty's newsletter and emailing Taja, my social media freelancer, about adding the discount for referrals and current clients to Monty's social. Before I could email Monty the newsletter mock-up, Bill called.

"Did you receive my email? I've compiled a wealth of data, including metrics from Kris's previous marketing campaigns. I've attached detailed reports and an outline. Let's schedule an online meeting to organized everything into an irresistible pitch. After that, I can create a pitch deck."

"Wow! I owe you. Thank you."

"Thank *you*. I need to be useful."

I got off the phone and created a meeting link for a video conference to email Bill, but I noticed I hadn't emailed Brian. It was already four thirty, so I quickly emailed Brian before he'd stop working at five.

With Monty's account cared for, I sent the link to Bill. Within five minutes, we were videoconferencing on Kris's pitch. By the time we finished, I was Rocky, eager to fight Apollo Creed. I thanked Bill with a "Let's do this!"

I polished the presentation until two in the morning then drove home to Jennifer's to get a few hours of sleep.

My phone alarm woke me up at six the next morning. I touched snooze, wanting to sleep for another fifteen minutes, but all I could think about was my metastasizing credit balance. I threw the duvet off my body and sat on the edge of the bed, wishing it was Sunday. "You can do this," I muttered as I stood and trudged to the bathroom.

Once I arrived at the office, I couldn't wait to start working. The time flew by so quickly that when eleven o'clock rolled around, I thought only an hour had passed. Though Kris's office was only eighteen miles away, I left now for our noon appointment. I'd wait in the parking lot or grab a coffee while I practiced the pitch.

While I sat at a stop light, Monty called. "Celine! You need to fix this!"

"What?" Oh no. I didn't email him the newsletter mock-up. At least the campaign went out. Brian emailed me he'd have it live by six this morning.

"You messed up. The email campaign says that my current clients and referrals get $1000 off a lawn package for June. It should be $100!"

In my shock, I pressed the gas pedal hard and slammed my brakes even harder. *Screech!* Addy stopped inches from rear-ending a cherry-red Jeep in front of me. Once I caught my breath, I said, "No, I'm certain I had $100. I would've caught that mistake." I pulled into a parking lot then checked my inbox.

"You didn't. Five clients called expecting $1000 off their lawn service."

Sure enough, I had typed $1000 in the newsletter. I couldn't believe it. I slapped my forehead. Why now? "Tell them your marketing consultant made the mistake."

"I told them it was a typo we're correcting now. Four people understood. But the fifth is a new account in an exclusive golf course community. He insisted I honor the deal. Otherwise, he'll leave a negative review on Google and report me to the Better Business Bureau!"

"I'll write an apology email stating that it was an unfortunate typo, but that we're still offering a terrific deal. Refer a customer or add a service valued at $1000 to receive $100 off."

"You better get that emailed now. I don't have time for troubleshooting your mess with my customers."

"I'm on it. And again, I'm sorry, Monty. It won't happen again."

"I'll call you in twenty minutes."

It was a quarter after eleven. If Isla weren't in Dallas, I'd ask her to write the apology, so I could make Kris's appointment on time. But I needed to get this right. Using a speech-to-text app, I composed an apology post, adding humor to smooth out the mistake to Monty's customers. After I double-checked it, I called Brian, so he could send it out ASAP.

Now I had twenty minutes to reach Kris's office. I'd cut it close but should make it on time. Once I got on the highway, I recited his pitch, trying hard to forget about my mistake.

Fifteen minutes later, as I turned onto the exit two miles from Kris's office, Monty called. "Since you've broadened my reach to a more affluent market, I need a firm with more staff."

Think of an irresistible incentive. "How about I give you $500 for your resident in the golf course community? Tell him you'll meet him halfway and give him a $500 discount for June. That'll be a win-win. He'll get an unbeatable deal, and I pay for the customer's discount."

"I hope it works."

"Me too."

"Bill vouched for you, but considering the saturation of competitors in my field, I can't afford these mistakes. Although I don't want to add insult to injury, I'll need a refund for June as well."

"Why? I've never made such a mistake before. And I've already corrected it."

"For starters, you didn't double-check your work. Nor did you email the mock-up; otherwise, I would've caught that error. Finally, you didn't check the email campaign after it was sent. I'm not shelling out thousands of dollars for an assembly line of workers that don't know what the others are doing."

My hands shook. I set the phone on the passenger seat and put in my earbuds. "I'll throw in a free month of social media services."

"Too late. I've texted Jordan to set up an appointment with Grassly. I've got to get back to my crew."

As I pulled into the fence company's parking lot and parked near the office, I held back tears, not wanting bloodshot eyes or smeared makeup. Why couldn't Monty extend grace?

After a few minutes, my body was dead weight. My mind blanked.

The buzz of a text coming in brought me out of my haze. I checked the message.

> Just heard from Monty. So sorry. But
> focus on Kris. You're a rock. Go get 'em!
> 

I didn't have much choice. As I emerged out of my car, Jordan's voice resonated in my head. *Ha! None of my referrals stayed. I knew you'd fail without me.*

CHAPTER 29

I ambled to Kris's office, trying to recite my pitch in my head. But a pebble from the unpaved lot worked its way into my right shoe. Dirt swirled as a pickup with an attached trailer passed me. The *beep beep* from a small bulldozer moving gravel behind the office demolished my concentration.

Best to get inside in time. I got the pebble out then entered the modular office building with three minutes to spare. I sat in a metal chair, grabbed a tissue from my handbag, and wiped the dust off my pointed pumps. I lightly ironed the creases in my navy pinstriped shift dress.

The young woman behind a waist-high counter asked if I was Celine, I nodded, and she assured Kris would meet with me soon. While I waited, I closed my eyes and made a mental checklist of the major points of my pitch.

Within a few minutes, Kris appeared. He shook my hand firmly and led me to his office down the hall. His contagious warmth put me at ease. By the time we reached his spacious office, I was ready to land this account.

I was professional and poised. We lost track of time until his wife came with his lunch. After introducing her, he promised he'd be in touch soon. I was confident he would've signed on the spot if he wasn't meeting with Grassly.

From Kris's office, I drove to a vacant parking lot. I emailed him a creative brief I'd already written, summarizing the main points I covered. Hopefully that would show him I was prepared.

You should've given that much effort to Monty's account. Where did that thought come from?

As I pulled back onto the street, I vowed I'd never drop the ball again. Anything to drive the accusing voice out of my head. Confidence in the face of adversity was the only choice against Jordan and Grassly.

I headed to the sub shop near my office, listening to alternative rock, so I wouldn't think about the loss. The music helped enough that I was composed when Kris called.

"Celine, thank you for your brief. I was impressed by your preparation and passion. You suggested a slogan I want to use, 'Just like our fences have a lifetime guarantee, so does our service.' Brilliant. I'm shooting a commercial next Friday, so I'd like your help revising the script. Can you meet Thursday night around seven? I'll pay you for your time and use this experience to evaluate hiring you."

I paused, so I wouldn't come across desperate. "Of course."

After we got off the phone, I tapped my steering wheel. "I got this."

Kris texted me the meeting info. When I saved it to my phone's calendar, I saw John's game in the same time slot on June 7th. I had blown it last year by not attending his game. Could I blow off my nephew again and live with myself?

I leaned back, resting my head on the headrest, then closed my eyes. Suddenly, I recalled pics of Kris's kids on his wall in his office. In one, he posed with kids in baseball uniforms. I called him back.

"Is it possible we could meet either before six or maybe around eight thirty on Thursday night? I promised my nephew I'd attend his baseball game."

"I respect your family commitments, but I can't do either time. Perhaps—"

"I'll be there." I was concerned he'd contact Grassly and have their copywriter add my slogan to the script.

"I can email you the current script today, and you can provide edits. Will that work?" His offer was considerate.

"Thank you but count on me for Thursday night. We'll work more efficiently in person."

"I agree. See you Thursday evening."

I called Aimee. "I'm sorry, but my prospective client needs me at his office in Owasso to prep for a production shoot. Unfortunately, the only time he can meet is next Thursday night at seven. Hopefully, it'll only last thirty minutes to an hour."

"Don't worry about it. I'll let John know."

"I'll make it up to him. I promise."

"Like I've said before, don't promise, just come." Her calm tone irked me more than if she had raised her voice. She had probably expected me to bail.

"Once my business gets stable, I'll be around for pizza night and the boys' events."

"I hope so. Best on your business. I've got to take John to practice."

My stomach churned as I thought about how I was disappointing John. I'd find a way to make it up to him, even if I couldn't for months.

CHAPTER 30

When I arrived at the office, Lauren's car was there. She emerged and waited near Addy. As I got out, the sun cast a warm sheen on her floral sundress. She gave me a hug, holding a to-go bag from a local restaurant. "Have you eaten lunch?" she asked.

"I just picked up a sub." I held up my to-go sack then opened the office door.

She walked inside. "I texted you about an hour ago to verify our plans." Her voice was strained. I could barely hear her say "Is this a bad time?" Was she frustrated with me for not responding to the text?

"I'm sorry," I said. "I was meeting with a prospective client. Is everything okay?"

"I'll share when we eat."

I led her to the conference room, where she sat next to me, then spread out her food—two spring rolls and a burger with a fried egg.

"Shane and I got into it earlier today. We worked it out, but that sickening feeling of sadness still lingers." She placed a napkin on her lap.

"About your video campaigns?" I asked.

"No... I'm frustrated with my infertility journey. Our journey, that is. These past five years, we've suffered two miscarriages."

"Oh my gosh! I'm sorry. That's so difficult." I took a sip of coffee, unsure what else to say.

"This morning, Shane got upset I booked a consultation with a reproductive endocrinologist without discussing it with him. Since insurance doesn't cover IVF treatment, we agreed to pursue less-expensive options first. Shane found a naturopathic doctor specializing in infertility. Six months later, I'm overwhelmed with tracking my ovulation cycles, avoiding this food and that, and taking all kinds of supplements, yet with nothing to show for it. When a friend referred me to a fertility specialist yesterday, I made an appointment immediately. What would you have done if someone showed you the Promised Land?" She took a bite of her spring roll then her burger.

I could so relate to nervous eating. And, honestly, to her impatience. I would've made an appointment without consulting my husband too, but I wasn't about to take a stance between them. "Shane will come around." I winced at how trite my statement sounded.

She frowned. "It's hard when I wear my emotions on my sleeve. I lost my cool, telling him he's insensitive. Before I could stomp off, he set me down and explained he's not against pursuing this route and wants to attend the appointment." Her pain emitted the same energy as her exuberance.

"Looks like you've snatched a good one." I took a bite of the sub, buying myself patience.

"He is! He prays with me every night, telling me how much he values me. But sometimes..." She set her burger down. "Sometimes, I'm angry at God, asking him, 'Why can't you fix me? Why do *I* have to suffer from infertility?' I'm ashamed for being ungrateful."

Empathy was never my strength even on a good day. "I didn't know you were enduring something this difficult. You're usually giving me hope. But I understand the pain of feeling that you're not enough."

Lauren hugged me tight; I sucked in my breath. When she released her embrace, I exhaled quietly.

"You encourage me. You always seem like you've got your life all together." She paused. "I need to focus on what I *do* have. Shane got checked, and he's cleared. I'm sooo grateful. So, I'm fine most days, but when I see a mom with her little child or a friend tells me she's pregnant, I have a mini meltdown and wonder why I can't have a baby. I want to hope, but it's difficult when you know something's wrong with your body. Sometimes I feel alone, as though I'm the only one dealing with infertility." Her blue eyes looked grey. The despair and desperation in them were too familiar. "I shouldn't feel this way, should I?"

"If my opinion means anything," I said, "you're so positive, I know you'll find a way."

"I hoped food would cheer me up, but it's not working." Lauren placed the half-eaten burger on her plate.

Bursting through my discomfort, Maman's voice echoed. *Tell my story.* I was relieved it occurred to me.

"If you want to talk to my mom about infertility, I'll provide her number. She had three miscarriages after my sister was born, but here I am. Guess I'm the miracle baby." What a joke. I wasn't an angel.

"That'd be amazing! I've discussed my journey with my mom since she suffered from infertility too, but she doesn't like to relive that pain." She clapped. "I can wait if I have a daughter as beautiful and generous as you."

I tightened my body. No, she didn't need a daughter like me.

"Maman has encouraged many women. But she has a thick French accent, so ask her to speak slowly." I texted Lauren the number.

"Thank you!" Lauren grabbed her phone on the table. "Got your text and can't wait to talk to her." We each ate a bite. "And then there's Garrett."

I raised my eyebrows.

"My parents and Garrett join us for dinner on Mondays. When we were under the same roof for a Christmas vacation in Michigan a few years ago, I had such a ball, I thought it'd be great to have them at my place every week. Well, the past two weeks, he's canceled on us. I don't have a problem with that, but when I ask why, he just says it's nothing. It irritates me when he won't tell me why. Shane tells me to let him be." She furled her brows. "I can't stand how men think they don't need to explain anything."

"My sister and her family have pizza Fridays at their place, but I haven't gone faithfully for a few years." On commitment to family, I was so callous compared to Lauren and Aimee.

Lauren touched my hand. "Once you get married, family rituals become more significant."

And there it was... Marriage, the key to enlightenment. "That's what most married people say to singles."

She winked. "Must be true, then. When you are ready, I want you to meet my friend Peter. We're in the same Life Group. He's handsome and has a heart of gold. And he's cultural. He's a member of the Philbrook. You'd be an ideal match." She held her head high, as satisfied as if she'd handed me the keys to a designed house. So, this was how Garrett felt.

"It's too soon." I bit my lip. She was threatening our professional boundary. Was I a project to distract her from her personal issues?

She waved her hand. "When you're ready."

"Anyway, I reviewed your latest metrics on the recent ad, and I—"

"Oh," she continued, "Peter's a plumber with a great reputation. How about I introduce you two and see if he'd hire you to promote his business?"

"I'm in as long as there's an understanding we wouldn't connect—romantically—if we have a working relationship."

"What if you connected romantically as well? Shane helps me in business. I don't see why—"

"No! Absolutely not. It's hard enough to cross professional boundaries and be a friend, but I won't threaten a work dynamic. It'll lead to a disaster." One I knew too well. I turned away to compose myself. My face felt hot.

"Are you uncomfortable with our working friendship?" She asked.

I turned back to face her. Her lower lip trembled. Great, I've offended her. I should've insisted on rescheduling. I shifted, angling my knees toward hers. "You're such a supportive client, and I can't thank you enough for all you've done to promote my business. But as I'm losing clients, I'm concerned about getting too close. What if you need to move on from me?"

"We'll cross that bridge if we get there. I've gained lifelong friends with clients; it's about honoring the client and maintaining communication. It can be done, but if you're apprehensive with me matchmaking, I can tone it down." She pursed her lips.

"I'd like that. Thank you." I grabbed my paper sack, partial sub, and napkin, and took them to the kitchenette. How much colder could I be?

She approached as I tossed the paper in the trash. "I better go. I can see you're frustrated with me."

"I'm not great company today, I'm afraid." I touched her arm as she looked away. "I'm sorry about your struggle. I really am."

She faced me and gave me a side hug. "I'll be praying for your business."

I accompanied her to the front door and gave her *bisous*. She didn't seem like she'd drop me, but nothing was certain anymore. I returned to work but wondered what I'd do if I didn't land Kris's account. I might need to reach out to Specter for a job.

CHAPTER 31
JUNE 3

I drove to Jordan's parents to return the bracelet. They lived in Jenks, a suburb in southwest Tulsa. Far removed from Jordan's high-rise condo, their home was in a family neighborhood with a community pool, playgrounds, and walking trails. Even if he got along with his dad, Jordan would loathe visiting here, especially losing patience with kids riding their bikes on the street.

As I got out of my car, the garage door opened. Someone was backing out, so I waved. The car stopped, then Jordan's mom emerged from the driver's side. She clutched her purse, her brows knitted.

Leaving the car door open, she waved. "Hello, Celine." She glanced behind. Was she expecting her husband to come outside? She looked at me. "Is everything okay?"

"Hi, Mrs. Sterling." I smiled and wondered if she despised me. "I'm sorry I stopped by unannounced. But I'm returning something that belongs to your family."

"Oh?" She headed toward me, barely moving her petite feet, until she stood five feet away.

I opened the jewelry box and showed her the bracelet. With the midafternoon sunlight touching the gems, rainbow rays rocketed in all directions. I didn't want to return it.

"She's a beauty, isn't she?" I asked.

She shook her head. "I've never seen it before."

I held it closer to her face. "Jordan said it belonged to your mother."

"Oh, that's impossible." She placed her hand on her chest. "My parents were poor."

I closed the box and carefully placed it in the purple sack Jordan gave me with the bracelet. "Unless I misunderstood your son. Could he have meant his paternal grandma?" *Please say no.*

"I doubt it." She rocked on her sandaled feet.

"Do you want to verify with Mr. Sterling?" I asked, wanting to slam all doors leading to Jordan.

She kicked a small pebble with the front of her sandal. "Maybe. Hold on."

I handed her the sack with the bracelet then glanced at the front yard.

Their home had pleasant curb appeal, giving an impression of a happy couple. A paved sidewalk led to the farmhouse-style front porch. Pinkish white peonies, green variegated hostas, and deep purple hyssop lined the flower garden below the porch. I assumed it was Jordan's mom who nurtured the plants and flowers, probably as an outlet. I admired how she maintained some form of creative expression.

When she returned, she handed me the bracelet. "My husband's never seen it before. Obviously, Jordan wanted you to have it."

Of course, Jordan's dad wouldn't have held onto an heirloom if he could've made a nice profit. I looked down, the kindness and understanding Jordan's mom showed me—the one who broke it off with her beloved son—endangered my desire to keep the bracelet. "But I broke up." I glanced up, but she didn't flinch. "I'm sorry we didn't work out."

"Maybe it was for the best." She patted my arm. "I've got to go." She trotted to her car.

Jordan lied! Where *did* he get the bracelet?

Once I arrived at Jennifer's, I returned the bracelet to her safe. An hour later, while Jennifer and I watched a movie downstairs, Jordan texted.

> When are you coming by with the bracelet?

"Should I text him back?" I asked her.

"What do you have to say? His mom would've told him."

"What if she's staying out of it, especially because he'd get angry that she didn't play along... I wouldn't have made the gesture if he hadn't lied about it being an heirloom."

"The bracelet is the last stronghold he has," she said. "I suggest letting it go, *for your sanity*."

I stood. "I'm no longer giving him everything he demands. He bossed me all throughout our relationship, and I've got to draw a line. Show him his bullying doesn't work."

"You already did."

"He hasn't backed down. He'll find another way to retaliate, even if I return the bracelet. For now, are you comfortable keeping it in your safe?"

"Sure, unless he continues to harass you." She looked at me with a narrowed eye.

"I'll handle it, but until then, thank you."

Did I want to have a hold on Jordan? Maybe. But while I couldn't put my finger on it, there was something about the bracelet itself that called to me.

Jordan phoned around eight and left a message demanding the bracelet back. Instead of responding, I blocked his number. Something I should've done weeks ago.

CHAPTER 32
JUNE 6

I met with Bill at my office, even though initially when we scheduled the meeting, I requested he come on the sixteenth, after the walls were painted and the furniture delivered. He said there was no time like the present and preferred to come earlier. Honestly, he might have been bored since he was in between jobs, so I figured I might as well take advantage of his open schedule.

As I gave him a tour, I recalled our conversation at Shades of Brown, when that woman interrupted him. "When we ran into each other at the coffee shop, you were about to say something about my look?"

He placed his hand on his chin. "Let me think... Yes. You look even softer than at Specter. More accessible."

Words I needed to hear. Content, I led him to Monroe, where I was most comfortable.

He scanned the room. "This is as professional as your Specter office."

"I think so too. My designer client painted the bookshelves and my file cabinet navy for free. Said it was an office-warming gift."

"Sounds like you're connected to some personable clients."

I shifted my feet. I might as well hear his take on my client relationship with Lauren. "Freelancing has broadened my client relationships. I know more about this designer in a month than I did with our clients at Specter in a year. Like you always taught, the soil that sprouts sustainable client relationships is trust, not just exceptional work."

"Glad you're getting well acquainted with clients." He tugged at his wrist as if wearing a white button-up shirt instead of a beige V-neck. "When you're working as closely with a client as you are, the lines can get blurred. Continue communicating openly, especially about her expectations of you as her consultant. Don't assume she wants you to be as vulnerable about your personal life as she is with hers. Let her set the tone while you tread with caution. And no matter how transparent she is, don't talk bad about your competition, your other clients, or her clients. If you bad-mouth others, she'll suspect you have no discretion in bad-mouthing her."

"That's helpful advice."

"I hope you understand the nuance in it. I like you dropping your guard a little. It's something I wanted to see. If you're unsure about boundaries, a good rule of thumb is to always be professional and prioritize the client's marketing needs."

"Probably even better advice for a professor." I tapped his arm.

"Trust me, I've hired a veteran secretary who'll keep me in line. My sister answered the bell."

Once again, Bill proved his integrity and wisdom. "I've got another tip for my student," he said.

"Teach away." I sat back in my chair.

"Hire a data scientist as your marketing consultant."

He was right that I needed another consultant. But I couldn't afford one. "I have a marketing assistant who keeps me organized and conducts research. She has completed her digital ads certification."

"Since you're close to signing a large account with Kris, you'll want to train another consultant now. If you acquire Kris, don't rest on your laurels. Maintain a well-balanced portfolio with sole proprietors and small businesses. Once you can handle two to three consultants skilled in digital technology, land more mid-level clients." He pointed at me. "Would you be interested in hiring someone with an IT and marketing background? She works at Specter but is looking for a smaller marketing team."

"Is she interested in freelancing?" I asked, swallowing my pride. "I can't afford to pay benefits."

"It'd be best to discuss that with her."

Of course he wouldn't speak for her. I nodded. I'd have to acclimate to our new dynamic of an equal playing field. "Send me her info." I looked away after saying it, wondering if I could afford to even hire her as a freelancer, especially if I couldn't land any more accounts this month.

"Are you working long hours like when you were at Specter?" He leaned back in his chair. I hadn't noticed when I saw him at the coffee shop, but without a constant strain across his forehead, he appeared five to ten years younger.

"Not like when I also moonlighted as a consultant. But yes, I'm working hard to build up my business."

"You've always expected results immediately. Give yourself time to rebuild your clientele. You're a brilliant marketing mind, hardworking, and poised."

Letting his words sink in, I held up my head. Boy, I missed his encouragements. "I needed to hear that. When you're working for yourself, it's hard to get positive affirmation. I haven't made the time to hear it though especially since working for yourself incites urgency. I want to keep lights on, freelancers paid, and software subscriptions up to date."

Bill hiked his leg across his knee. Cecil the Turtle socks peeked from the hem of his trousers. Nice.

"Take some advice from an old man and plan a two-week vacation for the end of the year or sooner. That way, you'll have to rest.

And delegate work, so you can average a forty- to fifty-hour work-week. You'll have time to give back. Invest in a charity and volunteer at a community outreach. You might think you can operate with your foot always on the gas, but you'll have to pump the brakes sometime. Best not to be forced to slam them."

No one in crisis planned a vacation. Should I have reached out to Stella at Specter to mentor me? Bill was at a different stage in life, where he could afford to retire. "That'll happen, but for now, I need clients; otherwise, I'll be asking you for a job referral."

"Getting away two weeks won't break your bank, no matter how desperate you feel." He covered his watch. "You were always striving to get ahead but ask yourself what's at the top. Once you get there, it's not as fulfilling as you expected."

I turned away. At the mountain summit, you could see what lay ahead and behind. You have the satisfaction of knowing you gave your full effort and dedication. And you have the experience to help others reach the top. Yes, it'd be worth the sacrifice. "I need to lead in a significant way—at least push my skills, intellect, and creativity to their limits. Then I can help others reach their summits." I glared at him, hopeful I'd said enough. "After building a leading marketing firm in the city by age fifty, maybe I'll live part-time in France."

I hadn't considered a retirement plan, but I was certain I'd reach my career goals by then if I followed Dad and Papa's motto. *Work hard now, so you can play harder later.*

"You need margin to spend time in a community outreach. How about speaking to my students in the fall."

"I'd like that."

"And most important, make sure you enjoy life with someone you love." He winked, wearing a half smile.

CHAPTER 33
JUNE 8

On Friday morning, Aimee texted that John hit the walk-off home run in last night's game. Great, I was the wicked aunt, absent as always. I responded with a GIF—the word POW in a jagged bubble.

Even though Kris and I created a persuasive script (he thanked me three times), I should've offered to email the edits, so I could leave our meeting earlier. I could've gone wild in the stands, high-fiving Aimee when John blasted the baseball into the stratosphere.

Confident I at least earned Kris's account, I called Kimberly, the referral Bill provided and scheduled a meeting for the eighteenth. I did need to hire another consultant.

Midmorning, Richard from Midwest Appliances texted:

Refund me

I replied right away.

> Since you didn't give me a heads-up about not renewing, I already spent the money. I'm sending a contract assuring I'll refund you in thirty days.

> Refund me today

I didn't respond; let him wait.

Two clients sent emails requesting refunds. After depositing money into my checking to cover those refunds, I was left with only two grand in savings.

An hour later, I presented a pitch to an attorney prospect in my conference room, excited to use the technology I'd shelled money to install. He signed with me on the spot, but as he leaned over to shake my hand, he accidentally spilled coffee on my laptop.

Though he gave me a hundred dollars to cover my deductible for the repair, I'd let my care package expire. At a shop midafternoon, I charged seven hundred dollars on my credit card for the repair, while paying a hundred for a refurbished tablet.

When I returned to the office, I sipped on a glass of rosé. As my body calmed, I threw myself into work. Within an hour, I received an email notification about a bank withdrawal. I logged into my account. Sure enough, the $2,500 withdrawal was made by Midwest Appliance.

Desperate, I transferred the rest of my savings to pad my checking account of any further withdrawals. I blinked several times as the zero in the savings balance seemed to grow bigger and overtake all the figures on the online bank balances screen. How could I cover the upcoming credit card balance of thirteen grand?

I checked the investment account at Raymond James. I'd have to withdraw money from there to cover my burgeoning credit card bill, or just pay the minimum balance until Kris paid me for the year. I had never paid interest on my credit card. Just how I was raised. But I'd rather eat Gra-Mere's duck livers than deplete most of my investment account. Draining it would feel like betraying my grandparents. I knew how hard Papa worked to leave a financial legacy for his grandchildren.

"Just eat the livers, Celine," I said out loud.

Deciding to offer my most aggressive deal ever, I began asking my remaining clients to prepay for July, starting with Lauren. She greeted my call with her usual exuberance. I went along then dove into my offer.

"I'm running a Christmas-in-July deal. If you prepay for July services, I'll toss in a free month of social media and gift $100 toward ads. You'd save $600."

My stomach churned. I came off like an infomercial. Desperation squeezed out decorum.

"I've received two clients through your ads, so sign me up. Do you need the money today?"

"This week," I said, grimacing. I didn't want to be like that relative hitting you up for money—saying it'd go toward basic needs, but you know it'd go to pay off the bookie.

"I'm praying for you. How's your business?"

I've never had a client like her, praying for me and truly invested in my well-being. Her kindness tapped into my code of honor. I couldn't put on a front. Squeezing my free hand, I opened up.

"I lost all my clients Jordan referred, so I'm rebuilding… Sorry, I don't mean to dump on you. I'm confident I'll land a lucrative prospect."

"Oh Celine, we've all experienced hardships. One time, I got sued, so I worked a side gig to pay legal fees. Another time, a client accused me of purchasing higher-end pieces than agreed on and refused to pay. Fortunately, she'd already signed the proposal itemizing the furniture, but it was a long process to get reimbursed the ten grand. And I have other horror stories I'd rather not share. Just too painful."

"The audacity of people, right? Sounds like that client was hustling you."

"I don't know, but I forgave her."

Conviction hit as I recalled Bill's advice. *Don't bad-mouth her clients.* "Sorry for assuming the worst," I said.

"No, I had the same thoughts. Is there anything else I can do to help?"

I thought about my abstracts. Oh, I couldn't sell those. They were centerpieces in the three rooms. But were they worth losing Isla and Taja?

"Maybe. Do you know anyone who'd buy the Evan Painter abstracts?" I asked.

"I might have a client who'd be interested, but are you sure?"

"No, but I can't afford not to."

"Alright. I'll be in touch."

"Thanks. You're a lifesaver."

"So are you."

After I hung up, I made a list of items I could sell online, hoping to find buyers over the weekend. If I could get enough money, I wouldn't need to sell the abstracts. I posted gifts Jordan gave me—except the bracelet—on a secondhand retailer site. Hopefully, the Hermes scarf wasn't a knockoff he bought from his uncle's pawnshop.

I struggled to post my Louis Vuitton handbag Jordan bought at the Manhattan flagship boutique. It set him back three grand. I tried to justify keeping it—I'd selected it myself as an impressive piece for meeting affluent clients. But I needed the money.

In late afternoon, I contacted freelancers, asking if they'd want to sublease a space in my office. All preferred to work from home. But I wouldn't give up. I'd pull money out of some hat.

CHAPTER 34

n my way home, I texted Aimee,

When I entered the condo, pop music and giggles diffused in the air. Jennifer emerged from her bedroom, a vision in a fuchsia maxi dress flattering her hourglass figure and dark skin. If I hadn't lost so much weight, I would've asked to borrow it.

"Hi," she said, putting on pearl earrings. "Good to see you. You've been MIA recently."

"Working late. Where are you headed in that hot number?"

She smiled. "Taking Sienna and her best friend to dinner to celebrate Sienna's acceptance into art camp. They're having a sleepover here tonight."

"I'm so glad!" For days, Sienna moped, worried about getting accepted.

"Would you like to join us?" Jennifer asked. "We have reservations at eight."

"No, I'm headed to Aimee's."

"Good." Her face beamed.

"Worried I've neglected my family? Or happy my sister will fatten me up?"

"Both."

"Do you have a moment?" I asked.

"Sure." Jennifer sat at the dining table nearby.

It was six thirty, and Aimee tended to run late. In her words, she didn't run her home like a drill sergeant. I was a bit militant about time. Growing up, I nearly lost my mind insisting we eat dinner by seven, since Maman struggled to have dinner ready by eight, the common time in France.

I sat next to Jennifer. "Would you be okay if I deferred paying rent until July? Then I'll pay for two months. Most of my clients dropped me and requested refunds for prepaid services."

"I'm sorry." Her shoulders slumped as though she was experiencing the loss herself. "You don't owe me anything."

"No. I gave you my word, and it'll boost my self-respect."

"Okay. But promise me that when things improve, you'll take a day off every week. I'm concerned you're not maintaining boundaries with work and leisure. You come home late at night, go to work early in the morning. I understand you're rebuilding your business, but how can you support clients if you're running on fumes?"

"I'm in crisis and need to take things a day at a time. I'll relax when I can." I pursed my lips.

"Just make sure you do it before you're too invested in the system to slow down. Before you have to rely on coping mechanisms to handle the stress. Taking sleeping pills, living off caffeine, avoiding community—that's not an abundant life."

"Speaking of abundant life, you also don't make time for yourself." I pointed my finger at her. "Do you date? Take a spa day?"

"Don't deflect. We can discuss my issues later." All the lightness in her voice left.

I stood and stepped away from the table. "I'm headed upstairs."

"Are you angry?" She remained in her seat.

I stopped and faced her. "I'm tired of everyone lecturing me about work-life balance. I can only take life a day—an hour—at a time. But no one understands."

She stood, approached me, and placed her hand on my arm. "I'll meet you upstairs. There's something I need to share." I would've told her to hold off, but I could sense she needed to get something off her chest. Her hand emitted electricity up to my bicep.

"I'll see you up there," I said, nodding.

I sauntered upstairs, curious, tired, and sad. Strange bedfellows. After slipping into yoga pants and a tank top, I sat on the edge of the bed, not wanting to slow down, just needing life's challenges to quiet down.

Within five or ten minutes—I wasn't sure how much time— Jennifer appeared at the bedroom door.

"Ready to talk?"

I glanced at my phone. It was a quarter to seven, but I doubted Aimee would notice if I arrived a few minutes late. "Sure."

Jennifer sat next to me. "After I divorced A.J., I went into frenetic mode. I worked crazy hours to support myself, while trying to be supermom to compensate for the divorce. I ran on steam, and to cope..." She glanced at her clasped hands. "I connected with a handsome client. We had this great chemistry and started seeing each other during the house-hunting process." She grimaced, still staring at her hands.

"A few days after he closed on a house, a colleague had seen us celebrating, so she told me that he was married with kids." Jennifer looked at me. "Oh Celine, I was in such denial, calling her a liar, even accused her of being jealous. But she provided evidence. Once I believed her, I almost ripped up my commission check. Discovering the home he bought was for rental income, I drove to his residence to confront him. Fortunately, I came to myself and left realizing I was trying to alleviate guilt."

Silence echoed as I processed her words. After a long pause, she continued. "I was craving attention and moving too fast. I ignored signs I normally would've sensed from a mile away." Her hand shook like a windblown leaf. "I've asked God to forgive me, but the hardest part was forgiving myself. It was a long, long process."

"Why didn't you tell me this when I first left Jordan?"

"I considered it, but you were hell-bent on doing your thing."

I frowned. "I suppose I was." I took her now still hand in mine. "Thank you for being vulnerable. I don't want to be the only mess in this life."

"You've made a brave choice by leaving Jordan and moving forward. Be proud of that."

I hugged her tight. "The reason I don't want to take time off is because I've lost so much and don't have anything to show for my hard work. I've lost most of my clients. You're my only friend, which I'm so grateful for. And I don't have a house to my name."

Leaning farther into her chest, I sobbed. Faces and the pain associated with each scrolled through my mind. Jordan, Monty, Richard, Elise, my childhood dog. Worthlessness, carelessness, betrayal, shallowness, and loss.

"Let it go... Let it roll through." Jennifer patted my back.

The dam collapsed. Everything rolled through minute after minute, until my wailing sputtered into short sniffling. I grew quiet, shoulders arching up and down with my breathing. Jennifer handed me a tissue.

"When I confided my mistake, that angel I told you about advised me to make a gratitude list daily."

I pulled away. "I'll do that... Thanks for always being here for me."

"Sometimes one true friend is worth an entire social circle."

I smiled, wiping sticky strands of my hair from my face. "Don't I know."

Needing to leave for Aimee's, I stood. "How about a compromise? You go on dates occasionally. Or at least indulge in a spa day. And I promise that once I survive June, I'll aim to stop working by six."

"I'll take that for now," she said.

"Tonight, I'll stay at Aimee's, so Sienna and her friend can have the Haven."

Jennifer waved her hand. "No, they'll be fine. They'll enjoy squeezing into her bedroom. Remember how we'd stay up all night?"

"Exactly. Consider it my gift, so *you* can sleep in peace." I knitted my brows.

"Alright. You're determined."

"And when you go on a date, wear that number. You'll have that man eating out of your hand. You shouldn't hide that figure under a bushel."

"Know any candidates?"

"I wish."

My phone rang. "Oops... It's Aimee. I better take it."

"Love you."

Aimee had to cancel pizza night. A family situation arose that they needed to address. I was relieved, because all I wanted to do was sleep. I packed a small suitcase and headed for the office after Jennifer and the girls left.

CHAPTER 35

At the office, I placed my suitcase in a closet in Monroe. I put fresh sheets on the pullout sofa then headed into the bathroom to get ready for bed. As I put my toiletries into the medicine cabinet, Maman called. I put her on speaker before placing the phone on the bathroom counter.

"Did something happen to Dad?" I asked, concerned. Although a night owl, she rarely called me this late. It was ten thirty in Florida.

"Père's asleep, so I can talk."

"What's going on?" I set the nearly emptied toiletry bag on the counter.

"You never ask us for help financially. Please let us pay the office rent. We want to invest in you, and this is the best way. You give us a return on our investment by taking better care of yourself. Not working long hours."

"Is this Dad's prompting or yours?" I wanted to take the money so desperately, but would I lose my self-respect?

"What he's asked, I'm enforcing. I know how badly you want to prove to everyone, especially yourself, that you can manage your business. We know how smart you are, so we don't doubt your abilities. The situation is giving us a chance to express to you how much we believe in you."

Instead of resisting, I relaxed. I didn't realize how much Maman cared about my business success.

"Is that a yes?" she asked.

Take it, Jordan said in my head. *You need Daddy's money to make it without me.* Gah! If I took their money, would my ex's words grow to an oak, shading any sunshine the money would provide?

"How about letting me borrow money for July rent now, and I'll reimburse you back once my client pays me a windfall on the first?" I grabbed my toothbrush from the toiletry bag then too zealously squeezed a dollop the size of a dollar coin on my toothbrush.

"Your sister lets us help her. We have an education fund for the boys and paid for all their airline tickets to France."

I dropped my toothbrush in the porcelain sink. I'd had no idea. "Is Heath struggling in business?"

"He's doing well. But we're spending our children's inheritance now, so we can enjoy how it blesses you."

Her argument was logical—and generous. "In that light, I accept. And in exchange for your generosity, how about I gift you airline tickets to France for next year?" I wouldn't purchase them for a few months, not until I'd rebuilt my business.

Maman clapped loud. Too much stimulation for me, so I lowered the phone's volume "Oh, *mon petit chou*!" Her voice accelerated. "You'll come to France with us?"

"Summer 2019."

"Père will transfer the money to your account, but we'll pay for the tickets. I love you."

And with that, much of my financial stress eased, though I'd still need to hustle. I had to beat Jordan, prove to Bill I was a team player, show the world that we Monroes could achieve the highest accolades in business, and encourage myself I could play with the big boys. Only then, could I silence the fear that I was just getting a handout.

CHAPTER 36
JUNE 9

Bill swung by my office with lunch. We sat in the conference room, eating Asian takeout. In my time of financial desperation, the complimentary meal tasted even more savory.

As we ate, he dove into business. "Sorry about Monty, but even more about Jordan."

"Yeah... After my conversation with Richard Pine, I walked with my eyes opened into this world of patriarchy. Up to now, I assumed men viewed me as an equal."

"The intelligent ones do."

"Thanks, I needed that reassurance." I paused. Richard's misogynistic remarks still clanged in my head. "I should be judged on my own merits, regardless of my gender."

If I were a man, though, would I have let Jordan take over my business and, really, my life? That a man probably wouldn't get in that situation made me angry at myself. I bit my lower lip. I didn't want to see myself as weak.

"There are places where women are treated equally. Specter is one of them," Bill said.

I grimaced. "Do you have to remind me? They filled your position with a woman from outside instead of promoting a woman from within. If I were a man, would I have gotten the promotion ahead of an outsider?"

He shook his head. "No. They hired her on the spot when she reached out."

"What?" My stomach soured, the Mongolian beef beginning to taste rancid. I stopped eating. "You told me they put her through the same interview process as me, and that the only reason I wasn't hired was because I needed to learn not to micromanage."

Bill maneuvered his chopsticks and took a bite of sweet and sour chicken. I wanted to wait him out, but he wasn't in a hurry to talk.

"Tell me the truth," I said.

He set his chopsticks on a napkin. "While you tended to micromanage, you were teachable. I had confidence you'd grow into the strategy position. The executives were going to promote you, but Stella called the owner and sent her résumé. The rest is history."

Now I understood why Bill hesitated on the day when he explained why I wasn't hired. And why he had seemed to downplay my experience when I ran into him at the coffee shop.

"I shouldn't have given you the impression your tendency to micromanage prevented your promotion, but I wanted you to stay. We needed your talents, and I wanted you to develop in patience and resilience. All of us were passed over at one point in our career. Trusting the process gets you to the top. I could tell that things came easy for you, because you're intelligent, shrewd, and a hard worker. But—"

"Are you saying that marketing came easy for me? Or I could handle obstacles in stride? Or were you concerned I'd eventually eclipse you and get promoted over you?" I stood as a myriad of emotions especially betrayal, confusion, frustration, ran through me.

"At that time, my goal was that I'd eat your dust one day and why I encouraged you to apply for my former position. But when I learned they hired Stella, I was partially motivated by the desire to instill character." He hung his head. "I shouldn't have misled you, but shot straight and let you handle your response."

"I wish you had too because I despise people thinking they know what's best for me. So, did you assume I wouldn't stay because they stopped considering me once Stella put her hat in the ring? I might've given my two-week notice, or I may not have."

"Yes, I knew you could find a job easily especially with your talent, zeal, and ambition." Bill remained sitting, eating his food. I supposed he was too acquainted with this type of conflict to get tense.

His admission disarmed my anger, but I still couldn't eat. "Did you also want me to stay because it'd be easier to have me support Stella?"

"Yes." His Adam's apple moved up and down as he wiped his forehead.

"I appreciate you bringing lunch," I said, as I headed to the conference door. "But I need to be alone with all this. Please."

He stood, brushed himself off, and ambled toward me, head held high. I escorted him to the front door. As I grabbed the knob, he extended his hand. I shook it out of courtesy.

Once he left, I put my takeout in the fridge, collapsed onto the chaise lounge, and became aware of the stillness in the office. I might've lost my mentor. Anyway, I wasn't sure if I wanted his wisdom.

CHAPTER 37

After Bill left, a loud pop reverberated through the office. I went outside, wondering if I'd heard a car exhaust. Isla pulled up and parked her car next to mine. She emerged looking relaxed in a peach sundress. A few loose strands of caramel hair hung from her messy bun.

"Do you have any car issues?" I described the popping sound.

"No, thank God."

Once inside, we stood in the entry.

"Celine, I wouldn't normally press and am not inclined to now, especially because you're in a tight bind. But my wedding gown came in today, and I need to cover the balance."

I gently slapped my forehead. "I forgot to pay you. I'll rectify that." As I'd lost money, I'd paused all automatic payments, including her paycheck. I led her to Monroe.

After I gave her a check, we discussed a prospective lead, a commercial photographer coming to the office at three. I practiced a mini pitch. She fanned her face.

"Is everything okay?" she asked, looking around. "It's warm in here."

"I better check the thermostat."

She followed as I trekked to the hall. The temperature was seventy-five, but I kept it set to sixty-nine.

"I'll check your unit," she said. "My family is in the AC business."

I followed her to the door, remaining by the entry while she inspected the appliance. "It's not running. Call your landlord ASAP."

"I doubt I can get someone here before the lead arrives," I said, looking at the time on my phone.

"Depends on what's wrong. How about I call the lead? See if he can reschedule or meet somewhere else, like his office?"

"Do that," I urged.

I called Russell, who assured he'd make calls and let me know about the repair. Isla, unable to contact the lead, called her brother. "He can come now, but he'll have to charge an emergency service fee."

I nodded, trying not to panic. I'd have to charge the service call on my credit card. "I don't have a choice. Tell him thank you."

Looking for emergency funds, I contacted Lauren, asking if she'd found a customer to buy my collection of Evan Painter's artwork. "I was about to call you," she said. "I have a buyer who can pick up the paintings on Monday for ten grand." I wouldn't have to touch the inheritance. What a relief!

Isla's brother arrived in twenty minutes. While he worked, I checked the secondhand retailer site. Thankfully, the handbag and Hermes scarf had sold. The buyers would deposit $1500 into my account by next week.

"Not a major repair," reported Isla's brother. "Just needed Freon and a thorough shower." My account two hundred dollars lighter, the AC was fixed.

After they left, I rushed to Monroe, dripping and sticky with sweat. It was two, so I took a shower and changed into a sleeveless cream peplum shirt and wide-legged black trouser pants. I applied a fresh round of makeup and pulled my hair into a slick bun.

When the lead rang the doorbell at three, I strolled to the entry, assured myself with a glimpse in its beveled mirror, and took a deep breath. Then I opened the door.

What the hell! Jordan's silhouette darkened the door as a tremor traveled from my head to my feet. I blinked rapidly until my eyesight cleared. I tried to slam the door shut. He put his hand on the side of the door and pushed his way through, grazing my arm.

As he stood in the entry, he removed his aviator sunglasses. I wished he'd keep them on. I didn't want to see his serpentine eyes.

"How dare you impersonate a lead," I said.

"Too easy," he hissed.

"You're trespassing."

He tucked his sunglasses into his shirt collar then lifted his head, a periscope scanning the environment. "Decent digs, although it's a little hot. Can't afford to keep the air tolerable?"

My back stiffened. "Leave!"

Staring at the painting that greeted visitors, his eyes constricted. "Displaying your lover's work?"

I shook my head. "Is that your best shot?"

"I never cheated on you." His voice drifted as he slithered down the hall.

"I have nothing to discuss." Not wanting him to reach Monroe, I ran past. That space was too personal.

He stepped into the conference room. "This place is larger than I expected. What do you pay, three to four grand a month? Too bad you lost all my referrals."

I approached the entry to the conference room. "It pains you that I acquired this office without you."

He laughed as he walked toward me, stopping only a few feet away before breaking into a snide song. *"Rich Girl, you can't make it without your old man's money."*

Through narrowed eyes and gritted teeth, I spat out the words, "Get out."

"I once had a client—a trust-fund baby—who arrogantly thought she could outperform me. She withdrew all her money and, six months later—tsk-tsk—she lost it all." Jordan shrugged, as if my demise was inevitable. "Now, she's working as a barista at her parents' coffee chain."

"Good thing *my* client knew how to run a business before she dated a loser. She's about to acquire a mid-level account. Kudos to her."

"Doubt he'll stay." He walked toward the hall. "What do we have here?"

I sprinted toward Monroe and blocked the entrance. Again, he stopped a few feet away. "You can't tolerate I don't need you," I said.

His hazel eyes flashed with streaks of yellow. "How ignorant do you think I am? You just replaced me with another. Did Evan Painter refer his patrons to you?"

"Leave."

"The tour's not over. Why don't we sit inside that space and talk?"

"I'm calling the police."

He smirked. "Don't be dramatic. I won't be long. I want to discuss you returning my bracelet, then I'll be on my way."

"It isn't an heirloom, is it? You gifted it to entice me to invest in the condo."

"You know that it belongs to my—"

"Maternal grandma? I tried to drop it off at your mom's, but she hadn't seen it before."

He pulled his shoulders back, eyes widening, and the hall seemed to darken. "How dare you harass her!"

The likely truth hit me. "Uncle Sonny sold it to you, didn't he?" I pointed my finger in his face.

He swiped it away. "No." He turned on his heels and headed

toward the entry. I followed, relieved he was leaving. But he stopped in front of the abstract in the sitting room, leaned over the console table, and grabbed the sides of the frame.

I rushed to him. "What are you doing?" Stretching my body to avoid hitting the table, I grabbed the right and bottom side of the frame as he removed it off the picture hook.

"I'm taking it as collateral until you return the bracelet."

"You're not taking it!"

"Let go," he said, pausing to glare at me.

I dug my heels into the hardwood floor, gripping the frame so tightly that my knuckles turned dead white.

He yanked the painting out of my grasp, raising it high above his head. I lost my balance and fell—*whack!* My back slammed hard on the hardwood floor. In the chaos, my feet tangled with his. As if in slow motion, the painting slipped from his grip, landing face down on the sharp tip of a glass trophy resting on the console table—a replica of an advertising award my team at Specter had won. The painting and trophy crashed to the floor.

I stood and ran to inspect the painting. The tip of the trophy punctured the center of the abstract.

"I told you to let go," Jordan said from where he'd landed.

"Why? Why? Why?" I knelt on the floor, looking at him.

He stood quickly, brushed his pants with his hands as if to wipe dirt off, and scowled. "I have nothing left here."

"You better reimburse me!" I said.

"I'm calling us even. You don't have your painting; I don't have the bracelet." He narrowed his eyes. "I commissioned an artist who used crystals and faux pearls."

"Why so adamant to get back a fake?"

"You don't deserve the effort I put into having it made." He bent toward me and whispered. "I was the best thing in your life."

Still kneeling on the hard floor, I shook my head and pointed to the door.

As he stood, I wanted to swipe his legs from underneath him and watch him fall flat on his face. What good would that do?

After he left, I jogged to the door, slammed and locked it, then ran to the window, watching his silhouette in the summer sun until he sped away. Hand on my aching back, I turned to study the tear in the painting. I no longer harbored guilt for keeping the bracelet.

CHAPTER 38

When I grabbed my phone to call Dad, I noticed Maman had called a few hours ago. Maybe they deposited the money. Should I decline payment? Jordan's words against me resonated too true.

I listened to her message. "Celine, I'm at the hospital with Père. Please pray."

For a few seconds, I blanked. Then her words slowly penetrated my mind. *Hospital. Pray.*

She didn't answer my return call, so I phoned Aimee. "I got Maman's message. What's wrong with Dad?"

"She thought he might've had a heart attack, but the EKG is negative. They're doing an echo now."

I clutched my heart. "What are his symptoms?"

"Heart racing, pain in his chest."

"How long will it take before they rule out a heart attack?" I asked, recalling my recent talks with Dad—his complaint of heartburn, pale face, heavy breathing.

"Unsure, but I'll keep you notified... Oh, hold on. Maman's calling me."

After Aimee put me on hold, I wished I had insisted she include Maman in a three-way call, but everything happened so fast. Poor Dad! Lying on the hospital bed with probes sticking out of his chest.

I rushed to Monroe and checked flights to Sanford, the airport nearest them. It wouldn't be cheap, but money problems were nothing compared to Dad's health.

"Celine?" Aimee asked, returning to our call.

"What did Maman say?"

"She's relieved. They're probably going to release him today. His vitals are normal, and he no longer has pain."

"I'm flying there to help."

"No, no, no. Dad needs zero stress for the next few weeks."

"That's why I need to be there. Make sure he relaxes."

"Seriously?" Her voice cracked.

"I promise not to add to his stress."

"Just wait until Maman approves. She's got a lot on her plate, so let her call you."

I frowned, frustrated by my sister's boss mode. "I will. Next time you talk to Maman, include me in a three-way call."

"I'll try. I've got to go."

I stood and paced the floor. Shortly, my phone pinged.

A bank notification: Zero balance in checking.

I logged into my bank account again, only to see zeros staring at me from checking and savings.

I texted Lauren.

> Would the buyer be open to purchasing two of Evan's paintings instead of three?

She texted back within ten minutes.

> Just checked with the buyer.
> Unfortunately, they want the three
> paintings for their new home as a
> collection; otherwise, they'll purchase a
> different collection from Evan directly.

My heart sank. I had no choice but to tap into my inheritance. I emailed my financial advisor, requesting a twenty grand disbursement from my investment account. Hopefully, the proceeds from the sale would hit my checking account before the fifteenth, when my credit card payment was due.

At least, I had fifty dollars cash.

After finishing a bottle of rosé, I craved something stronger. But I didn't want to be alone, concerned I'd get so wasted that I wouldn't be able to work tomorrow. I changed into white leggings and a black tank with a scoop neck then contacted a rideshare. The driver dropped me off at Charleston's, a nearby restaurant with a bar.

CHAPTER 39

An intimate gathering of people had collected along the bar. I dodged in and out among them, looking for an empty stool. The only one available was at the end of the counter.

A middle-aged man in a ballcap sat on my left. Cheap musk cologne wafted up my nose, reminding me of my high school boyfriend on prom night. My juvenile date was more debonair than this dude in a graphic tee with the word *Move* in red font.

"What do you need?" the bartender asked. He resembled a construction worker, biceps bulging from his short-sleeved shirt under a crew cut.

"Shot of whiskey," I said.

"Alright." Once he handed it to me, I downed it fast to the rhythm of the crowd and the nineties rock music in the background, but Jordan's voice in my mind pounded louder. *She lost it all.*

I scoured the people at the bar, some seated and others standing, all with drinks in their hands and smiles on their faces. Most of the women wore tight-fitting dresses; the men donned short-sleeved polos. Their homogenous head-tipping at someone's joke and faux smiles were just another rendition of my prior social circle. We gathered at bars, drinking imported wines and expensive cocktails. Our ambition was understood, never spoken.

"See anyone familiar?" asked the bartender.

"What?" I faced him as he cleaned a shot glass.

"You're looking longingly at them," he said.

"I'm not." I furrowed my brow, irritated he acted like he knew me. "It's just... Doesn't matter. Give me another whiskey, please."

"How about a Tree of Life? It's a bar favorite."

"What's in it?" I asked.

"Vodka, apple cider, lime juice, ginger beer, a few secret touches to make it *pure*fection." He kissed his curled fingers.

I rolled my eyes at his pretension. "That's a mule."

"It's a Tree of Life. I add a few twists of my own."

"Straight whiskey, please."

"Coming up."

"I'll try one," said Graphic Tee.

"What's changed?" The bartender leaned toward the customer.

"Got a job interview on Monday." The customer flashed a wide smile, which the bartender returned.

"This one's on me." The bartender squinted at the man. "I could make it a virgin."

I curled my toes, wondering if this customer might deck the presumptuous bartender. *What the heck?*

"No." Graphic Tee glanced at his hands. "Cut the alcohol in half."

The bartender tapped the counter. "You'll really like this one."

After the bartender gave me my whiskey shot, I observed the intimate group again. As one woman glanced at her drink, a small frown spread across her face. Sensing my stare, she looked at me then quickly turned away. She flicked her hair with her hand and laughed, unhappiness hid behind her smile.

In our circle, our personal lives were a wreck. We told each other we could have it all—rising careers, enviable relationships, and philanthropic endeavors. We were all with someone, so we considered ourselves power couples. Date nights were with our circle, so we didn't have to pretend we cared for our partner.

"I'll have another shot," I said to the bartender.

"Tree of Life?"

"Just whiskey." Why was he making this difficult?

"Last one for you tonight." He mixed someone else's drink.

"I have money."

"I'm sorry, but that's the limit." He leaned toward me. "You'll thank me, I promise. You don't really want all that." He tapped his heart in a sign of solidarity.

Before I could respond, the air wafted of backyard summer nights. A waitress set a plate of burger and fries in front of Graphic Tee. I scowled, turning toward the window. The counter seemed to move.

The bartender laid the shot in front of me. I downed it, hoping it'd evict Jordan's taunts. *You'll fail without me.*

I screamed silently, pressing hard on my temples. *Get out of my head!*

"Geez," Graphic Tee said. "This is incredible."

I turned, wondering if he meant the burger, but he was sipping on the Tree of Life.

"Told you." The bartender pointed to him.

"I'll have another after I'm done. But make it a virgin."

They conversed back and forth. "How's Esau?" Graphic Tee asked.

The bartender's eyes brightened like a polished diamond. "He's in remission. Thanks for asking."

"That's the best news I've heard all day." Graphic Tee extended his arm, and they exchanged a fist bump.

I stared at the bartender. I thought I had problems.

"This is my last night serving customers," he said. "I'm dedicating my energy to my woodworking business now that we paid off our medical bills."

"No insurance?" Graphic Tee asked.

"We got it through my wife's job, but it didn't pay for all the treatments. That's why I moonlighted here. I'm going to miss you, but congrats on the interview. Give me a holler if you land the job." His full-face smile illuminated the bar. Who was this guy?

I needed another shot, but I'd have to go to another bar. A little tipsy, I stood slowly and sauntered to the restroom, where I hid longer than I wanted, wondering how I could get another drink. I needed to return to the office, but I'd have the driver make a pit stop at a liquor store.

As I headed to the bar, a blonde woman sat in a vacated barstool. The man who stood to her right looked familiar. I did a double take. It was Lauren's brother. I slunk back to my seat at the bar.

The bartender approached Garrett and his date. She asked for a rosé, Garrett for a virgin margarita. As the bartender filled their order, I whispered to Graphic Tee. "Would you get me a Tree of Life? Here's cash. I'll throw in a few extra dollars." I batted my eyelashes.

"No." He stiffly shook his head, like a child not wanting to get in trouble.

"I'll get an Uber."

"Shhh." He covered his lips with his finger and darted his eyes toward the bartender.

"If I whisper, he won't hear me." Why was Graphic Tee making a scene?

"You're louder than you think."

"Is everything alright?" the bartender asked.

I nodded.

"Could you get her a virgin Tree of Life?" Graphic Tee asked.

"Half the gas," I said. "I've an Uber." I pointed to the door.

Garrett's girlfriend whispered something. He glanced at me.

My stomach churned. I whispered to the bartender. "Please."

He crooked his finger, beckoning me closer. I leaned against the counter, our faces just inches apart. "I'll tell you what," he whispered. "How about I order you a chicken salad then let's see how you fare?"

I shook my head, not wanting to spend money on food.

"Alrighty. I've got something good for you." He turned, facing the drinks.

He mixed, churned, and spun the mixing bottle then tossed it in the air. I clutched the counter, mixing, churning, and spinning inside. He handed me a glass. "There you go. On the house."

"I pay."

He smiled and walked away. I didn't see where he went, because I wanted to down my drink. But it was a virgin mule. I located the bartender and waved. "I need another, with gas."

"Ma'am, I can get you anything to eat, but nothing with alcohol."

My stomach growled, but I needed another drink. The odor of grease, heavy cologne, and sweet perfume climbed up my nose. Graphic Tee took a bite of his thick burger. Yellow cheese clung to the sides of the bun then dribbled down his mouth and onto his chin. I fought dry heaves as my stomach churned.

Had the space shrunk? Everyone talked over me. Laughter boomed. Did I have my office keys?

I reached for my purse hanging from my shoulder, but I struggled to unzip it. Tugging harder, I lost my balance and landed on my butt. That area was already sensitive from my earlier fall in the office. I painstakingly heaved my body up. The room spun faster as women and men laughed at me.

Someone grabbed me from behind. I swung my arm to defend myself.

"Ma'am?" a man said. I turned to face him. Garrett stood so close I could see the golden specks in his eyes. "Do you have a ride home?"

"No. Uber." I worked hard to be clear. "I'm fine." I tried to pull myself up but couldn't get my balance.

He gently grasped my arm. "Let me." He tilted his head, eyes piercing mine. "Have we met?"

"No." I didn't want him to know I was Lauren's consultant and friend. Yet, I couldn't stop staring at him, wishing he was my designated driver. I tried not to lean on him, but the counter was far, far away.

He did something with his phone then informed me an Uber was on its way. I still heard laughter. I didn't look, afraid I was the butt of the crowd's joke.

"Thanks," I said.

He smiled but stayed by my side. I wanted to disappear.

"I'm fine. Please." My eyes were moist, my mouth dry.

"How about we just get you outside?" He pointed toward the door.

A stranger tapped Garrett's shoulder. "I'll take this young lady home." The stranger approached on the other side, so I was sandwiched between them.

"Thanks, Jackson," Garrett's girlfriend said, still seated on the stool. She turned to face Garrett. "Let my cousin take her."

Jackson wrapped his hand around my waist, so Garrett slowly released his arm off my shoulder. "Your Uber should be here any moment," Garrett said.

I nodded, unsure if Jackson, a stranger, was safe.

"I've got it, Garrett. It'd be better for me to drive her home than to trust an Uber driver." Jackson slid his hand up my back and around my shoulder.

As Garrett walked away, was he zigzagging across the bar? Or was my eyesight that impaired? He approached his girlfriend. Her long legs were like chopsticks peeking through her miniskirt. Did she kiss him?

"Ready?" Jackson asked.

I pointed toward Garrett. "He got Uber." My feet scuffed along the floor as Jackson led me onward. Once we were outside, the hot air hit. I almost passed out.

"Whoa," he said, gripping my shoulders tighter. "I got ya. You'll be safer at my place."

I shook my head as safety sirens went off inside. His place was a foreign land, remote from Jennifer, Aimee, Lauren. I stopped, looking for an Uber.

"Come on!" he said, petting my hair.

"No!" My life depended on someone hearing me.

"You're safe." He dragged me along.

"Noooo!" I tried to wrangle my arms away, but his grip was a bulldozer claw.

"Shhh," he whispered. "No need to make a scene."

I kicked him in the leg, but he gripped me tighter. His fingers dug deeper into my skin. "Don't do that, you slut."

I scanned the parking lot. "Help meeee!"

He covered my mouth. "I'm keeping you safe."

"Let go of her, Jackson!" Garrett's voice echoed. I managed to turn toward him. He gripped the man's shoulder.

"I'm taking her to safety," Jackson said, "but she's confused."

"Your cousin wants to talk to you. She's got someone she wants you to meet."

"Nah," Jackson said.

"Now!"

I shook with the force of Garrett's words. Jackson released me abruptly, and I fell, knees scraping the concrete.

"Sorry." Garrett lifted me carefully to my feet. "I didn't expect him to let go like that."

Too ashamed to respond, I looked at the ground as tears ran down my face.

"Let's get you home safe. It's difficult when the world's spinning out of control. We've all been there, haven't we?"

I nodded. He glanced at his phone then walked me to a Jeep. He opened the passenger door, carefully hoisted me in, strapped me in the seatbelt, and asked for my address.

"I'll drop you off," he said. "Unless you'll feel safer with the Uber."

I pointed at him, then rested my chin on the door and stared out the window, watching as he approached a car parked closer to the restaurant. He gave the driver something, and the car drove away.

The blonde and Jackson came outside. She was red-faced, yelling, but I couldn't make her out. She pointed to Jackson. Garrett said something. She placed her hands on her hips, pointing at me. Garrett glanced my way. Finally, she stormed inside, Jackson following her.

When Garrett got in the Jeep, he smiled. "Ready?"

Somehow, I directed him to my office. He led me inside, where I gave him my phone and showed him the code for disabling the alarm and stopping the constant clanging.

"Are you good with me helping you to the love seat?" He pointed to the sitting room.

I nodded, relieved he led me to a resting spot. Once I laid across the love seat, I waved.

"I'll enable the alarm," he said, turning toward the door. Then he looked back at me for a few seconds, though it felt more like hours as his eyes searched mine. What was he seeing?

"Be at peace." He left, closing the door behind him.

CHAPTER 40
JUNE 10

I woke in the middle of the night, almost sliding off the love seat. For catching myself, I was rewarded with a pounding headache, sore neck, and stiff back. I stumbled to the kitchen and drank a glass of water. Then I climbed onto the sofa in Monroe and drifted to sleep.

Bang, bang, bang! I sat up, squinting against daylight and gripping my temples. Was that the constant beat of my throbbing head? I staggered to the bathroom, brushed my filmy teeth, and combed my hair. Yet, the banging didn't stop.

I walked slowly to the kitchenette, needing coffee. The banging grew louder and louder. Was someone knocking? I tiptoed to the front door in case Jordan was there and glanced through the peephole.

Lauren! I inspected myself. Still in the same outfit from last night, I reeked of sweat and alcohol.

I ran to Monroe and grabbed my phone. It was dead, so I texted her a message through my tablet.

> I'll be there in a moment. Long night working.

Take your time.

Nearly tripping on a pant leg as I kicked off my leggings, I gasped. My knees were black and blue. Scenes from my fall last night replayed. I inhaled then slowly stripped off my top and put on the first pair of clothes I saw in my suitcase—black yoga pants, a burgundy tank, and a yoga shrug. After I washed my face, spritzed perfume on my neck, and put my hair in a pony, I trudged barefoot to the front door.

"Hello," I said with a bright smile.

"Everything okay? I was on my way to church and saw your car in the parking lot." Her brows lowered. "I was surprised you'd be here on a Sunday morning."

"Come in," I said, looking down.

As she entered, she grabbed my hand. "Seriously, you look like you pulled an all-nighter. Your shrug is inside out." She pointed to the tag on the front. "I'm sorry for banging constantly. I called several times and rang and rang the doorbell. When you didn't respond, I thought it was broken. That's why I knocked. I worried that... that you'd..."

"What? I'd what?" I asked.

"Working too long. Alone and isolated. I don't know."

I turned and walked toward the sitting area. "Um... just in a hurry to get my day started." I sat in the armchair facing the entrance.

Lauren sat on the love seat next to my chair. "I've been feeling like you're in need of care. Do you have too much work on your plate?"

"I'm fine." I couldn't smile.

"I'm sorry for pushing Peter on you. You were right. I tried to distract myself from my problems." She went on and on, dizzying me with her talking. The pounding in my head synchronized with her every syllable.

I stood. "Excuse me, I need water. Would you like some? Or coffee?"

"Water's fine."

In the kitchen, I popped two aspirins and drank as much water as I could.

"What happened to the painting?" she asked.

I turned toward the chaos on the floor. The abstract looked as though the trophy stabbed it in the heart. I held my breath, so I wouldn't scream in disgust.

"Were you trying to remove it from the wall?" She frowned.

"Kind of... It's a long story... Fortunately, the other two are safe."

"I'm sorry this one got destroyed."

"Me too." I was too depressed about everything to ask if she could find another buyer. I'd probably ask her another time.

She stood and approached the kitchenette. Once she was inches away, she extended her arms. "What's up? You look... well, hungover."

I stared at the shrug's tag. I couldn't hide my night from her. "Have you ever done something rash, desperate, to drown the voices in your head and escape pain?"

She nodded. "Many times. I've laid in bed for a whole day, eating and binge-watching HGTV because a client dropped me or loathed my design."

I handed her a water. "But something in public?"

"Can we return to the sitting area?" she asked.

I followed her to the love seat, sitting a few inches away.

"When I was a sophomore in college," she said, "my parents were struggling in their marriage. I was distraught, not knowing how to deal with the drama. So, I started to smoke pot off campus. One night, friends and I were at this public park, when my professor ran by. She was training for a marathon with her husband. My friends and I ran the opposite direction, hoping she didn't see us. A few days later, she asked me what was happening in my life. She didn't judge but listened. After that, she served as a mentor."

Struggling to free my arms from the shrug, I nodded. "I was at Charleston's last night."

Lauren pulled the shrug off me and laid it on the back of the love seat. "I wish I would've known. You could've met Garrett."

"I was getting wasted. Garrett found me and gave me a ride here."

Her blue eyes got large, almost angelic. "That was you?"

"Yes." I closed my eyes like when I was a little girl. If I couldn't see her, she couldn't see me.

She hugged me, but I kept my eyes closed. Her body was warm and her jumpsuit soft. Her touch spoke healing, removing shame. I hung my chin on her shoulder as she talked about life. God. Love. All a blur.

"Shane left for an overnight business trip today," she said, coaxing me to come over and stay the night. She assured me she'd enjoy my company.

CHAPTER 41
JUNE 11

The next morning, I woke disorientated, the way I imagined I'd feel if I was blindfolded, stuffed in the trunk of a car, and held captive in a strange place. Suddenly recalling the menacing face of the stranger from the bar, I sat straight up in bed. The memory of him dragging me toward his car flashed like a Service Engine light.

Wrapping my arms across my chest, I closed my eyes. I recalled Garrett patiently leading me to his cherry-red Jeep. "You're safe, you're safe, you're safe," I said out loud.

Eyes opened, I tapped the baby-blue lamp then examined Lauren's guest bedroom. A turquoise vase filled with pink hydrangeas sat next to the lamp on the nightstand. The walls were a greyish slate blue, each featuring a pastoral picture of Jesus with sheep.

Once I slid out of the four-poster bed and my feet hit the shaggy white rug, I dug my toes into the wool fibers, soft like a Persian cat.

I entered the adjoining bathroom. My toiletry bag sat on the counter next to splashes of Lauren's hospitality. A beige wicker basket with an unopened bar of lavender soap. Travel-size bottles of shampoo and conditioner atop a fluffy white towel and washcloth. An unopened toothbrush and tube of toothpaste in a holder with a blue toile pattern.

After brushing my teeth and putting my hair in a bun, I slid into shorts and a casual tee. Wanting to check emails, I searched for my phone. I couldn't find it in my purse or in my car.

I must've left it at the office. Yet, I wasn't ready to face loneliness at the office, so I'd just stop by to pick up my phone and laptop then work at Lauren's home. I'd explore her design and make suggestions for her YouTube series, *Step Into the House of a Designer.*

I sat at the bay window on a padded seat, its blue toile pattern matching the duvet. I pulled up the slate-blue Roman shades and drew the white linen curtains, sheer like a bride's veil. Darkness from outside surrounded me. I made out the shadow of a tree near the window and pressed my forehead on the glass, cool and refreshing. A morning choir of sparrows sang of summer as I listened, unmoving. Once the sun ascended over the horizon, filling in silhouettes with color and shape, I stretched my legs.

Lauren's backyard reflected her vibrant style: a magnolia in the center, a spectrum of pastel blooms in the flower beds, and blossoming pink hydrangea bushes. Would I have a backyard like it if I'd married one of my exes before Jordan? I'd probably be outside chasing kids. Pushing our little girl on the swing or smiling as our son dug for earthworms. On occasion, I regretted not marrying, especially as the yearning for a family quietly grew. Now, I acknowledged that my career wasn't filling that void.

I left the window seat, made the bed, and headed toward the kitchen in search of coffee. The lights were on, but I didn't see Lauren. Her home was serene and stylish, each room painted in a different but complementary shade. The kitchen was Wedgewood blue, the living room golden cream, and the sitting area daisy yellow. We could create many vlogs here.

Above the white fireplace mantle was an eleven-by-fourteen

wedding portrait on canvas. The sun set behind Lauren and Shane. I walked to the built-in bookshelf, searching for pictures of Garrett.

There was only one. I leaned toward the four-by-six. He smiled, eyes slightly low as if weary. I smiled back. It was him with a short, scruffy beard and curly brunette hair peeking out from a forest green beanie. A camera hung around his neck and the padded blue straps of a backpack rested on his shoulders. He stood in a depression with a waterfall cascading down the mountains behind him. That same intangible feeling I'd had about him at Woodward Park returned. He seemed compassionate, composed, and chill.

"Good morning." Lauren emerged from the kitchen pantry.

I jumped, hand on my heart. "Hi." Once I recollected myself, I pointed to the picture. "Where was this taken?" I asked partly out of curiosity about the setting, but mostly afraid she'd caught me gazing at her brother.

"Let me see." She approached and picked up the mother-of-pearl frame. "That's in the Pyrenees."

My jaw dropped. Once I recovered, I smiled. "Is it the Cirque de Gavarnie?"

She clapped. "You've been there?"

"My Gra-mere lives in Gavarnie-Gèdre, a village close to the Cirque."

"What a coincidence! My cousin married a Frenchman, and they live in Toulouse. We visited her last summer." She touched my arm. "How are you this morning?"

"I'm fine. Thank you for letting me stay here. I slept like a baby."

"I'm glad... Do you want breakfast?"

"Sure." It occurred to me that it was Monday, and I thought about her schedule. "What are your plans this morning?" I asked.

"I canceled my morning appointment, so we—"

"No! Please don't modify your life around mine. I can work at the office."

She waved me off. "I want to visit with you. My client's on pregnancy leave anyway and doesn't mind if we postpone."

Her voice had caught on the word *pregnancy*. I frowned. "Is it difficult for you to work with a pregnant client?"

"I'm good."

"You have so much going on; you don't need to worry about me." Guilt pelted down like a rainstorm.

"You're the bright part of my morning. Plus, I could use a diversion." Her tone was soft.

I laughed. "Now I'm a diversion?"

"A welcome one," she said.

"You were a beautiful bride. Was Garrett Shane's best man?"

"Just a groomsman." She knitted her brows. "I'll be happy when I frame a picture of Shane and me dolled up at Garrett's wedding."

"Is he dating anyone?" I asked coyly, wondering if she knew about his girlfriend.

"Why don't you sit at the island counter while I make breakfast. I've got a lot to share."

I followed her into the open kitchen and sat in a cream barrel-back chair pulled up to a wide island. She stood on the other side. "Do you like biscuits and gravy?"

"Who wouldn't?" I said, smiling. This was exactly how I'd envisioned Lauren at home, the impeccable hostess.

"Good." She poured flour into a metal bowl. "Where do I start? Well, Saturday night—it must've been right after he dropped you off —Garrett came by here. He told Shane and me that he'd been seeing someone. That's why Garrett had missed Monday dinners. I don't remember her name. Anyway, they were at Charleston's to meet her family when he ran into you."

"I see." I gripped my hands, wondering what Garrett told Lauren about my state that night.

"His girlfriend's cousin was at the bar, so she summoned him over to help with you. Garrett hesitated but figured he'd leave you to the cousin's care if you were safe. He couldn't get rid of this sensation that something was off, though, so he excused himself and followed you outside."

"He's that intuitive?"

"He's sensitive to the Holy Spirit."

Just before Garrett had come outside, I'd pleaded silently to God for help. I wasn't sure if God would answer, but I didn't know what else to do. I didn't imagine him warning Garrett, though.

"Just so you know, you were Garrett's angel too—"

"What? How?"

"I'm getting there… I'll skip the parts you know. When the girl-friend came outside, she got belligerent, asking what he was doing. Her cousin had told her that Garrett was hooking up with you. She yelled at Garrett that he was embarrassing her in front of her family."

Lauren added, blended, and whisked ingredients in the mixing bowl. "I'm proud of him for how far he's come. Normally, he would've politely explained how he needed to help you. This time, he broke up there and then, saying they weren't compatible anyway and that her cousin tried to take advantage of you."

Lauren transferred the ball of dough onto the floured granite counter.

I exhaled, releasing built-up tension. "That's a lot of drama for one night. Was he upset I interfered with their date?"

Squish, pat. Lauren gently formed two large squares of dough. "Hardly! Because of you, he saw her true colors."

I covered my face. "I humiliated myself, even fell on the floor. Everyone laughed." I dropped my hands. "Garrett must think I'm an addict."

Wielding a bench scraper like Gra-Mere did, Lauren made four smaller squares from one piece of dough and repeated the cutting from the remaining dough. "I doubt it… But even if he did, he wouldn't judge. He struggled with an alcohol addiction in high school and college. We had to stage an intervention."

That explained his empathetic comment. "I didn't expect him to have struggled like that."

She pushed a biscuit cutter into the dough. "He had lots of counseling, group therapy, and prayer."

"Good for him." Knowing he'd struggled that way only made him more authentic and appealing.

"Do you want coffee? I almost forgot to ask."

"Sure, but I'll get it." I stood.

"The coffee maker is just to the right of the sink. Make yourself at home. Raid the fridge, stroll in the backyard, or watch TV."

"I don't want to impose."

She scowled, indicating her offer wasn't up for negotiation.

"Yes, ma'am."

"Oh, I just remembered something I meant to ask you. Our Life Group's meeting is next Saturday. Would you like to come? You might benefit from networking with people who are as honest as the day is long."

"I don't think so but thank you." She sounded like Aimee.

"It's held at the Marches' home."

I set my mug on the counter as I recognized the name.

"They're entrepreneurs who've made a fortune in investments," Lauren added, "and their home's incredible."

"Wait. Bryant March?"

"Yes. And his wife, Viviana. Do you know them?"

"Not personally. My ex applied at Bryant's investment firm out of college but didn't get hired. Ten years later, he tried to get a meeting with Bryant about investing in a company, but Jordan's contact couldn't get it to happen." I laughed. "Jordan complained that it'd be easier to meet the pope than Bryant."

"The Marches are mindful of their time, but if you're in their circle, they're generous and approachable."

"I'll attend, if nothing else but to say I met Bryant." What an interesting turn of events.

"Terrific! I'll give you more details over the weekend."

"Thanks for the invite."

At this rate, I wasn't sure who I'd run into or what unexpected events could happen next.

CHAPTER 42

After we ate the flaky biscuits, I showered and got ready for the day. As I walked down the hall to the living room, Mittens, Shane and Lauren's golden labradoodle, approached and nudged my leg. I squatted toward her, petting her woolly fur and scratching the back of her ear. My bestest pal growing up was a red labradoodle, Penny. She got hit by a car when I was in college. I never got another dog, unwilling to suffer that pain again. But as I interacted with Mittens, I realized how much I missed having a pet.

Lauren's phone rang. "Hi, Gare," she answered.

I stopped petting Mittens, remaining in the hall, unseen.

"Just checking on how you did by yourself last night," Garrett said. Lauren had him on speaker.

"A friend stayed with me."

He listed a few friends. "No," she said. "You haven't met her formally." I crossed my fingers. *Please don't remind him how we met.*

"What do you mean, *formally*?" he asked.

"She's conducting my marketing campaigns—the attractive woman I told you about."

Shoot! I wanted to run to the bedroom, but I also wanted to know what Garrett would say.

"She's as much a friend as a consultant," Lauren continued. Would she reveal I was the drunk woman he rescued?

He laughed. "Did you pitch that staying overnight would be like a slumber party? You probably should explain how you loathe staying by yourself."

"I already did. Just so you know, we weren't watching chick flicks into the wee hours of the night. We went to bed by nine, probably earlier than you."

"I get it's not normally my business," he said, "but I feel like it's my duty to look after you while Shane's out of town."

Mittens licked my hand. I'd forgotten about her. I sat on the floor and scratched her belly as I listened.

Lauren laughed. "*You* look after *me*?"

"Sarcasm aside, maybe you'll lay off of me working so hard now."

"We weren't working. She needed a place to stay right when I needed someone to stay with me."

"Why did she need a place?" His tone was skeptical. He was right on the mark to ask, wondering if someone might be taking advantage of his sister.

"I won't go into details, but that woman you helped at Charleston's the other night? You dropped her off at her office?"

I covered my face like they were looking at me.

"Yes, I've been praying for her. Wait... Is she the marketer?" His tone went slightly higher pitched.

"Yes but, honestly, we've become close beyond business. She's going through a lot right now. Anyway, Charleston's and the bottle served as therapy."

"Glad she's with you... It's a small world. I'm fairly sure I have seen her around the city. What's her name?"

Would he have recognized me from Woodward Park? That was over a month ago, and I went incognito in my ball cap and huge sunglasses. As a photographer, though, he might be acutely observant.

"Celine Monroe," Lauren said. "Poor thing. She's facing backlash for moving out of her ex's. He sounds like a piece of work, referring all her clients to her competitor. What loser does that?"

"Tell her I'm glad she's safe. I'll stop by this afternoon to see how you are and properly meet this friend."

"Sounds good."

Once they said goodbye, I went to the guest room and changed my shirt, so I wouldn't appear to be eavesdropping and walked into the kitchen. Mittens followed closely, tail wagging.

Lauren looked at me. "Oh, you look like a blooming peony. I've never seen you in pink before."

I glanced at my blush-pink tee. "Since I'm not seeing clients today, I can be casual."

"Feel free to hang out here all day. I just got off the phone with Garrett. He's relieved you're safe. He's stopping by later if you are up to meeting him." She took a sip of coffee.

"No. I left my phone at the office, so I need to check messages and start working." I didn't want him to see me *recovering*. I'd already created quite an impression, staggering, stammering, and slobbering.

Later, after I left, I wondered if I'd regret not meeting him formally. It would be my opportunity to make a better impression and show him how fun and cool I was. Yet, I knew better. I still wasn't recovered from Jordan's surprise visit or Jackson's sinister encounter. Best to wait until I was in a better state of mind to officially meet Garrett.

CHAPTER 43

At the office, I got chills as I headed toward Monroe. I stopped and stared at the empty wall where Evan Painter's abstract had hung. The punctured picture lay on the floor.

Fetching the abstract from the conference room, I hung it in the empty space. I'd contact Evan eventually and ask if he could restore the damaged painting. Jordan couldn't win. If Kris would sign with me and prepay for the year, I'd keep the paintings. After all, Evan's work fit my style and this space. I vacuumed the carpet, erasing all signs of the accident.

Once I got settled in Monroe, I peeked toward the closed door as the phantom scent of Jordan's cologne wafted into the space. I added more lavender to my diffuser on my desk, hoping to chase away any trace of his presence. I needed to work, not walk in fear.

My phone, that I was charging, rang. I answered it. Javier confirmed that his crew would come tomorrow to paint. Perfect timing. Still spooked by Jordan's visit, I preferred not being alone at the office. I could work at Jennifer's condo until Javier finished the job.

After I hung up, I checked my voice messages. I'd missed several calls and texts, especially from Jennifer, Lauren, and Aimee. Before I could listen to any messages, Jennifer called.

"Girl, I called you all weekend, but you didn't answer. Early Sunday morning, I called Aimee, but she hadn't heard from you either. I came by the office, but you didn't answer my knocking. By the time we swung by again on our way home from church, your car was gone."

"Sorry for scaring you. I went to Lauren's."

"A friend from your former social circle?" Jennifer sounded hurt.

"Not at all. A client who's become a friend... You know what? Why didn't I think to connect you two earlier? She's an interior designer."

"Give me her number for the future. But back to you. Is everything one hundred?"

"No." As I recounted the gory details of my weekend, I felt like we were in high school, swapping notes about how we got in trouble in class. Her for talking, me for working on homework instead of listening to the teacher.

"Are you returning here?" Jennifer asked.

"Yes. I'll come now."

At Jennifer's, I checked Aimee's voice messages, but she didn't provide any updates about Dad. She pleaded for me to call, asked why I wasn't answering, and said how scared she was, considering Jennifer hadn't seen me over the weekend.

When I called, Aimee wanted to FaceTime. She rarely did that. When I switched to FaceTime, she was in her sewing room. "Celine..." Her voice sounded too controlled, as if holding back fear. "What's going on? Are you flying to North Carolina?"

"Why there? Are *you* okay?" Maybe she needed a getaway.

"Maman and Père are flying there today. They're staying with friends in their cabin in the Blue Ridge Mountains. Maman hopes the quiet will help Père."

"Did the doctor confirm it was just an anxiety attack? What if it's something else? Is he in any shape to fly, much less endure high altitudes?"

"Maman called Dad's primary, and he assured a getaway would be ideal, especially because they'll unplug... You might as well know about the family drama on Friday."

"Is everyone alright?" I hated being in the dark, but this time it was my own fault for leaving my phone at the office.

"Père and I got into it on the phone about John. Heath wants John to work in the office, but I want him to wait until he's sixteen. Père pushed for John to get experience now, so I yelled at him for taking Heath's side. When Père defended himself, I accused him of neglecting me for work when I was young—"

"Why did you throw that in his face?"

"Calm down. I'm only sharing to help you understand what's going on."

"Fine." I wanted to hang up, unsure if I could handle her negative filter about Dad.

"He justified himself by saying he made an effort to resolve that. So, I told him I still felt discarded as a kid because I wasn't interested in his business, even when he was home. I said how it was obvious he favored you. John yelled at me for mistreating Père. Heath took John to another room, so Père and I could continue duking it out."

"You're the one who never tried to know him."

"I know him as well as you do. I've spent years studying him, so I could earn his approval."

I narrowed my gaze. "You make him sound like a tyrant."

"I regret that Père and I haven't addressed our issues in a healthy way. Friday's spat reflects our usual pattern when we don't agree. I tell him I feel neglected or misunderstood; he defends himself instead of listening reflectively. It's been a vicious cycle, but I'm going to work on changing me." With a yellow headband in her hand, she pointed to her chest.

"He does listen, but you assume he doesn't care because he doesn't say what you want to hear."

"Let's focus on the issue. He needs peace. Maman's asking us to refrain from reaching out until they call."

"I'll join him in the mountains and work remotely."

"No. His responses have gotten so bad that the morning after he went home from the hospital, he turned on the news and immediately complained of palpitations. Then he asked Maman about you. When she said she hadn't heard from you in a few days, he grabbed his throat and said he was suffocating."

"They should've seen a cardiologist. What if he's about to have a massive heart attack? I don't care what the tests say. I've got to fly there—"

"Maman called Uncle Karl, and he saw the test results. He's leaning toward Père suffering from a nervous breakdown. Again, help Père by letting him get away. Stop trying to be the answer." She chopped her hand toward me, emphasizing her command.

"I'm slightly relieved by Uncle Karl's opinion, but I'm going to text Maman that he needs to see a cardiologist in person."

"I'm not arguing with you. Promise you won't contact them and will wait for Maman to call."

"Hearing from me will ease his mind."

"Maman will keep him updated." She paused. "His anxiety comes because he tries to be Superdad, commissioned to rescue us. You and I need to set boundaries. Can you do that?" She glared at me, probably doubting I would.

I lifted my chin. "I've been trying, this year especially."

"If you want to help Père, encourage him to get counseling. Neither of you are great at acknowledging your emotions. That's what's gotten him in trouble."

"Whatever." I picked up my pen and doodled big circles on a notepad. "I don't have a problem telling Dad what I'm feeling."

"You both struggle with sitting in sadness. You stuff that emotion because you can't handle being unable to push through an obstacle."

I drew a face with a zigzag for the mouth. "I've been facing sad ever since I've lived with Jordan."

"Accept you can't fix Dad, no matter how difficult his situation is. By facing his mortality, *he* can change his course."

I tossed the pen on the desk. "Quit telling me what to do. Sounds like you need convincing more than I do. I didn't trigger his panic attack."

"I'm advising all of us to get help. Heath and I signed up for marriage counseling."

"Really?" I would've never expected Aimee to admit *she* was wrong.

"Just be open. K?"

"How about we work on not dumping our problems on our parents and trusting that each family member can handle his or her own drama?" I needed business advice, not a therapist trying to pry into my darkest childhood memories.

"That's part of the problem. You assume pulling yourself up by the bootstraps and 'being stronger' works, but it doesn't. You need..." She pursed her lips as if catching herself.

"God?"

"How about we discuss this in person Friday night?"

"K." I needed to focus on Dad not argue with her. "How long will Dad and Maman be away? Will they disconnect the whole time?"

"They'll unplug for a week then take it a day at a time. Père's not going to France."

"I'll stay with Dad in Florida while everyone's in France."

"No, wait... They're handling the plans. Maman's flying here from North Carolina on the twenty-ninth, since she's packed for France already. Dad will stay at the cabin, and hopefully Uncle Karl will accompany him back home. It's all getting sorted out, so do not contact Maman and try to force what you want them to do. Promise?"

"Why am I left out of this committee?" I asked.

"I wasn't consulted either. Maman has run herself ragged with packing and consulting with Uncle Karl, their pastor, and the Paynes —the couple who own the cabin—all while keeping Dad somewhat stable. Cut her some slack."

I shuddered. What did Aimee mean by keeping Dad stable? "Can't Maman cancel Tulsa and meet you at the connecting flight on the tenth?"

The tenth of July, when the family was leaving for France, was a date branded on my brain. Maman and Aimee had talked about that date as if it was Christmas.

"I suggested that, so she'd have one less trip, but..." Aimee tilted her head and looked at me with compassionate eyes. "She wants to see you, alright? When she discovered Jennifer and I hadn't heard from you, she panicked. She didn't bombard you with texts and calls because I asked her to focus on Père and their trip. I had to remind her that God would protect you; otherwise, she was about to report you missing."

I held back tears, wishing I hadn't added to Maman's stress, touched that her response showed she did love me as much as Aimee. "I'll call her next."

"No, let me. I know your intentions, but... Hearing from you might give Maman some relief, but if Père realizes you're talking to her, he'll move heaven and earth to join the call." She shook her head. "We're trying to keep him laying low with minimal contact. At least, not until he's found some relief with palpitations and the panic attacks." She gave me the stink eye.

"Fine." I pouted.

"I'm glad you're safe. See you Friday."

I went downstairs and asked Jennifer to hold me accountable to not contact Dad. She prayed for us all, and I returned to work. An hour later, Aimee texted.

> Maman so so relieved you're safe. Also, she wants to stay with you, so please ask Jennifer if Maman can stay there. Dad's better.

After Jennifer signed off on Maman staying here when she'd fly to Tulsa, I got excited about bonding with Maman.

CHAPTER 44
JUNE 15

Since Javier and his team painted the office walls three days ago, Lauren—eager to see the finished job—joined me on Wednesday to get my office in order especially to prepare for the new furniture.

When she arrived to check out Javier's work, I nearly cried, raving about how talented she was. Instead of my office resembling a bland atmosphere of a doctor's waiting room, the office now hummed with energy of an emerging marketing firm. I could almost feel the vibrancy pulse through the walls.

Now, three days later, I was eager to see the office outfitted with the new furniture. Fortunately, my office was the delivery crew's first stop. As they unloaded the pieces and placed them in the designated rooms, I was confident clients would feel assured that I was creative, contemporary, and cool. After the delivery crew left, I sank into the plush armchair and imagined myself conducting a strategy meeting with a mid-level company, exuding confidence and authority.

I texted Lauren.

> You were right! The area rug doesn't look too busy but brings in the colors from the abstracts and the walls. I love, love the space and the furniture. Everything's on point.

I attached pictures of the completed rooms.
She texted back shortly.

> I can't wait to see it in person. Love it too!

I stood and walked through the sitting area, taking pics. Afterwards, I posted them on my social accounts.

New look, same commitment to transformation! Our office just got upgraded, and we're ready to bring that same energy to your business. Let us transform your marketing strategy and achieve incredible results together. #marketingagency #digitalmarketing #strategytransformation #brandgrowth

Shortly after, Kris called.

"Celine, I'm about to improve your day. My assistant will email you the signed contract for July. I'll pay for the month of July, but will pre-pay for the remaining year in August. I'm looking forward to coming up with an effective strategy to market my expansion."

I clenched my fist in triumph and raised my hand in the air. "Thank you, Kris. I'll sign the contract and email you a copy. I'll also include a scheduling link, so you can sign up for our first consultation. Would you like to meet at my newly designed office?"

"I'm afraid my schedule is hectic, so it'd be best to meet here."

"Alright. Sounds good."

We hung up shortly after. I was elated, relieved, and slightly disappointed he wouldn't pay until July. At least, his signing eased the two-ton weight on my shoulders. And with the disbursement from the investment account hitting my checking today, I could pay off the credit card balance. I gave myself a pat on the back for avoiding any interest fees. In August when Kris prepaid for the year, I'd replenish the inheritance funds.

I called Isla, relieved to give her the great news. "We landed Kris's account!" I said.

"Thank God! When will he pay?" She was direct like me.

I needed to tread carefully, so I wouldn't alarm her. "He's prepaying for the year. That should bring you income for your wedding and your house."

"That's what I needed to hear!"

I winced, hoping to temper her expectations. "But he's not starting until July. My push for a more significant discount if he paid in June was a no-go."

"Okay." Her voice trailed off.

"Are you concerned?"

"I have to pay the remaining balance to several vendors, and Logan's car requires three thousand in repairs." Light sniffling came through our connection.

Uh-oh... Was she crying? She usually kept her emotions in check. I gripped my pen in my free hand. I should've been more careful after leaving Jordan.

"Are you thinking you might need to get another job this month?" I asked, fighting to maintain an upbeat tone.

"Yes, I maxed the credit card and refuse to just pay the minimum balance, but I'm sooo tempted. It's hard when you don't have many options. Both our parents are already helping with what they can for the wedding. We can't ask them for more money. And Logan's working two jobs already, so I'll have to pick up a side gig."

Needing her to be available at a moment's notice, I'd pay her with the money I received from selling Jordan's gifts. "Since Kris is prepaying in July, I'll float you for this month."

"Alright. Thanks." At least her voice projected hope.

I slumped in the armchair, feeling as though a jury had convicted me of pride and greed, especially of prioritizing impressing clients over protecting my savings and maintaining my marketing team. I needed a sustainable future, not a beautifully decorated office that no one would see.

CHAPTER 45
JUNE 16

Lauren called Saturday morning, confirming I was joining her for Life Group that night. Even though I told myself I'd go, I got cold feet, especially when I asked her what to expect.

"They start with dinner," she said, "followed by a check-in."

"A show-and-tell?" I asked.

"More a sharing of your high and low from the week."

Was I supposed to report how I got rip-roaring drunk, almost forced into a stranger's car, and rescued by Lauren's brother? Though I didn't tell Lauren my worries, she dismissed that I should be intimidated, saying I didn't need to get too personal with the check-in.

My desire to meet the Marches, however, outweighed my discomfort over sharing about myself to a room of strangers.

I got ready around four thirty. Anxious to please, I put on a grey jumpsuit with stilettos, but that gave a look of trying too hard. After changing into high-rise navy pants and a white off-the-shoulder top, I inspected myself in front of a floor-length mirror. I appeared relaxed, even though I was anything but.

An image of a granny with a body-sized Bible and ankle-length dress popped into my head. "She's baring a shoulder," she whispered to a fellow gossip. I replaced the top with a white boyfriend shirt, slid into block heels, and headed out the door.

Since I was a first-time guest, Lauren insisted that I shouldn't bring any food. I arrived at Lauren's with fifteen minutes to spare. We were riding together, so I wouldn't have to go alone. She opened the door with her hair in rollers.

"You look chic," she said.

"Thanks, but am I too dressy in heels?" I asked.

"They're darling. I usually take my shoes off and walk on their sheepskin area rug. Wait till you experience the softness under your toes."

After I came inside, I put my suitcase that was beginning to feel like an appendage into her guest bedroom, where I was spending the night since Shane was out of town till Sunday.

No longer surprised when she was running late, I waited in the living room and played with Mittens. By fifteen after five, Lauren strolled out of the bedroom in ripped blue jeans, a cherry off-the-shoulder top, and navy flats with a red bow. She'd added relaxed curls to her normally straight hair. Was I dressed too conservative, as if attending an all-girl social?

We didn't leave until six thirty, when the group was supposed to start. I hated that we'd be late. Everyone would stare when we arrived.

Lauren drove us to an affluent, gated neighborhood. She input a code, and as the gate opened, my heart beat harder. When we turned into the driveway, my mouth gaped. I expected a high-end home— maybe four to five thousand square feet with a meticulously land-scaped yard. Not this pillared palace.

We parked along a driveway circling a grassy knoll, where a wrought-iron fountain spouted water high into the air. As I emerged out of Lauren's car, I counted six vehicles around us and six more on the side street. My breathing was shallow.

I took slow steps toward the house, a few feet behind Lauren. As I approached the three stone pavers leading to the portico, I turned toward Lauren's car. Why didn't I drive separately, so I could leave?

She faced me, holding a ceramic food carrier filled with her homemade Cowboy Chili. "Are you alright?"

"Just nervous. Their home is more opulent than I expected."

"Once you meet Viviana March, you'll feel welcomed."

Lauren's hands were full. Since I only held a smaller tote with her sides, I rang the bell. Then I stepped aside, so Lauren could enter first. An elegant, middle-aged woman appeared. Brunette hair, slightly wavy, laid on her slim shoulders.

"Lauren, you look darling in red." The hostess extended her hands, slightly crouched, and gave Lauren *bisous*. Viviana's accent sounded Eastern European.

"Thank you." Lauren turned to face me. "Viviana, this is my friend Celine Monroe. She's joining us tonight."

I extended my hand, but Viviana greeted me with *bisous*. There was no need for her to crouch, since I was just an inch shorter. Inhaling her rose and citrus perfume was like sipping orange pekoe tea in a botanical garden. Even though she was dressed casually in white skinny jeans and a plain navy tee, her tennis bracelet glistened with the sun behind us and spoke luxury. I wanted to say, *I'm Celine of the English Monroes and French DuBois.*

"Thank you for joining us," Viviana said. "You're stunning. Do you model?"

"Oh, no, no…" My cheeks warmed. Normally, people would say that about Aimee. "I'm a marketing consultant, with my own growing agency." Great. I sounded like Jordan did when he met VIPs.

"Welcome to our home." She extended her hand toward the entry. Did she emphasize *home* as code for *No business tonight?* I followed behind Lauren, determined to keep my lips zipped about business. Probably best to keep a low profile.

Viviana escorted us inside an oval entryway with a cathedral ceiling. She and Lauren stopped in front of the circular staircase and chatted. Too nervous to participate, I took a few steps forward, standing in front of a small table.

A large, crystal vase was filled with orange gladiolus, Nana Monroe's favorite flower. She grew rows of different varieties in her backyard. These must have been artificial, since glads weren't in season now. I reached to touch a tepal, but a chime like church bells sounded and echoed. I jerked my hand away then glanced behind me. Viviana excused herself from Lauren and glided to the front door.

"Ready to eat?" Lauren asked.

I glanced at the glads again. The tepal was imperfect. They were real.

Lauren led me into a gourmet kitchen, where people stood along twin islands of rose quartz. I didn't recognize anyone but was surprised to see a variety in ages and ethnicities. I'd expected white, middle-aged professionals but preferred the mélange of backgrounds and cultures. It made for less of an echo chamber, something I wanted to avoid, considering my former social circle.

Once I placed Lauren's sides on a counter, I left the crowded kitchen and walked to a solarium with two tables filled with people eating. I went to the back window and looked outside.

Maman would be in heaven on the lawn, as green and immaculate as a golf course. Japanese maple trees, azalea bushes, and a stone walkway bordered the koi pond, and green shrubs hung over it. They'd replicated Woodward Park. The oasis was so naturally situated, you'd think it grew that way.

Someone tapped my shoulder from behind. I turned to face a man with Mediterranean skin and donning a backward-facing ball cap. He apologized for surprising me. His charming wide smile with narrowed eyes disarmed my anxiety. Holding a paper plate of food in his right hand, he extended his left, giving me a firm handshake.

"I'm Peter," he said. He had a slight rasp on his *r* as if a jazz singer. Bet he's the guy Lauren wanted to set me up with.

"Celine," I said.

"First time here?" he asked.

"Yes. I'm friends with Lauren."

"Well, any friend of Lauren is a friend of mine, although that's broadening my social connections." He laughed heartily.

I smiled. "She's quite the social butterfly."

"How do you know her, if you don't mind my asking?"

"Work. I'm a marketing consultant."

He pointed his finger toward me. "Celine?"

I nodded. Did she invite me, so I'd connect with Peter the plumber? He was charming, but I didn't need to add a man to my complicated life.

"She's told me about you, especially how you've expanded her reach. I might have to get marketing tips. I own a plumbing business and do well through word of mouth, but I don't want to sit on my laurels."

With his calm tone, he could do his own voice-over. I reached into my purse, grabbed my business card, and handed it to him as if at a networking event. "In case you're interested," I said.

"Thanks." He put it in his wallet. "Would you care to sit and eat?"

I gritted my teeth. *This is a Bible study, Celine.* "Sure, why not?" Normally I would've declined and told him I'd wait on Lauren, but after my minor gaffe, I felt obligated to act as though I was here for the right reasons.

Only one seat was vacant. "How about we sit in the dining room?" Peter tilted his head to the left. "It's not usually crowded there."

I followed my tour guide through the Marches' home. We went to the left, and he opened a door into a narrow long room, bordered with more arched windows on the right.

A mahogany dining table filled most of the formal dining room. Each setting had a gold charger, rose-pink cloth napkin, and sparkling gold silverware. Gold pillar candles and pink-edged, yellow tea roses in glass vases served as centerpieces. No one else was in the room.

Peter pulled out an ivory upholstered chair, and I sat down on the plush seat. He pushed the chair back in before sitting next to me, a gentleman.

Preferring to discuss business, I asked him how he marketed his plumbing business. He shared word of mouth then dove into anecdotes from servicing customers. Considering my gaffe with the business card, I just listened instead of veering back to marketing services. His stories were so entertaining that I eventually lost track of time.

I looked at Peter's untouched plate of food. "Please eat," I coaxed, irritated this felt like a date.

He stood. "How about I get you a sampler of food?"

Urgh! "No one likes cold food. Please eat. I'm unsure what I want anyway." I hadn't been to a church gathering for so long that I was too nervous to eat.

He leaned toward me, not seductively but in camaraderie. "As a bachelor, I'm used to eating food at any temperature. I'd feel better serving a guest. I brought tortilla chips, guac, and salsa, if you'd like to try some. Got the guac and salsa recipes from a buddy friend who owns a restaurant in Dallas. What do you say?" He flashed a smile.

Lauren entered the dining room and set her plate of food on the table near me. She tapped my shoulder, "You're in for a treat. Peter makes the best guac and salsa."

Not wanting to argue with Peter, I just said, "I'll try Lauren's chili, along with your salsa and guac and chips." I eyed Peter's plate. "And cornbread."

Peter smiled and left.

Lauren sat next to me and asked what I thought about Peter.

"He's very engaging." I held my hand in front of her. "But I'm not interested beyond getting acquainted as a friend."

She smiled. "I won't push for anything." She took a bite of her chili, to my relief. I didn't feel any chemistry beyond an acquaintance. Not that I would in ten to fifteen minutes, but I didn't experience any butterflies or intrigue like I had with Jordan the first time we met. I didn't mind the lack of attraction though, making my new acquaintance safe to befriend.

When Peter returned, he set a bowl and plate in front of me. After taking a few bites of Lauren's chili, I realized I'd hardly eaten all day. "Compliments to the chef. The chili's savory and spicy."

"Thanks." Lauren smiled.

I tried the guac on one chip, the salsa on another. "Peter, Lauren was right. This is delicious. Good as any restaurant." Hmm, he was a decent cook. A great trait.

After I ate the chili, my eyes felt heavy. I hadn't eaten this much in a few months. If dinner was just the evening's Round One, I didn't know how I'd make it to Round Two.

CHAPTER 46

Since I ate too much, I excused myself to the bathroom, where I stared in the mirror, holding tightly to the outer rim of the sink. I had to endure the physical discomfort.

"Hang in there, girl." I caressed my stomach. "I won't do this to you again. But I need you to settle down, just for another hour."

I took yoga breaths, hoping the heartburn would ease, then popped an antacid from my purse. My stomach needed to stop sending gastric shocks through my abdomen. Thankfully, I wore my stretchy pants. I'd endure.

After a few minutes, I ventured to the living room, as spacious as the Grand Hall at The Mayo. Its lux furnishings reminded me of the home of Jordan's boss. Instead of marble statues of Greek gods, though, tall botanical plants in marble pots stood in every corner. Family portraits hung on most walls, replacing fine art, except for a replica of *The Last Supper* adorning the east wall.

Everyone gathered on the north side, where Bryant March stood in front of a beige stone fireplace. Guests congregated in a U around him, seated in coordinating furniture sets. I sat next to Lauren in a twin high-back armchair, while Peter sat to my left on a padded fold-up chair.

People held Bibles and notebooks in their laps as they looked at Bryant with eagerness. How long until they knew I didn't belong?

"How are you doing?" Lauren tapped my hand.

"I'm fighting discomfort since I ate too much."

"Oh, I'm sorry. Do you need me to take you home?"

"No, I'll endure."

Viviana approached her husband. Bryant, about six foot, had light blond hair with greying on the sides. His athletic frame looked sporty in a salmon golf shirt, light denim jeans, and grey slippers. Nothing about him seemed unapproachable or elitist, so I was unsure why Jordan couldn't get an appointment a few years ago.

Bryant raised his hand. Instantly, people quit chatting. Once the room held a monk's silence, he apologized for not joining us for dinner, explaining he just flew in from overseas.

Why would he host a meeting after such a long flight? Were these people that important? As I pondered these questions, he opened in prayer.

Then Viviana introduced me. I smiled, unsure if I was supposed to stand, wave, or share. Since my knees knocked, I sat still. People said they were glad I came.

"Thank you for joining us, Celine." Bryant clapped as if I had accepted an award. "I hope you return."

"I will." The two innocuous words flowed out of my mouth. Would I? I wasn't comfortable, but I was curious.

Bryant asked us to go around the circle and share a high, a low, and a prayer request. When my turn came, my face burned with embarrassment. "My high is I'm here. Low is I've eaten too much." Laughter from the group. "And my prayer is that I can be a good person." I bit my lower lip. A pacifying answer when you felt uncomfortable about people praying for you, especially strangers. Most responded with "Thanks for sharing."

Bryant's high—he was home safe after a great trip overseas. His low—complications with expanding their nonprofit. His prayer—the orphanage they sponsored in the Czech Republic needed more staff and volunteers. Viviana must be Czech; Bryant was American or had lived here long enough to lose an accent.

For my sake, Bryant explained we'd each pray for the person on the left. I hadn't prayed out loud for a few years, but it wasn't like a rusty door needing WD-40. I could take Peter's request, add "God, do this," and voilà.

Lauren prayed that I'd receive from God's love more and more, that I'd find freedom and joy, and that God would continue to bless my business. Since we were asked to hold hands, I squeezed hers in appreciation. Now I needed to pray, but my tongue stuck to the roof of my mouth. I swallowed, then closed my eyes as I prayed for Peter's request that he'd treat his customers well and be a good witness.

After prayer time, I laid my head on the armchair's padded back. An invisible blanket wrapped itself around me. I dug my toes into the area rug, plush like a labradoodle's coat. In the cozy ambiance created from eucalyptus diffusing through the room and from the mesmerizing rhythm of lit candles, I fought to keep my eyes open.

Bryant and Viviana sat on folded chairs near the fireplace. With a large Bible in his hand, he shared about grace and forgiveness. Between my upset stomach and fatigued mind, I had a hard time focusing.

After the meeting ended, I didn't want to pretend to be a believer, so I dashed past Peter to the front door. I sat on a porch swing and texted Lauren where I was and to take her time. She didn't text back. Her phone was probably dead.

As the warm wind touched my face, I gently pushed the swing back and forth with my feet. Recessed lights spaced throughout the porch ceiling cast an enchanting glow. Spurts of iridescent yellow from fireflies flashed around me as mockingbirds whistled in the near distance, all taking me back to my parents' deck where we'd sit and talk for hours. At those times, I enjoyed just being.

I lost track of time, until the appearance of Lauren reminded me where I was.

"I hope you haven't been waiting too long here," she said.

I straightened my back. "No… Just enjoying the night air."

"I wanted to introduce you to Bryant, but I couldn't find you."

"Sorry, I'm tired."

"No worries." She nudged my side. "Peter thought you were lovely."

"I enjoyed meeting him. And you're right, he's intelligent and cultured. But I'm not ready." I hoped I wouldn't have to remind her of that if I returned to the Life Group.

She put her hand up. "Don't worry. I won't push. And he's a gentleman. He won't push either."

"Thanks."

Once we returned to her home, she explained about the meeting hosts. Bryant was semiretired from his investment company since his son took over. Viviana, a Czech native, launched a nonprofit to help orphans in Eastern Europe. They started this Life Group about a year ago.

Now, I could say I met the Marches in their home. If only Jordan knew.

CHAPTER 47
JUNE 17

I woke in the night from a dream. I was at a masquerade party at Jordan's condo, where we donned costumes suitable for the court of Louis XVI and Marie Antoinette. As I approached guests with a tray of hors d'oeuvres and wine, I could see their faces through their elaborate masks.

Some uninvited guests arrived in elaborate ivory costumes but without masks. When I asked if they'd like foie gras, their eyes became Swarovski crystals. I could see my reflection. Realizing I was naked, I shrieked, dropped the tray, and ran.

The dream was so real, I touched my face, expecting to feel a papier-mâché mask. It took a few seconds before I realized I was in Lauren's guest bedroom. I glanced at the clock on the nightstand. It was four in the morning.

I decided I might as well get up, knowing I wouldn't fall back asleep. I took a long sip of water, hoping to refresh my mind. After brushing my teeth and hair, I returned to the bedroom and sat on the bed. Wanting a distraction, I scoured social media feeds on my phone, mostly pausing at motivational quotes to inspire me to work and at dog videos to raise my dopamine levels.

I got ready for the day then joined Lauren in the kitchen as she made a pot of coffee. After a few niceties about how we slept, she handed me a full mug.

"You're welcome to hang out here this morning or, if you're up for it, attend church with me. I catch the nine o'clock service and then usually go out to lunch with someone."

To avoid blurting no, I took a sip of coffee. I needed to act open, even though I wasn't. Attending the Life Group had expired my tolerance; I wouldn't step foot in a church. "I'll take a rain check. I've got to get work done."

"On Sunday?"

I nodded. "Yep."

Lauren shrugged. "I grew up practicing Sabbath. It's necessary, especially as a reset from the week."

"I see."

"I'd love for you to join us tonight. It's Shane's birthday, so I'm making his favorite meal. Lemon risotto with scallops. Inspired from our time in Sorrento." Her voice trailed off as though she were transported there. Not wanting to interrupt her revelry, I waited. She sighed, returning back to the present. "And Garrett and my parents are coming."

Nope, I didn't want to meet them. Even though Lauren wouldn't introduce me as the woman Garrett rescued at the bar, I'd wonder if the parents knew.

"I need to spend time with Jennifer," I said. "It's tempting, though. I had the best lemon risotto in Italy when I was"—I paused, pondering how old I had been—"twelve or thirteen."

She smiled. "We have so much in common! Shane and I try to visit Italy every five years. We have a family friend who owns a restaurant in Amalfi, so we get the royal treatment every time."

"The locals are kind there—or so I remember. It's been ages."

I smiled at a memory from Amalfi. Dad and I got separated, and a boy close to my age, his father, and a local helped us reunite. The local owned a restaurant and treated us to an incredible spread. Although we never returned, I've always wanted to.

Lauren put homemade biscuits into the oven. "If you can stay for an hour, we can enjoy biscuits and gravy for breakfast."

"I'm game." I raised my mug.

"Great! Excuse me for a few minutes, I need to finish getting ready."

As I headed outside, I stopped in the living room and stared at that same picture of Garrett in the Pyrenees. This time, I focused on the dark, craggy sides of the mountains. The greying clouds crowded out the blue expanse of the sky. Above Garrett's head, a hawk flew, its wings spread in their full glory.

How difficult was Garrett's recovery journey? Did he relapse? Was he an angry, jovial, or reclusive drunk? I didn't remember being so intrigued by a man before.

I went outside and sat on a wooden bench facing the spacious backyard. Mittens laid by my feet. Peace set a table there, so I didn't contemplate anything. I enjoyed the choir of sparrows awakening the neighborhood. The rows of pink hydrangea bushes pointed upward. The magnolia sat in their center like a statue, its well-pruned limbs extending umbrella-like over a congregation of hostas. It was about thirty minutes before Lauren peeked her head out the back door, informing me breakfast was ready.

A bouquet of pink hydrangeas brightened the kitchen table. Lauren placed grape juice, coffee, and water in front of my plate. The biscuits sat in a white woven bread basket, a ceramic gravy boat nearby. What better breakfast could there be than this communion of flavors and fellowship? This morning, though, I'd eat in moderation.

"While you were outside, Garrett popped by to drop off my extra key." Lauren passed me the basket of biscuits.

"Oh!" My heart raced. That was too close.

"He would've stayed and eaten breakfast with us, but he had to rush off to shoot a wedding brunch at The Mayo."

I smiled, wondering if we both raced through life at a frenetic pace. "He doesn't take a Sabbath, either?"

"Mondays are his Sabbath. You can find him on a hiking trail on those days."

"So, he's the backpacking and camping type."

"Very much." She scrunched her nose. "Not me. I prefer running water and a hot shower."

"I can rough it for the right view, especially in the mountains or on a beach. But I prefer the luxury of a hotel or a cabin."

"A girl after my own heart." Lauren took a sip of her grape juice then retrieved a gold key from the counter and handed it to me. "I wanted you to have it, so you can just come in and out when you need to."

Was this a good thing? I placed the key in my pants pocket.

CHAPTER 48
JUNE 18

Around eleven on Monday, I left my office to interview Kimberly at Coffee House on Cherry Street, since she craved their monkey bread. I would've preferred meeting at the office, so Kimberly would get a sense that my firm was thriving yet relaxed. While I couldn't afford to hire Bill's referral full-time, I hoped she'd freelance. I needed her unique skill sets.

I arrived early, wanting to enjoy a latte. The aromas of freshly ground coffee beans and bakery goods wafted, clearing my mind of financial problems. As I approached the counter, I was met by the graphic food porn of pastries in glass displays. All the cakes tried to seduce me, especially the peanut butter and tres leches. Just as I settled on the latter, the monkey bread beckoned, pecans and caramel glaze oozing down its sides.

The male barista wore pink sunglasses, a matching pink plastic necklace, and a black tee. I'd enjoy writing copy for CHOC. After I ordered, I tipped him twenty percent. I might as well be generous, so karma would take effect.

I sat on a couch along the wall leading toward the side door.

Lauren would be horrified with the incoherent decor—red coffee mills, hanging gas lamps turned electric, and Gibson girl prints on the walls. Today, I liked the Victorian vibe.

My eyes widened when Garrett entered from outside, decked out in dark jeans and a forest-green button-up shirt, untucked. He pulled off casual like it was trendy. As he inspected the room, I smiled, but he didn't notice me.

He sauntered to the register and perused the food in the glass displays like he had the day to burn. His sculpted biceps peeked out of his short-sleeved shirt.

Unlike Jordan, who'd be checking the stock market or complaining about the wait, Garrett stood still, phone out of sight. Once he ordered, he chatted with the barista. When another patron approached, Garrett stepped to the side and waited for his order. His transparent ocean blues, jawline chiseled like a mountain's peak, and athletic frame could land him a cover of *Outside Magazine.*

I needed to redeem myself. Speak to him and show him I wasn't the drunk girl at Charleston's but Lauren's consultant and an intelligent conversationalist.

To collect myself first, I went to the restroom and stared in the mirror. "Hi, I'm Celine." *Too fast, girl. Slow down.* "I'm Celine Monroe. Are you Garrett? I know your sister, Lauren." *No, too stalkerish.* "Hi, you don't happen to be Garrett?" I'd see what he'd say after confirming. If he didn't recognize me, I wouldn't mention the bar but would dive into my relationship with Lauren.

I practiced looking calm, giving a half smile with wide, engaging eyes. Men have said my eyes could launch a thousand ships. Although I laughed off their pickup line, saying that I have no interest in starting a war, it wouldn't hurt to use my striking baby blues today. After I applied sheer lip gloss and iridescent powder, I walked out of the bathroom with increased enthusiasm, despite some major jitters.

As I turned the corner, my heart deflated. Garrett was hugging a sophisticated brunette. Where did she come from? Was she a bride? In her black mini, white silk blouse with bow tie, and black Louboutin heels, she was too cosmopolitan for this coffee shop.

Embarrassed, I turned away and sat in my seat. She finished greeting Garrett with *bisous* then sat across from him at the table for two. Her brows, perfectly arched, framed her oval face.

This brunette couldn't be a date. He just broke up with that other woman Saturday night. Lauren's words echoed—*Mondays are his Sabbath.* So, the brunette couldn't be a bride, especially since I didn't see a ring on her finger. Who was she?

"Celine?" I turned toward a voice from behind and faced a twenty-something in khaki shorts and a lavender short-sleeved blouse, strawberry blonde hair sticking out of her beige beret. Oh, I liked her artsy style.

"Kimberly?" I asked.

"Yep." She gave me a firm handshake.

"Nice to meet you," I said. "Bill raved about you, highlighting your creativity, drive, and intelligence."

"Likewise. He said you'd be ideal for me to learn under."

I led her to the sofa where I'd settled, and we talked for nearly an hour. When I occasionally caught myself glancing at Garrett and the mystery woman, I mentally rebuked myself and gave my attention to Kimberly.

We closed a deal where she could freelance as a consultant for me and the other clients she had already. The best part was she'd start training in my office in two weeks then work remotely. I was relieved to have her help, and she was excited for the opportunity.

Sipping on water after Kimberly left, I texted Bill and thanked him for her referral. I peeked at Garrett. His eyes were glued to the mystery woman as he nodded, laughed, and showed her something from his phone.

Was it longing I saw on his part? Had he already rebounded to the next woman in line? Nah, he didn't seem that type. Whatever their connection, he was relaxed and focused.

I left while they were still visiting. Surely I'd have another opportunity to "meet" him.

CHAPTER 49

Despite the pleasure of writing a well-crafted strategy to market Kris's expansion, the afternoon at the office dragged on. I couldn't stop thinking about Garrett. Once I finished work, I paced Monroe.

Who could that woman be? Was she a wedding planner who could only meet him today despite his "sabbath"? Or was he diving back into the dating pool, not wanting to stay dry? Was she someone he already knew and was attracted to?

I would've never pegged him with someone so elegant, porcelain complexion enhanced by monthly facials. Surely she wasn't his girlfriend, but she stared at him like she was.

Bill called. Although still hot under the collar that he misled me at Specter, I appreciated him referring Kimberly. Considering all the people who gave me second chances, I answered on the third ring.

"Hi, Celine. I thought you and Kimberly would be a good match." He was even-tempered, like nothing unpleasant had happened. That was so Bill. He could've been a poker champion.

"Thanks for the referral."

"Of course. Look, I just got off the phone with Kris. He told me how well you handled yourself at the shoot. So, I pushed him to take the deal you offered earlier and prepay today. He should be contacting you."

My nerves snapped into place like a shoulder joint clicking back into its socket under an ER doc's hand. I could pay my bills!

"I haven't heard from him yet but thank you. I thought he already spent his budget for June."

"That's his story to tell. And you're welcome. But that isn't why I called." He paused. "I owe you an apology. When you asked me at Specter why you didn't get the promotion, I would've served you better if I'd laid out the landscape honestly, asked you to stay because you'd be an invaluable asset to the agency."

"Thanks for owning that."

Another giant had fallen off a pedestal I had erected. Could I trust Bill to represent truth when it was to his hurt?

"Still pondering the situation?" The fatherly tone he usually took with me had returned.

"Yes." An eerie silence descended. Neither party wanted to make the next move. We couldn't both wait it out, and the ball was in my court. "Was your motive for keeping me at the agency to serve Stella?" I asked. "Or to make your job easier?"

"I wish I could say it was one or the other, but I had many cards in the game. I wanted to retain you for my ego. You enjoyed working for me and the agency so much that I expected you'd take one for the team. And I wanted the agency to thrive. Retaining you meant less work for Stella and an easier adjustment for the team. My thinking then is a credit to your gift as an assistant. No, more than that. As a VP in training." He sighed. "And, in the end, I wanted to look good among the execs."

I turned toward the window; my reflection stared at me. Would I have done any differently if I were in his shoes? Probably not. Yet that didn't lessen the blow to my ego. I wouldn't have struggled vocationally if I had stayed. I would've eventually achieved my goal of climbing to the top—validating Papa and Dad, both overlooked for the CEO position. But I walked away.

"I appreciate your transparency," I said quietly.

"But?" he asked.

"I don't know." How much did he trust me? Did he want to continue serving as a mentor because he was concerned about my ability to run my own business?

"You've surpassed my expectations with your consulting firm. Your talents are impressive. Add your drive, work ethic, and boldness, and you can go far. That's why I'm asking if you'd let this old man advise you from time to time, maybe send case studies to you. It can work as a two-way street. You could help by occasionally talking to my students. Share what a day in the life of a marketing consultant looks like. Up for it?"

"I'd enjoy sharing in your class." My formality kept me from exploding with gratitude and tears. His affirmation was gold.

"Great. Well, I better let you return to work. Enjoy."

Shortly after we hung up, Kris texted.

> I just prepaid for July. I'll pay for the year
> on August 1st. Looking forward to
> working with you.

I logged into my bank account and saw the deposit pending in my checking. $2,500. Yippee!

As my daily gratitude items in the journal app on my phone, I added Kris paying me for July, Kimberly coming on as a consultant, and Bill admitting his error.

I wanted to call Dad. That I'd been tempted many times during the week reminded me how much I relied on him. At least, I had mostly uplifting news to share.

CHAPTER 50

After I got settled in a love seat at Jennifer's, Dad wanted to FaceTime. I answered immediately.

He sat outside on a green Adirondack chair, the sapphire shadow of mountains behind. "Hi, Dad. Maman allowing you to talk on your getaway?"

"I'm doing better up here." He waved his finger at the screen. "And I needed to check on you. We haven't talked to Aimee yet, either."

Was he worried more about me? "I want to know about you first," I said, "although I have only good news to share."

His aquamarine eyes became clear as a freshwater lake. Creases across his forehead disappeared.

"I'm improving daily. We're staying at the mountainside cabin owned by the Paynes. I take long walks every morning, sometimes with Maman or Stewart. Sometimes all four of us go. Here, I'll show you the path." He turned the phone toward the mountains in the close distance. Thick evergreens crowded the towering stone structures. Blue skies were still as fluffy white clouds drifted by.

"Is nature helping?" I asked as he turned the phone back around.

He nodded. "That and unplugging. I've connected with God a lot, and I'm learning where I can slow down."

"Good." I leaned my head on the loveseat's back.

"I promised Maman I'd join a support group when we return. And if I still need counseling, I'm open." His eyes shifted to the left slightly, probably indicating discomfort at the idea of being vulnerable.

Despite everyone around me taking up counseling like the latest trend, I disliked the idea. I'd heard those who need therapy become therapists. I wasn't ready for someone to project their struggles as mine. Jordan psychoanalyzed me enough; I didn't need to pay someone to do the same.

"Speaking of groups, I attended a Life Group with my friend Lauren."

He clutched his heart. "I like this Lauren gal and how she's connected to a healthy community."

"She is... I'm unsure if I'll return, but I appreciated meeting genuine people."

Dad studied my face. "Have you felt free to explore what *you* believe? Talked to a pastor or another believer? Had an honest exchange where you can express your doubts, fears, and beliefs about God openly without judgment?"

"That talk stopped once I quit attending church."

"Has anything turned you off about God, church, or people professing to be Christians?"

"I don't know." Tightness spread over my body. I didn't want to admit out loud the offenses I carried toward God, especially since I hardly addressed them myself. If I heard myself say them, would I sense God's anger?

"Thanks for your honesty."

"I went to Lauren's group for the business networking." I winced, wondering what he'd think.

"That's a start." He pointed to me. "At the end of the day, your motive is between you and God."

Wanting to hold Dad's hand, I wished he wasn't hundreds of miles away. "I'm also afraid to return to the Life Group because I'm not like them." Dad wouldn't want to hear that his daughter remained a skeptic, but he'd discern if I tried to hide that from him.

He rested his free hand on his cheek. After about ten seconds, he nodded. "Let's take it a day at a time, alright?"

"Maybe."

"Speaking of Lauren, she called Maman. I don't know what they discussed, but Maman was impressed and is happy Lauren's your client."

"I figured they'd hit it off. When did Lauren call?" I was surprised she hadn't mentioned her talk with Maman.

"Yesterday." He took a drink of water then smiled. "How's business?"

"Improving. My new mid-level client prepaid for July and will pay for the rest of the year in August. So, I can retain Isla and Taja. I'll be training a freelance consultant in two weeks. And I've lined up meetings next week with two potential clients."

"I'm proud of you." He extended his fist, so we gave each other a virtual bump. I sat up straighter.

"I'm proud of you too. It's been difficult to not call, hasn't it?"

He nodded. "I was fine with canceling France, not wanting to endure jet lag, acclimate to the time change, and whatnot. But not talking to my two girls was the pinnacle of the challenge. I don't like that." His voice sounded winded.

"You won't be alone during Maman's trip, will you?" I wanted to solicit my caretaking services, but my life wasn't conducive to serenity and solitude.

"Karl's flying here on the thirtieth and will fly out with me to Florida on the next day. He'll stay two weeks. I told him that he's working too hard at retirement, so I need to keep an eye on him." Dad leaned toward the screen. "Are you still worried?"

"That helps."

"I've been concerned about you."

"I'll be fine." I waved him off, not wanting him to borrow more trouble.

Dad paused, probably brainstorming. Shortly, he smiled. "How about you fly to Florida for a rest?"

"That might be good. I'd need to work, though."

"Alright. I miss my girl."

"Miss you too."

CHAPTER 51
JUNE 19

When Lauren came for our nine o'clock meeting, she gushed over the office's transformation, rekindling my excitement about the new interior. "Prepare to get busy," she said, raising her hands in the air.

"Think clients will be that inspired?" I asked, surprised by her confidence in the space.

"I've showed the Marches and Peter how you've transformed my marketing strategy. They're impressed. And when I chatted with Viviana on Sunday, I raved about how I've acquired ten leads this month." Lauren jerked on my arm. "They will be referring clients to you."

I hugged her. "Thank you!" I was impressed those people were interested in my business after just one visit to the Life Group.

"Before we get started with work," Lauren continued, "I've got amazing news! Garrett connected with someone opening a new art gallery in Oklahoma City. She wants to feature his wildlife portfolio."

I pointed toward Lauren. "Have you met her?"

"Yes."

"Is she a brunette with a short bob? Stylish, like she shops on Fifth Avenue?"

Lauren narrowed her gaze as if someone had leaked classified information. "Yes. Did you contact him about marketing his wildlife business?"

So the mystery woman wasn't a dating prospect. "No. I saw him meeting with that woman at CHOC on Monday."

"Did you talk to him?"

My heart beat irregularly. "No," I said meekly, considering ways to deflect Lauren's focus off me. "You have to be thrilled he's following his passion."

"Yes, and that he's finally listening. His wildlife shots are breathtaking, each telling a story about a creature's dignity. He could go on to sell at other galleries, art shows, and online."

I laughed, imagining Lauren designing during the day and managing her brother's art career at night. "Will his big sis represent him?"

"No," she said, seeming to take me seriously. "I want you to market him." She grabbed her phone. "Hold on, I'm calling him now."

Taking a step back, I nearly tripped. I copped a half smile, troubled with my uncertainty. When I went full-time into consulting, I vowed I'd never date a client. Was I that interested in Garrett romantically? Could I afford to be?

"I'll go to Monroe to give you privacy," I said.

"It's about you." Her extended hand told me to stay. But I waved and walked to Monroe, shutting the door, so I wouldn't hear her.

To keep from talking myself out of taking Garrett as a client, I started jotting down ways to increase exposure for his art. I immediately wrote Contact Evan Painter. He'd be a great source for inspiration and networking opportunities. A sudden stream of ideas hit, so I did a mind map. Within a few minutes, a page in my notebook had filled with cloud-shaped thought bubbles floating close to each other, one or two words of action written in each. We'd boost Garrett's business until he could shoot and sell wildlife photos full-time.

This was why I loved my job! Helping clients reach their goals, especially while working in the fields they were passionate about. All my other motivations, like ambition and validation, were molting off me like a lobster's shell.

Shortly after I finished mind-mapping, Lauren knocked on the door to Monroe.

"Come in," I said.

She entered with stooped shoulders. "Sorry, but the art dealer connected Garrett with a marketing agency who helps artists. He's already reached out to them."

I shrugged. "No problem."

Although disappointed, I was concerned about how I felt about Garrett. Why was I relieved his choice for consultation left open the option of us dating? This man unknowingly had me in all sorts of feels. Maybe the best of them was optimism I was healing from Jordan.

CHAPTER 52
JUNE 22

I finally made it to pizza night, feeling relief when I texted Aimee that I was on my way to spend time with her and the family. Hopefully, we'd find common ground.

"Aunt Celine!" John met me at the door, standing taller than when I last saw him. Kids are bittersweet memos reminding you of time passing quickly.

"Hi," I said. "Sorry I missed your game a few weeks ago." I wanted to vow I'd attend his next game, but Aimee's insistence not to promise rang in my head. "I'll do better."

A cool kid, he shrugged. "No big deal. I have football in the fall."

"Thanks. What else is going on?"

He leaned closer and whispered. "Mom's all cray cray trying to get us ready for France. Maybe you can help her chill."

I laughed. "I'll do my best."

Mentioning the Life Group might settle her. But would she blast me with invites to her church again? Life Group was all I could handle.

As I walked inside, nostalgia and sadness enveloped me. Aimee and Heath inherited my parents' home—the one I grew up in—and while I appreciated they kept it in the family, memories sometimes hit hard.

Was that why I avoided coming over? I could see my parents praying over us before Dad left for work. Them reading the Bible out loud at lunch. Dad praying over dinner, Maman during the bedtime ritual. Their ghosts reminded me how far I'd run from the Christian values they instilled.

I took a deep breath and followed John into the kitchen. Aimee stood by the refrigerator, an empty glass in her hand. John introduced me like a royal herald. "Aunt Celine's here."

Yep, the spinster aunt was here. Suddenly I felt old.

Aimee filled the glass with water. "Hi, sis. Heath and Daniel went to get the pizza. Do you want a glass of wine?"

I wanted to say yes, but I'd been cutting down since overindulging at Charleston's. "No, just sparkling water."

"Flat or gas?" Aimee winked.

I laughed.

"John," she said, "when Celine was about six, a waiter at a restaurant in Rome asked her what she wanted to drink. When she said water, he asked if she wanted flat or gas. Her little eyes became big like a Susan B. Anthony coin as she turned toward Mamie and Papi for explanation. She almost cried, but—"

"I was too embarrassed to answer. I envisioned the server passing gas in the water pitcher to create bubbles. No thanks!" I giggled, having forgotten that memory.

"That's funny." He looked down. "I wish you were coming to France." John and I always got along, both of us creative, driven, and self-assured. Well, I was working to restore that last trait.

"I wish I were coming too. But good news. I'll be there next year."

"Seriously?" Aimee stopped pouring water into a glass.

"I promised Maman, so it's a done deal."

Aimee handed me my glass of water and gave me a stern look. "You can't back out now."

"Oh, I know."

She touched my arm. "Hey, let's sit in the living room until Heath and Daniel return."

"I'm going outside to play with Jake," John said. His golden retriever at his heels.

"I'll text when the pizza's here," Aimee told him.

We walked into the living room, where a wall of windows faced the spacious backyard. Almost everything in the room was white—walls, furniture, whitewashed hardwood floors. Pops of color came from the grey buffalos that decorated the throw pillows and from green succulents in white ceramic pots. Also from the family photographs on the gallery wall behind the sectional, where Aimee and I sat.

She pointed to my head. "I like how you're growing your hair out, especially letting the blonde roots play."

"It's less maintenance." I smiled, knowing she preferred a natural look.

"It gives you a softer edge. I hate to say it, but the blunt brunette made you look like a femme fatale." She tucked her legs underneath her.

"With a knife hidden under her thigh?" I asked.

"Exactly." She laughed.

"Hey, what if I bought a handsewn Aimee headband? It'd keep my bangs out of my face, especially when I run."

"How about sky blue like your eyes? I'll add a white border. All on the house."

"Perfect."

"Anything new from the last time we talked?"

I held my breath, hesitating to tell her about the Life Group. I'd made strides but unsure if my baby steps were enough to satisfy her. "Yes and no… I'm working on having more of a work-life balance."

Aimee squeezed my hand. "I needed to hear that."

"I figured."

She squeezed again. "John called me out on something the other day. I admit I was accusing you of bailing on us after you didn't answer my calls for two days…"

"And?" This might be good. I couldn't imagine John confronting his mom about me.

"He said since I expected Père to understand me, I needed to try to understand you. He helped me realize I treated you the way I felt Dad treated me." She released my hand. "I'm sorry."

I pursed my lips, wanting to live in the moment. For so long, I've wanted her apology for not accepting me.

"I also realized why I was adamant about you attending church with us and why I wanted you to have a family." Aimee looked down at her feet.

"Oh?" *Welcome to a night of revelations, Celine.*

She glanced at me. "I didn't want to lose you."

I jerked my head back, wondering what she meant. "Like die and go to hell?"

"No. Ever since Maman and Père moved to Florida, I was afraid of you and I drifting apart, especially when you stopped attending church with us. I pushed for you to have a family because I hoped you'd want to stay connected if you did."

"Your fear must've accelerated when I moved in with Jordan."

"Afraid so."

I crossed my arms across my chest. "I wish you had explained this, although I'm unsure how much it would've helped once I was with him."

She waved a hand at the room. "Living here reinforces my fears, especially as I get nostalgic. Memories come—like when you'd run into my room and lay beside me at night when a bad storm hit. Or when we'd run through the sprinklers. Or when I'd help you get ready for a date."

I glanced away. "When my guy friends or boyfriends would see you, they'd say, 'You're pretty, but your sister's a supermodel.' I didn't feel like I'd ever be enough."

Aimee tilted her head. "All this time, I thought you considered yourself above me because of your business talents, eye for fashion, and high-brow tastes. Heath would ask if I was jealous of your refined manners."

"Could we make a pact? That we'll try to find common ground, and if we can't, we'll just agree to disagree? We're so different, yet we need each other."

She leaned into me. "Absolutely. I miss my little sis. And relying on each other more will hopefully alleviate some of Père's need to rescue us."

"I'd like that." I touched her knee. "You'll be happy I attended a Life Group recently. Lauren—my client and friend—invited me. It was at the Marches' house, an affluent couple that, ironically, Jordan wanted to network with. That was the reason I went." I shrugged. "I'm unsure if I'll check out Lauren's church, but I'm considering it."

Aimee raised her hands in front of her grin. "I'll work on not asking how that's going."

"And I met a guy Lauren's trying to hook me up with..." I shot Aimee a warning glare. "But I'm not interested in him that way. And still not ready to date."

"It's a start."

I rolled my eyes.

She laughed. "It'll take me time to learn not to be the pushy older sister."

"One who always knows what's best?" I raised my brows.

"I won't apologize for being right, but I'll try not to ask about your love life."

"Thank you."

Heath and Daniel walked into the house. While Aimee chatted with them, I studied her, unable to imagine a better conversation between us. Hopefully, we'd established a precedent.

CHAPTER 53
JUNE 29

I almost left Maman in a parking lot. After I picked her up at the airport, we met Aimee and her family at a restaurant. After we finished eating, I headed to my car by myself, forgetting Maman wanted to stay with me at Jennifer's condo. From the rearview mirror, I caught Maman waving at me as she stood near Aimee's car.

Later that night while Maman got ready in the bathroom, I lay on my bed, scrolling social media. I received a notification that I'd been tagged. Hoping it was a client, I checked the post.

What I saw floored me. I didn't know Jordan had any social presence outside of LinkedIn. His post featured a carousel of six images. The first three were of me at my worst.

In the first image, I was sitting in a chair in PJs, smoking a cigar, feet resting on Jordan's desk. We had just moved into his condo.

The second was from when we attended the New Year's Eve soiree at The Mayo two years ago. I was sprawled on a couch drunk, my mouth wide open as though I was screaming, my short hair in sweat-induced spikes.

For the third photo, Jordan had somehow gotten a shot from my recent outing at Charleston's, when I was clinging to that jerk Jackson outside. I was dragging my feet, mouth open, and arms flung over his shoulder.

The last three images were of his girlfriend, the receptionist. In the first, she stood smiling on the condo balcony, dressed in a white button-up blouse and black dress pants, her hair pulled into a chignon. The next was her in a white Easter dress with small pink flowers, standing in front of a cross at the church I used to attend with Jordan. The last one showed her holding a bouquet of red roses.

Jordan's caption was the worst.

When you upgrade from a Honda @celinemonroe at @monroeconsulting to a Bentley @haleighblossom. #upgraded #ditchedtheloser #lifeisbetterwithyou

Are you kidding me? Doubt Haleigh Blossom was his girlfriend's legal name but her social media handle. I couldn't imagine him with someone so boho. I paced the floor but couldn't get my heart rate down.

Obviously, Jordan became indignant I ignored his texts and didn't return the bracelet. But how did he get that pic of me at Charleston's? Just as my life was on the rise, he was working tirelessly to drag me back down to his den.

A cigar-toting woman, one of the boys, comfortable in a boardroom and with any executive—that was how I viewed myself. He mocked me, telling me I didn't belong.

Memories of me walking into Papa's lux office at the oil and gas company flooded. I was only five, but it was like yesterday. I clung to Dad's hand until I saw Papa sitting in his chair, then I ran to him. He hugged me tight. After a few niceties, he carried me to the window of the thirtieth floor. "Celine, the sky's the limit for you one day." He patted my nose. "Your dad says you like going to work with him?"

I nodded, eating all the validation treats Papa gave.

"Good, because you'll go where your dad and I won't. You could be the CEO of a Fortune 500 company."

That was the biscuit I needed. I'd break the barriers that kept my family from ascending. The CEO of the corporation where Papa worked gave the position to his son-in-law instead of Papa, the COO at the time. So, I blamed nepotism for Papa's ceiling.

Dad got snubbed for the CEO position because the other, younger candidate was a master manipulator. He moved in close to the founder, called Dad the old man, and rallied employees under Dad to jump on a campaign to pursue mid-level clients over the mom-and-pop businesses Dad preferred. When the founder retired, the younger candidate got the promotion. I nearly quit serving as an intern. But Dad talked me into staying, saying I needed to learn resilience.

I guess I didn't. Once I faced adversity at Specter, I didn't push through. Unable to make it to a VP position, I started my own business, so I could be "on top".

But was I? Jordan and I sketched out my five-year and ten-year plans. I'd start small, consulting with mom-and-pop outfits. Then I'd hire more staff and reach more mid-level clients until I had a fledgling marketing firm. I still had confidence I could grow, though I wasn't sure if I could reach my goal on the timeline I wanted.

Maman sang a psalm as she approached the bedroom. "You know when I sit and when I rise; you perceive my thoughts from afar."

I scurried to turn off the light switch, but she was in front of me suddenly.

"*Mon petit chou*, what's wrong?"

"Nothing." I shook my head.

She narrowed her eyes, scrutinizing me. "You're scaring me."

I smiled wide, as if my mouth were frozen in place. "I'm tired."

She wrapped her arms around my shoulder. "Jennifer's still up. Let's confide with her."

"No." What if a client or lead saw Jordan's post? This couldn't be happening. I lightly pushed her arms off and paced the bedroom.

Maman called for Jennifer.

I walked into the Haven as Jennifer came upstairs. Maman sat on the loveseat. I paced the perimeter of the space until Jennifer stood in front of me.

"What's wrong?" she asked, her hand on my shoulder.

"Everything," I said.

"Can you sit down?" She pointed to the couch, our usual debriefing spot.

I shook my head and resumed pacing. Jennifer sat on the couch. The next hour was show-and-tell, but I was the only one with something to share.

Jennifer lashed out, insisting I report Jordan's post to the social media powers for bullying and harassment. I didn't expect her to get so animated. I loved it!

Maman sat silent, which I also didn't expect. I stopped to study her, not recognizing the woman who usually wore her emotions on her sleeve. When she didn't say anything after Jennifer finished speaking, I ranted that just reporting Jordan on social wasn't enough. He'd find another way to retaliate.

I continued pacing, angry how brutal he was. Why couldn't he just leave me alone?

Maman cleared her throat. I snapped to attention.

"*Mon petit chou*, you're wound up. The vein on your forehead is jutting like a guitar string. Calm down." Her eyes appeared dilated. She held a hand over her heart and took short breaths.

Her look of terror drove me to a mirror, where I touched the vein jutting out. I took long breaths to calm down and returned near Maman.

She reached her hand toward me. "*Assieds-toi*, Celine. Please sit." I hesitated, preferring to expend my anger by pacing. "And take deep breaths," she said.

I joined her on the loveseat. She laid her smooth hands on top of mine and sang "Amazing Grace." Her singing calmed my swirling angst enough that the images posted by Jordan stopped flashing through my mind like a PowerPoint presentation.

When she finished singing, my body stopped trembling. I grabbed my phone, untagged myself from the post, and reported it as harassment. What an empowering feeling!

"If he pulls another stunt like that, he better watch out," I said. "He's not the only one with a dark side."

"Don't contact that boy or retaliate." Maman caressed my arm. "He's not your problem."

"Trying to ignore him led to him embarrassing me on social. If a lead saw that post, they won't sign with me. Worse, if a current client saw it, they might drop me. And that's Jordan's strategy. I've got to do something that'll make him stop."

"Focus on supporting your clients and being the intelligent and hardworking daughter I know and love." She gently stroked my hair. "The right people will understand."

I shook my head. "But the post reflects who I am and why I was attracted to Jordan. I'm drunk on ambition, stepping over everyone to get ahead. Insecure, needing work and status to validate me. And shallow, overlooking the socially awkward. I've never done anything sacrificial, ever."

"No," Maman said. "That's what he wants you to believe. You got swept up in your career, but you still are my considerate and tenderhearted angel."

Mothers always believed in their children. I turned to Jennifer, needing her confirmation. "You think so?"

"Yes." Jennifer said with a nod. "Don't let your ex define you. The jilted will accuse an ex of all kinds of bad behavior to make themselves look good."

I collapsed onto my side and cried into the arm of the loveseat, wanting to believe Jordan's images didn't represent my character yet thinking they did.

"Would you give us space to talk privately, Jennifer?" Maman asked.

"I'll be downstairs."

"Thank you."

Once Jennifer's footsteps on the wood stairs weren't resonating through the Haven, I sat up.

Maman wiped the tears from my eyes. "Do you know why we named you Celine?"

"It's French?" I whispered.

"Yes. It means 'heavenly'." Her eyes penetrated mine as if drilling a hole in my irises.

I smirked. "Okay." I'd figured it was something celestial and weird.

Maman pushed back a sweat-filled bang. "You're my answer to prayer."

My back straightened. "How?"

"After Aimee was born, I wanted another child, but that became difficult. I had those miscarriages, and my body didn't cooperate. One gynecologist hinted about needing a hysterectomy, but I refused. I suffered depression for the next three years. Poor Père—he was so scared. I carried myself well enough during the day to care for Aimee, but in the evenings, I'd escape to the bedroom, lying in bed for hours like a zombie. Some nights I'd cry in his arms. Other nights, I'd turn away from him, curled up in a ball, unable to talk. I felt like I wasn't a complete woman. All I ever wanted was to be a wife and mother."

"You've told me." And many others. She liked to share her fertility story with friends or new acquaintances.

"But I haven't told you that I had a dream a few weeks after the third miscarriage. In the dream, a little girl with pigtails approached, cupped my chin in her tiny hands, and kissed me on the forehead.

Immediately, I woke up, overwhelmed with peace and hope. I woke Père and told him we were having a girl."

"Was he excited?" I grabbed Maman's hand.

"Of course! We held each other and cried. We'd wanted to believe, and in that moment, it was as though God kissed us."

"Oh." All my life, I'd fought Maman's affection, not fully embracing her love. I longed to be as tender and reassuring as the girl in her dream.

"Once I got pregnant with you, I never faced depression like that again."

Heavy regret clung to my body like wet clothes. How many years had I wasted being hurt and angry, assuming she favored Aimee?

"You're sad," Maman said. "Why?"

I wiped the tears off my cheek. "I've never understood you. I've said hurtful things. I'm sorry."

"I'm sorry too. I was overly protective of Aimee from the beginning. As a preemie, she was the size of a kitten. But you? A little late and hearty at eight pounds and twenty-one inches long. So strong, *mon petit chou*."

"Doesn't mean I wasn't vulnerable."

Maman curled her fingers back and forth between us, signaling me to snuggle. I inched toward her and laid my head on her chest. "You were always Daddy's girl, while Aimee took to me from the beginning. I'm afraid I haven't let her fly out of the nest, even after she married Heath."

"Doesn't she balk at your mothering?" Having to ask awakened me to how little I paid attention to their dynamic. Because they got along like best friends, I assumed they didn't have much conflict.

Maman laughed. "Of course. But it doesn't stop me, does it? I'm learning to just be there if you two need wisdom on life. Just like Gramere still does with me."

"I'll always be your *petit chou*."

"Yes, no matter how old you are." She caressed my hair. "I always knew you'd be fine, even after you moved in with Jordan."

I covered my face. "I thought you despised me for not following Christian values."

Maman pulled down my hands and stared into my eyes. "I hurt because you were living with someone who didn't love you. I wanted you to be with a man who saw your value enough to marry you."

When we finished talking, I planted a big kiss on her forehead. I'd work on understanding her better. Valuing myself would be much more difficult.

CHAPTER 54
JUNE 30

I woke up the next morning with a voice message from Jordan. "My coworker captured that flattering shot of you at Charleston's."

His coworker was at the restaurant? I started to text him, but since I had blocked him, I wouldn't receive his text responses anyway. I deleted the voice message.

Lauren called. "I saw Jordan's post," she said. "It grieves me you have to endure such a hateful man, so I have to do something. Let me shoot a testimonial for my social, raving about your marketing services."

Her empathy spoke volumes, reiterating how much I valued her friendship. So, when she asked if I'd bring Maman to Life Group, I caved, assuring her we'd be there.

At the Marches', everyone embraced us with open arms. Of course, Maman endeared herself to all, leaving no strangers in her path.

I was clear-minded throughout the meeting, especially as Bryant shared about taking off our masks and being authentic. He made the process seem natural, as though everyone could live that way. I wanted to, but it was safer to exude the perfect, controlled persona—the "false self," as he called it—than to expose my imperfections and weaknesses.

After the meeting proper, Peter kept Maman company while Viviana chatted with Lauren and me. The three of us sat in a sitting room resembling a greenhouse. Vases of blue hydrangeas rested on every side and coffee table. Acacia trees in beige stone planters stood as sentries in the corners of the room. On one wall, a gilded frame presented a giant picture of a full-bodied tree.

Lauren and I shared a dusty-blue love seat. Sitting across from us on an armchair, Viviana leaned forward, hands clasped together. "Celine, would you be interested in joining a D-group? I want to limit it to six women. So far, we have four of us, including Lauren."

I'd heard about discipleship groups at the prior church I attended. Not wanting another time commitment, I never joined. But no way could I resist sitting under Viviana, gleaning nuggets about finances, friendship, and faith.

"I'd be honored," I said.

Viviana smiled as though I'd made her day. Who was this woman?

"Terrific. I want you to be comfortable, so I'd like you to invite the sixth woman to join us."

Viviana was full of surprises. I couldn't wrap my mind around someone like her being so humble, wanting me to help form the group. If I were in her shoes, I would've only asked women I knew.

I sensed Jennifer would fit in the group perfectly. "Sure. I have someone in mind. When does the D-group start?"

"In August, after Moriah returns from her honeymoon."

"Moriah's my invitation," Lauren said. "Garrett suggested I ask her. She's his assistant and has been wanting to join a D-group. And I want to get more acquainted with her." Lauren tapped my knee. "Hey, you could give her tips, since she runs his social media, emails prospective clients, and writes his blogs."

"I'd be happy to." I wondered when I'd meet Garrett formally. Once I got acquainted with Moriah, it'd feel even more as though I knew him.

Lauren winced. "Speaking of Moriah, I need prayer."

"Oh?" Viviana leaned back, hands resting on her crossed legs.

"I called her, asking if she might set up Garrett with one of her bridesmaids for the wedding. I got flustered once I discovered Presleigh is her matron of honor and is bringing Ciaran to the wedding. Now I especially don't want Garrett to be alone." Lauren shrugged as though being overly protective was an older sister's right.

"Where's the wedding?" Viviana asked.

"Portugal. My uncle married a Portuguese woman who owned a vineyard, so they run it together. Kind of cool since we're of Portuguese descent. Anyway, once Moriah, who's half Portuguese, discovered our uncle has a vineyard in Lisbon, she wanted to get married there. Of course, Garrett's shooting the wedding."

"Who's Ciaran?" I asked.

"Sorry." Lauren took a deep breath. "Ciaran is Presleigh's husband. I think I mentioned to you Garrett was engaged to Presleigh—"

"Will Garrett be okay?" I imagined how humiliating it'd be to attend a wedding with Jordan as a groomsman and with his receptionist as his wife, especially if I was dateless.

"I'm concerned about Garrett's headspace." Lauren straightened her back. "Presleigh dated Ciaran in college, but he broke up with her abruptly. Six months later, she started dating Garrett. After Presleigh broke off their engagement, she moved back home and served in her dad's church where Ciaran's the youth pastor. The rest is history." Lauren crossed her arms.

"Have you talked to Garrett about seeing his ex?" Viviana asked.

"I didn't tell him about my talk with Moriah, but I asked him how he'd handle seeing Presleigh. He said he'd figure it out. But I know better. When she got married, Gare sulked for a few days. How will he handle seeing her with Ciaran?"

"We'll be praying for him. He might need the closure." Viviana winked. Lauren sat erect, as if offended at Viviana for downgrading the problem.

To douse water on Lauren's flames, I quickly asked, "Does Moriah have someone lined up?"

"No. At first, she minimized the issue, saying Garrett wouldn't care. Then..." Lauren's face flamed pinkish red. She grabbed my hands and glanced at Viviana. "Please you two, don't think bad of me when I say this."

Viviana spoke first. "Family can bring out the best and the worst in us."

"I've been there," I said, considering Lauren's request easy given my long list of iniquities.

"Moriah corrected me, saying he wouldn't want a date since he'll be focused on shooting. I accused her of being too preoccupied with her wedding to see Garrett's dilemma. I felt terrible when she cried and said all the hassle was so much she wanted to elope. I've never seen her so discombobulated before. She's normally a cool cat." Lauren plastered her hand on her forehead. "Boy, it sounds worse as I share this out loud."

"The bride doesn't want to be pitted against two people she cares about," Viviana said.

Lauren waved her hand. "I apologized, admitted sometimes I get carried away, and assured I'd ask my cousin to find Garrett a date."

I envisioned a lithe blonde with a dewy golden complexion walking arm and arm with Garrett. To not get preoccupied by this conjured supermodel, I thought of how much he must be struggling about seeing his ex. "I'm sorry he has to endure that," I said.

"Thanks for understanding." Lauren squeezed my hand tight, cutting off the blood flow. I grimaced. After she released her grip, I massaged my hand.

"I shouldn't be too concerned," Lauren continued, "because he'll be living it up at the vineyard for a month." She half smiled, as if convincing herself.

I stood. "Oh, when will he return?"

"August tenth. Doesn't that seem long?"

Viviana stood. "Portugal is a beautiful country with engaging people. He'll have a great time."

What if he did, especially connecting with a supermodel? What if he planned on moving there one day? And what was any of that to me? Why was I so enthralled with someone I hardly knew?

CHAPTER 55

Realizing I needed to find Maman, I excused myself as Viviana asked Lauren about renovating a spare bedroom. I walked outside and joined Peter and Maman on the front porch.

"Thanks, Peter, for entertaining my maman." I stood near them as they sat on the porch swing.

"Best thirty minutes of my night." He got up and hugged me. Sandalwood and sweat wafted. "Here, have my seat."

I couldn't move as my eyes caught on Garrett emerging from his cherry-red Jeep in the driveway. Shutting the door, putting his sunglasses on, wiping his forehead with his hand—everything he did was in slow motion. He approached with a fluid gait, smooth and relaxed, like a ballroom dancer.

His chiseled chest and boulder-muscled arms showed through a white button-up. His long legs filled grey slacks. Unable to resist a fine-looking man in business attire, I turned away, wondering if he noticed me gawking.

"Garrett!" Peter piped up. "You're late for the Life Group."

"A little event interfered." Garrett threw his arms to the side.

"Knocked the brunch wedding out of the park?" Peter asked.

"More like it knocked me out. Par for the course." Garrett's eyes drooped.

Once Garrett stepped onto the porch, Peter put his hand on his shoulder, escorting Garrett toward us.

Shoot. I wished I had applied a fresh layer of lipstick after dinner.

"Mrs. Monroe," Peter said to Maman, "meet Lauren's brother, Garrett." Peter turned to Garrett. "Mrs. Monroe is from the Pyrenees region."

Maman stepped off the swing and approached Garrett. He took her hand and kissed it. "*Bonsoir*, Madam. It's a pleasure to meet you. The Pyrenees is one of my favorite places I've visited."

Maman's brows raised as she studied Garrett. "*Bonsoir*, Garrett. What part did you enjoy?"

"Gavarnie, with its hiking trails and Cirque. I would've liked to spend a year there." His eyes brightened, erasing any signs of exhaustion.

"*Oui*, I'm from Gavarnie-Gèdre, about fifteen minutes from the Cirque. If you return, please stay with my *maman*. She'd enjoy hosting you for as long as you like. And your wife if you're married."

He flashed a toothy smile, eyes narrowing. "Wow, I'd like that. The locals were very friendly." He grimaced but quickly resumed smiling. "I'm single."

"*Oui*." She turned to me. "This is my daughter Celine. She's from Tulsa."

For goodness' sake, Maman. Try to be subtle.

"Oh." Garrett turned to face me and paused. I held my breath, wondering what he'd say, but knowing he wouldn't mention the incident at Charleston's.

"Glad to meet you. You're friends with Lauren, right?" He shook my hand but didn't let go right away as if someone hit the pause button. His hands were smooth, unlike what I'd expect a photographer to have. And his grip was firm. So, I didn't let go.

"I've always said that Garrett is the type of man any woman would want to introduce to her parents," Peter said to Maman.

I released my hand slowly. Once my arms laid by my side, I became stiff, hardly moving, as though my feet were nailed to the porch.

"*Oui*," Maman said.

Needing to show my chill side, I smiled wide. "I've wanted to meet you as well." Oh no. I meant to say *Good to meet you as well*. I looked down, unsure what else to do.

"I've gotten to know Celine through the Life Group," Peter said. "She's becoming a regular here."

I flashed Peter a smile for his thoughtfulness.

Garrett winked. "I'm glad to hear that."

Undone and uncertain what else to say, I just replied with a thank-you. Our eyes stayed locked on each other.

The door opened and Bryant stepped outside. "Garrett, thanks for stopping by."

"I'll catch you later, buddy," Peter said, patting Garrett on the back.

Garrett turned to face Peter and gave him a fist bump. "Yeah, we're overdue for lunch."

"Just call," Peter said.

"Will do." Garrett took a step toward Maman. "It was a pleasure meeting you."

She gave him two *bisous*. "The pleasure is all mine. I hope we can connect again."

"Definitely." He turned to face me, scrutinized me for a while, then smiled. "Have a good night." Had he been about to say something, but changed his mind?

"Yes." I waved and watched him go inside with Bryant.

Yes? Who are you tonight, Celine?

CHAPTER 56

Maman went inside to say goodbye to Viviana and Lauren. Peter walked with me toward my car. As we passed Garrett's Jeep, a stack of mail, *Outside Magazine* on top, laid on the front passenger seat and food wrappers littered the floor. Large, black duffel bags were on the back seat. I was taken aback by the clutter, assuming he'd be neat like Jordan.

Peter spoke first. "I'd like to meet with you about promoting my plumbing business. My LinkedIn profile could use updating."

"I'd gladly unclog archaic posts, drain your profile of unnecessary clutter, and connect your account to more collaborative networks." I winked.

He laughed. "It's good to see your humor... I hope I'm not out of line, but I'm sorry for the negative post you were tagged in."

I tightened, embarrassed that he'd seen those images.

"We all have mug shots," he said. "They didn't change my view of you. Only showed me what a louse your ex is. I asked Lauren about him, but she didn't have much to share." Peter opened my car door. "How bad was he?"

I touched the edge of the car's roof. "I'd prefer not to get into that, but he was a mistake."

Peter nodded. "The enemy tries to remind me of the man I buried. I used to resort to certain coping mechanisms, work being a primary one, food another." He patted his stomach. "You can laugh."

I smiled since I couldn't laugh. "Really?"

"Three years ago, I weighed fifty pounds heavier. I asked Jesus to help me to cope, and I got counseling to deal with my wounds. Those were my first steps to freedom. When I start to resort to food to cope now, I remind myself that I'm a new man. While I still struggle from time to time, I'm not controlled by gluttony anymore."

I stared at the ground, unable to see the me from Jordan's pictures dying, much less dead.

Peter reached for my hand and shook it. "Consider me your honorary brother. You know what?" his voice elevated. "How about we snap a pic now for my social, so I can tag you? I'll say something like 'Meet my sister from Bible study. She's a sharp marketing consultant. I'm hiring her, so check her out.' "

I shrugged. "Why not?"

He took several pics then asked me which one I preferred. I selected the second to last, where I'd finally relaxed into my natural smile. After he posted it, I liked his post and shared it on my Stories.

"So, this is what having an elder brother is like?" I asked.

"I'm not that old! Thirty-six. You're what, thirty?"

"Thirty-two."

He chuckled. "I always wanted to antagonize a younger sister."

"Oh, you have no idea how I can retaliate." I jabbed his elbow.

"Watch it." He pointed his finger. "I'll report you to Maman."

We went back and forth until Maman emerged.

During the drive to Jennifer's, Maman raved about the Life Group. At a stoplight, she feebly attempted a casual tone. "Why hasn't Lauren set you up with her brother?"

I was shocked she didn't say Peter. "Garrett's fresh off a relationship, so probably not interested in dating."

"Don't think I didn't catch him holding onto your hand as he stared long into your eyes," Maman said, ignoring my analysis. "Peter's ready to marry but too upbeat for you. Garrett is more melancholy and laid-back. Your type, with his mysterious sky-blue eyes, high cheekbones, and chiseled jawline. *N'est-ce pas?*"

"Whether it's so or not, I'm not ready to date... I am attracted to him, for some strange reason. He's so different from the guys I've dated." I wrinkled my nose, still wondering why I couldn't shake off my attraction for him.

"You're tapping into who you are. Maybe that's why Garrett appeals to you." She waved her hand as if swatting a fly. "Jordan was a counterfeit. When you're open, God will connect you to the real thing."

"Garrett or a man in general?" The light turned green.

"Garrett, of course. He's got it all. Handsome, great family, faith, and that..." She snapped her fingers, searching for the right word. "*Savoir-vivre.* He'd handpick a bouquet of seasonal blooms at the local florist instead of grabbing a dozen red roses at the grocery store. Take you to a cozy eatery where the owners talk to their patrons. Custom design your engagement ring."

The more I was made aware of Garrett's strengths, the more the gulf between our characters seemed to grow. "You're generalizing because he's a photographer. Meeting him for five minutes doesn't make you an expert."

"I experienced his impeccable manners. And you heard how he talked about the beauty of the Pyrenees, especially the Cirque. He'd take you to visit Gra-mere every year! That'd lift the song of my heart."

"I already plan on visiting her next summer, so I don't need a man to convince me."

"Gra-mere would adore him. Why not make yourself alluring to him? Nudge him your way."

"I'm sure a drunk woman he rescued is not Garrett's desire for a mate." Why did I blurt that? The incident at Charleston's still haunted me. "You saw the photo."

"If he's a man of honor, he'll know that was a lapse in judgment. You hit bottom, but you're climbing out. Lauren can testify to that." Maman touched my arm. "You're starved for true love. You need to eat. *L'appétit vient en mangeant.*"

"My appetite will not come as I eat. That attitude got me in trouble." I jumped too soon toward the security, charm, and ambition Jordan promised. Had I waited and gotten acquainted first, I would've seen through his facade before moving in with him.

"The appetite for the real thing will come once you get acquainted with him. Garrett's the first man I can envision you happy with."

Maman had either conveniently forgot her relentless push for me to accept Lance's proposal—a former flame—or was feigning indifference about my refusal.

"I'm not saying it'll happen soon. But I hope it will one day." Maman's tone was so high pitched, I could practically see her mentally arranging my wedding bouquet.

There wasn't anything else for me to say. I just couldn't have her optimism that Garrett would be attracted to me. Fortunately, she let the conversation die. We remained silent until we reached Jennifer's.

After I turned the car off, Maman cupped her chin with her slender hand. Her porcelain skin and baby-blue eyes radiated as the guard light from the garage cast a slight shadow on her face. I reached over and gave her a hug. "You're stunning."

"So are you. You've come so far from that cold, impersonal look you had with Jordan."

"Thanks." I looked down. "I'm sorry for getting irritated. I'm having a hard time."

"You're like a Monet displayed behind protected glass. People can see you, but you don't allow healthy suitors to get too close." She kissed me on the cheek. "I believe you'll get to the place where you shatter the glass and embrace someone who will love you the way you deserve."

That place sounded good. I didn't know how to get there, though.

CHAPTER 57
JULY 10

When I dropped Maman off at the airport for the trip to Paris, I struggled to say goodbye at the TSA PreCheck, where Aimee and her family already waited on the other side. My teary eyes must've inspired Maman to focus elsewhere.

"Now that you're growing your hair, you should wear bright colors. Vary your wardrobe. Add a chiffon sundress with floral patterns. And a tangerine linen jumpsuit."

"We'll see." I smiled, not minding the unsolicited advice.

"Promise at least a sundress, if just to wear in the heat." She nodded, expecting me to comply.

I gave her *bisous*. "Love you."

When I got into my car in the airport parking lot, I posted on my social about dropping her off and how much I'd miss her. Then my curiosity got the best of me. I checked Jordan's social, hoping those terrible images of me were gone since I'd reported him days ago.

His account had disappeared. Either the social media company suspended his account, or he had only created a temporary one to harass me. An unsettling thought accompanied my relief that post would no longer be seen. What if he'd created another account with the same images and caption without tagging me? I knew better but navigated to his girlfriend's account. She had it set to private. Should I create a pseudo profile and follow her?

As I brainstormed witty handles, Maman texted.

God's speaking! Look who's on the same flight to Atlanta?

I gaped at the attached picture of Garrett at the gate counter. Could I get away from this man? What were the odds he was flying on the same flight as my family? I texted back.

Don't be obvious.

I started to resume creating a new social account, but the interruption had knocked sense into me. *Forget Haleigh Blossom the receptionist, Celine. You need to focus on moving forward.* I headed to the office to start working.

A few hours later, Maman called while she and the family were at their gate in Atlanta, waiting for their flight to Paris. "I sat next to Garrett," she crowed, before summarizing their conversation revolving around me. Her report spun in my mind through the afternoon.

Chatting with Jennifer in the Haven after dinner, I invited her to the D-group. Unfortunately, she couldn't join. I didn't know who else to invite, but I'd face that issue later. It was a relief to confide in her about Maman's conversation with Garrett on the plane.

"If I wanted to land a date, Maman did her part. She shared how I'm benefiting from Lauren's friendship, which is obvious. And the kicker—she told him I plan to visit the Pyrenees next summer and will hike the few remaining trails I haven't explored."

"What did he say?" Jennifer asked.

"He focused on his sister, especially how she's found a supportive single friend. Since most of her friends are married with kids, my friendship's a refuge for her. And he said he appreciates I'm holding Lauren accountable to not set him up with someone. It's obvious he was hinting that he's not interested in me." I shrugged, disappointed I wasn't on his radar.

Jennifer tilted her head. "I think he was just giving you a compliment. He probably notices Lauren letting him be because of you."

"What happens if I get thrown into his path a lot more as Lauren and I become closer friends?" I pouted, wondering how I could let this fire die.

"Let's cross that bridge when we get there. I know you're still taking things slow with God, but what if... Just go with me."

"K..."

"What if God has brought you and Garrett together for mutual benefit? Maybe just as friends for now? Can you sit with that?"

I took a deep breath. "I'm unsure because I'm definitely attracted to him. You should've heard me barely utter a coherent sentence to him at the Marches."

"If it might remain only platonic, what do you have to lose?"

I touched my chest as palpitations grew. "He's gone for the month, so I'll see how I feel when he returns."

"Sounds like a plan. What has become of the social media fiasco?"

I was relieved she changed the subject, albeit to a less favorable one. "Jordan's account is closed. I think he created one just to retaliate after I embarrassed him about the bracelet."

Jordan was so vindictive. I couldn't imagine Garrett ever acting that way. Was I only fascinated by Garrett because he was a contrast to Jordan?

CHAPTER 58
JULY 14-20

Dad bought my airline ticket to Florida and scheduled the trip for two weeks, insisting I take the second week off to relax. Concerned I'd get behind, I worked twelve to fourteen hours for several days leading up to the trip. Kimberly came to the office every day and stayed for eight hours. While I enjoyed training her, the responsibility added to my to-do list.

Thankfully, Kimberly was a fast learner. She and Isla helped me get campaigns set up, reports run, and clients' needs met. I assured my team I'd be available if they needed anything during my trip. We'd communicate on the project management app. Other than Lauren, I didn't inform my clients I'd be in Florida. Since I'd acquired most of them recently, I didn't want them thinking I was unavailable.

Dad and Uncle Karl picked me up at the Sanford airport. As we stepped outside the terminal, a mild breeze and the mid-nineties temp whisked me away from the hundred-degree inferno Tulsa had become.

As I lay on a padded lounge chair the next day on Sunday, my mind raced through work like a horse on the manicured track of Pimlico. After Dad and I dropped Uncle Karl off at the airport

Monday morning, I continued sprinting around the track, losing myself in work for my first week in the sunshine state. Friday afternoon, a migraine sucker punched me in the face.

I sat in Dad's office, the window shade down and blue-blocking glasses on, running mid-month reports. Nausea swept over me, so I moved to the Murphy bed next to a low-light lamp in the corner, my laptop propped on my lap, a hard pillow behind my back.

My fencing client called. "Hi, Kris," I said, gritting through the constant hammering in my temples.

"Celine, what's going on?" His panic invaded my room.

"What do you mean?" I quickly pulled up his latest ad campaign. The ad was humming, with five hundred clicks to his website in the past week.

"I'm not receiving any email inquiries or phone calls, despite all the clicks we're generating. No one has entered the giveaway. What have you done?"

"Are you sure?" Oops. I meant to say, "How could that be?"

"Where's your head?" he asked. "*You* should've called *me* about this."

"Let me check the link." I had double-checked it before I left for Florida. The link took you to his site's contact form. Visitors who supplied name, phone number, and email would be entered into a five-thousand-dollar giveaway including fencing and installation. We ran the ad to people living within one hundred miles of metro Tulsa.

"I was willing to overlook that post you were tagged in," Kris said.

I stopped looking at the ad. My fingers froze a few inches from the keyboard. Was he talking about Jordan's post?

"My daughter was impressed by our latest reel your social media manager created and wanted to promote it on her personal account. As she looked at her feed, she noticed that post where you were tagged. When she showed it to me, I assumed it was a prank someone pulled or a friend oversharing. But now I'm wondering about your professionalism."

Hopefully, earning Kris's confidence with his account would lighten my indiscretion. "I'll address that post in a moment... Oh, I've received a message on the Contact page of your website. It says that the account has been suspended."

"What?" he blurted. "What's going on? Your graphic designer set up that page."

I texted Brian a screenshot of the message. "I'm contacting him now," I told Kris. "We'll get to the bottom of this."

"I don't toss two grand in the trash. You've got to make this right, because I'm losing confidence in you and your team."

Brian didn't respond, so I reached out on the project app, sent him a direct message on social, and emailed him.

"My team and I will investigate," I said. "I promise we'll get this resolved within the hour. I'll call you soon."

"You better." Kris ended the call.

Dad knocked on the door. "May I come in?"

"Yes," I said quickly, then resumed staring at my phone.

I called Isla. She didn't answer, so I left a voice message. "Call ASAP. Crisis with Kris's account."

Dad entered the room and handed me a tall glass of ice water and a chocolate bar. "Figured you'd need a snack."

"I'll wait on the chocolate. I've got a relentless migraine and nausea." I took a long sip of water, hydrating my parched throat.

"I'll get you an aspirin." He turned around and disappeared.

I slid out of the bed, set my laptop on the desk, and called Brian again. Still no answer. An online search for reasons a website account would be suspended yielded three possibilities. I leaned my head back and considered each.

First, if someone hacked Kris's website, we'd have bigger issues on our hands. Second, I doubted that Kris hadn't paid his account fees. Third, overuse of server resources might be it. Yet, a few weeks ago,

Brian informed me that Kris had upgraded to the cloud server with his hosting service.

As I jotted notes, my head pounded harder with every movement of the pen. Sweat dripped down my forehead and chin and onto my neck.

When Dad returned with an aspirin, he accidentally let the door slam behind him. The noise rammed into me like a violent swell of waves in a storm, each pounding churning through my body. I held on to the desk, so I wouldn't fall.

"You need to see. That's part of your problem." He turned on the light.

"No lights!" I blocked my eyes with my arm. "Migraines cause light sensitivity."

"Sorry." He turned it off and sat at the desk. I handed him my laptop, asking if he'd take over my online searches. I couldn't look at the computer screen anymore.

Isla returned my call. We talked for about ten minutes. She had checked all the campaign details, but she didn't know much about managing websites. We were acting productive while helplessly waiting for Brian. I lay on the bed, waiting for the hammering in my head to ease.

Dad served as my nurse, filling my water glass, handing me my notepad, and navigating online to sites I directed him to. When his phone dinged with a notification, it might as well have been a bullhorn. I plugged my ears as another wave of nausea hit.

Like a novice sailor enduring a violent storm at sea, I bolted to the bathroom. When I returned, I found Dad with beads of sweat on his forehead, the whites of his eyes showing. Great—I was stressing him into another panic attack.

His finger hovered over the Power button on my laptop. "Call it a night. I'm shutting everything down."

I ran to him, frantically waving my hands. "No. I'll lose this client if I don't fix this. He's keeping my business afloat." I took a deep breath. "I won't be long. Why don't you relax on the lanai? I'll join you shortly. Please."

He gritted his teeth, but I refused to let him stare me down. "Fine," he said. "But only for another hour. I'll be reading in the living room."

As he was leaving, Brian called. "Despite my advice, Kris didn't want to upgrade to the cloud until August, assuming his website would accommodate the increase in traffic. Obviously, it didn't. I'll call the web host and Kris."

"I'll call Kris." I wanted to convey the news to our client.

"I advise you wait, in case there's something else going on. This is a hunch, so—"

"The client needs to hear from me," I said.

"If you promise a resolution the hosting provider can't achieve today, that'll anger Kris. If I were him, I wouldn't appreciate anyone getting my hopes up prematurely."

"I know what he needs." I raised my voice, the hammering grating on my patience.

"Your call, boss." Brian's tone was caustic as a Brillo pad.

After we disconnected, I started to call Kris, but Bill's voice resonated in my head. "Learn to delegate. Trust your team."

I gripped a phone, wrestling with what to do. I could handle this myself, but my stomach was in knots. Instead, I lay my phone on the desk, sat on the edge of the bed, and waited in torment. If I lost this account, I'd have to start recruiting another mid-level client. Worse, I'd have to remind Dad to pay my rent for the year.

The steady clicking of Dad's watch from his desk penetrated my chest as if setting my heartbeat. *Tick, tick, tick...* I wanted to toss the watch across the room. He'd received it as a retirement gift from the firm. His souvenir for forty years of service and loyalty.

After an hour of waiting, I got restless and went to the living room. Dad sat in the armchair, staring, not reading or doing anything as far as I could tell. His face remained pale.

"Is it resolved?" he asked.

"No."

He stood. "Just shut it down then. Shut it down."

Kris called. "Hold on," I told Dad. "This is my client." I ran back to the office, so Dad wouldn't have to listen.

"Celine, I apologize for my panic. Brian explained I had to upgrade to the hosting provider's cloud server. The site is up and running."

"Thank you for calling..." I wanted to say more, but it hurt my head to hear myself talk. The aspirin hadn't kicked in yet.

"I owe you an apology for accusing you of negligence. And I should've extended grace about that post." His quiet delivery eased my aggression toward Jordan.

I needed to lay it out honestly. "That photo with me at Charleston's..." I cleared my throat, trying to find the words to clarify what happened without painting a picture of a reckless partier. "After I left my ex, he referred my clients to my competitor as retaliation. That night, I tried to drown those losses with whiskey comfort. His co-worker recognized me at the bar, took the pic, and shared it with my ex."

"Was this recent?" he asked.

I paused, wanting to say it was several months ago. But I couldn't. "A few weeks ago."

"Thanks for admitting that. Your confidence and poise outshines a momentary personal lapse. Kudos to you for taking your ex's mistreatment while remaining professional in business. I'm in good hands."

"So, everything's good with your campaign? Your website?"

"Yes. I'll check in next week about the giveaway."

"Sounds good." Except I'd promised Dad I'd rest. "On second thought, do you mind calling Isla, my assistant? She is great with ad campaigns, so she'll be the best one to handle any questions or modifications you want to make. I'm in Florida with my dad. He suffered a health issue, and we're both needing rest. I'll only be on leave for a week."

"Take two weeks." Kris's tone was serious.

"Thank you for your generosity. But if anything dire comes up, don't hesitate to call."

"Just enjoy your family."

"Thank you."

I messaged my team a big thank-you and reiterated I'd be on leave. I'd periodically check messages and progress on the project app next week, but I asked they only reach out if there was an emergency. I emphasized that I trusted them.

After shutting down my laptop and phone, I joined Dad on the love seat in the living room. "It's resolved." I raised my hand in victory, hoping to alleviate his stress. "How about watching a documentary on the Gilded Age? See how Rockefeller, Ford, and Vanderbilt ruled America?"

"In a minute... I need to apologize."

"Why?"

"I'm sorry for exposing you to work too early and not encouraging you to be carefree. I'm sorry for—"

"No, I'd cry if I didn't go to work with you on the weekends."

He held up his hand and said, "Let me finish."

I nodded in resignation, so he continued.

"When I didn't break the ceiling that Papa couldn't, I lived vicariously through you, hoping you'd break it to vindicate the family. I'm sorry for feeding your ambition."

"I can't blame you. I've been ambitious all my life."

"Even if my desire for your success wasn't consciously expressed, you felt it, right?"

"I suppose."

"While in the Blue Ridge Mountains, I realized that in my pursuit to be CEO, I had forgotten what was more important." He frowned.

I scowled. "No, you didn't. You prioritized the mom-and-pop shops and your employees."

"I served our clients well, so I justified my zeal. But I didn't just work to serve them. I spent time and energy trying to prevent the new CEO from destroying the firm's vision. That effort prevented me from investing in the employees under me."

"I witnessed you mentoring them." I couldn't let him paint an inaccurate picture of himself.

"I expended too much energy trying to implement my vision, instead of establishing an empowering and sustainable culture. I knew the need for employee training in interpersonal communication, in-house therapy, community outreaches for low-income business owners, and rotating employees to provide pro bono consulting."

"The new CEO would've killed or at least stifled all those initiatives."

"But I didn't even try."

Not wanting Dad to continue thinking about those painful memories, I waved a hand between us. "Where do we go from here?"

"I'm going to avoid offering you unsolicited advice. But I'll be here if you want to ask me anything."

"All I want is your confidence I can run my business."

"You proved your competence even before Jordan." He narrowed his gaze. "Do you promise to take off work next week?"

I laid my head on his shoulder, still his little girl even though I could adult.

CHAPTER 59
JULY 22

While I thought I'd welcome rest, I woke up anxious on Sunday, my first actual day of vacation. I could only endure lying by the pool for a few hours before I wondered what to do with myself. I listened to leadership books, read marketing articles, and watched documentaries, hoping that'd get me through to dinner.

I missed noise. The stillness in the house paralyzed me, especially when Dad left for lunch on Monday with his buddies. I distracted myself with calls to Lauren, Jennifer, and Maman in France. When I sat on the lanai, I got up and watered Maman's hibiscuses and birds-of-paradise. They were drooping as if stricken with arthritis. Though my parents used a cleaning service, I dusted the outdoor grill, swept and mopped the tiled floor, and shined the acrylic windows.

Tuesday night, when Dad fell asleep on the couch, I turned the movie, *The River Runs Through It,* off. I've seen it before anyhow. As I sat in the armchair in silence, thoughts ran through my head. Why did God take Papa and Nana? Would I make it to heaven to see them? How long did I have with Dad and Maman? How could I endure life without them, especially if I never married?

Despite my aversion for introspection, I wrestled with those thoughts like Jacob going toe to toe with God. After about ten minutes of getting nowhere, I got up and tapped Dad on the shoulder.

"Why don't you go to bed," I said.

He opened his eyes and smiled. "I'm praying."

I smirked. "I see."

"Was I snoring?"

"No, but you weren't stirring."

"I see the restlessness on your face that I experienced in North Carolina, so I'm praying for you."

"Sorry, but your prayers aren't working. I can't keep thoughts from ambushing me. I was less stressed trying to salvage my business."

He tapped the seat next to him. "What thoughts?"

I sat, giving myself space between us. "I've never said this out loud, but I've blamed God for Papa and Nana's death. They were on their way to church. And they'd only done good all their lives. Why them?"

He nodded in solidarity. "I've never put two and two together. I didn't think how their death could affect your view of God. I should've, because I blamed him for a short time too."

"You did?" I scooted closer to him.

"I blamed God and the other driver. Until I could sense my heart was calcifying. I nearly stopped attending church, but Maman walked with me through that journey."

I struggled to accept that God could do whatever he wanted, without love, logic, or loyalty. That was a tyrant.

He put a finger under my chin. "It was just an accident. As much as I wanted to blame the driver for losing control or God for allowing it, I didn't find peace there." He set his hand on my shoulder. "Death doesn't discriminate but snuffs out the right-eous as much as the unrighteous. Have you grieved that the world is unjust? Have you accepted that sadness is a valid emotion?"

I scowled. "Do you think tragedy is some character test God expects us to accept, so we can face sadness?" I'd faced plenty of sadness since leaving Jordan, but I didn't like the idea of being tested.

"Let me say this. I—"

"How about we dive into it tomorrow?" I stood. Hopefully, he'd forget about this talk by then.

He touched my leg. "Let me finish."

I glanced toward the guest bedroom. "I'm not in the frame of mind for heavy conversation."

"I won't be long, but I have to get this off my chest." He pursed his lips as he stared hard at me.

I sat, biting my lower lip. I wanted to say that it'd be a waste of breath, since I wasn't ready to hear.

"Thank you." He smiled, but I crossed my arms as he continued. "I didn't realize how much fear I bore after my parents died. I gathered you, Maman, and Aimee like a hen gathers her chicks, but control only made things worse. Forgive me?" He extended his hand.

I grabbed it, wanting to soften the blow, excuse his behavior as being a protective father. But was that for the best? Ultimately, hadn't my defending him caused friction between us?

"Your lives are a burden I shouldn't have carried," Dad continued.

"No, you don't need to."

"There's a good chance I'll falter, so be patient with your old man as I learn to let you go." He took back his hand, removed his glasses, and wiped his eyes. His chest heaved as he recovered his composure. "Lately, Maman and I've been reading Psalm 139. Appropriate to my letting go, because she'd sing that while pregnant with you. She'd hold her belly and just fill the room with her song."

I smiled. "For years, those verses were stuck in my head." Every night, Maman would sing part of Psalm 139 when she tucked me into bed. As an adult, I didn't like to hear that psalm and be reminded of the faith I ran from.

"Missing your Maman this morning, I read verses eleven and twelve... In summary, it says darkness is light to God."

Dad's words were hard to accept. I turned my chest toward him. "If you think God uses darkness to shed light on things, would you say he worked through me dating Jordan? Because that was the only way I'd realize that ambition at all costs is a dead end?"

"Wasn't God there the whole time?"

My eyes searched the room for an answer and landed on an eleven-by-fourteen gilt-framed pic of our family. Though my grandparents had passed away only two weeks earlier, Maman insisted we keep our scheduled photo shoot, saying Nana and Papa would want us to. I barely smiled for the photographer.

Yet you couldn't detect our sadness. The golden hour created a halo effect around our heads, and fall leaves nestled near our feet. That family photo had become one of my favorites.

CHAPTER 60
JULY 28

When Jennifer picked me up from the airport, I mistook her for a fashion blogger. She was dressed in navy velour joggers and a coordinating top with a gold streak across the shoulders.

Her auburn brown eyes were bright; I could see the layers of color in her irises.

"Celine! I've missed you." She stopped and stared. "You are absolutely radiant with your sun-kissed glow." She shook her finger. "Someone chilled by the pool."

"Guilty as charged. I spent the last week enjoying Dad's company and learning to embrace solitude. That's why I barely texted."

"I'm proud of you. And I would've ignored your calls and texts." She hugged me then stepped away. "Did you buy this tropical beauty in Florida?"

"Yes." I glanced at my cream-colored sundress with orange glads. "I figured I might as well be comfortable when doing nothing." I eyed her. "What's up with you? You're abnormally perky, like it's sorority recruiting day. You're not that enthusiastic about my rest."

"I'll give you the scoop in the car."

Once she drove away from the airport's parking lot, I couldn't wait any longer. "So, spill."

"My toilet got fixed." She winked.

"What?"

"A week ago, my toilet wasn't flushing. I was about to call a plumber, when your client Lauren called about staging one of my homes. Anyway, I asked if she knew a great plumber, and she referred Peter."

I laughed as she blushed. Now, we were getting somewhere. "I never thought about setting you two up!"

She fanned her face. "We hit it off, and he asked me out on a date for this Friday."

I turned my body toward her. "What?"

"I know. Who knew a plumber could be so hot! Honestly, I blushed when I first saw his strikingly exotic face. I blanked for a second."

I clapped. "I love this!"

"We talked like we've been friends for years. He's so funny. Had me rolling... And his voice is alluring, like—"

"A jazz singer, right?"

"I could listen to Peter talk all day."

"Uh-oh. How long did it take to fix the toilet?"

"Fifteen minutes, but a good hour for the house visit."

I clutched the side of my head, hardly knowing what to say. "What does Sienna think?"

"She hasn't met him yet. But I told her about him, so she wants to see if he passes the grade."

I glanced at my watch. "Drop me off at the Marches. I have time to make the Life Group and want to talk to Peter."

"Wait until our relationship is a sure thing. I don't want to get my hopes up."

I stared like she was someone I didn't recognize. Normally, she'd want a spy report, urging me to ask him about her.

"Are you worried it might not work out? That Sienna might not jive with him?"

"I never felt this giddy about anyone before, not even A.J. I was attracted to my ex, but never infatuated. I'm so nervous I can't think."

"How about this? I'll wait and see if Peter says something about you at Life Group. If he doesn't, I'll play it cool and thank him for responding to your plumbing emergency." I raised my brows.

"No, don't mention anything about me unless he does first. Promise." She wagged her finger at me.

"I think you're overthinking this. It's not a big deal if I fish around to see where he stands."

"He knows you're my close friend, so he'll talk. Promise you won't initiate anything."

"Fine." I wanted to cross my fingers behind my back and ask Peter about Jennifer anyway, but I'd uphold my word.

"And I want to enjoy your company on your first night back," she said.

Not going to Life Group would make it easier for me to do as Jennifer asked. "Alright." I wanted to at least call Peter, but I'd honor her wish and wait a week. By then, I could ask how he thought their date went.

I couldn't believe how fast life could turn. I didn't know if I was happier for Jennifer, because Peter was an authentic gentleman, or for Peter, because Jennifer was a once-in-a-lifetime catch.

At her condo, I unpacked while she fixed dinner. Sienna was with her dad, so we had a quiet meal.

It occurred to me that if Jennifer and Peter became a couple, his friendship with Garrett would make my life closer networked with Garrett's. Even if I wanted to, I couldn't avoid Garrett now.

CHAPTER 61
AUGUST 5

Dad and I were holding each other accountable. While he promised to attend counseling beyond his support group, I vowed to check out Believers Church, where most people from the Marches' Life Group attended. He wanted me to get resourced with a broader group of people, especially for social events and ministry opportunities. I assured him that even if I wouldn't return to Believers, I'd attend the Life Group regularly.

Once the weekend hit, though, I came up with valid reasons why I shouldn't go to church on Sunday. Lauren was vacationing in Michigan, and I didn't want to sit alone like a new transfer at school, strange faces swimming around me in their sea of cliques. Plus, I preferred sleeping in on Sunday morning.

At Life Group, however, Bryant discussed pushing past your comfort zone. He shared that his father offered to partner with him if he started his own investment firm. But Bryant was too comfortable working for a large investment company, where he had a corner office with tall windows and a great boss. Why leave that secure job? After his dad died unexpectedly, Bryant took the leap, realizing life's fragility.

After Bryant's message, I told Peter I'd attend Believers, and he assured he'd save me a seat. For the record, I didn't initiate conversation about Jennifer. There wasn't time before Peter started drilling me with questions.

"What's her favorite flower?"

"Orchids."

"What's her favorite pastime?"

"Skydiving!"

His eyes got large. "Really?"

"No, although she's already crossed that off her bucket list. I think the one time was enough." I smiled. "She enjoys attending sporting events. Football, baseball, basketball."

"I knew I liked her." His dimples appeared. How sweet.

On and on, he interrogated. After exhausting his questions, his face turned pinkish red. "Thanks, Celine. I needed to know all that because I want to plan unforgettable dates. Last night was a blast! It's just too cool that Jennifer's your best friend."

I laughed, hardly able to contain my joy. I'd never experienced this much fun cheering for a couple. Later that night, I asked Jennifer to come with me to Believers, so I wouldn't be alone. Jennifer couldn't come since Sienna was in a skit at their church.

When I nervously entered Believers Church that Sunday morning, a female greeter welcomed me like we were long lost friends. Her warmth eroded some of my walls. But as I walked through the long hall, I could hardly hear myself think. Hordes of people headed toward the sanctuary. Others chatted in groups while kids weaved through. In the faint distance, drums and singing echoed, directing me toward the worship ahead. Overwhelmed by all the stimulation, I stopped.

I'd just text Peter that I couldn't make it. As I grabbed my phone, Maman sent a WhatsApp message with pics of her and Gra-mere sitting in the humble church in Gavarnie-Gèdre, followed by a video of the melodic church bells ringing, something I always enjoyed about European churches. Maman's face glowed, making me glad she hadn't returned to the States with Aimee and the family but was staying a month.

Since she had been at church much earlier today, was her share now a timely hint for me to attend here? Boy, Maman would fall on her knees praising God if I shared a pic. Fine... I headed through the open double door and into the sanctuary as laughter and the buzz of conversation replaced the music. A sea of strangers mingled in clusters. I turned toward the hall; I'd return next week.

"Celine." I spun around. Peter gave me a hug. "I'm glad you're here. I saved you a seat."

He led me to the middle section, two aisles from the front. I wished we were in the back. But I captured a shot of Peter and me with the church's stage in the background and sent it to Maman then Dad. Shortly, the worship band started the service. Once I endured the praise session, the pastor encouraged us to greet each other. Urgh, why not just dive into the sermon?

Someone approached Peter and asked him a plumbing question, so I sat alone, reading Maman's message.

> Jesus is alive! Tell Peter the Pyrenees is calling. And thank him for being a good friend. Have you heard how Garrett's doing? Is Lauren there? I miss you. Will call later, so you can talk to Gra-mere again. She loves you!

Dad's message was more subdued.

> I better hold up my end. Call later.

"Celine." I looked up at Viviana as she and Bryant approached. We chatted until the pastor resumed the service.

During the sermon, he spoke about mental health and the value of ministries and resources for inner healing. He conducted a Q&A

with a counselor from Plumbline Ministries. The church sponsored attendees who obtained a pastor referral to receive free counseling. Nice! There was a place for someone who needed counseling but couldn't afford it.

Although I still wasn't ready to sit alone with a counselor, spilling my deepest, darkest memories, I was open to their ten-week classes on topics like safe people, boundaries, and codependency. Their one-day courses appealed most to my schedule. Since they offered a one-day class on marriage, I considered raising my hand and asking if they taught a class on how to manage singleness in a world valuing marriage. But I was sure they didn't.

After the service, Peter invited me and the Marches to lunch at The Tropical, an Asian fusion restaurant nearby. Bryant needed to stay for the second service, but Viviana joined us. As we headed toward the parking lot, Peter got a call. A burst pipe required an emergency visit.

I didn't mind having one-on-one time with Viviana, since I'd longed to get more acquainted with her. Yet, I was nervous wondering if she'd discern my weak faith. I wouldn't be able to fake it with her.

CHAPTER 62

At The Tropical, Viviana and I sat in a spacious booth. The padded leather seats were cool and firm, easing the church stress out of my legs. A scant smoky musk wafted from a tea light on the table, the short flame seemingly swaying to the rhythm of the restaurant's instrumental music resembling soft rain. Lime-green palm fronds hanging on the wall whisked my imagination to a Thai resort. Although tempted to order a mai tai, I got jasmine tea instead. Since my infamous night at Charleston's, I avoided liquor, only occasionally enjoying wine.

After ordering, we chatted casually about my business and Viviana's nonprofit. Until now, I hadn't realized the magnitude of her presence. Because of her cordial demeanor, you could easily underestimate her. Yet, her violet eyes, resembling Maman's lavender, wielded an intensity, as though Viviana could see beyond my congenial smile. I sat on my hands to prevent them from fidgeting, wondering if she could see into my depths.

We chatted casually about my business, until our waitress brought Viviana's order of stir-fry with scallops. Once the waitress left, Viviana leaned toward me across the table.

"Have you asked anyone to join the D-group?"

Her tone carried her calm manner, but I felt agitated since I was unsure who to ask after Jennifer declined my invitation. Aimee came to mind, but she'd prefer a group focused on parenting rather than business.

"Yes, but my friend can't make it." I paused to sip my tea, pondering what else to say. I didn't want to hold Viviana up, especially because there must be a waiting list of eligible women dying to join. "Do you need to ask someone else?" I asked.

"Take your time. We can launch the group with five of us. Although I'd like the sixth person to start from the beginning, it's not a dealbreaker if they join shortly after."

I stopped fidgeting. When some people say there's no pressure, their frustration of having to wait on you rumbles under the surface. But with Viviana, her placid countenance didn't change. Her eyes were still bright and engaging.

"I appreciate that, although I'll let you know by Friday." I made the promise for myself, since I operated better with a deadline.

"Like I said, take your time." She cut small slices of scallop with her knife and took a bite with the back of her fork facing up, the European way. "It's important you ask someone you trust. I formed this group to serve as a refuge where we can share, heal, and grow."

I winced, not expecting the D-group to be a communal therapy session. I would've preferred laying low as I learned from Viviana.

"I see." I scanned the room for the server, realizing she hadn't mentioned when my food would be ready.

"Did you have something different in mind?" Viviana asked without any defensiveness.

I straightened my posture, sorry she'd discerned my disappointment. "I assumed it'd be more of a mentorship where you'd share about business, faith, and relationships."

"Oh no." She waved her hand, dismissing my expectation. "I want everyone to contribute... You have much to give."

Contemplating whether I did, I scouted a family at a nearby table. An adolescent girl sat between the couple. While the mom ordered, the daughter reached across to grab her father's phone and knocked over her water glass. He bit his lip, probably wanting to rebuke her, then wiped the water up with napkins.

In Viviana's group, I'd be like that girl. With the other women further along in their faith, wouldn't they have to correct my misunderstanding of scripture and not dive deep because I couldn't understand?

Our server walked by, so I stopped her and asked about my order. She bowed her head. "We are so busy, I forgot. My apologies." She beelined toward the kitchen.

"Hopefully, they have your order ready." Viviana set her utensils on her plate.

"Please don't wait on me." I waved my hand.

"I don't mind." She gave me a firm smile.

I sipped tea to ease my nerves. "I want to join the D-group, but honestly, I've kept my distance with God for many years. As a college student I focused on academics, so I didn't make time for discipleship. Over time, my faith got diluted. I didn't want to believe all the scriptures about mammon, worldliness, and surrender. It wasn't convenient." I tapped my feet on the tiled floor, ashamed of my pride. I'd lived selfishly most of my life, and where had it gotten me?

"We want to be our own god, don't we?" Viviana's head tilted as if she were nodding toward the potted tropical palm tree to my right.

"Yes." In one sentence, she'd summarized what kept me from drawing near him. The candle on the table flickered higher as the waitress approached with my tropical chicken fried rice.

After the waitress left, I faced Viviana. "I'm curious. Why did you invite me to the group?" I took a small bite of food.

Viviana extended her left hand, not touching mine, but still showing support. "I asked certain women from different stages of life, backgrounds, and experiences, so we could all grow."

Great. I'd be the little tugboat they'd have to pull along.

"I'm in a complicated transition," I said, "so I don't know how much I can contribute, at least for a while." I frowned, hardly believing my transparency. Something about her pulled truth out of me.

"Don't underestimate yourself. You don't take things at face value but want to understand and explore what you believe. Because of that, your faith comes from the heart and isn't just built on what you were taught. The Bereans were commended for studying the scriptures to verify what Paul said was true."

I gave her a faux smile, mostly because I wasn't as devoted to truth. "I'm getting there."

"Perhaps it'll help to know why I asked my daughter-in-law to join us. She comes from a Greek Orthodox background, so she can offer a different perspective." She played with her bracelet. "Also, I wanted to connect with her through the group. Since she's an introvert and laid-back, I've struggled to understand her. I subconsciously did only the little necessary to maintain a relationship and didn't dive too deep. Now, I realize how much I'm missing from not knowing her and learning from her."

"Is she excited to join?" I wondered because Viviana's admission brought to mind how I viewed Aimee.

"She nearly cried, having sensed but never asked why I never wanted to do anything with her that didn't involve my son." Viviana shook her head. "I felt like I failed my son and our family in my effort to protect my heart."

"I understand playing it safe." And now I knew who to ask to fill the sixth spot.

For the rest of the lunch, I asked Viviana about Prague, since I hadn't visited her home city. Listening to her paint beautiful word pictures of that historical site of revolutions, art, and progress, I felt like I was there. She dove into describing her sister, who resided there. Viviana shared how they talked daily. I envied how tight they seemed though they lived so far apart.

When the waitress brought the bill, Viviana procured it immediately. She placed a crisp hundred in the leather bill holder with a half smile. "That should cover lunch." I thanked her without feeling indebted or patronized.

After we left the restaurant, I sat in my car and called Aimee. Once I confirmed I'd be at her place Friday night, I closed my eyes, telling myself to take the plunge before I changed my mind.

"Also, I joined a new discipleship group that will meet every Friday at noon. It's held at Viviana March's house, only about a few miles from you. Viviana and her husband host the Life Group I attend on Saturday nights." I paused, wondering if I'd regret what I'd say next. "I'm inviting you to join."

She didn't say anything for a few seconds. "Really?" Was it good or bad that my invitation caught her off guard? "Is the group spiritual or business? Co-ed or just women?"

I smiled, wishing I could see her surprised face as I continued. "Spiritual deep dive with only six women."

"I've been praying to join that type of group, but I never expected my sister would invite me. Let me talk it over with Heath. When do you need an answer?"

"Before Friday, so I'll have time to ask someone else if you can't make it. The first meeting is on the seventeenth, and Viviana will provide lunch."

"Gotcha... Hmmm."

Why did she hesitate? Was she unsure how serious this group of women would be? "Viviana is a devoted believer and wants us all to learn from one another. Lauren, another strong believer, is attending too. I've never met the other two women."

"Sorry, I'm remembering a conversation I had with Gra-mere."

"Care to share?" I envisioned Gra-mere in her kitchen adding goose fat to her cast-iron pot while Aimee sliced carrots.

"She said God rewards love, not longevity. She warned me to not look down on eleventh-hour laborers."

"What does that mean?"

"I've prayed for you for so long, but now that you're changing, I need to acclimate. Will you be okay if I struggle if these ladies view you to be as spiritually mature as I am? That sounds so arrogant, doesn't it?"

I cleared my throat, not expecting she'd feel threatened. "You realize, sis, that I only have my toes dipped in baptismal waters, while everyone else is already submersed."

"Trust me, it won't take you long. Remember when we hung out at the neighbors' pool when you were six and just learning how to swim? I held your little hand as we walked toward the shallow end. I told you to stay close as we'd step into the pool. But when we walked past the diving board, you slid your hand out of my grip, hopped on the board, and jumped in feet first. You doggie-paddled around the pool in your arm floaties. I yelled for you to get out of the water. But you looked up at me, sweet smile on your face, telling me to get in."

I laughed, envisioning Aimee with hands on her hips and face boiling red. "I barely remember."

"Well, I wholly remember." She laughed too. "I'll let you know by tonight. I do want to join."

"Let's dive in and struggle together," I said. Now, I couldn't think of anyone else I'd want for the group's sixth spot.

Later that evening, Aimee texted a diving emoji. I texted back.

Let the adventure begin.

CHAPTER 63
AUGUST 15

Even with Lauren in Michigan, we texted nearly every day. She sent pics of the vacation home they were purchasing, its hilltop view, and the quaint city of Gaylord, where her in-laws lived. A few days after she returned home, she invited me over.

To my surprise, Shane answered the door. I'd never been at their house when he was, although I had met him at Life Group. Even though he was quiet, I'd learned to listen whenever he talked, expecting a clean joke, a nugget of wisdom, or a keen insight on life. He and Lauren were a good balance, his temperate spring to her blazing summer.

"Come on in," he said, his copper-brown eyes bright. "Lauren's chomping at the bit to see you."

He led me into the living room. Vanilla citrus wafted from a candle on the coffee table as Chopin played in the background.

Lauren emerged from the guest bedroom. "Celine!" Shane implored her to be careful as she bolted toward me. Give him a few more years with Lauren, and he'd sprout some grey locks on his head.

She hugged me tight. "You look refreshed! Eyes clear, skin glowing. And hair ethereal. When did you start curling it?"

"I figured you'd approve of forest siren over boardroom exec." I touched a curl near my neck. "All with the aid of my hair wand."

She clapped her hands together. "Wait until Garrett sees you." Surprised by the comment, I glanced at Shane. His calm demeanor didn't clarify whether Lauren was pushing Garrett and me together or if Shane approved. "I'm not saying this to hook anybody up," Lauren continued, "but Garrett asked how you've been and complimented you."

"Oh?" My hands tingled.

"I showed him images you texted from Florida. He thought you seemed different."

"Really? In what way?"

"How did he put that? Like all the angst left. He said your serene smile and your mole reminded him of someone. But he dropped the conversation there. He can be a man of few words."

Garrett had noticed my change. When our eyes locked on the Marches' porch, I wondered if he stared because he couldn't believe my transformation.

Switching gears, Lauren talked a million miles an hour about her trip then mentioning there was good news about Garrett. I straightened my posture as she got my full attention. Did something happen on his trip? Did he connect with Miss Portugal?

Lauren had texted me captivating pics from his trip. Every wildlife photo from Arrábida Natural Park revealed his respect for nature and patience to capture the quiet and dramatic moments. His passion to tell meaningful stories showed from the lone pine on the edge of the limestone cliff, the humble fishing boat straying deep into the Atlantic, and the pods of dolphins flipping in the air.

As Lauren rattled on about her trip again, I patted her shoulder and said, "I got bits and pieces of all that. Let's pick one topic to dive into."

She sat on the sofa and motioned me to sit beside her. After I joined her, Shane settled on the armchair nearby.

"Oh, the good news about Garrett," Lauren said. "He survived meeting Ciaran, Presleigh's husband."

"Oh good." So much had happened lately, even our conversation about Garrett shooting Moriah's wedding felt long ago.

"He came over last night. I'm so proud of him. It sounds like he handled being around Presleigh and Ciaran like a champ. So... I've got to slow down." She took a deep breath. "Gare planned the all-day bachelor event. And of course, he packed it full of adventure—rock climbing, rappelling, cliff diving." Lauren shook her head. "Garrett invited Ciaran."

Shane tapped her leg. "It was a nice gesture; otherwise, the guy would've been hanging out by himself."

"I guess," Lauren said, "considering Presleigh threw the bachelorette outing that same day. Anyway, Gare said Ciaran was charismatic and likeable. But I'm not impressed. Ciaran had the audacity to ask how Gare survived wedding planning with Presleigh. How rude! Presleigh and Ciaran deserve each other."

Smiling, Shane said, "Ciaran's question provided Garrett with the best punch line though. Garrett said he didn't survive." Shane glanced at Lauren. "Actually, babe, asking a question like Ciaran's is what I would do if I met one of your exes. Find common ground and tell a joke."

"Strange how men handle delicate situations," I said. If I saw Jordan's girlfriend at a party, I'd give her the cold shoulder. If she approached, I'd let her know how relieved I was to have escaped his abuse. Whatever it took for her to know I was better off.

"I would've confronted him," Lauren said. "Asked why he interfered with my engagement."

"Ladies," Shane said, hand extended. "Let me explain men. We use humor to disarm a situation. Ciaran showed Garrett respect, assessing he could hang. Got it?"

"Not really," Lauren and I said in unison. She gave me a high five. Then she grabbed his hand. "The best part is Presleigh apologized for mishandling the situation when Gare called off their engagement for good. She said she'd wanted to reach out to apologize but was too ashamed of her behavior not just when he called it off but throughout their engagement. Zealous about having the wedding of her dreams, she didn't acknowledge his needs. And she said she didn't regret their relationship."

"Did her apology help?" I asked.

"He appreciated the closure, but seeing her, especially with Ciaran, triggered insecurities. He's going to get counseling at Plumbline and work through issues he assumed were already healed."

"Good for him," I said.

So healthy and mature. Where did this guy come from? Unfortunately, the more I knew about him, the more convinced I was that we were incompatible. I wasn't afraid of heights, but I wasn't into extreme sports. You couldn't pay me to rappel down a mountain relying on just a piece of rope.

Lauren smiled. "Speaking of dating, has seeing Jennifer with Peter softened your heart toward getting back out there? It's been three months."

"Honestly, I'm learning so much about myself it's like getting oriented with a new me. I'm unsure if I'm ready to date yet." I shrugged, hoping she'd understand.

"That's your cue to let go, babe," Shane said.

She frowned. "Don't rain on my parade." She turned toward me. "Don't worry. I'll work hard at not setting you up with Garrett, unless it's obvious you're meant for each other."

I raised my brows. She was definitely compelled to put Garrett and me together. "Obvious to me or to you?" I asked.

Lauren giggled. "Touché."

Later that night, as I sipped on herbal tea in the Haven, I shared with Jennifer what I'd discovered about Garrett's trip to Portugal.

"Suddenly, Lauren's pushing us together. But I'm unsure if I'm his type. I don't know what his type is. I guess what I'm trying to say..." I exhaled. "I don't want to act like a swooning teenager, especially since that mentality got me in trouble with Jordan. I fell hard, losing my judgment."

"Jordan was more about your ambition than your hormones. From what Peter's shared, Garrett's a godly man—big difference there. Why not enjoy having feelings toward a great catch?"

"All I catch is myself wondering what he's doing. Imagining him shooting wildlife in the mountains. And his transparent blue eyes staring into mine." I covered my face, embarrassed.

"Should I prescribe a Garrett antidote?"

"I'll say this since I'm thinking it anyway. If anything does materialize, the four of us need to double-date."

Jennifer laughed. "Peter already called it. And I haven't said anything about your interest, but the other night, he mentioned how you'd be ideal for Garrett."

"He did?" I sat up straight.

"Said you're a unique blend of creativity, pragmatism, and zeal—all traits complementary to Garrett's. Of course, I had to probe for clarification... Men!" She rolled her eyes. "He said Garrett would give anyone the shirt off his back, so he needed someone pragmatic to stop him from giving away the house. He's also time blind, so he needs someone punctual to help him make it to his own wedding." We laughed.

"Considering what Lauren said about his spontaneity," I said, "maybe Peter isn't far off."

"Here's the kicker," Jennifer added. "He has a labradoodle."

I raised my arms. "I have to marry him now."

Jennifer elbowed me. "I advise you to wait three months before asking to walk his dog."

"No promises."

We giggled and latched our pinkie fingers anyway, like in grade school.

CHAPTER 64
SEPTEMBER 14

Glancing out Monroe's window, I reminded myself to slow down, appreciate the beauty of the season, and embrace change. If anyone had told me that attitude would become mine within four months' time, I wouldn't have believed them. So much had occurred. Between recording the highlights and adding to my gratitude list, I'd filled two journals.

The Celine from four months ago wouldn't have welcomed all my new extracurricular activities. Between the D-group and Life Group, Aimee's pizza night and the boys' activities, and a ten-week codependency class and church, my calendar was as full as a college student's. And I had a ball participating in a Q&A for Bill's marketing class at TU. The eager students reminded me of myself from my university days. Giving back felt rewarding.

After wrapping up work around five, I stopped by the condo to change before heading to Aimee's for pizza night. When I entered the condo, everything was still. I didn't see anyone. As I headed upstairs, Jennifer spoke.

"Celine... is that you?"

I turned toward the couch, where she laid on her back, hand covering her eyes.

"Yes, I'm changing clothes and headed to Aimee's."

"Do you have a few minutes to chat?" She sat up and patted the seat next to her.

"Sure." I sat, wondering if she was under the weather. "Is everything okay?"

"Yeah, I just have something important to discuss with you."

"Oh?" Instinctively, I clutched my heart. Did she break up with Peter?

Her chest heaved up and down. "First, tell me about your day."

I gave a summary as dull as a butter knife. That way, she wouldn't inquire further, keeping me in suspense. "So, what's your news?"

She took a deep breath. "Some of Sienna's friends live in Jenks, so she's been begging me for a few months to move there. She wants a dog, a backyard, and a neighborhood pool. But I've kept it in my heart, unsure if I wanted to move right now, especially since I like the low maintenance of the condo. Even though I hadn't told anyone I might be considering a house, a Realtor friend called early this morning and said I came into her mind last night. She asked if I'd be interested in buying her house in Jenks. Sienna and I visited it this afternoon, and it checks all the boxes."

Screech! Whop. Jennifer's news had the effect of a minor collision.

She bit her lower lip. "I would've said something sooner about Sienna wanting to move, but she's always saying that she wants this and that. Like kids do... Anyway, I'm giving myself the weekend to consider it, but I'll probably let the Realtor know by Monday."

I wanted to say something, but words weren't coming.

"Celine, I'm sorry this happened so fast."

"When do I need to move?" I asked, still reeling.

"If all goes well, within forty-five days. Unless..." She rubbed her temples. "A Realtor friend always told me if I put my condo up for sale, she'd buy it. I haven't contacted her yet, in case you'd be interested."

I closed my eyes and laid my head on the back of the sofa. "I don't know."

"If you're not interested, my friend would pay cash. I could sell this condo within two weeks then pay her rent until I close on the house."

Kaboom! The impact of her plans escalated into a head-on collision. I opened my eyes. "Two weeks from today?"

"No, from the time we sign a contract."

She laid her hand on my shoulder. "I hate to pressure you, but I'd like to close on the condo first, so I could apply the payout to my down payment on the house. You're welcome to move into the house with us. Or if my friend wants to lease the condo, you could rent it and buy yourself time to look for another place."

In shock, I envisioned flying dollar bills migrating out of my bank account. "This is a major pileup." Though I'd tried to just think them, the words had come out.

"Just move in with us until you find a place." Jennifer was too perky, as though I wouldn't be inconvenienced by a move to Jenks.

"You need an answer by Monday, then?" I asked.

"If I put an offer on the house."

"K." I glanced at the wall clock. "I need to get ready and go to Aimee's." I stood and started upstairs. A little miffed Jennifer hadn't warned me about a possible move, I was still grateful she took me in without a second thought. I stopped after a few steps. "I'm happy for you."

She nodded as if relieved. "Thank you."

After pizza and a board game at Aimee's, I asked if I could talk to her and Heath alone. The boys scurried upstairs, chattering about a video game.

"What's going on?" Aimee asked.

I dove into Jennifer's news. "I'm unsure what I want to do. I prefer not moving, especially since my business is rebuilding. Having lived in condos since college, I'd like a backyard for a dog and entertaining."

Aimee sat deep in thought. Heath drummed his fingers on the game table between us. "Would you be content paying rent in the condo for a year before shopping for a house?"

His idea was one I'd thought of, with a twist. "After paying rent for over ten years without anything to show for it, I want to own my next place. I could buy the condo and lease it when I found a house."

Aimee narrowed her gaze. "Do you want to invest time as a landlord?"

"I'd hire a property manager." My shoulders slumped. Aimee was on the right track. I'd rather build my business than trouble myself with a real-estate investment.

"When does Jennifer need to know?" she asked.

"Probably by Monday or Tuesday."

"You could look at houses to see what's out there," Heath offered. "That might help you decide what you want to do."

"I've got so much going on. I'm not thrilled about adding house shopping to the list."

"How about we ask God to reveal what's in your heart?" Aimee asked.

I smiled. "I'd like that."

After the prayer, I didn't get a warm feeling or an answer. Not that I expected an audible voice. I'd just hoped for an inclination toward one option.

"Whatever decision you make, we support you," Aimee said as she and Heath walked me to their door.

"And I know a great agent who'll give you a deal on insurance, especially if you bundle." Heath winked.

I laughed. "I better get the family discount."

Back at the condo, I had a difficult time falling asleep. Hopefully, by Monday, I'd have a sense of direction.

CHAPTER 65
SEPTEMBER 17

While I was at the office Monday morning, Dad wanted to FaceTime. Since his anxiety attack, he called only once or twice a week. Now, I eagerly awaited our chats since he didn't offer unsolicited advice but reflectively listened.

After we caught up on our days, I told him about my housing conundrum.

"What would you do if money wasn't an issue?" he asked.

"I'd buy a house."

"Maman and I have been talking, and we want to visit around mid-October through Thanksgiving. How about we look at houses together then? See what's out there?"

My heart leapt, knowing both my parents would visit for that long. "If I leased the condo, you two could have the upstairs."

He looked away, mouthed something I couldn't hear or make out, then turned back to me. "Maman just came inside. Can I call you in an hour?"

"Of course."

Once I hung up, Jennifer texted.

I texted that I was on my way then went outside. She was on the phone and jumped when I knocked on her car window. She hung up and opened her door.

"Sorry. That was the Realtor interested in purchasing the condo. I'm buying the house, for starters, and wanted to talk to you in person—"

"Must be serious." Was she here to talk me into renting the condo?

"The Realtor's son wants to live in the condo, so it's not a rent option."

I took a step back as if the ground beneath me shifted. "Narrows my choices."

"I'm sorry. Like I said, if you don't want to buy the condo, you can move in with us. I'm meeting Peter at the new house now, if you'd like to see it." She flashed a wide smile. Was she just excited for Peter to see it? Or did she also hope I might remain a roommate?

"Maybe this weekend I can give it my stamp of approval," I said. "I've got a full schedule today."

We hugged before she left. I returned to Monroe and dove into work, not wanting to consider my options. Just as I got into a steady flow, Dad FaceTimed.

He and Maman sat with big smiles on the sofa, flush like conjoined twins and slightly farther from the screen than Dad had been earlier. He must've set his phone on a table or tripod. Uh-oh— they prepared for this call.

"What's up?" I asked.

"We have a proposition," Dad said. Maman clapped.

I flinched. "K?"

"If you decide to buy a house, we'd enjoy going house shopping with you. And if you find something, we'll cover the down payment." Dad nodded as if urging me to agree.

"With Père's health scare, we never paid your rent on the office," Maman said.

"That's too generous. I'm making it on my own." I curled my toes. I'd been making strides toward independence and didn't want a handout.

Dad leaned toward the screen. "But—"

Maman tapped his shoulder, so he leaned back, pursing his lips.

"This has nothing to do with your inability to pay. It's about our desire to bless you, *mon petit chou*." She blew me a kiss.

"But don't expect us to pay your mortgage." Dad wagged his finger.

I grinned. "Using reverse psychology?"

"Well?" he said.

Jordan's taunting about accepting handouts from Dad echoed through my mind, but his opinions were dung, overruled by something said in my codependency class. The leader said that long, dark corridors could lead to unexpected rooms of healthier relationships. She emphasized applying tools, receiving inner healing, and awakening to lies and replacing them with truth. Recognizing what drew us to these toxic relationships was an important first step toward growth.

I smiled. "I'll think about whether I want a house now, and if I do, I'll accept the offer."

"We'll take that," Dad said.

My heart swelled. "I can't wait to spend a month with you two."

After I got off the phone, I resumed working. Two hours later, I went outside, needing fresh air. The geraniums in the navy pot Maman had bought and placed near the office entrance were still ruby red and happy. I took in the neighborhood sights as cars passed, people entered shops, and pedestrians strolled by. Life continued no matter what we endured. And I needed to take the next step myself.

I called Jennifer. After a few niceties, I asked, "Ready to find me a house?"

"Music to my ears," she said.

On Saturday, I toured her new house. Seeing it helped me to accept that she and Sienna were moving, especially because the home suited them perfectly. Its three thousand square feet gave them space to grow. An enclosed patio overlooked a manicured backyard, a wrought-iron fence, and a view of a neighborhood pond with a fountain shooting water high into the air.

I was tempted to move in with them. But I'd find my own paradise soon.

CHAPTER 66
SEPTEMBER 21

At every D-group, the breakthrough moments shared by the other ladies illuminated how they were light-years ahead of me spiritually. While on board with Jesus, I struggled to follow his ways. Mostly, I got hung up on things like doing unto others as I'd like done to me, especially when driving on the highway. Balancing a work ethic with overzealous ambition, I couldn't even begin to address all Jesus said about not serving mammon.

As we sat in Viviana's sitting room Friday afternoon, Aimee shared how God was restoring her and Heath's marriage. Through counseling and participating in D-group, she was learning to embrace marital challenges with grace.

Moriah said she appreciated our support as she transitioned into married life. She reported growing closer to God, especially leaning on him to love and respect her husband.

It was my turn to share struggles and successes. "I don't have much to say, except I want to find a house when my parents visit."

"You look sad," Viviana commented. "Do you feel unsafe to share further?"

"I just..." I couldn't say it.

"Do you mind if I talk to Celine alone?" Aimee asked the group.

"Don't mind at all." Viviana stood.

"We can help clean the kitchen," Moriah offered.

Viviana led the three other ladies out of the sitting room.

"What's going on?" Aimee held my hand.

"I'm not offering much to the group. I hate feeling like I'm so far behind everyone else."

Aimee pushed a strand of hair off my face. Her soft touch reminded me of our childhood, when she'd fix my hair before church. "You're missing the truth. You're catching up on discovering scripture, but a spiritual life is less about having lots of knowledge than about living what you do know. I'm proud of the difficult choices you've made to get to this point."

I held her hand gratefully. "I needed that reminder. I'm afraid I'm not growing spiritually like you ladies. The other day, I cussed at someone for cutting me off on the highway. And this week, since I wanted to land an account badly, I exaggerated to a potential client about my experience working with mid-level companies."

"Seriously?" Aimee half-smiled. "The old Celine wouldn't have experienced conviction for lying, much less exaggerating."

That was true. "I did call him back and admitted I only serviced two mid-level clients as a consultant but had worked with several at the agency. He appreciated my clarification and wanted someone with more experience. Kind of stung."

"Sorry. I know how much acquiring clients means to you."

"I'll find another."

"I don't doubt it." She nudged my arm. "Hey, what about the great call you made last week in attending John's game?" I hadn't hesitated to take a rain check on a dinner with a prospective client, and I felt rewarded when Peter brought Jennifer and Sienna to the game, so we could all root for my nephew.

After giving Aimee a hug, I pulled away with a half frown. "I didn't land that client either, but it was worth it. Even though I nearly lost my voice cheering in the stands." We laughed.

Letting the potential client go was worth witnessing John throw for three touchdowns, including the game winner. I high-fived Aimee and Jennifer each time, and it was great to see Peter with Jennifer and Sienna. He was a smart man to take an interest in Jennifer's friends. If his relationship with Jennifer didn't already have my enthusiastic vote of approval, it certainly did now.

How much would I have missed if I hadn't invited Aimee to join the D-group? The friendship I longed for as an adult had finally materialized.

After D-group, I drove Lauren to her home. As we pulled away from the Marches' house, she said, "Remind me I can't get involved with Garrett's decision-making."

"What's happened?" I asked. "Does he want to move to Portugal?"

"No, it's about his love life. I'm so tempted to set you two up, especially because he's struggling with resurfaced rejection, unworthiness, and grief over not being married."

The sharpness of my heart's ache for him caught me off guard. "Is counseling helping?"

"Yes, especially to process his feelings. He's such a feeler that his emotions overwhelm him at times. So, I see the pain on his face."

A principle I learned in my codependency class tapped me on the shoulder. "Pain isn't bad to experience."

"I know, but I want him to enjoy a healthy relationship and get loved well by the right woman." She paused. "I *need* prayer because just as he's longing to get married, he's going on this three-month sacred cleanse."

I shook my head. "What's that?"

"For the next three months, he's abstaining from three things distracting him from going deeper with God. The first is dating."

"I haven't heard of anyone fasting from dating." I narrowed my brows. "Too bad I wasn't on that fast when I met Jordan."

Lauren looked at me with wide eyes. "Alright... That puts Garrett's fast into perspective. He did assure me fasting will help temper his emotions, help him gain freedom from throwing himself into any relationship like he did with Presleigh. Makes sense. It's just... He's also avoiding social media and chocolate."

"Oh, not chocolate." I covered my mouth, suppressing a laugh.

"Pray he can stick to the fast without too many withdrawal symptoms," Lauren said. "I don't want him coping with something else as a substitute."

I winced. "Of course. Is he doing the fast with others?" Just what were the dynamics of a three-month cleanse?

"His buddy in Colorado is leading the cleanse. Everyone's meeting at a retreat center next week to launch the challenge. They equip participants to walk through different mile markers with God and each other, and they have partners to hold each other accountable. Andrew, Garrett's best friend, is his partner."

The support impressed me. "I'll be praying... After I moved out of my ex's place, Jennifer advised me to wait three months before making any major decisions. In hindsight, I realize I needed at least three months to cleanse my mind of old thinking. This might be the best path for Garrett."

"I think so, but I don't want him to carry guilt if he can't follow through even with the chocolate."

"If he succumbs, he can try again the next day, right?"

She extended her hand, tapping my arm. "Thanks for the wisdom."

Her thank-you ringing in my ears, I entertained the idea that I had something to offer after all. While that notion encouraged me, Garrett's fast and my immediate thoughts about it intrigued me. Three months would give me time to become healthier before he was back on the dating scene. But would he then have a clearer mind for seeing incompatibilities between us?

CHAPTER 67
OCTOBER 7

I spent Sunday evening at Lauren's. After dinner, we sat in the living room listening to Johnnyswim's song, "First Try" pipe through the speakers. Lauren and Shane sat on the love seat. I laid my head on the back of the adjacent armchair, eyes closed, as I sang along quietly about knowing what I need.

Once the song finished, Lauren spoke. "We have something to ask you, Celine."

I opened my eyes and sat straighter. Shane turned off the music. She handed me a narrow box with a velvet ribbon, smiling so wide I could see most of her teeth. "Here."

"Is this an early Christmas gift?" I imagined Lauren saw something for me and couldn't wait.

She shrugged, so I opened it. Beneath the layer of tissue paper inside lay a thin, silver cross necklace. I held it up and smiled at Lauren, appreciating the symbol of my renewed faith. "Thank you."

"That's not all... I can't believe I've kept this secret for weeks." She exhaled. "I'm pregnant!"

My jaw dropped. I stood and walked to her. She got up from the love seat, and I gave her a tight hug. "I'm so happy for you.

Congrats!" My heart beat fast as it occurred to me that I'd witnessed a miracle. While Lauren and Shane had seen the fertility doctor, Lauren hadn't tried any medicine yet.

I returned to the armchair, Lauren to the love seat. "You're a month along?" I asked.

"Yes. I got tested about three weeks ago because I felt off and I missed my period. We had our first natal visit last week. Outside of family, you're the only one I've told."

I shook my head, unsure what to say. "Wow." I stared at the necklace.

"After the gender reveal, I'll have it engraved with our baby's name."

"Okay." I gave her a side-eye that asked for explanation. Why would she want her child's name on my necklace? It was too big to be the baby's necklace.

Lauren grabbed a tissue and wiped her eyes, so I looked to Shane for the explanation.

"Give her a minute," he said.

Lauren broke out in spontaneous laughter. Once she regained composure, she looked at me. "Will you be the godmother?" She exhaled. "I got it out! It's so exciting to think we'll have godparents for our child!" She hugged Shane.

Stunned, I touched the cross. "I'm unsure if I'm qualified. I know nothing about being a godparent."

"You won't be handling all the load," Lauren said. "Garrett's going to be the godfather. He's sooo excited! He's going to be a terrific uncle."

Shane waved his hand. "Babe, please explain the responsibilities and give Celine a chance to consider them."

Lauren calmed. "We want your support as our child's spiritual covering. You'd attend her baby dedication, support her with prayer, and be present in her life. That's why we'll put her name on the cross, as a reminder to pray for her." She glanced at Shane. "Or him."

"I don't want her decorating the nursery for a girl if we have a boy," Shane said. "I'm looking forward to either." He held Lauren's hand as he looked at me.

"I'm beyond honored you'd ask me... But I'd like you to reconsider and ask someone else. I'm not the most qualified in your community. It's only recently that I'm following Christ."

Lauren extended her free hand, so I grabbed it. "We prayed about this decision... When I first met you, I saw a bright light around your head. God spotlighted you, revealing you'd play a special role in my life, though I would've never guessed how dear of a friend you've become. And I value your authentic faith journey. We're not looking for spiritual giants, just someone with a heart for our family. I know you'll love and support our child well."

"That's good to know." I squeezed Lauren's hand lightly before letting go.

She tapped her belly. "I can't wait to have this baby. Can you believe I'm finally going to be a mother? And I can finally decorate a nursery for *our* baby!" Her eyes sparkled as she smiled at Shane. I'd have to pray for his patience, as she was likely to wear it out just over the nursery.

Lauren clapped. "You'll be the best godmother. I can hardly contain myself. You and Gare will be amazing together. You two can plan the gender reveal party! No... I want to organize that. But you could know the gender and arrange the actual reveal. I'm struggling with having to wait for that until the first of the year."

"Do you promise you won't badger me to reveal the gender after you give us the sealed report?" I gave Lauren the stink eye.

She frowned. "It'll be sooo hard, but you are too obstinate to give it away. Garrett might, so you'll need to remind him to not let the cat out of the bag, because he doesn't want me to boss him about anything anymore."

Shane laughed. "Celine, please pray for Garrett's patience."

"I think we'll need to pray for each other," I said.

"I'm sad he's on a three-month fast. I want to double-date with you two so bad! Oh my gosh! It'd be perfect if the godparents were dating when our baby's born."

Shane touched her knee. "Let things happen naturally."

"Only for the time being. When it's the new year, I'll drop some hints."

Shane's steely brown eyes penetrated Lauren's. "We'll talk about this later."

I was grateful Shane was tapping on Lauren's brakes. Was I ready to become friends with Garrett soon? Now I'd have to be. So, I'd need God to take my attraction to Garrett away or assure me that everything involving Garrett and me would work out.

CHAPTER 68
OCTOBER 20

Growing up, I had a crepe myrtle outside my bedroom window. I called that large bush in our front yard Beatrice. When I was four, I grabbed one of her pink fluffy buds and ate it, expecting it to taste like cotton candy. I nearly gagged. How could something that colorful taste like glue?

Every day, I'd sit on the window seat of my bedroom and tell Beatrice my secrets, my fears, my joys. When lightning struck and split her into two pieces, I wanted to move to a different bedroom.

Beatrice was on my mind as I looked out my bedroom window on this mild October twentieth morning. I'd been living at Aimee's since the first, when Jennifer closed on the condo. Although Jennifer paid the Realtor rent until she closed on her new house on the fifteenth, I hadn't wanted to be in the way while she and Sienna were packing.

Later today, my parents, Jennifer, and I spent the afternoon touring houses. As we got into Jennifer's SUV after the tenth place, I threw up my hands. "This is harder than I thought. No place gives me that intangible sensation of home." I looked at Maman. "Like the aroma of your simmering Garbure soup filling the house. Or like sitting on a a porch swing as the wind blows lightly on my face."

"Sometimes you need to tour several houses to narrow down what you want," Dad said from the back seat.

"Exactly what I tell clients." Jennifer looked at me as she tapped the steering wheel. "Like kissing a bunch of frogs to find your prince. Is your mind too overwhelmed to continue looking today?"

"Yes. Are there more open houses tomorrow?"

"There are." Jennifer started her SUV and pulled out of the driveway.

I was naive, assuming we'd find the house in one day. Everyone knew that patience wasn't my virtue. But I didn't want to spend days or weeks house hunting. I had too much going on.

As we rounded the street corner, I noticed an Open House sign in front of a two-story, English cottage.

I pointed toward the driveway. "Turn in there! I want to check that listing."

"There?" Jennifer pointed to the house.

"Yes."

"Oh!" Maman said. "Look at the porch swing."

With the slight breeze blowing, the Nantucket-style swing moved slightly forward and back, as if someone sat there.

Jennifer pulled in next to a white sedan. "Let's hope the car belongs to the Realtors and not the owners. The Open House was over at four."

The car clock said it was 4:15 p.m.

"It's still early, so maybe," Dad said. "Otherwise, we can look at the listing tomorrow."

A fashionable couple emerged from the house, holding hands. We got out and Jennifer introduced us, then asked the husband-and-wife real estate team if we could take a tour since I was a serious buyer. They agreed.

As we walked toward the porch, sweet honeysuckle perfumed the air. In the entryway, I elbowed Dad and tilted my head to the left, where French doors opened into a study. We approached the room. The bay window showed the front yard, the street, and, most important, a fuchsia crepe myrtle. I walked into the study and stood at the window, gazing at the resplendent reminder of childhood.

Jennifer poked her head through the study doorway. "The Realtors are offering us a tour now. They can answer any questions you might have."

Dad and I followed her and the husband-and-wife team past the staircase and into a spacious living room on the right. The wife pointed out details like the white tiled fireplace, updated to accommodate wood and gas. Even though my nostalgic side wanted to burn wood, the pragmatist wanted the cleaner option of gas. Check!

The kitchen, the most remodeled space, sat in the back of the house, closed off from the living room. I'd host dinners here, fixing crudités on the antique oak table, grabbing seasonings from the white Shaker-style cabinets. The black-and-white diamond-tiled flooring reminded me of The Mayo Hotel. Check, check!

All the bedrooms were upstairs. The floor-to-ceiling windows in the renovated master faced the backyard. I'd put a window seat there. Across from the bed was a fireplace, perfect for cuddling if my future included a husband.

The ivory claw-foot tub in the en suite bathroom reminded me of a tub Nana and Papa had. I was giddy when the Realtor explained the owners had restored the original tub. I'd light a candle and enjoy an Epsom salt bath.

The backyard was the clincher. Maman hugged me. "Look at that southern magnolia! You'll have the most gorgeous white blooms."

Even though I was blocking Dad behind me, I couldn't move. The magnolia, placed in the center of the yard like the tree of life, was magnificent despite having shed its blossoms for winter. How glorious it must be in the spring and summer!

I walked ahead, laughing as Maman gawked at the hydrangea bushes along the house, the garden beds, and the honeysuckle hanging near the privacy fence. The house called her name and mine.

After the tour, we drove to my office. Dad and Maman sat across from Jennifer and me in the conference room. Jennifer fanned documents on the table and asked what I liked and disliked.

"I want to put in an offer on the last house now," I said.

She stopped jotting notes on her tablet. "Are you sure? Do you want to tour it again with a more discerning eye?"

I shook my head. "It's mine. Hopefully an inspection will find any issues that need addressing. I want to put in an offer before it slips away."

"Will you look at the disclosure form before we draw up a contract?" She narrowed her gaze.

I looked around. I'd rented this space after only seeing it once. "I'll look while you draw up the contract, if it'll make you feel better." I grabbed the disclosure form the sellers' agents had provided.

"What do you think, Dad?" I asked, confident he loved the house like I did.

He rested his left foot on top of his right thigh. "I'd like to tour it again. The floors creaked. A few windows looked aged. How old is the roof? And when was the house built?"

Jennifer handed him the flyer from the open house. "In 1935. According to the disclosures, it was renovated in 1975 and 2005."

"You might have structural issues because she's just old." Dad crossed his arms, so I crossed mine.

"Its age is why I want it. Modern homes won't have custom features such as the casement window or the azure door with the mailbox slot and the diamond-shaped leaded pane."

"How much do you want to offer?" Jennifer asked.

"What are the comps?" Dad asked.

She listed them off, along with recent sales, then handed me her tablet with the information. The more Dad and Jennifer talked business—talk I normally enjoyed—the more irritated I became.

"No matter what the comps are, it's my house." I glared at Dad, then checked myself. Had chilling and trusting Dad flown south?

"I just want to make sure we get a fair price," he told me. "We don't want to pay more than we should, considering the possibility of repairs." He looked at Jennifer.

"The sellers have priced it competitively," she said. "I'd —"

"Dad..." I waited until he looked at me before finishing. "Let's offer five thousand below their asking price now. They can always counter."

"Alright." He scowled.

"The house is within my budget. I've replaced all seven clients I lost, so I can afford this. And I just acquired the Marches' landscaper." I flashed a smile.

"Add the renovations to the final cost," he said.

Maman patted his arm. "She can afford it now that we're helping financially."

"Can you give us a moment, Jennifer?" Dad asked.

"Sure." She grabbed her tablet and left, shutting the conference door behind her.

Dad wasted no time. "I don't doubt your intentions, but I need to know this is what you want. I like the features and character, but are you willing to tackle a high-maintenance home?"

I leaned toward him. "If I add a contingency where I can opt out after the inspection, will that give you peace of mind?"

"Can you give your dad and me a moment to talk?" Maman asked.

Not saying anything, I left and joined Jennifer on the love seat in the sitting room. "What do you think of the house?" I asked her.

"It hits all the top items on your list, although these older homes require maintenance. I'll get the best inspector to shake it around a bit. But what matters is you want that house."

"Thank you."

After about five minutes, Maman appeared, asking us to return. Once I walked into the conference room, Dad stood. Jennifer and I returned to our seats.

He cleared his throat. "I'm trying to protect you from anything that could go wrong, but I've got to trust God and you."

"Thanks." I looked at Jennifer. "Let's get this offer in."

Within twenty-four hours, the sellers agreed to my asking price. As I waited for the inspection, I made a renovations list in a computer file.

> Add deck (hire Qwinn)
> Paint walls (hire Javier)
> Repair fence (hire Kris's team)
> Remove wood paneling (hire Qwinn)
> Clean hardwood floors (hire Nathan)

Oh boy. My fingers crossed. I hoped the inspection wouldn't require too many repairs, because I wanted to invest my money in renovations.

CHAPTER 69
NOVEMBER 3

Late afternoon, just Dad and I visited Woodward Park. We hadn't spent much time alone since my parents arrived in town.

A cool breeze carried the redolence of fall's final breath through the park. I always enjoyed the musky amber aroma, evoking memories of family campfires, apple cider, and cashmere cardigans. Leaves of auburn red, pumpkin orange, and burnished gold danced on the catwalk of branches above us. The chorus of migrating warblers, grey mockingbirds, and black-capped chickadees filled the air. Fall was showcasing its finest collections.

As we neared the rocky terrain of the woodlands area, Dad nearly tripped on a stone step.

"Do you need to sit?" I asked, grabbing his arm.

"Wait until we reach the pond."

As we crossed the bridge, he held onto my arm, supporting me like old times. Approaching the lily pond, I remembered my first impression of Garrett, taking photos of an uneasy bride. That moment seemed longer ago than six months.

I followed Dad to the bench where I'd sat on that day. Seated next to him, I leaned my head on his shoulder and closed my eyes, listening to his heart beating like a clock.

After a short while, I opened my eyes. His were closed, his face serene. Not wanting to interrupt his meditation, I stood and strolled near the pond. Garrett consumed my thoughts. His intense focus on the bride, his affirmations easing her nerves, his steady demeanor that lacked urgency even when I got in the way.

I rejoined Dad at the bench.

"What's on your mind?" he asked. "You're restless, although nothing compared to when you first came to Florida."

"I've got a lot going on."

"Until the inspection report comes through, you'll have to sit and wait."

I shrugged. "That's not it."

"What is it?" He turned to face me squarely.

"Remember our father-daughter dates?" I asked.

"You always chose fine dining, saying those restaurants were where successful women ate."

I laughed. "I asked Nana where we should eat. She gave me a list. And I loved going dress shopping with her, so I'd look my best."

He touched my cheek, something Nana did. "You remind me so much of her, classy and poised."

"Where did I go wrong? On our dates, you demonstrated how a gentleman should treat me. You also talked about adult subjects like I was your peer. Do you remember? You'd converse about college, career, other life choices."

"I didn't realize you were paying such close attention."

I waved him off with my hand. Although I no longer heard most of Jordan's accusations in my mind, I couldn't shake them when it came to my appeal. "What if Jordan's right?"

"About what?" He narrowed his eyes.

"He told me that no man would want me." I held my breath, so I wouldn't cry.

"He's a liar." He kicked a pebble with his shoe. "I hate what he did to your confidence. You never doubted yourself with men before."

"He repeated that lie so many times during our last six to nine months of living together. At first, I didn't buy what he was selling, but hearing the same words over and over wore down my resilience until I started believing them. The fact that he cheated only reinforced the lie." A wilted brown leaf fell on my boots.

"I'm proud of how you've invested in your mental health these past six months. Keep focusing on truth. You'll wake up one day and realize you've buried Jordan's words six feet under."

"What if I'm rejected by a man I want?" I wrapped my arms around my chest.

Dad rested his hand on my knee. "Is there someone?"

"I'm kind of obsessed with someone I hardly know. Lauren's younger brother, Garrett."

He smiled. "Really?"

"This past spring I stumbled on him shooting a photo session here in the park. He looked so confident and content in his element that I couldn't stop staring. And he's the guy who rescued me at the bar."

"Maman mentioned talking to him on the plane."

"Maybe I'm lonely. It might be time to date."

"You're healing," Dad said. "After meeting Lauren, I can't imagine her brother being less than honorable."

My parents attended Life Group and church with me. Although I wasn't surprised how well everyone hit it off, I was still overjoyed my parents embraced my new community.

I tucked my arm under Dad's. "What should I do?"

"Take it a day at time and work on understanding how amazing you are. You've got to know that your worth comes from being you. No man can validate or define you."

I glanced at the grass. "I'm working on that."

"If Garrett's not interested, my first instinct is to say he's ignorant." Dad frowned. "My second is that he's just not the one for you. Whoever you end up with, know he's the one who's striking gold."

"Thanks."

"I can ask around The Villages to find someone with an eligible son or grandson. Someone close to your age."

"That's unnecessary. I'll use a dating app or speed date."

"I can't help you there. At times like these, I feel old."

"I just needed a sounding board. You're doing great."

The breeze blew through his receding bangs. "Seems like only yesterday you were my little girl, standing by the door every night when I came home from work. You'd squeeze my leg, then raise your arms, expecting me to hold you. When I asked what you wanted, you'd say, 'Tell me I'm beautiful, Daddy. Say it, Daddy.' "

"And you'd tell Aimee and me that we were the most beautiful, creative, and kind daughters in all the universe."

He touched my chin with his index finger. "Life can knock confidence out from under your feet, but it doesn't change the truth. Beauty forged in the heat of iron radiates more."

"Thanks." I gripped his hand.

Maman called him, wondering where we were. While I stared at decomposed leaves collected on the fading grass like stacked bones in an ossuary, Dad explained he lost track of time.

We headed back to Aimee's, dead brown leaves crunching and flattening under our feet, reminding me of the past seasons that were gone. Yet, those seasons still impacted the ground below, providing a protective layer over the soil and releasing carbons necessary for plant growth. Could I accept death to what had been, so my past could nourish what was to come?

CHAPTER 70
NOVEMBER 27

Since I closed on my house the Tuesday after Thanksgiving, I took the day off. My parents, deciding to extend their stay in Oklahoma until December, accompanied me to the closing. We'd all fly to Florida together for Christmas, and I'd return to Tulsa with Aimee and her family just before New Year's.

Holding house keys in my right hand and the sale contract in my left felt like redemption. I posted a carousel of pics on my social, starting with me gripping the keys at closing, ending with me standing in my front yard and pretending to eat a flower from my crepe myrtle. My exhilaration was evident in the caption.

Bought a house today! A 1930s cottage with original flooring, fireplace, and claw-foot tub. Some renovating but maintaining classic elements. Tune in later for before and after pics. Which room is my favorite? Guess in the comments. #midtownTulsa #Tulsamarketing #digitalmarketing #MonroeConsulting #Tulsabusinessowner

Having a project where I could collaborate with clients and post my renovation progress on my social helped me embrace not being able to move into the house right away. I was grateful to continue living with Aimee.

Leading up to the closing, Lauren and I created a vision board for each room of my new home. She immediately started recommending decor in transitional style at locally owned shops. I gave Maman and Aimee the task of picking up these reserved items and bringing them to the house. I'd wait on the furniture. With Lauren and my hectic schedule, we hadn't made final decisions on that front.

After the closing, I dropped Dad off, so he could get a jump start on the renovations while I picked up lattes and French pastries. When I returned to the house, Dad and Lauren were in the backyard, so I summoned them to the kitchen.

We sat around the antique table. Lauren and I enjoying our *pain au chocolat*, while Dad, operating in high gear, dove into listing necessary repairs. "The roof needs to be replaced."

I calculated costs in my head. "There are higher priorities on my list. I need Kris's team to repair the fence and Qwinn's to renovate the house and install a composite deck. Once I add cleaning the fireplaces, painting walls, and varnishing the staircase, I'm spending nearly all my reno budget."

"Unglamorous repairs like a roof and windows are items you don't want to consider when first buying a home," Dad said. "But they become major headaches when water leaks onto your hardwood floors. Or when your heating and air bills skyrocket because you can't cool or warm your house efficiently."

"I'll replace the roof and windows in a year or two," I said. "I want to spend my money transforming my house into a sanctuary."

Lauren pointed to the wall shared between the kitchen and dining room. "Do you want the contractor to remove walls, so the living, dining, and kitchen areas are open?"

I shook my head. "I prefer the closed-off style. It retains the look of the thirties, and the rooms will stay quieter and more private."

"Open spaces allow for more air circulating when you're hosting guests," Dad said. "And when you have a family, you can see what your children are doing if you're in another room."

"Exactly!" Lauren chimed. "If you're fixing dinner, your husband and children can interact with you if they're in the living room."

I glanced at Lauren. "I'm single and have no idea if I'll marry." I frowned. I didn't mean I didn't want to marry, but I felt cornered by the family-related comments.

She wrapped her arm around my shoulder. "I know a guy."

Dad winked. Was he hinting to Lauren that I liked Garrett or was the wink meant for me? Either scenario was awkward. I didn't want Lauren assuming I was obsessing over her brother; otherwise, she might try to set us up before his dating fast was over. Or worse, blurt to him that I was attracted.

"If I'm reclining in your living room," she said, "I'd enjoy visiting with you if you're cooking in the kitchen."

"I can open rooms later. For now, I want a composite deck for entertaining. I'll put a grill there, string Edison lights along the railing, and install a gate to protect your baby." I tilted my head, hoping Lauren would side with me.

"Let's do something productive," Dad said. He hadn't touched his croissant but had finished his latte. Like Jordan, Dad spoke the language of action and results. As I watched him stand, I flinched, recognizing that trait as one reason I was attracted to my ex.

Thankfully, with Dad's panic attack and my setback, we were learning action wasn't always the answer. Contemplation and patience were as necessary. Dad wasn't in a patient gear right now though, and I didn't mind. He seemed to enjoy being useful.

"How about a compromise?" Lauren said, still sitting. "Replace the windows and roof but wait on the deck. You can use furniture, stepping stones, and cypress or tall shrubs to create a cozy sitting area outside. It'd be much cheaper than a composite deck."

"Maybe." My head spun, my mind now unsure what I wanted most.

"At the end of the day, it's up to you," she said. "I'm offering options to help you get what you want, especially the most important items on your list." She touched her belly.

"I know. It's just all overwhelming."

Lauren stood. "How about we regroup by walking from room to room and reviewing the design choices you wanted?"

"That's a good idea." I grabbed my phone, where I stored my design notes.

Dad patted my back. "I'll tour the house while reviewing the inspection report. There are minor repairs, like replacing outlets to conform to GFI standards. I can make a list of loose doorknobs to tighten or replace, fixtures that need new light bulbs. Things like that."

"Thanks, Dad."

Armed with a clipboard and paper, he headed toward the living room. Lauren and I went to the study.

I pointed to the wall across from the bay window. "I want a large abstract painting there. Since I'd like an art deco study, how about a glass desk? I know it'll be a bear to clean fingerprints daily, but it'll give that thirties vibe."

"Glass isn't very kid-friendly," Lauren said.

I crossed my arms. "Are you injecting yourself in this study?"

"I'm..." She shrugged.

"Oh... thinking of your child visiting or staying with me."

"Yes." Her eyes narrowed. "Do you want glass furniture throughout the house?"

"I might... You wouldn't be comfortable with your baby crawling around glass tables, would you?"

"I'd try to be." She scrunched her face, trying to disguise her discomfort with a bachelorette home.

I always liked Nana's rattan furniture in her solarium. "I also like rattan. Let's go with that."

Lauren perked up. "Then we can layer different materials."

I paused to envision that look elevating the space, giving it a transitional feel. "That'll work."

As we went through the house, Lauren sprinkled ideas to make every room look like an image out of *Southern Living*. I couldn't wait to entertain, especially because my home would reflect who I had become.

Midmorning, Dad approached with a long list. The majority of the items on it were straightforward and inexpensive, but some required professionals and money. I didn't want to compromise on my renovations. Before we could dive deep, Maman and Aimee arrived, Aimee's SUV loaded with household items and takeout. Putting off hauling the items inside, we paused for lunch.

While we ate, Maman wanted the lowdown on what we'd accomplished in her and Aimee's absence. Dad reported his laundry list of repairs. I shared a speech I'd already given Lauren to justify my wants for the reno budget, ending on a positive note about the design progress Lauren and I made.

"If the roof leaked," Maman asked Aimee, "would homeowner's insurance pay for repairs?"

"Not unless it was caused by hail or storm damage." Aimee looked at me. "How about compromising by repairing one item on Dad's list and waiting on one repair you want?"

"I like that idea," Dad said.

I didn't. I bit my lip, buying myself time.

"How's your money?" Maman asked.

"The repairs are threatening to rob my reno budget." I smirked.

"You've mentioned your business is growing, and you're making more money than when you were with Jordan."

"I'm doing better." I flashed a smile, appreciating Maman's

attentiveness to my business. For many years, it'd seemed like she didn't care to know.

"Could you put money away and make more renovations in a year?" Her tone suggested impatience was a vice.

"I suppose."

"A lot can happen in a short time, so make space for lifestyle changes." Maman formed a heart with her hands.

"Right!" Lauren said.

Oh Lord, give me patience. I was outnumbered and needed to divert the focus before Lauren and Maman conspired to invite Garrett over soon. "I can get on board with Lauren's alternative to a deck. I'll work with my landscaper client and make it flow with the rest of the backyard. What does everyone think?"

All gave me a thumbs-up except Maman who stood and gazed out the kitchen window. "Add window planters, large pots of perennials, and landscaped floral beds bordering the sitting area. The options are endless."

Aimee rolled her eyes. "If we keep up this brainstorming, Maman will make sure you spend your entire reno budget on landscaping."

I turned to Dad. "You're right about the roof. I don't want to put up with water leaking on my hardwood floors, but I'll wait until next year to repair the windows." My jaw tightened.

Dad bobbed his head, and my jaw relaxed. Why had I expected an I-told-you-so smirk? Or worse, a rebuke for standing up for myself through compromise?

Breaking through the noise in my mind, a memory of a late Saturday afternoon emerged—Jordan and I were in his condo, discussing an office space we had seen about an hour ago. While he sat in the living room, I was in the kitchen slicing cucumbers to infuse our waters. Despite my enthusiasm, he insisted the property was too large and costly. When I suggested I could share the office and split the rent with a graphic designer I subcontracted, Jordan's cheeks got crimson as he accused me of harboring feelings for the designer. Fed up with his jealousy, I told him to grow up. He ambushed me with verbal assaults, so I ran to the balcony, desperate to escape the sense that the condo's walls were caving in on me.

Clearing my throat, I looked from Dad to Lauren. "I realized one reason why I prefer closed-in spaces. Since Jordan's condo is an open concept, I didn't have any rooms to escape a fight except the balcony or the spare bedroom."

Maman kissed the top of my head. "I'm sorry you went through that."

"What a piece of work Jordan was." Dad tapped the table.

I wrung my hands, scared about what I was about to say, yet certain I didn't want to be pigeonholed to my past. "Opening the kitchen and living room will make it better for hosting guests and for babysitting my godchild."

"Yes!" Lauren said, forming a victory fist.

"My little sister's moving forward." Aimee gave me a high five.

There were no more disagreements. I called all the necessary contractors and scheduled the repairs. Hopefully, I'd be able to fully furnish my home in the three weeks before Christmas.

CHAPTER 71
NOVEMBER 30

I didn't sleep well in silence. When I stayed at Gra-mere's farm as a child, I'd have difficulty falling asleep in the still house. Sometimes I'd drag Gra-mere's down comforter and feather pillows outside and sleep near the barn. The neighbor's sheep bleating and baaing, cats mewling as they roamed, and the croaking frogs serenaded me to sleep.

Silence in my dating life had a similar effect. Although I had walked through so much healing, abstinence didn't help with insomnia. I missed tender kisses and nightly debriefing about the day. Since I'd been so lonely with Jordan, I didn't expect to yearn for the simple pleasures of a relationship as I was now.

My longing started while I stayed at Aimee's, especially while observing the teamwork between my parents and between Aimee and Heath. Once I closed on my house, the longing heightened. When I touched on it in casual conversation with Lauren, she insisted I was nesting.

As we pulled into Viviana's driveway on Friday, I told myself to hang in there. I wasn't in the mood to spill my guts about my loneliness. But as I opened the driver's door, Lauren asked me to wait.

"I'll meet you inside," I told Maman and Aimee.

After they walked away, Lauren smiled. "A client gifted Garrett four tickets to the New Year's Eve event at The Mayo. The theme is Avant Garden Soiree, so I can't resist donning a magnificent floral gown and headpiece. Please will you go with us?"

"What?" Was I ready to connect with Garrett?

"He invited his best buddy, Andrew, plus Shane and me. Andrew would've only had to buy a ticket for his wife, but they can't make it now. I assured Garrett I'd find a fourth person."

"Does he know you were going to ask me?"

"No. I didn't want to put you on the spot."

I clutched my heart. "Thank you."

"Well?"

"I'm unsure. I might be more comfortable getting acquainted with him at your house. Something quiet and intimate."

She waved off my suggestion. "A party is perfect because there won't be any pressure. There'll be tons of people around, so you won't have to talk just with him."

For the moment, I needed the focus off me. "Are you sure you're up to staying out past midnight?"

She rubbed her belly. "I want to celebrate late while I still can. How about we book adjoining suites in case I need to leave the event early? Garrett and Shane can stay in one, you and I in the other."

Jordan's photo of me lying drunk on a sofa in a Mayo suite flooded my mind. I wasn't that disillusioned woman anymore, but I didn't want to wrestle memories of my time with Jordan at the hotel while getting acquainted with Garrett.

"I'll take a rain check."

"I won't push. But you'll have to cash in that rain check when helping with the gender reveal." She winked.

CHAPTER 72

After D-group, Viviana summoned me to her study. The room exuded warmth with its pearl-white furnishings and curtains complementing a herringbone oak floor. Extending her arm, she invited me to sit in a dusty blue armchair adorned with gold tufted buttons.

"I have a housewarming gift for you." She handed me a gift wrapped in purple paper, topped with a large gold bow.

"Thank you. I'm flattered you troubled yourself." I placed the present on my lap.

"Look inside and you'll understand." Viviana stood next to me.

I let my imagination simmer in the mystery as I carefully unwrapped the gift. Something substantial was nestled inside. Could it be a crystal vase? A Bible with my name engraved on the cover? A gilt-framed picture of the D-group?

There was a narrow, lavender jewelry box of velvet. I lifted the lid to reveal a crystal skeleton key, polished so well, I could see my reflection.

"It's Swarovski crystal, crafted by a beautiful woman." Viviana turned on her gold desk lamp, and light illuminated the key's prismed sides. "She was rescued from sex trafficking over twenty years ago. A few years later, we connected, and she expressed interest in designing jewelry. I referred her to a talented craftsman. Now, she has her own jewelry line and even a storefront in Prague."

I clutched the key to my chest, appreciating the jeweler's resilience and Viviana's thoughtfulness. "This means so much."

"Look on the other side."

I turned the key over. *Your Home Is Safe* was engraved along the shaft in an elegant font.

"Your home will be a sanctuary for many. I see you hosting people needing a refuge even for one night. And..." She took one of my hands in hers. "I dreamt you'll have a supportive husband by your side."

Looking away, I glimpsed a vibrant red juniper outside the study window. Dad once told me junipers were ideal in Oklahoma because they were drought and cold tolerant, able to grow hearty in clay soil. Could I grow to be as hearty? Even offer sanctuary?

"Does my dream give you hope?" Viviana asked.

"Maybe... I've never gone six months without dating. I'm glad I could invest in me, but with this dry spell..." I squirmed in the chair. What was with this woman? She illuminated dark crevices I wanted to keep hidden.

"You wonder if any man will accept and love you," she said.

I released my hand. "Yes."

She walked over to her dusty blue leather office chair behind her pearl white desk adorned with gold knobs. A bouquet of burgundy glads brightening the desktop. "You remind me of myself when I was your age."

"Really?" I leaned toward her. "How so?"

"At thirty-two years old, I flourished in business, having launched my own jewelry line. I was selling the collection all throughout Europe, especially at Christmas bazaars and festivals, and wanted to expand to North America. A friend connected me to Bryant, who agreed to invest in my company and help me expand to the US market." Viviana pulled her sleeve up on her left arm, exposing a gold chain-link bracelet I'd seen her wearing several times. I could see names engraved on the links. "Here's something I designed," she said. "These are my kids' names."

"I prefer meaningful jewelry like that. I see why your business excelled."

"Thank you."

"Was Bryant attracted to you off the bat?" I leaned toward her.

"Oh no." She shook her head. "He was thirty-six years old, raising two teenage boys, a recent widower not interested in marrying again. His housekeeper kept his home in order. He didn't think he could find someone as amazing as his wife."

"Were you interested in him?"

"No. I had come off a broken engagement and was a no-nonsense pragmatist, determined to stay single and focus on growing my business. I couldn't let *any* man hold me down, even one as charmingly handsome as Bryant March."

I smiled, hearing my own beliefs in her words. "Yet here you two are."

"Plus, I was an agnostic and thought his faith in an intimate God childish. I didn't tell him that, but my skepticism kept me at a distance."

"What happened?" I asked.

"His sons interned at my firm one summer. The eldest was assigned to help me prepare demographics, read census data, and analyze research. We hit it off. One day, he told me I should marry his dad." She drew her head back as if amused. "Flabbergasted, I asked if he wanted a stepmom. He said only if it was me." She pointed to herself. "I made it plain that it was one thing to work closely together in business but another to be a family."

I nodded, impressed by her sharp answer.

She hung her head. "He turned away and quietly said, 'I work for my dad.' I understood what he meant. He had gotten close to me and had projected how we might be together at home. Realizing my insensitivity, I explained how I wasn't equipped to serve as his mom. He didn't skip a beat. 'How can you know if you don't try?' he asked. 'Is parenting much different than running a successful business?' You see how brilliance runs in the family?"

"Did that alter your view of Bryant?"

"It made me consider what an amazing job he was doing as a father. Despite working long hours, he prioritized his boys."

Her description of Bryant reminded me of my dad. "So, you fell for him through his sons?"

She touched her bracelet. "I observed him closer and liked what I saw. But because of that whole faith piece, I didn't pursue him. I didn't want to let go of my religious philosophy."

"For how long?"

"About a year. After his son recommended me as a dating prospect, Bryant saw me in a different light, recognized his attraction to me, and softened to the idea over time like I did. We worked closer on my business. He invited me to the boys' birthday parties and other family functions. Then invited me to church to hear a Czech missionary speak. Missing my home country, I went."

"Was there an overnight conversion?"

"Not at all. It took a few years before I embraced Christ. In hindsight, I noticed God had planted seeds when I was a little girl, through my days at Charles University, and after. By the time I met Bryant, I was a full wheat stalk, ready for harvest."

"How long after your conversion did you start dating Bryant?"

"A few months."

"Was it difficult to date someone more spiritually mature?"

"In the beginning. I didn't understand what I could offer him spiritually. About six months in, I embraced the risk and surrendered my concern to God, trusting him to lead me through. Bryant was patient, especially answering my endless questions."

I sighed. "Normally, I embrace risk. But after the fiasco with Jordan, I'm leery about entering a new relationship. I want one, but fear is holding me back. I'm afraid of getting out there socially at all."

"Lauren informed me that she invited you to the New Year's Eve event at The Mayo. We'd enjoy connecting with you there."

"I told her no. I have some bad memories with my ex there."

"Join us and make good ones."

CHAPTER 73
DECEMBER 1

On Saturday morning, my parents were visiting friends. I called Jennifer and asked if I could help her settle into her new home, hoping I could get her advice about the New Year's Eve soiree. Almost moved in, she told me to come over anyway.

In her living room, Peter and Jennifer held hands as they shared the love seat. I sat on an oversized beanbag, sinking into its core as I wrapped up in a burgundy sherpa blanket. Sienna was visiting a friend.

A lit candle on a side table effused with evergreen. The TV played classic holiday tunes and showed an image of a white-lit Christmas tree near a roaring fireplace, red stockings hanging along the mantle.

Peter stood. "Anyone want hot chocolate?"

"I'm good for now, love," Jennifer said.

I smiled. "You're letting Peter play host now?"

"It comes naturally," she said.

"Hot chocolate, Celine?" he asked.

"Sounds perfect."

Once he was in the kitchen, I extended my hand toward Jennifer. "You couldn't have found a more suitable gentleman."

She grinned. "Destined, wasn't it?"

Within a few minutes, he brought me a curved Christmas mug resembling a snow globe, painted with images of snow-tipped evergreens. I took the mug carefully, so I wouldn't upset the tower of whipped cream capping the drink. "This looks amazing. Thanks."

"Got to impress the best friend." Peter smiled.

"Let's see." A small sip transported my imagination to a Parisian café with massage-your-tastebuds drinking chocolate. "Alright, you're a keeper."

"The judge has spoken. You're stuck with me, babe." Peter kissed Jennifer on the cheek.

She blushed and looked at me. "What's the latest with you? No talking about the house or your business. Give us the scoop on the ever-changing life of Celine Monroe. What do we need to talk about?" She knew me too well.

I grimaced. "Garrett has four tickets to the New Year's Eve soiree at The Mayo. Lauren invited me to be the group's fourth, but I said no."

"Why?" Jennifer asked.

"I'm haunted by memories from spending New Year's Eve there with Jordan. Although I don't remember most of that night, I have impressions, especially of the two of us arguing. He spent most of his time talking investments with Matthew and other businessmen. The next morning, he left our suite before I even woke up. I assumed he had booked for another night, so I didn't set an alarm and woke up to housekeeping coming into the room. I was livid and embarrassed." I took a longer sip of hot chocolate.

Jennifer raised her brow. "Lauren's invitation sounds like a great opportunity to make new memories."

"That's what Viviana said." I was more comfortable to probe the advice with Jennifer. "What if being there conjures up more of that awful night?"

"How about the four of us attend the Festival of Lights at the Philbrook next Friday?" Peter said. "That way, you'll be more comfortable for the soiree."

"That's a terrific idea." Jennifer smiled.

I wanted to wait on getting acquainted with Garrett, but if I continued to object to opportunities, could I stand to watch another woman swoop in? Maybe Miss Manhattan, the gallery owner I saw him with at CHOC?

Peter grabbed his phone from the coffee table. "I'll text Garrett." I watched as if Peter moved in slow motion. "If it helps," he said as he texted, "I told him you've made many strides in your faith. And how fun you are."

"How did I come into conversation?" I asked.

"Let me think." He took a few seconds. "As I told him about Jennifer, I plugged you as her best friend."

"Did Garrett seem interested in getting to know Celine?" Jennifer asked.

Peter looked at me. "He seemed happy you're doing well. But I didn't promote you that way, because he's still on his dating fast."

"Is he coming off it for New Year's?" Jennifer asked, brow furling.

"Yeah, that should be three months." Peter winked at me. "Good timing, Celine. He says that backing off his drive to always be dating has surprised him with a deeper desire for connection. Quiet but steady is how he described that longing. He's not rushing anything but is open to what God chooses to unravel for him."

Jennifer glanced at me. "I think it's already happening."

My cheeks heated.

"I could see it working out," Peter said. "You're different than Presleigh."

"You knew her?" I asked.

He nodded. "She was someone who'd enter a room and capture the energy. And she was hilarious. We'd get each other cracking up."

"Unforgettable?" I asked. His description and Lauren's seemed to depict different women.

"That but, with her assertive personality, she could be polarizing. I liked her, just not for Garrett. You seem more his speed—congenial and creative."

"I haven't always been this way." I looked at Jennifer.

"You are in general until you want something badly. Then you're a lioness." Jennifer clawed the air.

Peter raised his brows. "I haven't seen that side. But it's probably a good complement for Garrett since he's a golden retriever."

"I hope he's got some bulldog in him." Jennifer elbowed Peter. "Some pushback is good for Celine." She stared me down. Her comment was fair.

"He's got a spine and conviction," Peter said. "And won't let a woman run over him this time."

"Bad experience?" Jennifer asked. I smiled, as if she had read my mind.

"He learned the hard way with Presleigh, but he stood up for what he wanted in the end."

I held up my mug. "If we could double-date beforehand, I'd be more comfortable attending the New Year's event."

"That's my girl!" Jennifer said.

Peter looked at his phone. "Garrett just texted."

I leaned toward him, my pulse racing as he read the text out loud.

"Sorry, bro. Would enjoy that but booked every weekend and then have a family trip. How about a rain check for January?"

I tapped the beanbag. "Lauren told me the Bettencourts spend Christmas in Michigan."

"Why not on a weeknight?" Jennifer asked.

"He's probably busy, babe. That's why he was specific about the rain check."

"Thanks for trying," I said. "Hey, what are you doing for New Year's? Having the two of you join all of us at the soiree would be fun."

"Peter's parents have a place on Grand Lake, and my parents are coming."

"Wow! It's getting serious." I made a heart gesture.

They looked at each other. "Yes."

"I couldn't be happier." I stood and gave Jennifer a hug.

"So?" Jennifer asked.

"What?" I retorted.

"Tell Lauren you can attend before she finds another candidate for Garrett." Jennifer pointed toward my phone on the coffee table.

"Or Celine could wait until she's comfortable." Peter placed his arm around Jennifer's shoulder.

"I know how to motivate Celine."

"I'll let her know now," I said before I lost my courage.

I texted, and Lauren called within a minute. I could hardly get her to calm down. It was settled. I had a date for New Year's Eve.

CHAPTER 74
DECEMBER 29

I moved into my new house after Christmas, its renovations almost finished. The kitchen and living area was now one open space, and the roof was replaced. Although unopened boxes and a few opened ones littered nearly every room, my bedroom and closet were accessible.

Lauren and I would furnish and decorate after I got unpacked and organized. Today, it was more important that she and Aimee help me decide what I'd wear to the soiree.

"How about Nana's emerald taffeta?" I said as we stood in my spacious walk-in closet. "I wore it at the 2016 soiree, so it'd be a full circle moment."

Aimee shook my shoulders as if knocking apples off my branches. "No! You were with *him*." As she released her hands, her eyes widened. "Oh my gosh. You have to wear Nana's red gown."

I clasped my hands together. "Of course."

Nana wore the cherry-red taffeta when Papa first approached her at a New Year's party at The Mayo. My family kept the gown in an airtight box at Aimee's.

"How about I retrieve it?" Aimee offered. "So you can see if it fits?"

I touched my chest. "Yes, thank you."

After she left, Lauren focused on styling me. "What jewelry will coordinate with the gown?" she asked.

"Check this out." I took her by the arm and led her to my jewelry chest on top of the dresser. "I'll wear Nana's pearl necklace and her pearl drop earrings."

"Perfect. Do you have a coordinating bracelet?"

My heart raced. I lifted the fake bottom of my jewelry chest, grabbed the purple sack I'd placed there, and slid the bracelet box out of the sack. "I have just the right one." I carefully opened the box and held it in front of Lauren, so I wouldn't get fingerprints on the bracelet. "Isn't it a stunner?"

She gasped.

I touched her arm. "Are you having pains? Do you need water?"

"Where did you get this?" Lauren leaned closer to me.

"My ex gifted it. He told me it was an heirloom, but he lied."

"It looks like my Granny's bracelet that got stolen. Exactly like it!" She covered her mouth.

"What?" I blanked and stumbled backward.

"You okay?" Lauren asked.

"Yeah, yeah... Just shocked."

"Me too. Do you mind checking the serial number?"

"Of course."

I grabbed a magnifying glass from the drawer where I stored my jewelry cleaner. I liked to use the glass to inspect for scratches on Nana's pearls. "Why don't you check?" I suggested, dazed over the mystery bracelet's potential journey.

With trembling hands, she carefully lifted the bracelet out of the box with the velvet cloth. She placed the magnifying glass to her eye. "I see the number, but I don't know it. I'll call Dad first. Otherwise, Garrett—who inherited it—will get his hopes up. I hate to see him disappointed again. He's been desperate to find the bracelet."

My mouth gaped. I would've never expected him to own such a vintage piece. Every time I thought I had him figured out, I discovered unexpected sides to him. He truly was an enigma.

She placed it back in the box then grabbed her phone.

"Do you want me to wait in another room?" I asked.

"No, stay."

When her dad answered, Lauren put her phone on speaker. After a few niceties, she tapped her foot on the hardwood floor. "Dad, please don't say anything to Mom yet, but would you give me the serial number for Granny's bracelet?"

Within a few minutes, he texted an enlarged image of the bracelet with the serial number visible. I waited in anticipation while Lauren made the comparison. Shortly, she started to cry and fanned her face as if too overcome with emotion to speak.

Were her tears of joy or disappointment? Either way, I understood how hope deferred made a heart sick. Waiting for the promotion. The right clients. The compatible boyfriend.

Finally, she raised her arms. "This is it!" She clutched the bracelet to her heart. "It's Granny's bracelet, Dad!"

"God is faithful," he said. "I told Garrett God would return the bracelet if it was meant to be."

Lauren arched her brow. "How did he take that?"

"It was hard at first, but eventually, he agreed to let it go. If God didn't return the heirloom, it was meant to be on someone else's wrist."

"Did you or Garrett persuade Mom to surrender it too? After we returned home from our first Christmas in the farmhouse, no one mentioned the bracelet and the investigation. I told Shane that Garrett must've persuaded Mom to never bring it up."

"I asked your mom to only discuss the bracelet with me; otherwise, Garrett would continue to suffer. With her not obsessing over it around him, Garrett found it easier to surrender its return to God. That's why he didn't insist on that woman showing him the serial number."

"What woman?" she asked.

I touched my chest, feeling a pierce in my heart.

"Do you remember Garrett approaching a woman at The Mayo? He was there for a bridal shoot and thought he saw a woman wearing the bracelet. He followed her outside and asked her about it, but the boyfriend shoved Garrett."

A memory flashed. Jordan gifted me the bracelet in the hotel suite. We changed into vintage costumes then headed to an Old Hollywood party. While we waited for the valet, a man approached, asking me about the bracelet. I assumed he was a pickpocket, although much more clean-cut than the stereotype. Uncomfortable, I glared at Jordan, hoping he'd intervene. I hardly saw the stranger.

"Yeah, Mom told me," Lauren said. "It sounded like nothing came of it."

"The part that Mom didn't know is Garrett saw the same woman wearing the heirloom on New Year's Eve, again at The Mayo. He introduced himself as the stranger who inquired about the heirloom earlier."

I covered my mouth as a second memory flashed. Another encounter forgotten because I was wasted after I ran into him.

"The woman didn't flinch. Said the jeweler who made it for her boyfriend probably created a dupe. That a client might've seen the original and wanted something similar."

"There's no way Garrett believed her," Lauren said.

"No, but he intuited she was going through a lot with her boyfriend. It sounded like she was financially dependent on him, so Garrett didn't expose him. We decided to keep that incident between us and not upset your mother. If your brother had to do it over, I think he'd do the same again."

As though I was watching a movie, scenes from running into

Garrett that New Year's Eve appeared in my mind. At first, I hadn't recognized Garrett at our second meeting. Our exchange was friendly, since Jordan wasn't with me on the rooftop. I thought the hotel hired the photographer for the soiree, so I asked if I could take a pic by the lit-up LOVE sign. He asked his client, a bride who rented the sign, if we could take a pic.

After he left with the newlyweds, I corralled Jordan, Matt, and Elise from the bar inside, and Jordan snapped a few pics of us four posing in front of the sign. Since that night was a disaster, I never asked for those images.

When Garrett approached later that night to hand me his business card, Jordan snatched it. Triggered by many things between us, I ripped into Jordan for taking my card. Elise and Matt told me to calm down. Jordan warned that if he saw that stranger again, he'd call the police.

Shortly after, Jordan talked to some business connections he made earlier. After I rebuked him for networking, he said the connections helped my business too. Then he called me childish and returned to the businessmen. I drank and danced the night away, trying to silence the impression that Jordan didn't care about me.

"Again, don't repeat this to Mom," Lauren's dad was saying. "She's unaware and freer because of it."

"My lips are sealed," Lauren said. "I have an idea. Promise you won't tell Garrett or Mom that the bracelet is found. I have the best way to return it to him... Let's just say it involves New Year's Eve at The Mayo. But this time, the story has changed."

"I trust you, sweetie. I'll hold off for Garrett's sake." He laughed. "God is good. With New Year's coming up, I recently mentioned the bracelet to Garrett, just saying how proud I was of him for letting it go. Honestly, he hardly could recall those two run-ins with that woman."

"He does possess an uncanny knack of forgetting unpleasant memories."

"Garrett prayed that God would erase it from his memory so he could move on, especially since he shoots several weddings at The Mayo. God answered. I felt bad for bringing it up again, but I think the nudge for me to do so was God preparing him. If that makes sense."

"You obviously didn't pray to erase your memory," Lauren said.

"It would've been in vain. Even if I'd forget, Mom would remind me. After Michigan, I asked her to stop bringing it up to people, especially Garrett. If she needed to vent or process the loss, I'd listen. She's hardly mentioned it anymore."

She chuckled. "That's a miracle."

"I'll wait until Garrett can show her the bracelet is recovered. She'll probably insist he keep it in our safe until he walks down the aisle."

"She needs to stop babying the heirloom," Lauren said. "Garrett can do whatever he wants with it."

"Be sensitive to her. When the bracelet got stolen, she felt as though she lost Granny all over again."

I stiffened, wondering if Lauren would think less of me for inadvertently playing keep away. If I were her, I might not care to understand my point of view.

"I'll be sensitive but don't give in to her." Lauren wagged her finger as if her dad could see her. "I don't mean to sound like you don't hold your own. You've come far. Just remind her that the jewelry is Garrett's."

"That's not your concern, sweetheart... Mom just pulled into the garage. Love you."

"Love you more."

As beautiful as the restoration of the heirloom was for Lauren and her family, I hung my head, worried how I was filling in the ugly shadows of the bracelet's journey.

CHAPTER 75

After hanging up her phone, Lauren hugged me. I lightly squirmed. She stared into my eyes so long, I turned away.

"I'm that woman." I hung my head.

"I'm thankful." Lauren smiled as we sat on the large ottoman in the closet.

"I'm still surprised Garrett didn't recognize me at Charleston's, especially because he knew who I was the second time we ran into each other at The Mayo." I narrowed my eyes at Lauren. I was skeptical of God erasing someone's memory of an incident as emotionally escalating as losing a precious heirloom, especially since most of my fights with Jordan were still fresh in my mind.

She waved her hand. "He's very sensitive to his emotions, especially around losing the bracelet. Even if God hadn't filed the confrontations at The Mayo away, Garrett might've naturally blocked them and your and your ex's faces out of his mind, especially since it's been two years."

"I'd assume a photographer would be very astute to faces."

"He has a very selective memory when it comes to unpleasant events. I had a roommate he met a few times while I was at college and he was in high school. When I later ran into her and discovered she was still single, I got them to go on a date at a coffee shop. He didn't recognize her when she arrived, so she had to introduce herself. Granted, she had cut her hair and highlighted it auburn after having long blonde tresses back in college. When I half-teasingly confronted Garrett about not placing her from when he'd visit me at college, he point-blank said, 'I've worked on forgetting those days.' " Lauren scowled. "Whenever he'd visit me at OU, he was more motivated to attend a party and get wasted than to be a dutiful brother."

Sometimes, Lauren's expectations of her brother seemed a bit much. "In fairness to Garrett, I looked so different that New Year's at The Mayo. I spray-tanned. Wore layers of makeup, eyelash extensions." I crinkled my nose. "Lip fillers—the works. And I was a brunette with a harsh, blunt bob." I grabbed my phone and showed her an image of me in the Old Hollywood gown.

"You look glammed up. I see how he wouldn't recognize you now... And I hope you don't mind me saying you look a little hard there."

"That's how I had to be with my ex. He convinced me that an ambitious woman should look professional, but I realized he meant cold." I shook my head. "I'm embarrassed I didn't recognize Garrett. I kept wondering why he looked familiar. I have broken memories since I got drunk on both nights after running into him at The Mayo." My face flushed. "Like at Charleston's."

She scrolled through her phone. "Gare's more rugged now," she said. "I can see why you wouldn't recognize him." She showed me a photo. "This is from when we were at my cousin's wedding in Michigan a few years ago."

"That's how he looked at The Mayo." My breathing tightened. "I can't believe how forgiving Garrett is. You too."

"The heirloom's restored now." Lauren wrapped her arms around my shoulders.

"I still need to apologize out loud." I stood and paced the closet.

"When Garrett first asked me about the bracelet, I got nervous, wondering if he was a pickpocket. That incident was chaotic. I don't remember too much of what anyone said. But I felt his desperation and got scared."

I fumbled with my fragmented memories. "After we left for an Old Hollywood party, I vaguely remember rebuking Jordan for being too aggressive. He said he feared Garrett was a druggie and might use force. Later, Jordan suggested the idea that a dupe had been made and lost." I stopped pacing. "I'm so sorry." Why would Garrett ever be interested in me?

Lauren narrowed her eyes as if lost in thought. "Gare and Dad probably kept that second run-in with you and your ex close to their chest, so I didn't have to worry about accidentally slipping the New Year's incident to Mom." She groaned. "Otherwise, poor Gare wouldn't have heard the end of it. My mom's loving, but she's assertive. Kind of like Presleigh."

"Your mom might not want to accept me as your daughter's godparent."

Lauren shook her head. "You're not to blame. You thought the vintage piece was Jordan's heirloom."

I sat on the ottoman. "It's behind me now. Let's return the bracelet to Garrett."

Lauren grabbed my hand. "Why don't you wear it on New Year's Eve and surprise him?"

"No, no, no. Won't seeing it on my wrist upset him?"

She smiled. "You heard Dad. Garrett's content letting God restore it. And you're the one God entrusted for its care. It's an amazing story."

"I don't see it that way. My ex gifted it to me, pretending it was his family's heirloom, but he must've bought it from his uncle Sonny. I wish I had returned it that New Year's."

"Exactly! You *are* returning it on New Year's. Go with me on this." Her squeeze of my hand emphasized this needed to happen her way.

I removed my hand from hers. "The bracelet has caused too much tension. Please take it to Garrett today."

"It needs to come full circle. Trust me, Gare will appreciate the gesture... You don't know how it got lost in the first place."

"Tell me," I said, curious.

"Wanting Presleigh to wear it as her something borrowed, Garrett insisted she take it to Vegas when shopping for her wedding gown... I don't know why, since she's not the type to select a gown around an heirloom... Anyway, Garrett escorted her into the airport. Before heading to security, she went to the restroom. She placed her carry-on bag on the airport's restroom floor while she washed her hands. What woman would risk her bag getting bacteria and who knows what?" Lauren stuck out her tongue. "To make matters worse, she left the bag in the restroom."

"The bracelet was in the carry-on?"

"Yes. Garrett wanted her to secure it in her purse, but she was careless... Oh, I better slow down. I'm getting angry all over again." Lauren took a deep breath. "When Presleigh returned to the sitting area, Garrett noticed she didn't have the bag. She checked the restroom, but it was gone. My heart flutters when I think what Gare must've felt in that moment." Lauren touched her chest and took several more deep breaths. "Where did I leave off?"

"Presleigh couldn't find the bag," I said.

Lauren nodded. "Right. Presleigh and the security guard rechecked the restroom and, voilà, found the bag exactly where she left it but without the bracelet inside."

"The thief must've removed the bracelet from the bag and took it to Okie Pawn," I said. "The owner, Sonny, is Jordan's uncle and my former client. He must've sold the bracelet under the table to Jordan."

"Garrett was right." Lauren slapped her knee. "He went to the pawn shop the next day, and the owner insisted he didn't have it. Garrett saw the purple sack and demanded to see what was in it, but the owner told him to leave."

"Was this a few weeks before Christmas?"

"Yes."

"Did Garrett report it missing to the police?" I asked.

"Of course. A detective checked the pawn shop's video footage from the day it went missing but didn't see anything conclusive. Garrett thinks the owner met the thief in the back of the shop or in the parking lot. Maybe she came desperate for cash when he was locking up." Lauren sighed. "There's a lot we may never know."

"I know my ex is a piece of work." I shook my head relieved to purge myself of that evil.

Lauren hugged me again. I listened, dumbfounded, as she thanked God for giving me the bracelet. I'd never experienced a family like Lauren's.

CHAPTER 76
NEW YEAR'S EVE

I walked around Aimee's house with her Velcro rollers in my hair as we celebrated the New Year's Réveillon. Despite the vast spread, I only ate foie gras and drank half a glass of imported French pastis—enough to satisfy my hunger pangs while I tried to be cool with changes in plan.

Shane hadn't come home from a production shoot until six that morning and felt like he was coming down with a cold. Lauren asked if I could pick her up, so we could get ready at The Mayo. Garrett would arrive separately.

Around 6:30 p.m., Lauren texted.

> Sorry, but I'm running late. Nausea hit suddenly. Garrett came over, so he'll just bring me. Is that okay?

I scrambled to reply.

> If you're not feeling well, please don't push yourself. Rest! I'll meet Garrett another time.

No!!! I CAN'T miss celebrating with you!

Alrighty. See you later. 😊

As Aimee handed me a garment bag with Nana's gown, I frowned. "I'm not picking Lauren up after all. I'll get ready here, so you can help me."

Aimee shook her head. "We don't want the gown wrinkled. I'll drive you and help there. I can pick you up tomorrow if you need a ride. Although I doubt you will." She winked.

I gave her a big hug, but she kept her head away from my hair. "I owe you, big time."

"Just enjoy yourself. That's payment enough for me."

By seven, I'd checked into the hotel suite, fortunately on a different floor than the one where I stayed with Jordan. My nerves spun me around like a turntable. I wandered to the walk-in closet and stared at the plush terry robe bearing the hotel's emblem. Would it be better to slip into that while I got ready? Or should I stay in my yoga pants and tee? I returned to the bathroom, wondering if I should just apply my makeup and get on with it.

"How are you doing?" Aimee asked from the other side of the bathroom door.

"Come in. I'm debating whether to put on the robe or stay in what I'm wearing."

She entered. "The robe, so you can slip it off without messing up your hair or makeup. Do you want help?"

I nodded and soon found myself relaxed in the plush robe, sitting in the living room chair Aimee placed in front of the bathroom counter.

"Thank you," I said, as she set my makeup on the counter. "I don't know what I'd do without you. Honestly, I feel like a nervous bride. But Garrett's not my groom."

"Yet." Aimee smirked.

"Oh don't say that." My cheeks burned. "I only want him to find me the most alluring woman he's met. Is that too much to ask?"

"He'll be speechless."

"I just hope I'm not. Otherwise, it'll be a short night." I sat on my hands so they'd stop shaking.

"Focus on what you can control. Enjoy his company." She leaned toward me. "When I'm done with you, he'll definitely be speechless."

"He better!" My tease squeaked from doubt.

As Aimee worked her magic, each stroke of the makeup brush revived memories of her dolling me up before a school dance. She'd instructed me how to attract boys with my eyes. How to ignore back-stabbing rivals. How to care for my adolescent skin. I cherished the resurrection of memories life's hardships had buried as though they never breathed life.

Once she finished removing the rollers and fluffing my high wavy bangs, my jaw dropped.

"Voilà!" she exclaimed. "Princess Bride beauty suits you better than the Bond femme fatale's look Jordan pushed on you."

She angled a hand mirror and showed me the waves tumbling from my crown to my midback. They screamed nineties supermodel. I blinked hard. That pretty woman was there all along, but I had tucked her away, fearing she wasn't enough.

Aimee pulled me into the suite's walk-in closet, where I stood in front of an elongated mirror as she helped me slip into the corset gown. Once the spaghetti straps settled on my bare shoulders, I felt an otherworldly force penetrate my body. The gown, almost animate, adhered to my natural contours. I felt weightless, as if floating a few inches above the tiled floor.

"Fits perfectly." Aimee's voice from behind brought me to earth. "Look at the back."

I turned and looked over my shoulder toward the mirror. The cherry-red taffeta flared majestically to the floor like a bridal train.

"Ready for the jewels?" She sat the jewelry boxes, holding the heirlooms, on the dressing table while she donned white gloves. First, she outfitted me with Nana's pearl necklace and pearl drop earrings. Then she slipped Garrett's heirloom bracelet onto my wrist and closed its lobster clasp.

Light from the closet's small chandelier hit the prism of the bracelet's gems. A luminous cloud of red, yellow, blue, and green shone around the gown.

"I'm FaceTiming the parents." Aimee grabbed her phone from the pocket of her ripped jeans.

I faced her as my parents answered.

"What do you think of our beauty?" she asked, holding her phone toward my body.

Dad covered his mouth.

"Tu es magnifique!" Maman blew me a kiss.

"You look like Nana," Dad said.

I touched the pearl necklace. "Thank you."

"Celebrate like it's the end of the world," Maman said.

"I'll try."

"I'm proud of your journey." Dad smiled.

"Me too," I said.

"Take pictures," he said. "I'd like to see what this young man looks like."

After we got off the phone, Aimee ordered me to the living space. "I need to capture the princess."

I posed for several pics. As soon as she air-dropped them to me, I posted a few on my social account with a chic caption.

Old World glam for Avant Garden Soiree at The Mayo. Donning my nana's gown and feeling like Grace Kelly. What are your New Year's plans? #NYE #TheMayoHotel #marketingconsultant #vintageismyjam

"I better go and let you join the party," Aimee said. "Unless I need to chaperone."

"Only if you could keep my nerves at bay."

"You'll be fine." She blew me a kiss from the suite's door. "Call tomorrow if you need a ride."

CHAPTER 77

S hortly after Aimee left, Lauren texted.

> Sorry, just getting ready. We should be
> there within the hour. I'll text when
> leaving.

I responded with a thumbs-up emoji then called Viviana, but she didn't answer. Not wanting to be in the Crystal Ballroom among strangers, I decided to stay in the suite until Lauren arrived.

Standing barefoot near the window, I looked out into a night sky lit by a crescent moon. The condensation of my breath on the glass registered the chill of winter. I scanned the street below and the hotel's entrance to the right, reflecting on all my memories in between. The tidy landscape was barren of green. Winter had killed off anything refusing to die in the fall. All that mattered for me in this moment was the life coursing through the gown, the bracelet's wild journey, and my steps forward.

My legs yearned for rest. I perched on the edge of the sofa, sipping on sparkling water. Just as I relaxed and nearly drifted off to sleep, Lauren texted.

We're on our way. See you soon!

The wall clock read 8:30 p.m. Tired of being cooped up in the suite, I slipped on my gold stilettos and took the elevator to the Grand Hall, so Garrett would see me as he emerged from the lobby.

I stood next to a deep-seated barrel chair, my hands on its high back, and faced the imperial staircase. Eyes closed, I envisioned the story Nana and Papa told me about the first time they met.

Nana, wearing the red taffeta, came down the staircase late in the evening. Unable to take his eyes off her, Papa stood and waited at the bottom. Just before she reached the last step, he extended his hand and aided her to the tiled marble floor.

"Why did you take so long to meet me?" he asked.

She blushed as she replied. "I'm meeting my fiancé."

Undeterred, Papa smiled. "Perhaps you just have."

Later, he asked her to dance and waltzed with her around the ballroom, making her forget about her date. Within a few weeks, she broke up with her fiancé and went steady with Papa, the only man she ever loved.

Their story moved me—not because of Papa's assertiveness, but because Nana knew her life began the moment she saw him. As she once said, "I knew I was asleep."

Eyes open, I thought about how I'd greet Garrett. "Hi, I'm Celine. Here's your bracelet."

Wrong approach. I'd have to explain the bracelet fiasco. How I broke up with Jordan. How I learned the heirloom belonged to Garrett—Lauren would interject that information. By the time we got beyond that story, his patience would be thin.

Dare I attempt a line like Papa's? "Hi, why did you take so long to meet me?" Lacking Papa's finesse, I'd jumble the words and laugh with nervous energy. It was probably best just to see where the night took us.

My gaze fell on couples at the elevator. Women in silk floral sheaths wore variegated hats suitable for the Kentucky Derby. Others had large pink and white roses in their hair. All were arm in arm with men, no one alone. I looked away, thinking about Jordan. Last year, we avoided the soiree and had a quiet dinner out, then we went home. He pretended to engage in small talk, but after an hour of sitting on the balcony and sipping champagne, he went to bed, too tired to kiss at midnight.

Weary of the fashion show, I called Lauren. Her cell rang and rang until it went to voicemail. I didn't have Garrett's number, so I texted Shane. No answer. If Lauren's nausea had grown worse, surely one of them would've reached out.

I called Viviana. Again, no answer. Should I search for her in the ballroom and mingle with the Marches? Thirsty, I needed something to drink and eyed the restaurant bar about fifty feet away. Before I could step toward it, Jordan and his receptionist girlfriend entered the hotel arm in arm. I dashed behind the hall's massive curtains and observed. Her sleeveless royal-blue maxi with plunging neckline highlighted a sapphire drop necklace surrounded by diamond baguettes. He wore a black tux with a royal-blue pocket square, like a coordinating prom date.

They headed to the elevators. Jordan's hand on her bare back exposed her taut muscles. He whispered something in her ear. She laughed, touching his cheek. He was never so tender with me.

Suddenly, the hotel reeked of bad memories. I opened the car-sharing app on my phone. Unable to rewrite history, I needed to go home.

Garrett's bracelet felt heavy on my wrist. I touched it. Would I ever get to wear his heirloom or Nana's gown again? Why should Jordan's presence rob me of pleasure in this night?

I closed the app, sidled up to the restaurant bar, and got a club soda. I returned to the Grand Hall and walked up the staircase to the second floor. Every step reminded me of my grandparents. What would Nana want me to do?

The response echoed in my heart. She'd want me to *live.* How many times had she told me to stop worrying about what everyone else thought? If someone gossiped about her, she'd wave her slender hand. "She can buzz like a bee, but she won't pollinate primroses."

I strolled to the glass display containing hotel memorabilia. Brass skeleton room keys, vintage restaurant menus, bellhop uniforms. All preserving days gone by.

If nothing else about the night turned out like I hoped, I could still appreciate the hotel's elegance, my family's legacy, and Nana's gown. At midnight, I'd toast in the ballroom under the crystal chandeliers with the Marches.

Ambling down the staircase slowly, I glanced at my phone. How much longer should I wait for Lauren? Still, she hadn't replied. A bit of the conversation we'd had over lunch on Saturday replayed.

"Garrett's looking forward to meeting you and hearing about your transformation over the last months. I didn't tell him about the bracelet, but I shared you have a surprise for him."

I didn't know how to respond. Was he excited about the surprise or about my transformation? "What if we don't hit it off? The way you think we will?"

"Then you'll be good friends."

"That's my aim." I nodded at her to assure myself. Being friends meant no pressure to perform.

"But be open too." She put her hands together in a prayer pose. "He said it was all so strange but wouldn't explain. He can be so stubborn. He whispered 'The Mayo was where...' He stopped talking, but I recognized his distant look when he sees something in the spirit."

"Oh," I said. I was as unsure what to make of that then as now.

What if he'd started to say that The Mayo was where he saw me being haughty and rude? Could he have suddenly remembered me and intuited I'd return the bracelet here? Would he move on after I returned it, and could I live with that? I'd be disappointed.

Focus on being friends, Celine. I'd have to tattoo that motto on my brain.

At the bottom of the staircase, I glanced at the heirloom. The Akoya pearls and bouquet of stones on the clasp radiated, nearly blinding me. My wrist became hot. I slipped the bracelet off, carefully placing it in my handbag. Was I delirious from this long, long night?

CHAPTER 78

The thought of Jordan and his girlfriend seeing me enter the Crystal Ballroom alone gave me pause. I remained in the Grand Hall, hoping to find the necessary courage before midnight. To preoccupy my mind with something else, I scrolled through social on my phone.

By nine thirty, I was bored, tired, and approaching livid. Could Lauren and Garrett have arrived while I wandered the second floor? I went outside and asked the valet if he'd seen a bright red Jeep. He hadn't.

Wanting to go upstairs to find the Marches, I returned inside and waited for the elevator.

"Celine," said a female voice.

I quickly turned, my heart pounding. The Marches approached.

"You are breathtaking and your gown regal," Viviana said.

"Thank you. Like always, you are so elegant." I admired her high-collared dress, its white top complemented by a Mikado navy skirt with large white magnolias.

We exchanged *bisous*, and she asked if I'd just arrived.

"No, I've been here for a few hours. Did you get my texts?"

She touched my arm. "I left my phone in the suite while we ate in the dining room. I'm sorry."

"Had we known you were here," Bryant said, "we would've invited you to join us for dinner."

He was dressed in a navy suit and bright red tie, a magnolia on his jacket lapel. We boarded the elevator, chatting about the night. Both checked their phones. They hadn't heard from Lauren or Garrett either and were concerned. But Shane hadn't contacted them, so hopefully no news was good news.

As we entered the Crystal Ballroom, I was spellbound by its transformation into a garden paradise. Ruby-red roses and faux grass covered the front of the stage. White LED lights strung through two maple trees with green garland illuminated the nearby deejay station.

The atmosphere was charged with energy. Strobe lights flashed fuchsia pink and electric blue through the ballroom. The steady booming of techno music increased my heart rate. Oh, how I'd tried to dance away anger here. Even though that was two years ago, it might as well be tonight. As guests danced, I turned to focus on the decorated stage. Otherwise, I'd be tempted to down shots.

A waiter passed with a small tray of champagne. I reached out as if to grab a glass. I withdrew my hand and instead approached the carved-meat station for a small cut of prime rib. Balancing plates and glasses of ice water, the Marches and I escaped into the quiet hallway. We toasted early to the New Year and our friendship.

Bryant turned aside as a couple approached. Jordan and his girl friend held hands. Laser-focused on Bryant, Jordan didn't notice me next to Viviana. I stepped a few feet away to lessen the chance he would.

Jordan released his girlfriend's hand and extended his. "Hello, Bryant. I briefly met you at a charity auction in May." They shook hands.

"Your face vaguely rings a bell," Bryant said. "What's your name?"

"Jordan Sterling." Jordan fiddled with his initialed gold cufflinks. "I'm the investment advisor who has studied your firm for years."

"I remember now. You plugged your buddy's tech company."

"What's your name, dear?" Viviana asked Jordan's girlfriend.

"Haleigh." She smiled at Viviana but didn't acknowledge me.

Viviana stepped my way and touched my shoulder. "Celine, this is Haleigh."

"I remember seeing you when I'd stop by the investment firm," I said with a half smile, testing if Haleigh recognized me.

"Okay." She shrugged.

Figured. She didn't seem the type to care about people outside of her acquaintance.

There were two separate conversations: Jordan and Bryant, Viviana and *her*. Jordan talked nonstop about the market and whatnot. He was nervous! I replayed his lecture about the importance of actively listening, especially with VIPs. *Glean their wisdom and show them you're focused. Opportunities avail themselves.* I smirked.

Viviana asked Haleigh where she worked, and Haleigh shared the investment firm's name.

"How long have you dated Jordan?" I asked.

"Since the fall." She ran her hands through her brunette wavy locks. "Before then, we were just friends."

I glared at her, incredulous she lied. Friends didn't hold hands across the restaurant table.

"Your necklace and earrings are stunning," Viviana said.

I glanced at the sapphires and diamonds. Did Jordan gift the set to her? They appeared real.

"Thanks." She touched the necklace. "A gift from my father. I don't normally wear them, since they were a bribe." She pursed her lips as if uncomfortable sharing with strangers.

Viviana didn't skip a beat. "Familial bonds can be complicated."

"After my parents divorced when I was ten, my father moved to Philadelphia. Now he wants me to attend Wharton Business School. He used the jewelry to entice me. It won't work." She placed her hand to her side.

Why did we have to run into her? I wanted her to stay the "other girl," but she was becoming flesh and blood. Knowing more about her could make it hard to hold on to my anger.

"Sounds like a challenging situation," Viviana said.

As so often happened to people conversing with Viviana, the dam broke. Haleigh mentioned she wanted to stand on her own without her father's money.

Her skin was flawless. I would've expected her to say she wanted to be an aesthetician. But she wanted to be an investment advisor. In a year, she'd attend TU and major in finance. For now, she was content working at the firm as a receptionist instead of sitting in a classroom. Her goals explained why Jordan took her under his wing. His apprentice needed him more than I did.

"Good for you," Viviana said. "It's refreshing to encounter young adults with resolve."

Haleigh glanced at her hands. "That's what Mom says."

The tables in my heart turned. Suddenly, I wanted to pull Haleigh aside and implore her to run. *Jordan is as controlling as your father.*

She turned to face Jordan and placed her hand on his shoulder. "Are you ready?"

He ignored her.

Viviana patted Bryant's arm. "I hate to break this up, but Jordan and Haleigh are here to celebrate the New Year, not to spend it with middle-aged curmudgeons like us."

Jordan said it was more enjoyable with them, but Bryant shook his hand. "With such a beautiful woman on your arm, it'd be a shame not to give her your full attention."

I fidgeted, searching for an excuse to walk away quietly without Jordan noticing. But I was too intrigued by the dynamic before me.

Jordan shook Viviana's hand then stared at me. His mouth gaped open. "Celine?"

I smiled, having envisioned the day he'd see me with the Marches. "Hello." While I found it satisfying he'd realize I was flourishing without him, my drive to prove myself to him was gone. He wasn't relevant to my life.

"What are you doing here?" He touched his neck.

Haleigh tugged on his arm.

"Are you alone?" he asked me.

"No," said Viviana. "Celine's our guest. She's being gracious for the moment until her party arrives."

"How do you know them?" Jordan pointed to Bryant.

"Church." Knowing that was the last thing he expected me to say, I wanted to laugh. But I kept a straight face.

"We've become close friends." Viviana placed her arm around my shoulder.

Running his hand through his slicked-back hair, Jordan barely moved his lips as he forced out stilted words. "Looks like you've made connections without me."

A hard knot of pain, resentment, and regret rose in my throat. I loathed that I'd ever wanted to be with this man.

"Jordan," said Haleigh, "let's dance."

"Alright, alright," he said, slightly raising his voice.

Triggered by his caustic tone even though he addressed Haleigh, I took a few steps back. Jordan turned to Bryant and handed him a business card. "If you want to discuss venture capital. I've invested in some promising start-ups."

Bryant took the card and placed it in his breast pocket. "Enjoy your night."

Viviana placed her arm under Bryant's. "It was lovely to meet you, Haleigh."

"You too." Haleigh's voice was strained.

I turned away, reminding myself not to pity her. She chose Jordan.

An older couple approached Bryant and Viviana.

"Oh, Celine." Jordan stood arms akimbo. "Richard Pine and I had lunch the other day. Grassley's killing it, so Richard's planning an expansion in Kansas."

I took another step away. "Tell him congrats."

"I will."

Haleigh placed her arm into his. "Jordan, I'm not saying this again—let's dance."

"Bye, Celine," he said coldly.

I nodded, then they walked away. But after a few steps, he turned to look at me. I walked toward the Marches. They were saying good night to some of their acquaintances.

Once their friends left, Viviana faced me. "Are you alright?"

"Just mixed emotions." I looked down. "I broke up with Jordan in May."

She took my hand in hers. "Sometimes God lets us see what we needed to release before we embrace something better."

"It's not easy," I said.

"No, it's not. I had to let go of my ex-fiancé and all the bitterness of a broken engagement. Bryant had to release his wife and all the pain of losing her to cancer. It can be done."

"Thank you." I squeezed her hand. "I'm going to rest in my room. I'm exhausted from moving into my new house, and it's been a long night. Do you mind?"

"No. We'll catch up at breakfast tomorrow. Text when you're ready. We'll probably sleep in until eight or nine."

"Good seeing you," Bryant said. "You made a great choice moving on."

I smiled. As I approached the elevator, I checked my phone. Nothing. What a disappointment. Maybe Lauren got too tired to come and forgot to call. Garrett might've lost track of time hanging out with Lauren and Shane.

Whatever happened, I was too frazzled emotionally to care. One day, I'd spend New Year's here with someone I loved, not stuck alone again.

CHAPTER 79

Once I entered my room, I wanted to get an Uber home. I grabbed my phone, but it rang in my hand. Lauren, finally!

"Hello," I said, anxious to know if she was still coming.

"Celine, it's Shane. I'm sorry we didn't call earlier. On the way there, Lauren had terrible cramping and dizziness, so Garrett took her to urgent care. I'm taking her home, but he's headed to The Mayo. Are you still there?"

"Wait—is Lauren alright?" Worry dissolved any disappointment.

"Yeah. She needs to stay off her feet, but she's talking a mile a minute now, ordering you to stay there... Hold on, Lauren's saying something." His voice became distant. "No, baby, I'm not putting her on speaker... You need to take it easy... I will, don't worry... I'm back, Celine. Are you still at the hotel?"

"Yes but tell Garrett he doesn't have to meet me here. He's had a long night. We'll connect another time."

"Garrett's getting his second wind. I gave him your cell, and I'll text you his as well." He spoke to Lauren again. Bless his heart. He might as well put her on the phone. "Celine, Lauren asked if you'd text her a picture of yourself. She insisted that Garrett also text a picture of the two of you. But in case he forgets—her words—she wants to see your gown."

"Alright. I'll send a pic once I get off the phone. Tell Lauren I'll be praying for her and not to be concerned for me. I'm doing well."

"She sends her love and will call you either tomorrow or the day after. Bye."

After I hung up, Shane texted me Garrett's cell number, and I responded with one of Aimee's pictures for Lauren. Needing to refresh my makeup, I scurried like a field mouse to the bathroom, where I powdered my face, then reapplied lipstick and gloss, carefully maintaining the Cupid's bow effect Aimee had created.

"You can do this," I told my reflection in the mirror. "Be natural." Still tense, I kept lowering my shoulders when they rode up.

Garrett texted.

> Celine, sorry about the holdup. Lauren's well but resting. I'm pulling into The Mayo now.

After reciting a short prayer, I headed out of the suite, hoping our time together would go smoothly. At the elevators, I opened my red handbag. A vibrant red light flashed from inside, almost blinding me. What the heck!

I nearly dropped the bag but kept it in my unsteady hand. As I waited for the elevator, I carefully retrieved the bracelet from the bag and slipped it on for a last time. The red light subsided, but warmth penetrated my wrist, not with discomfort or burning, but as if God had breathed life into the jewels.

The elevator door opened, and I stepped inside, trying not to overanalyze. Had my imagination played with the bracelet's glow?

Once the door closed, I became eerily calm. Redemption came to mind. My journey paralleled The Mayo—tearing down the irreparable parts, salvaging what could be saved, and rebuilding something stronger and more resilient.

My parents, especially Dad, embraced a new outlook. Aimee and I restored our relationship. Jennifer received a second chance for love. Lauren's hope restored with life growing within, and Viviana found life in Christ and then opening doors to a family.

"Nana, I understand now," I whispered, recalling our talk in the Grand Hall during my cousin's wedding. One of the cloud of witnesses, Nana was cheering me on.

When the door opened to the floor of the Crystal Ballroom, Garrett's blue eyes penetrated mine. "It's you," he said.

My resolve melting, I stared at the marble tile under his feet. What must he think of me?

"It's you," he repeated.

"Were you expecting someone else?" I asked, lifting my gaze slightly.

"No. It was you all along."

I extended my hand exposing the bracelet.

He stared at it and smiled. "The surprise."

Of course. He'd take the bracelet, and the night would be over. My stomach knotted. The moment of truth had come, and I longed to dodge my disappointment.

"Celine?" His voice was tender.

Meeting his eyes required mustering every ounce of courage I had. They sparkled as he smiled. Those eyes bore no anger, no judgment. There, I found kindness. And maybe something more.

"Wow!" He took a step back, gazing at me as if admiring a work of art. "You're even more breathtaking in person."

My whole body tingled. *Thank you, Aimee.* Fixing my gaze on the marble floor, I bit my lower lip until I felt the flush in my cheeks subside. Slowly, I allowed myself to look up. To look deep into Garrett's light blue eyes. My heart expanded. And just like Nana with Papa, I knew I was home.

EPILOGUE

In the Crystal Ballroom, Garrett and I danced until midnight. As clouds of balloons and showers of confetti drifted down, we held each other's gaze and exchanged *bisous* when the clock struck midnight. The gentle touch of his lips on my cheek was more intimate than anything I'd ever known with Jordan.

People lingered, basking in the newness of 2019, so Garrett took my hand and led me to the hallway. Here, we reconnected with the Marches to say goodnight.

Garrett turned to me with a half-smile. *God, help me.* He was so hot. His penetrating blue eyes, Greek-shaped nose, and angular jaw melded in artistic symmetry.

"Up to escaping somewhere quiet?" he asked.

"I'm game." I smiled, happy he wanted to spend time alone.

"How about the penthouse roof? I'll grab my down jacket in my room, for you."

"Thanks." I smiled, envisioning myself wearing his jacket. But what would he wear? "On second thought, I brought a long, wool overcoat."

Once armed with our coats, we headed up to the roof. Stepping outside, the brisk winter air jolted me into reality. Was the solitude worth the frigid temps? A crisp wind blew my hair into my face, and Garrett gently moved a strand out of my eyes then took my hand. He led me to the table, pulled out my chair, and waited until I settled in. I could tolerate an hour in this weather. He sat across from me, facing the door, while I faced the glowing skyline. The light from the full moon mingled with the deep red of the illuminated Mayo sign above us.

"Are you warm enough?" he asked, removing his jacket. "This would add another layer over yours."

"I'm good," I said, not wanting him to sacrifice his comfort for me.

He put his jacket back on. "Hungry? Thirsty?" he asked.

"Set for the night." Exhilaration filled my chest like champagne bubbles. Self-conscious as though I might expose my giddiness, I looked away. I had forgotten how compelling a man's attentiveness could be.

After a few moments of silence, Garrett spoke. "When I saw you at the Marches', I was drawn by your beauty." He leaned toward me. "But it wasn't until I drove home that night I realized—you were *the* Celine from The Mayo. You were so transformed, I hardly recognized you."

"What clued you in?" I asked.

"Definitely not your long blonde hair. No offense, but I prefer you as a blonde."

"That makes two of us." I flashed a smile, happy he preferred my natural look. "What else?"

"I put two and two together. How you ran a marketing business that your ex helped launch, your light blue eyes, and the mole."

"Did knowing I was *that* Celine turn you off or confuse you?" I asked.

"Confused, no." He shook his head. "After two years, I forgot what you and your ex looked like and really, much of the chaos of both incidents. So, like when blood rushes to a limb after it feels like it fell asleep, memories trickled in. Once those two nights at The Mayo became clear, I battled mixed emotions—wondering if you still possessed it and concerned about what you'd experienced with your ex." He looked behind and pointed to the right near the balcony's edge. "We stood near there, remember?"

"I'd rather not." I frowned.

"When you were certain the heirloom belonged to your ex, you gave me hope. I thought if I ever got the bracelet back, I prayed someone like you would value it." He frowned. "Unfortunately, my ex didn't appreciate it like I expected her to."

"Speaking of hope, how did you handle the uncertainty about the bracelet after realizing I was that Celine?"

"Not well at first." He winked. "Three counseling sessions later, I surrendered to letting it go again. You'd think after two years, I'd have moved on."

"Did knowing we'd be in regular contact, as godparents, help?"

He paused, moving his mouth to the side. "It opened up a different set of complications. If you returned it to your ex, how could I get it back? I wrestled with that option, hating the thought of him having it again. What if you still had it? Could I bring the topic up with tact? But God already had my back." He laughed. "If I had trusted, I could've avoided those counseling sessions."

"I'm glad you're happy with how this—let's call it an adventure —turned out."

"I'm dying to know. Did you value the bracelet because you thought it was an heirloom from him? Or you liked the bracelet itself?" He leaned toward me with eagerness, perhaps fishing for a particular answer.

"At first, I valued it because Jordan wasn't sentimental, so for him to gift an heirloom was special, at the time." I pulled my overcoat cuff back until the bracelet was visible. "But once the aura of him gifting it eased, I appreciated its uniqueness and craftsmanship. It reminded me of something my nana would wear, which only increased my attraction to it. After discovering it wasn't Jordan's heirloom, I wanted to keep it."

"Since the bracelet gravitated to you, hold onto it for now."

"But it belongs to your family." I looked away. "I'd feel…" I didn't want to disappoint him, but I couldn't imagine his mother content to let him gift the heirloom. I wasn't even his girlfriend. *Yet.*

"I inherited it," he said, "so it's my call. My family will be thrilled it's found. I don't think they'll mind you having it."

"Are you sure? If it were my maman…" I winced recalling his dad's talk with Lauren. When the bracelet went missing, Garrett's mom felt as though she lost her mother again. I understood feeling grief when something triggered a memory of a deceased loved one—hearing *Somewhere in Time* which I used to ask Nana to play on her baby grand, catching a note of her perfume on a stranger, or feeling the pearls of her necklace around my neck.

He leaned back on the chair with a half-smile, seemingly unfazed over how his mother might react. "I'll smooth out the situation with my mom." His voice strong yet calm. She'd have to go along with his decision, but would that put a barrier between her and me?

"Still, I think you should have it," I said softly.

Garrett frowned. His shoulders sagged like a dog rebuked by its owner. I wanted to take my words back. Assure him I wished to keep the bracelet for life. But I wasn't confident enough to say that.

"I cherish it, though," I said.

He studied my face. "God's plan is greater than our vision. My mom might not understand the heirloom's journey, but I trust God will ease her mind. Can you trust too?"

"I'd like to." If a serious relationship might develop between Garrett and me, I'd need to trust him.

"She'll adore you."

Suddenly, Nana's words echoed in my head. I smiled, as though she were here, counseling me.

If you knew you couldn't live without him, you'd fight to make it work.

"You drive a hard bargain." I winked. "I'll continue protecting your heirloom."

He slid his hand from under my palm and wrapped my hands in his. "Better keep these warm."

"With you, I don't think that'll be a problem." I smiled.

We stayed until we could no longer ignore the biting wind. He escorted me to the Grand Hall where we sat and talked for a while, losing track of time. When our eyes drooped, he finally escorted me to my suite, holding my hand—so natural, as if we'd been dating for months.

"Good night," he said. "Sleep well." He slowly released his hands and waited while I opened the door, then turned and walked away.

Inside my suite, the wall clock read a little after 4 a.m. I strolled to the window and looked outside. A streetlamp cast a faint pool of light in the dark, silent morning. I almost didn't want to go to sleep, afraid I'd wake up and find it all had been a dream.

After I woke around eight the next morning, I checked on the bracelet, reassured. Last night had been real. But as I got ready, I reminded myself to not get carried away like I did with Jordan. Even though Garrett wasn't him, I needed to enter into any relationship with my eyes wide open. Garrett hardly knew me, really. Once he did, would we work out? I didn't want to think we wouldn't.

I spoke out my mantra to stop focusing on my fears. "Conquer this hour, so you can conquer the day."

An hour later, Garrett knocked on the door. We were meeting the Marches for brunch. I turned off the light in the living room of my suite, anxious yet excited to see where 2019 would take us.

A Letter From The Author

Readers often ask where I find inspiration for my stories. For the *Mayo Love* series, the answer is personal. I married later in life, so my single journey provided a wealth of inspiration—heartbreak, loneliness, and redemption. I wrestled with feelings of unworthiness, plagued by lies like, "You're not enough" or "No one wants you". Through inner healing, I embraced the powerful truth: through Christ, I am enough.

The spark for *Love at The Mayo (LATM)* came from a desire to explore what redemption could look like for someone struggling with rejection. A vivid scene played out in my mind:

A single woman, still healing from heartbreak, agrees to a date with a friend's brother—a man she admires but doesn't know well. She waits for her party in The Mayo Hotel's lobby. But as the minutes tick by, frustration builds. An hour later, they haven't shown up nor answered her calls or texts—just silence. Dejected, she gets up to leave when her ex enters the hotel, walking arm and arm with the very woman he cheated with.

You'll recognize this moment as this novel's climactic ending scene. But how did this story become a series, and why isn't Book 1?

Initially, *LATM* was the first book I wrote. While it was in my editor's hands, I started working on *Christmas at Sonshine Barn (CASB),* to serve as a prequel. But after consulting with my trusted author circle, I realized readers would benefit from experiencing Garrett Bettencourt's journey first. Releasing *CASB* as Book 1 lets readers step back two years, setting the foundation for the love story to unravel more profoundly.

Writing the books "out of order" required adjustments. I wove key elements from *CASB,* like the heirloom bracelet, into *LATM.* And since my initial draft of *LATM* was over 130,000 words, I worked closely with my editor, Michele Chiappetta, to trim over 40,000 words without losing its heart.

CASB is available at major bookstores or through my Shopify store.

Get Christmas at Sonshine Barn

Looking ahead, Book 3, *Love Beyond the Mayo,* will feature dual perspectives between Celine and Garrett. As their relationship grows, they wrestle with trust issues, confronting complex family dynamics (especially surrounding the bracelet), and emotional wounds of their pasts.

If you haven't read "Rescue in Amalfi", a short story inaugurating the *Mayo Love* Series, now is the perfect time. The story plants Easter eggs that hatch in each book, and Book 3 will reveal a game-changing secret tied to it. You can get "Rescue in Amalfi" for FREE by signing up for my newsletter at: SarahSoon.com. (Check out my website to get Book Club resources, exclusive sneak peeks, and the latest updates.)

Get Rescue in Amalfi

Acknowledgements

Thanks to my editors. Mark Spencer, whose critiques helped shape the story. Kristi Bridges for her first draft editing. To Michele Chiappetta, your brilliant editing and advisement—especially helping me cut a major plotline—was invaluable. Jill Butler, your editing expertise helped bring this project across the finish line.

Thanks to beta readers—Karen Grunst, Laurie Salvacion, Erin Garcia, and Rachel Throp—for your insightful feedback. Appreciate Jennifer Owens for advising me on authentically portraying my African-American character, Jennifer. Shoutout to Unbreakable Spines, my critique group, for your feedback and a special thanks to Meg Perdue for providing weekly critiques for nearly half this novel. You're a gifted writer and critique partner.

Thanks to my ARC readers! Special mentions go to Steve Levon, Susan Marie Graham, Becky Green, Ina Soliz, Susan Hellenberg, Nancy Bliss, Wenonah, Dee Selby, and Jessica Freeman, for submitting edits.

To my fellow Lady Lits, Mari Eygabroad, Cindy Godwin, Susan Marie Graham, Linda Sammaritan, Janet Weiner, J. Bea Wilson for your support and expertise! I'm grateful to Nancy Ness for founding this amazing group. I miss you!

To Caroline Raschen, thanks for the tour of The Mayo Hotel, answering my questions about the hotel, and serving as a liaison. My gratitude extends to the hotel's legal team and its owner, Macy Snyder-Amatucci, for allowing me to use the hotel in my book title.

Thanks to Mike Tedford for capturing the stunning book cover image of the hotel.

Thanks Marline Williams and Dianne Severson for advising me on the marketing industry, and to Will Cleaver for your review of the financial advisor aspects of the story.

Finally, I couldn't have written this novel without my husband—you're my exceedingly, abundantly gift. To my family, friends, and church community, your timely encouragement helped me throughout the writing process. And most of all, my deepest thanks to God for providing the grace, joy, and fortitude I needed to bring this story to life.

ABOUT THE AUTHOR

Sarah Soon has helped authors share their stories. She has served as a contributing author in *Option Ocean,* a devotional anthology; ghost-written memoirs; written magazine articles for *Tulsa Lifestyle Magazine;* and edited non-fiction books on topics ranging from Tulsa's medical history to Christian living.

Now she writes transformative fiction, where characters experience inner healing to find love and renew their faith. The *Mayo Love* series is set in her hometown of Tulsa, Oklahoma, and Book 1, *Christmas at Sonshine Barn*, transports readers to her childhood home in Gaylord, Michigan.

In her free time, Sarah enjoys spending time with family and friends, exploring the outdoors, traveling, and discovering other cultures with her family.

facebook.com/SarahSoonWriter

instagram.com/Sarahsoon38

goodreads.com/Sarahsoon